HILL OF BEANS

} LESLIE
} EPSTEIN

HILL

of

BEANS

} A NOVEL OF WAR
} AND CELLULOID

High Road Books
An Imprint of the University of New Mexico Press Albuquerque

HIGH ROAD

*High Road Books is an imprint
of the University of New Mexico Press*

ISBN 978-0-8263-6259-9 (cloth) | ISBN 978-0-8263-6260-5 (electronic)

Library of Congress Control Number: 2020949940

COVER ART Floyd MacMillan Davis, *Bar in Hotel Scribe*, oil on canvas, 1944. Courtesy of the National Portrait Gallery, Smithsonian Institution.

Composed in 11.5/15 point Fanwood Pro, Acme Gothic Extrawide, Resolve Sans Semilight Wide, and Parkside Regular.

For Philip G. Epstein. My Father.

DISCLAIMER Many of the characters in this novel were once living. They often spoke and behaved in the manner depicted here; yet those words and actions have been so refracted by the author's imagination that any resemblance between how they lived their lives and what is printed in these pages is largely coincidental. Any resemblance to any other person not known to history is bound to be an illusion.

CONTENTS

ACKNOWLEDGMENTS

This book took many years to research and write and I owe a good deal to many people, too many to name here or, with my cluttered brain, recall. But some I wish to acknowledge especially:

Joe Kanon

Michael Mandlin

Jennifer Schlossberg

Elizabeth Frank

Jake Fuchs

David Kleinbard

Elise McHugh

Robin Straus

John Blumenthal

Bernard Katz

Rebecca Ginzburg

The generous Andy Marx and CeCe Bloum for, respectively, Groucho's letter and Jimmy Durante's song

And the no less generous and understanding people at Warner Bros.

Finally, the wonderful librarians at:

The Motion Picture Academy

Boston University (specifically Marci Cohen, Holly Mockovak, and Donald Altschiller)

Penn State University (thank you, Ana Enriquez)

University of Southern California

And to you others, my friends, my colleagues, and distant scholars, forgive my lapses and accept my thanks.

VOICE-OVER With the coming of the Second World War, many eyes in imprisoned Europe turned hopefully, or desperately, toward the freedom of the Americas. This is the story of how one nation, one industry, and in particular one man responded to that desperation and that hope.

Hedda Hopper's Hollywood: December 1941, Los Angeles

Since Hedy Lamarr has taken off those silks and satins and gotten into something that shows her chassis, she's certainly the life of the party in *Tortilla Flat*, with Tracy and John Garfield so hot after her it's enough to turn any girl's head. I mean for the picture, dearie—don't go getting ideas. Going to hotfoot it over to Union Station tomorrow morning to meet the Super Chief when the freres Warners' newest acquisition, German starlet Karelena Kaiser, arrives from Berlin. This nineteen-year-old blonde isn't well known over here, but she's featured in many ingenue roles and is quite a heartthrob in theaters across Europe.

Search me why such a rising young actress would want to leave Germany, which is making so many exciting pictures these days. Rumor has it that Warner Bros. and Jack Warner in particular were kind to her after the tragic accident that took the life of her father, a low-level studio employee. Whatever the reason, we're always happy to have such pretty young talent. Welcome to America, Fraulein Kaiser!

Spent yesterday afternoon Christmas shopping at Bullocks Wilshire with Rita Hayworth, who has made such a hit in *Strawberry Blonde*. "Christmas!" I declared to this sultry Spaniard. "Why today is only the Fifth: Christmas is three weeks away." "That's true, Hedda," she told me, "but I have so many new friends and fans I've got to start early." That red hair looks like the real thing to yours truly.

With censorship rearing up again, I hear that 20th will drape those nude Greek statues in *Tales of Manhattan* with plaster sarongs. Incidentally, in that one, Charles Boyer has three death scenes and comes out alive. Yes, IT HAPPENS IN THE MOVIES!

PART I

~~

TO THE GARDEN

1 } SALUTE, GODDAMMIT!

The Terrible Turk: April 1942, Burbank

The sons of the prophet are brave men and bold
And never a danger will shirk
But the bravest by far in the ranks of the Shah
Was Abdul the Terrible Turk

That's me. Maybe not so terrible now. But I can still outbox any man on the lot. Including the illustrious Errol Leslie Flynn. He wants to fight—in the army, I mean. Or the navy. Anywhere. But he's got a heart problem. 4-F. Julius Epstein, one of those writer twins, was a bantamweight intercollegiate champ. He's thirty years younger, but I've got sixty pounds on him. The idea is that I take on him and his brother. We're trying to arrange it. It'll be a fair fight. All for the war effort and the good of the country.

The sons of the prophet, and so forth and so on. That's what we shouted through the megaphone before every bout. My biggest was with Philadelphia Jack O'Brien: 2/22/07. I remember the dates of all my fights, especially that one. He was still the light-heavyweight champion. *Ring* ranks him number two in the history of the world. I won five rounds. My whole life would have been different. But we had to throw in the Turkish towel. Ho. Ho. Some joke.

My next biggest was when I was for a short time in the business doing silents for First National and even a feature called *One Round Hogan,* in which I played a guy named Sniffy and got KO'd by Jimmy Jeffries, who played himself. It was a real concussion caused by the ring pole and they had to shoot around me for two days. The Chief—but I didn't call him anything but Mr. Warner then—was mad as hell. "You're seeing double? So what if you're seeing double? I'm seeing red. *Red Ink!*" That was the end of my motion-picture career; it was also the beginning of my relationship with the Chief.

Yesterday he wanted to meet me at wardrobe. I thought he wanted to outfit his latest blonde, whose name is Karelena Kaiser, not the one the Chief gave her and not Miss Kauffman, which is the one she was born with. She's a beauty, all right, even though she hasn't got what you'd call an hourglass figure. Not much sand in the top. I can't help feeling sorry for her, being a refugee, and all of her family I hear or maybe only her father was shot. I wouldn't mind getting that Hitler in the ring. He'd be KO number four.

Anyhow, when I got over to the wardrobe department I was surprised to find out they weren't making a costume for the girl but were putting the pins and the chalk on the Chief.

"Hello, Abdul," said this, no joke here, knockout.

"Good afternoon, miss," said I, because I was embarrassed to call her by her first name, which is Karelena. I took the hand she held out to me, wondering for a second whether because she was from the continent of Europe I was supposed to bow down and kiss it. Instead I said, "Is that the outfit they made for you? For when you test for Ilsa? It's A-OK with me. Thumbs up!" It was a nice dress, with a zigzag pattern and little puffs at the sleeves.

She laughed. "Oh, this is off the May Company rack. The fitting today is for Mr. Warner."

Then, right on cue, from behind a curtain stepped the Chief, dressed in what I found out was a US Army Air Force uniform. He held up his arms and grinned, like a girl coming out of a cake, and his teeth were brighter than the brass buttons that ran up the front of his tunic. "Don't just stand there, dummy," he said, pointing at the silver oak leafs on his shoulders. "You better learn how to salute."

"You bet, Chief," I said, and put my thumb to my eyebrow, like in the movies.

"You bet, *Colonel*," said J.L., and he wasn't kidding.

"Colonel," I said, and saluted all over again.

"*Lieutenant* colonel, actually."

Then Rydo Loshak stepped through the curtain, I swear to God with the points of pins in his mouth. "You, too," said the Chief, giving him a nod; and when a wardrobe girl came out with the Chief's old suit over her arm, he said more or less to all of us: "What's the matter with you people? Don't you know there's a war on? Salute, goddammit! Salute!"

2 } GLORIA PALAST

Goebbels: *Last Day of April 1945, Berlin*

Our last hope, Mohnke, arrived an hour ago with the latest reports. Some good news: the Schlesischer Station has been recaptured. A brief celebration. Then bad news: the Russians have taken the Friedrichstrasse tunnel and have moved into the Vossstrasse, only a stone's throw away. The Führer heard these words without emotion. He had already received more important intelligence from Professor Haase, who informed him that when with a pair of plyers he crushed an ampule of prussic acid in Blondi's mouth, the dog died on the instant without a whimper of pain. *That* is the only news worth celebrating. Magda has arranged to get a supply from Stumpfegger. Not for ourselves. For the children. For tomorrow night. How they liked to romp about with that bitch's puppy. He would nip with his sharp little teeth but never do any real damage.

And after? Nothing of the Führer must be allowed to remain.

I have ordered Günsche and Kempka to bring 200 litres of petrol to the garden. We saw what happened to the Duce: hung by the heels, mocked and desecrated by the masses. The Führer is determined that he shall not suffer such a fate. To be forced to act in a farce, one in which the Bolsheviks can have a good laugh and the Jews with their hacked-off Schwänge can urinate on him through the bars of his cage. Linge has confirmed that a minimum of 180 litres has been secured. They shall have to find more for Magda and myself. Schwägermann will see to it.

The Führer has now completed his luncheon, a modest and calm last meal, differing in no respect from so many others; that is, with only Frau Trudle and Frau Christian, and Fräulein Manziarly, for company. There is true humility.

A knock on the door. Bormann. His criminal face is without expression. The head of the Parteikanzlei: "The Führer has summoned you and Frau Goebbels to say Auf Wiedersehen."

I try to hide my annoyance. What need of this ceremony? I said my own good-byes when I witnessed the Führer's last testament and, with flowing tears, added my own coda to it: a vow never to abandon him in his hour of greatest need. Still, I rise from my chair. Bormann turns. I follow him.

The farewell. Better to have remained in my den. The Führer, stooped and wan. Eva—now Frau Hitler—in a blue, white-trimmed dress. A handshake, weak, moist, and a word or two, *My dear Goebbels*, and the rest an inaudible mumble. Burgdorf steps up next. And after him Krebs.

Suddenly, strangely, from another time—from another planet, it seems—these wild words come to me:

> *Baby, what are you out for?*
> *Baby what am I in for?*

In English. American English. Sung by Neger. Written by Jews.

At last the Führer moves away. His arm, held behind his back, is shaking. Magda pulls at my sleeve. She tells me she is going to Günsche and ask to be admitted to the Führer's study. She intends to make a final plea: that he abandon the bunker, abandon Berlin, and lead the resistance from Bavaria. It is all I can do not to laugh in her face. I doubt he will even agree to hear her.

> *Baby, what am I in for?*

The jungle music. I know where it comes from. A film. Typical pablum from the Jew Warner, born Wonskolaser. *Twenty Million Sweethearts.* How bright and gay Charlottenburg on the night of that premiere. The Kurfürstendamm! Gleaming with the headlights and taillights of taxis and sedans. The shower of sparks from the number 6 trolley. All gone, all burned to the ground. Nothing but swaying walls and debris. The black smoke rising into the black sky. Our German folk running through the streets like ghosts.

> *Is my baby out for no good?*

A single stone was dropped that night. On the Kufürstendamm. Kauffman. The Jew Kauffman. And the daughter. Karelena. She might have changed everything. She almost saved everything. Instead the ripples that should have carried us to the triumph of National Socialism became the wave that has overwhelmed us. Our Reich. Our beautiful Berlin.

Dinner alone at the Ordenspalais and then the premiere at the Gloria Palast. I arrive ten minutes late and with my hat pulled low, lest one in that crowd of more than a thousand recognize me. I take the spot that has been reserved, off to one side of the balcony. On the screen the American actor Powell is making a clown of himself as he sings, for all the capitalists of the radio network, his beer-hall ballad—

Oh, he floats through the air with the
greatest of ease

I have, of course, seen this production before, just as I have viewed every film before approving it for our masses. I am aware that when Herr Powell sings his ballads to Fräulein Rogers, each of the women in his broadcast audience—those twenty million sweethearts—will believe that she and she alone is the one he loves. Our own audience of good Germans is no better. I hear them all around me, laughing and clapping and cheering for this yodeling buffoon. I can't wait until, like well-trained Zircus Seehunde, they will pull out their handkerchiefs as this Dick turns to this Ginger with the words:

All my life I've waited for an angel
But no angel ever came along

Our sobbing, weeping, sentimental folk, just like these Americans sighing over their Philcos, their Crosleys, and their ugly wooden Zeniths. I shall make certain that soon there will be no such empty-headed radio listeners in the Reich. Rather, they will all be listening to what I want them to hear. Twenty million sweethearts! I intend to guarantee that eighty million Germans fall no less deeply in love. What do the latest Volksempfänger cost? Fewer than forty Reichsmarks. I am determined that every home in the nation shall possess one—no, not one. Two. Three. A receiver in every room. And each will be tuned to a single station: the Deutschlandsender. And on this station there will be a sole voice, repeating, over and over, in one guise or another, the same message: *Ein Volk, ein Reich, ein Führer.*

Now, in the Gloria Palast, the time has come to act. With both hands I raise my hat from my head, as if the pressure from such pondering had made my skull swell inside it. Still too tight? I raise it again, to make sure the Dummköpfe have seen it. Then I stand and move toward the nearest exit. I pause, not looking at the screen but waiting to hear the words I know will come from the loudspeakers behind it. Dick Powell, at the microphone, utters them aloud:

And now, ladies and gentlemen, I have a real
surprise for you. Yes, sir, I'm afraid you
guessed it. It's the Mills Brothers!

At once the four Schwarzenneggers burst into song:

Baby what are you out for?
Baby what am I in for?
Is my baby out for no good?

"Alles Afrikaner rause!" shouts a voice from somewhere down in the orchestra. "Away with these Neger!"

Another voice, closer by, in the balcony, cries, "They are insulting the Aryan race!"

Some in the audience make shushing noises. A voice declares, "We want to hear the music!"

"*Music?* A German calls this music?" That is the fellow in the balcony. "Just listen. It is the sound of the zoo."

As if following those instructions, everyone does seem to listen. Impossible to translate into German how the black men, in their dark jackets and cream-colored pants, turn the lyrics of the song into chaos:

Rooty-a-tooty-a poop-droop-a-doop

"Ha! Ha! Ha!" A second man joins the first in the balcony. "Monkeys have learned to talk!"

"It is the love song of the apes!"

"Nein! The parliament of Africa!"

Now, at the front of the orchestra, a small formation of SA marches before the first row of seats. Together they point up toward the far-off projectionist's window.

"The filth must stop!"

"Turn off the machine!"

For a moment nothing occurs. The primitive rhythms continue while our Berliners watch and listen from their plush Gloria Palast seats.

At last one of our men in the balcony rushes forward and throws something that, trailing a stream of smoke, flies into the midst of the sitting crowd. A second man races ahead and hurls a similar missile. In seconds the smell of sulfur, accompanied by alarming sparks, spreads through the theater. Now people begin to stand. They push by the ones who remain stubbornly seated. Suddenly, a loud crash at the back of the room and the yellow beam in which have danced so many Warner Bros. dollars goes out. Simultaneously the houselights come on to reveal, at the front of the theater, a group of men wearing something resembling lab coats. Each carries a wire cage, the front latch of which he kneels down to open. The SA men are happy to offer an explanation:

"Here you are, ladies. Your favorite entertainers."

"The Four-Hundred Maus Brothers."

Immediately, scores—perhaps there really are four hundred in all—of white mice begin to run into the crowded auditorium. At the same time the houselights once more go out. In the pitch-dark all is pandemonium. Women scream. Men curse. Fistfights break out as people climb over each other to reach the aisles. Suddenly, unmistakably, a single shot rings out. It seems to cause everyone to take in his breath. Then all the doors, with a Brownshirt to either side, are flung open. The crowd streams out—some into the lobby, some directly into the street. In less than three minutes the great hall stands empty. Only one patron remains in his seat. When the houselights come back on, he is found slumped forward, the result of the bullet that has gone into one side of his head and out the other.

APRIL 1945, BERLIN

Magda enters without a knock. I see that she has been crying.

"The Führer would not admit you?"

She shook her head. "He admitted me. It was as if he were not there. As if I were pleading with the wall. Or begging a piece of furniture. You would be ashamed of me. I broke into tears."

"I am not ashamed. But I warned you. Now we must find our dentist."

"We have time. Tonight a normal sleep. Tomorrow night nothing must wake them. Not the loudest explosion."

"Send someone to the Chancellery. Alert him to come as soon as he can."

"And Stumpfegger."

"Yes, Stumpfegger. Tell him to bring—he will know what to bring. And cigarettes."

"*Cigarettes!* The condemned man wants his last pleasure."

I wave her away. "First the dentist. Then Stumpfegger. Make sure they get here in time."

AUGUST 1934, BERLIN

My presumption that the dead man in the Gloria Palast committed suicide was soon confirmed. For this we must thank the timely report from our Staatspolizei. Name: Joseph Kauffman. An American Jew. Geboren in Cincinnati, a leading city of the state of Ohio. Some will undoubtedly exploit this incident and blame the death on the SA or the Gestapo, but it was an undoubted Selbstmord. The fatal wound to the left temple was delivered by a short-barreled Mauser C96 military pistol.

That pistol had been purchased by Herr Kauffman after he had received a number of threats by telephone and the post. The weapon was found under the seat directly in front of the victim, who was—according to the testimony of his spouse, a Frau Hannelore Kauffman, of full-blooded Aryan descent—left-handed. After a diligent search, the coroner was able to recover the bullet, a 9-mm Parabellum round, from the plush material in a seat some eleven meters distant. Ballistic studies determined that it came from the victim's pistol. From the evidence of papers inside the jacket pocket of the deceased, it seems that the Jew was despondent at being unable to find employment in the new Germany. The inevitable conclusion of the coroner was that the fatal wound to Herr Joseph Kauffman had been self-inflicted. He leaves, in addition to Frau Kauffman, a daughter, Karelena, aged twelve. Mischling of the first degree.

One question still remained before us: How would the Americans, and in particular Warner Bros., respond to the death of their citizen and their employee? Would we be accused? The coroner's report noted that Kauffman could no longer find work. For that we could indeed take the blame—or as those in my ministry prefer to see it, the credit. We demanded that all six American film companies dismiss every Jew on their payrolls. They quickly complied.

For some time the Americans made no response at all. You would have thought the poor fellow had never existed. But a few days ago a dispatch arrived from Gyssling, our consul in the city of Los Angeles. In it was a clipping from the publication that likes to call itself "the Bible of the show-biz industry." It read as follows:

Variety—July 24, 1934

WB TO EXIT GERMANY

Acts after General Manager Killed in Theater

BY BERNARD KATZ

Studio Chief Jack L. Warner announced yesterday that he was closing all Warner Brothers offices and exchanges in Berlin and throughout Germany. He said this action was in direct response to what he claimed was the murder of his Berlin Branch Manager, Joe Kauffman, by Nazi toughs.

The six majors have been under pressure in Hitlerland since they were required to dismiss their non-Aryan personnel. Over the course of the last year each studio began replacing its Jewish representatives with Christian employees. The feeling here was that the Jew problem had been trumped up for popular consumption and would soon blow over. How wrong that assessment turned out to be was revealed when Kauffman was shot to death at the UFA Gloria Palast while tracking audience responses to his studio's *Twenty Million Sweethearts*, radio-comedy with Powell and Rogers and foreign grosses of 1.2 million.

"He died with his boots on," Warner declared at yesterday's press conference, "working loyally for his studio until the very end."

The exec went on to explain that he had urged Kauffman to transfer to a similar position in Poland or Czechoslovakia, or even to return to a new post in Burbank. "But Joe had come to love both Germany and its people. He married a fine German woman. They had a lovely daughter. Over the last few months the Nazis burnt his car, trashed his flat, and attacked him with vicious dogs in a back alley. They forced the twelve-year-old

Karelena out of her school. Still, he believed these thugs did not represent the true Germany and that he was not going to let them hound him out of what had become his own country. Now I wish that instead of sticking by him we had been wise enough to insist.

"We've made our own investigation. A gang of Brownshirts made a big fuss in the theater. When everyone was distracted they hunted Joe down in the dark. They snuck up behind him and shot him in the head. Warner Bros. is no longer doing business in the German market. I don't care what it costs us. And it costs us plenty."

No one at Para, MGM, Universal, Fox, or Columbia would comment on the Kauffman case, though the marketing execs made it clear that none of their studios was considering closing down its German operation at this time. A spokesman for Disney, reached by phone, said, "Withdraw from Germany? Why? They are a dynamic country, a friend to the United States, and they appreciate our product more than anyone else. Disney isn't going anywhere."

The foreign market makes up more than half of all studio revenues, and in that market no other country save Britain can come close to matching German grosses.

Gyssling offered the opinion that the other five studios will not follow suit, and that Herr Warner is a hothead acting entirely on his own. He underlined the statement by Herr Disney, who has been sympathetic to our cause, and said it more closely reflects the opinion of the studio magnates, even those of Jewish blood, than that of Herr Wonksolaser. I think we have little to fear—and in any case, once our own industry produces work worthy of the National Socialist spirit, we shall send them packing whether they wish to leave or not.

LAST DAY OF APRIL 1945, BERLIN

What was that? A shot? Yes—far off, muffled, but a definite report. Will there be another? Why isn't there another? The Führer—undoubtedly dead. Or is it—still difficult to say this word—Frau Hitler? Did one or the other lose courage? I refuse to believe it. But where is the second shot?

AUGUST 1934, BERLIN

Gyssling was correct: Warner is a hothead. But in addition there is no measuring the depths of his hypocrisy. I could learn lessons in effrontery, in absolute insouciance, from this master. I have not forgotten the documents found inside the victim's pockets. Some were nothing more than scraps of paper: for instance, an old receipt marked Zylinderhut Billard, which is evidently a pool-hall establishment. Also a half-page torn from the Berlin *Tageblatt* that contained most of the city's motion-picture theaters and the times of the main features. Some were circled in black ink, including that night's premiere at the Gloria Palast.

Of greater interest, however, were two letters, one long and one short. The first was written in the dead man's own hand and obviously never posted. It is addressed to Wonskolaser in Burbank, California. Of course, after making a copy we returned the original to the widow.

July 3, 1934

J.L.,

I just received your most recent letter, written on May 31st. The one-month delay was probably caused by the censors. God knows when this one will get to you, for the same reason. Nowadays they examine every word. I guess all I really want to say was how disappointed I was to finally read your reply once it arrived.

I haven't drawn a paycheck since last September, when the studio let me go. You had no choice. No hard feelings. You know that I still came to the office anyway—and right at nine a.m., by the way. I didn't want people to think the studio had caved in to Goebbels and the rest of that crowd. That was as important to me as I know it is for you. But since May there has been a guard at the door and a cop on the street. I can't get anywhere near the place.

I have no other paying job. Things are getting pretty rough. Last week Hannelore was forced out of the auction house. Blond hair. Blue eyes. Spotless bloodlines. Not good enough. I don't have to tell you the reason. Karelena is not going to be allowed to return to school at the end of the summer break. I am not so sure the Jewish schools are going to hold out open arms. They've got their bloodlines, too. What is to become of her? Twelve years old!

Back to business. Saw *Fashions of 1934* at the UFA Palast. You've got a big hit on your hands. There must have been two thousand people laughing their heads off. The key to the success of this picture, and just about every other Warners feature, is the Berkeley routines. They are a big hit with Herr Hitler as well. I've heard from reputable sources that he still watches *42nd Street* four or five times a week. Sometimes twice in a row. Predicted gross: two hundred and fifty thousand.

J.L., you've got no idea of what's going on here. If you have a Jew in the family, no matter how distant, it's a stain. You can't wash it away. Imagine if you've got a Jew for a father. A Jew for a spouse. It's curtains! I've got to figure it out.

At this time we have nothing for you in our offices abroad. You didn't write those words. You didn't mean them. We go back too far. Didn't I get you into Germany in the first place? With *Where the North Begins?* The Wolf Dog! I'm the one who shepherded Rin-Tin-Tin from one city to another. The Germans loved it! And besides, it's not true! Not true! I know there is an opening in Warsaw. I know it for a fact.

No, no. Of course you wrote those words, J.L. I'm the one who didn't mean what I just wrote. If this were in pencil, I'd erase it. I'd rub it out. I apologize!

Back to business! But I already said that. The long and the short of it is you can save yourself a lot of time and trouble by not submitting the Robinson picture. *The Man with Two Faces?* They hate them both. That's because he speaks out. He takes stands. Do yourself a favor: tell him and everybody else to put a sock in it. They cost you and they cost the studio. But can you just stop and think how much they are costing me? For God's sake, J.L., put yourself in possession of the facts!

I'd just like to say that it is my wish that my friend Alex Engelsing take care of my daughter in case anything happens to me. He is her "Uncle Engel."

Time and trouble: that's not all my advice has saved you. What about the money? A ton of money. That's how much my connections are worth. Ten years of connections. I know what's going on at the Reichsfilmkammer. People still talk to me. They like me. Nobody turns their back.

I think there has been a misunderstanding. I wasn't angling to become the branch manager in Poland. Maybe I didn't express myself clearly. I'll take any position—a rental agent in Prague or sales rep in Stockholm. Bring me back to Burbank. I'll sweep the floor of the writers' bungalow. You can't get any lower than that, right, J.L.? I'll be the guy who keeps an eye out. To make sure those guys come in at nine! You'll be able to meet my family. Hannelore is learning English. Bit by bit. I guarantee she'll be fluent by the time we arrive on the coast.

And Karelena: Blond! Like her mother. Not from me. Eyes blue, blue-grey. Also not from me. You would never guess she has a drop of Jewish blood. You should see her nose. Straight, I swear it. Like on a Greek statue. Like on an ancient coin. She speaks English, with hardly an accent. She's got a broad brow stuffed full of brains. Now they won't even let her play billiards! J.L, you'd never know she's my daughter. You would never know I injected her with poison. Jack! Jesus! They set the dogs on me!

Well, back to the grindstone! Tonight I'm going to the premiere of *Twenty Million Sweethearts*. It's at the Gloria Palast on the Kurfürstendamm. I'll hold on to this letter until tomorrow, so that I can add my impressions. There is not a single Jew in the cast. I don't think there's going to be any trouble. So long for now. And don't worry. I'm paying for my own ticket.

Your friend,
Joe

This is the second letter in the dead man's pocket, written one month before the first:

Date: May 31, 1934
Subject: Kauffman Employment
To: Mr. Kauffman
From: Jack L. Warner

Dear Joe Kauffman:
I am in receipt of your letters of April 4th, April 18th, April 27th, May 3rd, and May 22nd.
I am sorry to have to tell you that at this time we have nothing for you in our offices abroad. Where did you get the idea that we had any openings?
I have noted your reports on *Gold Diggers of 1933, 42nd Street,* and the other pictures. In future, if you have information to give us, please send it directly to Blanke or Sam Bischoff.
Regards to your family.

J. L. Warner

I am in possession of one last letter, written just a few days ago. We intercepted it—as we do all letters sent out of the Reich—copied it for our files, and then mailed it off to the recipient.

24 August 1934

Sehr Geehrter Herr Mister Jack L. Warner:
Here is the correspondence of my husband. He intended the next day to send it to you by the mail. It is called I think in English language a "suicide note."

Hannelore Kaiser
(*Vorher Frau Joseph Kauffman*)

LAST DAY OF APRIL 1945, BERLIN

Again Magda. This summons I cannot ignore. I follow her to the Führer's study. Günsche stands guard, with Linge and Bormann. I motion to Linge, who opens the door. The smell of almonds, bitter and sharp, is in the air. Eva and the Führer are both on the sofa. He has a bullet wound in the temple; she has swallowed the poison. The last of his women to take their own lives.

Everything now occurs swiftly. The Führer is wrapped in a blanket and he and his spouse are carried up the four flights to the garden. The shells from the Bolsheviks are falling near. Some have already landed in the grounds. Both bodies are doused with petrol. A shell lands to the left. A second one follows. I offer my matches. The wind—or is it the concussion from the falling bombs?—blows them out. Linge twists some papers together, which Bormann makes into a sort of torch. He throws it onto the bodies; they ignite with a rush. Another shell. We retreat to the Bunker door. There Krebs, Burgdorf, Bormann. Günsche, Linge, and I give the salute. Without a word we turn, bumping into each other in our haste to get inside. The heavy door closes behind us.

Is my baby out for no good?

After so many years, are these the words that are going to sound and sound and sound in my ears? They are louder than the thunder of the Russian guns. At least I will not have to bear them much longer. Weeks? Days? No: one more day at the most.

Fräulein Kauffman: 1935, Berlin

I knew Joe-Joe worked for Mr. Warner because he took me to all the Warner Bros. pictures. Even when there was school the next day. He once took me every night of the week, which made Hannelore, which made Mama, angry. I saw *Gold Diggers of 1933*. I was the girl in the window when Dick Powell sang:

> *In the shadows let me come and sing to you*
> *Let me dream a song that I can bring to you*

I was the one he blew the kiss to. Not that Ruby Keeler.

Oh, I was so jealous of that person! I already had a crush on Dick because of *42nd Street*. After Joe-Joe took me to that, I snuck away from school and saw it three more times on my own. The way he held her in his arms! The best was *Footlight Parade*. When Dick and Ruby sing "By a Waterfall" together. What a moment that was. All those beautiful girls sliding into the water. Swimming with their legs underneath and making a diamond necklace—that's what it looked like to me—on the surface. Shining. Shining and glittering. Like the pieces in Ein Kaleidoskop.

By a waterfall, I'm calling you-oo-oo-oo

Then he kissed her. On the screen. But it was my own lips that were open and hot. Oh, if Joe-Joe knew what I was feeling!

It wasn't all romance. We saw *Dracula*. We saw *M*. We saw the horrible *Doctor X*, where the murderer always laid his corpses under a full moon. Oh, the chunks taken out of their bodies. Kannibalismus! I was only ten years old. I wanted to run, to run, to run. Joe-Joe put his hands over my eyes and we stayed in our seats. But I had nightmares. Night after night. It was my throat the fangs of the vampire sank into. I took the balloon from the hands of the whistling Mörder. I saw my body, my girl's body, lying in the moonlight.

Joe-Joe, Papa, would come into my room. He would take the two ends of my bedsheet and hold them above me: and he would say, *You see? No one can harm you.* And he would flap the sheet back and forth. *With these wings you can fly away.* But I didn't believe him. Why didn't he fly away when they beat him? He just lay there in the street. So I knew I couldn't fly away, not from the Moon Killer.

In *Twenty Million Sweethearts* Dick wasn't the juvenile lead. He was the star. I could tell from his picture in the newspaper. It was summer. I wasn't in school. I begged Joe-Joe to take me to the Gloria Palast. *It's Dick Powell!* But he said no. I couldn't understand. He never said no. I lost my head. I told him he was a terrible father. It didn't do any good. Then I told him, *I'll drown myself! I'll put my head in the oven!* That didn't do any good, either. He smiled. He said, *Tomorrow, we'll play pool together. It doesn't matter about the Zylinderhut. We'll find a new place. You and me. You'll like that, won't you?*

He knew that I would. I even had my own cue stick. With my initials, KK, on it. But I said I wouldn't. I said I wanted to go to the Gloria Palast. I wanted to go that night. That moment. Now. But he turned and left me. It wasn't until the next day that I found out why.

3 } MAGIC
} HANDS

The Terrible Turk: November 1941 Washington, DC

I have been to the White House a lot since the president took office, and I think I'll be invited again. I like going. Everybody takes your coat and your hat. Mostly I go alone, but a few times I've gone with the Chief—only I don't call him that because that's really the president's job, head of the army and the navy and the whole country and not just the Burbank Studio. Instead, when I have to say something, I just go, "That's right, Mr. Warner"; or if the president asks about "my pal, Jack" I say, "Mr. Warner is fine."

The president calls him Jack and sometimes "Jack, old boy," or once when we were all fishing together, "Good old Jack-o." That happened when we, I mean Mr. FDR and me, were back in the stern together; he asked me to leave Warner Bros. and come to work for him. The Chief must have heard him because at that very moment he walked up holding this barracuda or some other fish he caught and he was smiling the way he does, with all his teeth. He said, "What about it, Abdul? You want to work in the White House and drink old-fashioneds?" The smile was because he knew I would say no. The president didn't give up. Another time he said, "Jack, old fellow, I'm going to make you ambassador to Norway and keep Abdul here for myself." But the Chief figured he was kidding and just said, "Norway? I couldn't afjord it."

One time, though, he got a real scare. We were going down a hallway, the president in that bicycle chair, when all of a sudden he stopped and looked up at the Chief and said, "You know, Jack, about Abdul here. I might have to make this a matter of national security." And the Chief, like he's in on the joke, said, "I know, I know. You are going to make me ambassador to Timbukto. But I already told you: I look lousy in striped pants." But this was no joke. "You don't understand," the president said. "I need him. Don't you see I am in pain?" The Chief did not say a word, which was, believe me, an unheard-of event, and I give thanks to God Mr. Roosevelt did not turn to me because I had tears in my eyes and in spite of the fact I love the Chief and never want to leave him I think I might have said *Okay, I'll come.*

Maybe you have figured out I am not a man of few words. *The Talkative Turk*, some people have called me. I'm going to talk now about our last visit to the White House, which occurred only one day ago. We got to Pennsylvania Avenue and were disappointed since we were told that the president was waiting for us over in the steam room and that meant no martinis and no old-fashioneds, which he always mixed for us himself and poured into silver glasses. He squeezed the oranges with one hand, so we could be impressed by how strong his arms were, which was, you can take it from an expert, plenty.

Then the Chief said, "You go, Abdul, and I'll wait up here and see the president later. Maybe somebody around here will take pity on a starving man and bring him a soda cracker. Between you and me that is, for these Episcopalians, a feast."

But right away Arthur, the president's right-hand man and of course a colored, which was the race he had a fondness for: Arthur came up and said that the Chief was supposed to come along, too. This was a first. I knew the sight that awaited me, but the Chief—well, I guess he had an imagination for it, because his face, which was as dark as mine because of the million years he spent playing tennis in the sun, all of a sudden was drained of its color, as if Mr. Roosevelt had squeezed it like one of those oranges or lemons. "Sure," he answered Mr. Prettyman. "Lead on, Macduff!"

The whole world knows that Franklin Roosevelt was a victim of the infantile, and most people did their best to forget it. Sometimes, because of his smiling with that cheerful cigarette and that chin, I thought Mr. FDR forgot it, too. But not the Terrible Turk. I should have said that Mr. Prettyman was the right-*leg* man of the president, and the left-leg man, too, since it was his job to get him into those braces with the straps and then into his pants and his socks and his shoes.

When we got to the steam room, which was really only one of the laundry rooms that had been fitted up with a bench and exercise rings, the braces were propped up against a wall. His suit of clothes was on a hanger. The president himself was face down on the rubbing table. You could see from his hair that he had been swimming in the pool.

"Hello, Jack, old boy!" This came out in a shout, or maybe the tiles on the walls made it sound like one. "Abdul! A sight for sore eyes!" He waved his left hand at both of us. The Chief made some lame joke—though maybe it is not good taste to use that word right now—about the president being in the swim or doing swimmingly, and I just said, "Hello, Mr. President. I am glad to see you. Would you like me to begin?"

"You bet!" he answered, which came out also in a shout. "I've been looking forward to this day. No one has magic hands like you."

An aide of some kind, he was wearing a navy uniform, stood just inside the door. But it was Arthur Prettyman—the Chief always called him the Roosevalet—who, the same as always, came to the table and folded the sheet up to the president's hips. It was, like I said, a sad sight. The Chief was looking up at the ceiling or down at the floor and every which way, including whether all of a sudden he needed a manicure, except at where those twigs of legs lay on the table, all grey with blue veins and so thin that it was hard to believe there could be human bones inside them.

"Pull up a chair, Jack," the president said, "and tell me what new picture you're going to send me for New Year's Eve."

Three wicker chairs were lined up against the wall. The Chief dragged one of them up to where he and Mr. Roosevelt were about eye to eye for their chat.

"You saw *Dive Bomber*, right? WINGS TO THE WIND: EYES TO THE SKIES! You saw *Maltese Falcon*, right? A MASTERPIECE OF MYSTERY!"

"Indeed I did, and it was absolutely grand. I am going to issue an executive order that you get the Academy Award. I only wish that Mr. Spade could work for the FBI. Between you and me and the wall over there, I wish he could be *head* of the FBI."

"No dice, Mr. President. We've got him under a seven-year contract."

Mr. Roosevelt gave a big laugh. It was strange to see—the difference between the pink and lively top of the man, his head, I mean, with his big shoulders, and the ice-cold sticks that I was rubbing for all I was worth, as if I could make them catch fire.

"I want you to send me something before anyone else in the country gets to see it. So I can make them secrets of state."

"How about *You're in the Army Now*? A REGIMENT OF ROARS! Silvers and Durante get drafted into the army by mistake and try to make this stick-in-the-mud general trade in his horses for tanks. We were going to release it at Christmas, but I guess we can hold it for New Year's Day. HERE'S A KISS YOU DON'T WANT TO MISS! The longest in movie history."

"Send it along! I'll invite the chiefs of staff. They could use a lesson on modernization—not to mention kissing."

"*Three minutes. Plus five seconds.* Reagan wanted to know how we got his wife to sit still for so long."

"Anything else in your treasure chest? What else have you got to cheer us up?"

"Well, in January we're releasing a picture about this guy, a real New York sophisticate, who drops in on this Ohio family of rubes to have dinner. Well, what happens is he slips and breaks a hip or a leg or something and spends the whole winter making an ass of himself going around in his wheelchair—oops."

For a long time, maybe as long as that record kiss, nobody said a word. I was too embarrassed to speak myself. Then the president—his head was turned so I could see his smile—said, "What's the matter, Jack, old boy? You look a little peckish."

Say this for the Chief: he was a master at changing the subject. "Remember when you were going to make me ambassador to Norway? Hitler got there first. What a diplomat! Now he's got ambassadors in Belgium and Holland and France. You'd better hurry up or you're going to run out of countries to send me to."

The president did not laugh. He said, "As a matter of fact, Jack, that's why I asked you to come over here for my hour with Abdul."

"Uh-oh. Where to now? Bangkok? I better go get a bow-Thai."

"Jack, I'm serious. I wanted to thank you, and Harry too, for re-releasing the Nazi spy picture. I've seen all the new scenes you added."

"*RIPPED FROM THE HEADLINES!* A fat lot of good that did us. It's banned in half the countries in the world."

"Not the half that matters, Jack. When our citizens see German soldiers marching down the Champs-Élysées they're going to make up their minds to stop them from marching down Broadway."

"Speaking of Broadway, we're doing the life of George M. Cohan. THE YANKEE DOODLE DANDIEST ENTERTAINMENT OF 'EM

ALL! It's plenty patriotic and everybody sings "Over There" and if you want to stir people up and get them in a fighting mood, that's your ticket!"

"Wonderful, Jack. Just wonderful. I—oh, *there*! Right there, Abdul! I feel it. I swear to you. Once more! And again! There's feeling at that spot."

The spot was on his right leg, just beneath the buttock. I dug in my thumbs. The president gasped. He always said he could walk ten feet farther after I'd gone to work on him. The trouble was, it didn't last. That's why I always had to come back. With a grunt he said to the Chief, "What I wanted to tell you, Jack, is that your pictures are performing a real service. They are going to hasten the day when this country makes up its mind to fight. That's why I wanted to see you. To offer my thanks."

"You don't have to give me a medal or anything. Well, maybe just a wee favor."

"Ask away, Jack-o. If I can do it, I will."

The Chief took an envelope from an inside pocket. "It's personal, you know. It involves a very good friend of mine. Now deceased. He worked for us in Berlin. He headed up our offices there. Joe Kauffman. As it so happens of the Jewish persuasion. So when the Nazis came to power they hunted him down. They cornered him in a theater and then shot him in the head."

"I am very sorry to hear that, Jack."

"Well, we paid the funeral expenses, naturally. We send money over to the family all the time."

"That's very good of you, old boy. You always do the right thing."

"Don't mention it. It's our policy to be loyal to our employees. Anyway, he had a daughter, who a friend of his at Tobis—a guy that's now under contract with me—took under his wing. By the way, Paramount and those other studios are still doing business with those bums. At the time the girl was only twelve, but today she's eighteen or nineteen, and she's had a few parts and she's on the verge of being a star, whether she's half of a Jew or not."

"It sounds like the happy ending to one of your pictures."

"Far from it. It's more of a tearjerker. And with an old-fashioned villain, too. Goebbels. He's got his eye on her. More than an eye. Do I have to say more? She's desperate to get out. And we'd like to have her in Burbank. To tell the truth she's a looker and we'll find work for her. Supposedly she's got an ironclad contract with Tobis; I write and write and get no answer to my letters. And at the State Department all we hear is no, no, no. They make it sound like there are a million people ahead of her. Every damned Jew left in Europe. So until now it's what in chess you call a stalemate."

"What they say is true, Jack. There probably are a million refugees. We can't let them all in. The country won't stand for it if they think we're going to fight a war for the Jews."

"Yeah, well, the thing is, we just got a letter—from this Fräulein Kaiser, that's her screen name. I've got it right here, and with it came her old contract all torn up. So it seems she's free to come and those bums at Tobis didn't want us to know. She wants to come. Isn't there some way to move her up to the top of the list?"

"I'd like to help, old boy, but I am afraid I can't. You have to go through Secretary Hull. If he can't do anything, neither can I. You know the president doesn't do these kinds of favors for particular citizens."

"I know, I know. But it's a matter of life and death. If you'll just let me read you—oh, dearie me!"

What happened was that when the Chief took the letter from the envelope, something slipped out and fell to the floor.

"See, Mr. President? Here's the contract, just like I told you, with a big X through it and—"

"Just a minute, Jack. Didn't you notice? You dropped something there."

But Prettyman had already stepped over and picked up the piece of paper that had fallen through the Chief's fingers. It wasn't paper, actually. It was a photograph.

"Ah, ha!" said the president, squinting through his little glasses. "What's this?"

This was the moment when for the first time I saw the face of Karelena Kaiser. It was a publicity shot: lots of dramatic lighting and one shoulder bare. The eyebrows were dark but the hair was blond, and the lips of the mouth were like—well, in my opinion, like someone who was about to welcome a kiss. Right away you could see why they wanted to make her a star: that combination of the girl and the woman, the unplucked bud and—every now and then I surprise myself at my own poetry—the wide-open flower.

"I don't know why she sent that," said the Chief. "It's immaterial to our discussion."

"Ho, ho!" The laugh was booming, like one of the Santas who were already showing up in the department stores. "You don't have to say anything else, Jack-o. Because with this picture—and what a picture it is!—you have saved yourself a thousand words. And now I am truly sorry: I simply can't do it, not even for ten thousand words."

"Well, there's more. There's plenty more that I—"

"Abdul! What are you looking at? Keep working. There! Keep at it. That's the spot!"

"Look, I won't pretend that I didn't think a girl like this might be good for business. It crossed my mind. But I swear that's not why I am begging, *begging*, for this favor. It's because of family feeling. The Warner Bros. family. The girl is in danger. She knows too much."

"You're not making, sense, Jack-o. Too much about what?"

"I don't know myself. I'm not sure. There's this letter. Where she says how much she wants to come and how frightened she is because she knows some secret about that Furor guy and that other women have died because of it and then—this is the funny part, the part I don't get—she says there's another secret, something about the fleet, she means the Japanese fleet, is going to sail, and there's going to be an attack on a Sunday, and somewhere here—let's see, yeah, right here, submarines are already on their way and—"

Here the president gave another big laugh. I could feel it under my fingers. "Ho, ho, now I understand! You want her to be in one of your pictures. Some big battle at sea. Is she going to be a nurse? In love with a sailor? And you want the cooperation of the navy, eh?"

"No, no. I mean, yes. We'd love to work with the navy. But listen. This isn't a picture. I mean, wait a second—here are her actual words."

With that the Chief put his finger down on the paper. "Let's see, hum-hum-de-hum. Oh, yeah: 'You must tell the president about Pearl Harbor and Admiral Yamamoto and Operation Z.' Yamamoto? Is that the guy Lorre plays over at Fox?"

But the president had pushed himself up with both hands. He turned to the navy guy.

"Lieutenant Fox!"

Now his whole body, except for his legs, was raised off the table. "Will you immediately escort Abdul and Mr. Prettyman outside?"

I never heard that tone of voice from Mr. FDR. The navy officer took hold of my arm with one hand and, with the other, took hold of Pretty-man. He marched us out of the room. When he turned to go back in, the president said, "No: you, too, Lieutenant. I want you to leave me alone with my Hollywood friend. Ha, ha, ha The things they think up in that town. Ha, ha, ha! *Submarines!*"

The next thing I knew Mr. Prettyman and the Terrible Turk were out in the corridor, and the navy man was standing with his two legs apart and his hands on his hips outside the door. On one of those hips was a gun.

How long did we wait out there? It seemed a long time, but in reality it was only a half an hour, tops. At first we could not hear anything—not a word and not a sound. But after awhile there were voices. And also a clank, a bang, a burst of laughter. Then came more clanking and something that sounded like maybe a waiter had dropped a pile of tin plates. After that, it became quiet again, but it was only the quiet in front of the storm, because all of a sudden the door flew open and the lieutenant jumped to one side and out came first Jack and then the president. He was wearing only the glasses on his nose and the steel on his legs, and he was walking, one foot and then the other foot, working his shoulders, swinging his arms, and he wouldn't let Jack or me or the colored touch him—he just kept walking and at the same time shouting: "By God! By God, Abdul! You've done it this time. You're a wonder! A miracle worker! A treasure! You have brought a dead man back to life!"

4 } ABOARD THE EUROPA

Goebbels: First Day of May 1945, Berlin

The end must now be measured not in days, but in hours. Yet some still cling to fantasies. There has been talk of the Twilight of the Gods. Did not monsters in that age storm the Citadel, even as they do today in ours? Flames devoured it. The sacred walls crumbled. All seemed lost. Ah! Suddenly a new Valhalla arises, more splendorous than ever before. Thus at the close of my life am I surrounded by children. Against all odds Frederick the Great was victorious at Leuthem; and so it follows in their syllogism we shall be victorious in Berlin. Yet even these prattling babes fall silent when the ground shakes over our heads. Nothing can be heard but the hum of the ventilator fans. Basso continuo. By Wagner.

The question is not: Have our enemies won? But: How long shall their victory last? That will be determined by the example we set here in our final refuge. The Führer, in declining to flee, has done his part. By dying with honor ourselves, with some part of the Führer's heroism, we create the legend that will break the chains that bind a Bolshevized continent. The myth of our perishing will make certain that National Socialism, the true Citadel of our time, will rise again, not just in Germany or Europe but in America itself. As for the Jews, they will meet their Cannae not in centuries but sooner than they, in their dancing and Purim merriment, could ever believe!

Fräulein Kauffman: March 1937, Berlin

My dear dear Onkel Engel came by today—even though he is a film star and a film producer he wears the same old suit and scuffed-up shoes—and he said he wants me to be in a movie! In lots of movies! I had to cry for an hour to get Hannelore to agree. Tonight she will put my hair in braids. Already I am staring into the mirror.

Goebbels: May 1937, Berlin

I spend the afternoon preparing my radio broadcast. Then to the Chancellery to watch a film with the Führer. It features Zarah Leander, who I feel is overestimated. She has the typical pinched features and limited range one finds in a representative of a small state. At the UFA reception I asked her whether Zarah was a Jewish name. She has no humor. She said, "Just like the name Joseph." I would not want to be a Swede. Only a member of a world power.

But in that film a brief scene with a golden-haired child, perhaps fifteen, in the Australian work camp. Charming in her braids.

JUNE 1937, BERLIN

I see that Mädchen again, once more in an Engelsing production. *Andere Welt*. She wanders down an obviously fake Oriental street, wearing the hat of a cooly. The hair is dyed jet-black and pulled back. But the eyes! They cannot be disguised. Even in black and white, an Aryan blue. A smile. One tooth overlaps another. Must contact Lehnich to discover her name.

AUGUST 1937, BERLIN

Uncut version of *Die Umwege des schönen Karl*. An empty comedy. That girl again. In a beach costume. Running in and running out of the waves. The swimsuit is in two pieces, which is becoming more common. We Germans are not prudes. I have asked the Reichsfilmkammer to give me her name. The idiots have not been able to perform this simple task. We might have to replace Lehnich sometime soon. The cameraman shows us the touching adolescent shoulders, the legs, der niedliches kleines Arsch.

OCTOBER 1937, BERLIN

I now watch each Tobis film with special attention. And my efforts are rewarded. Today, at a private screening, I see her sitting with her protector, Engelsing, at a café table. Smoke. Music. A laughing crowd. She has her natural blond hair but with an ugly smear of lipstick across her lips. Ah! When she smiles, there is that one tooth overlapping the other. The long swan's curve of the neck. Engelsing is under watch. Many dubious contacts. *Twice* observed at entrance to Soviet Embassy. But our child is growing into a woman.

Fräulein Kauffman: October 1937, Berlin

I am going to India! AND by myself! I mean, with Onkel Engel and all the actors and all the crew and the makeup man, but not Hannelore. She said the strangest thing: "If I go, I don't come back. You should not come back, either." But of course I am going to come back. She doesn't believe in the new Germany. She even says bad things about our Führer, who is working so hard for his people. Because we had to move from our flat. Because she doesn't work in the auction house. Because I can't go to school. Well, an actress doesn't have to go sit in a boring old classroom. And Onkel Engel said I am beautiful enough to be an actress. Only he does not want me to call him Onkel Engel anymore but just plain Alex. And now I am going to have lines to read and an actual close-up. Why should I sit in the stupid old höhere Schule, where all they can do is read about India and the Taj Mahal, but I am going to see everything for myself! I'll come and give them a lecture! About the temple dancers and the people who swim in the Ganges River and the tiger hunt. Now I must put to memory my lines. When Herr Theo, dear old Herr Theo, asks me where the Maharaja is, I am going to say that I am not allowed to tell that to the Sahib. *Sahib!* Ha! Ha! Ha! *Sahib!* And of course I have to dye my blond hair black; I practiced it last night and Hannelore—well, I thought she was going to slap me. She lifted her hand, but instead turned away and said, "Now you look like a verdreckt Jude."

I don't care. I don't care if I look like a Jew or a Gypsy or a kangaroo! I am going to India! And next year I will get a bigger part and we will have lots of money and no one will be able to say anything or do anything when I am a famous star. Of course I will have to change my name. I think I should also change my teeth.

Goebbels: December 1937, Berlin

This morning, at last, I find on my desk the dossier of the young Tobis actress—not from the inkompetenten at the Reichsfilmkammer, but from the SS. Strange the workings of destiny. That this young actress should turn out to be the daughter of that same Kauffman who shot himself in the Gloria Palast four years ago. *Twenty Million Sweethearts.* "En Musikkomedi från Warner–First National." All I had to do was raise my hat. Twice. Then our good German folk expressed their indignation.

Who would have guessed that our attractive Mädchen, with her noble brow and that Kussmund, was a Jewess? Well, if we have temporarily permitted Furtwängler to keep his hook-nosed violinists—like Gypsies, they have an affinity for that instrument—then we at the Reichsfilmkammer can allow this young girl to play her parts, especially since the bereaved widow has already resumed her Mädchen name of Kaiser, which her daughter has wisely adopted as well.

APRIL 1938, BERLIN

Tageskopie of *Der Tiger von Eschnaupuer* arrived this afternoon. For the first time we hear her voice. Theo Lingen, the comedian, strolls through a palace courtyard. He comes across a veiled servant with a basket of fruit on her head. "Wo ist der Maharadscha?" he asks her. "I am not allowed to tell that to the Sahib." Those are Fräulein Kaiser's first spoken words.

Here is what happens next. Lingen takes the fruit and peels away the veil. A close-up: the large, wide-spaced eyes; the cheekbones full enough to cast shadows; the thin upper lip and the pouting lower one. I know this face well; the actor, however, has never seen such a sight in his life. As the girl moves shyly away, he stands, thunderstruck: *She would be a good start for my harem.*

What is Engelsing up to? On the one hand, he gives his protégé some lines to speak. And he takes her all the way to India to deliver them. At the same time, he hides her away in these frivolous diversions for the masses. I intend to do something about that. It is time for me to turn this beautiful young girl into an actress.

Fräulein Kaiser: May 1938, Berlin

People Think Alex and I began our—what to call it?—our love story when we were in India, but the truth is it did not begin until we were on the steamboat for the long long long trip back. Together. Always together. With the light streaming through the round steamship window. How on earth all the world found out about it I don't know. There they were, waiting for us when we docked at Hamburg. The flash lamps! The reporters with their pencils and radio people with the microphones in our faces. And I only had a few lines. But of course my close-up. Is this what it will be like to be a star?

"When did you fall in love, Fräulein?"

"Was it at the Taj Mahal?"

I did not tell them the truth. I did not tell Alex the truth, which is that my feeling for him began long before the *Europa*. He does not remember, but I do: how he used to throw me in the air. Up to the ceiling, where I would almost hit my head. And Joe-Joe would catch me. Then Joe-Joe would throw me and my Onkel, my Engel, would catch me, the two of them laughing and I shrieking and pretending to be afraid. I really was afraid, but I could smell him then. The sweat of him. It is the smell, exactly, that he still has now. He is planning a new part for me. In our next film he is going to hold me, embrace me, and we are going to kiss.

Goebbels: June 1940, Berlin

Definite news of the cease-fire at Compiègne. Spent the night with Magda and a small circle of fellow workers at Lanke. The silvery waters. The silvery light. Champagne. I announce that in my opinion the war is over. Britain, without France, cannot fight on. Our unit filmed the ceremony. The Führer accepted the surrender in the same railway carriage in which Foch humiliated us in 1918. Great and glorious Germany!

Over the last eighteen months I have permitted the Kauffman girl, Fräulein Kaiser, to appear in three films. Each time with Engelsing. The newspapers cannot get enough of it. Die Opa Romanze, they call it, because they are living together offscreen as well as on. I only wish he *were* old enough to be her grandfather. His blood may be pure, but in our investigation of his ancestry, we uncovered his ties to the Soviets. This Onkel is quite likely a spy. Now he wants to take her off to film an epic in Poland. We shall see about that.

On this happy day, I have seen the fall of France and shall begin to truly shape this Fräulein's career, a career that began with a single moment. If I had blinked I would have missed that golden-haired child. But I never blink.

LAST DAY OF MAY 1945, BERLIN

A tap at the door. Tap-tapping. The children have come to say good night. I force myself to look at them. What pleasure they have brought me over these years. If I am honest with myself, I would say the *only* pleasure. The fall of France? Nothing. Everything: the girls, following Helmut, all in a row on their ponies. Now Hilde comes running in her nightgown and stockings. My God! With ribbons in her hair.

"Are you coming up to say good night, Papa?"

"No, not just now. You see I have work to do."

Helmut: "Is it your diaries? Is what you are writing?"

"Oh, I've put those Tagebücher away."

"But I thought I would be able to read them."

"Yes, yes. Some day you will. Here's a promise, my smart boy: I'll show you a page in the morning."

"Me, too?" This is Heide.

"What? Are you reading now? And only four?"

"But I will be five the same day as you."

"Aren't I lucky? We shall have a big cake together."

"Just the two of us?"

Hedda breaks in: "That isn't fair!"

"But don't you get a big cake just for yourself on your birthday?"

She puts a finger to her chin, thinking this over.

"I'll tell you what, my Liebsten. We won't wait for a birthday. Tomorrow we shall have cake for everyone!"

What a garland of smiles. What joy. As if they were already tucking their napkins around their necks. I have no choice but to turn away and say, more sternly than I wished, "To bed now. Mama is waiting. Don't make me count to ten. You know what happens when I do."

They all move backward. They all go out. Alone for the moment I attempt to look with objectivity at myself. What am I feeling? Disgust. In spite of everything, a life of heroic effort, of sacrifice—a hundred thousand arms thrust upward, a hundred thousand voices: *Totaler Krieg!*—I am no different than anyone else. In the end we are all good burghers, with our slippers and newspapers and a pretty child to bring our pipe. And let's have a cheery fire, too.

Ponies! A ribbon in the hair!

Fräulein Kaiser: December 1940, Berlin

The press follows us day and night. This morning they were waiting outside the door of our flat. "What about your next film?" The reporters hound mein Engel with their questions. "Will Karelena play your mistress? Will you carry her away in your arms?"

Alex only tells them that sometime next year our new film will be shot in Poland and that its name will be *Heimkehr*. He says that it will show how our people were persecuted there and why Germany had to invade that land in order to save them. Later, once they have gone, he says to me to pay no attention and that it is only more propaganda. But he has a secret plan. He really does want to carry me away—not to Poland but onward, to the east, over the border to the Soviet Union. He says there we will be safe. There we can make true films. There we can be true artists. Can that be? I don't know. I don't care. I will follow him anywhere.

Goebbels: First Day of May 1945, Berlin

Where is Stumpfegger? Has he not found the cigarettes? Or is he smoking them himself? He has a more precious treasure. Rarer than the Golden Party Badge that the Führer gave Magda. A gift for the children, a priceless gift, though not one of them is having a birthday. Oh, for a cigarette!

5 } A BULGARIAN!

The Terrible Turk: April 1942, Burbank

We all followed the Chief, or maybe now I should call him the colonel,
from the wardrobe department and outdoors. It was a nice spring day
in the valley, a blue sky, with what in Anatolia we call horse-tail clouds.
The Chief, as soon as he got outside, put his hand to the visor of his cap
and stared up at the sky. It was a habit he had developed—not to look at
the clouds but for the bombers and fighters of the Japs. We were right in
line with the aircraft plants in Burbank, which was why he had the set
painters splash a big sign with an arrow on top of one of the sound stages:
LOCKHEED, THATAWAY.

Anyhow, who should come past the guardhouse of the main gate but
Julius J. Epstein and his brother, Phil. This for the Chief was worse than
a flight of Zeros. He stopped short. So did the twins. They looked at
Mr. Warner. Then they looked at each other. Their two bald heads turned
pink, like eggs you color at Easter. Instead of doubling up in laughter,
they did the opposite. I mean, they stood up so straight they were bending
backward, and, as if they had rehearsed it, saluted. Then they saluted again
and were about to do it for the third time when the Chief—his arms were
already down at his side and twitching as if he were holding an invisible
whip—said, "All right, all right, knock it off."

The boys, which is what everybody called them, simultaneously said,
"Yes sir, Colonel, sir!"

"*Lieutenant* colonel, goddammit!"

Was that a snort from Miss Kaiser, just behind me, or was it a laugh?
No doubt about the two writers: they were struggling to hold it in. One
or the other of them—no telling which pea in the pod—said, "Hi there,
Hadassah!"

"Very funny, very funny," said the Chief.

By now everybody in Burbank knew the story. One of the boys had stolen a piece of stationery from the Chief's office and got a gofer to hand her a letter practically the first minute she stepped foot on the lot.

Date: December 10, 1941
Subject: Screen Name
To: Karelena Kaiser
From: Jack L. Warner

Dear Miss Kaiser:

This is just a brief note to welcome you into the Warner Bros. family. My brothers and I look forward to a long and fruitful association with you under your new name, Hadassah Felberbaum.

Regards to your mother in the old country.

J. L. Warner
(Please call me Jack)

They copied his signature, right down to the loop on top of the J and the slash mark underneath it.

The story is that back then, in December, the Chief came running up and grabbed the letter out of her hand. "Forget about this," he told her. "I know the wise guys who pulled this prank. I've already got a screen name for you. From now on you're Cheryl Charmaigne. That's what I call class." Class or no class, none of us knew that name would only last a couple of weeks.

Now J.L. turned to the writers and said, "I knew it was you two jokers."

To head off trouble I called to one of the twins. "Say, Julie, when are we going to have that fight? Five rounds. The Terrible Turk is going to take on both of you at once. It's all for war bonds."

"'Buy them and hold them!' Okay, we'll do it. But one at a time."

"No, that wouldn't be fair. You never had a professional fight."

"Not true," said Julius J. "I had one. It ended in a draw."

"Then how come you never had another?"

His brother chimed in: "He wanted to retire undefeated."

The two of them started in with the same kind of laughter, each one topping the other.

The Chief all the time was frowning down at his watch. "Do you two have any idea what time it is? Let me be the first to inform you: 2:02."

"Thank you, Jack."

"We had no idea."

"I'll give you an additional piece of information. Your contract says you have to be in your office and at work by nine a.m. You aren't fooling anybody. I know damn well you stroll in after lunch every damn day. Don't you know we're trying to get out a picture? Right now we're on our way to test Miss Kaiser and thanks to you we don't have a single line for her to speak. But at least she's working. I'm working. Rydo here is working, too. What makes you two so special? I'm getting tired of it. What were you doing? Playing tennis at Roxbury? Don't lie to me! We've got our spies!"

"We weren't playing tennis, Jack. But we do need a fourth this Sunday and—"

"Goddammit! I'm getting worked up. A butcher arrives at his butcher shop at nine. A clerk sits down at his desk at nine o'clock, too. Even bank presidents start work at nine."

"Fine," said Julie—or maybe it was Phil. "Then why don't you hire a bank president to finish this script?"

"I'll tell the jokes around here! As of today this stops. I'm going to tell the guardhouse to write down whenever you two come in and send me a report. After two! Two p.m.! And with a war on!"

"Well, we'd have been in sooner, except that Hal told us to go over to Culver City."

"What the hell for? Do they have better courts over there?"

"Didn't he tell you? We're trying to talk Selznick into loaning us Bergman for the picture."

"Selznick?" said the Chief, looking up at the sky once more, but this time for inspiration. "Bergman?"

Little Rydo came forward and whispered something in the colonel's ear.

"Oh, yeah. Ingrid! Well, what happened? And make it snappy."

The Epsteins started in.

"He was eating lunch."

"Right at his desk."

"Soup."

"Tomato."

"With a spoon."

"For Christ's sake, why don't you tell me what he had for breakfast, while you're at it? What the hell happened?"

"Well, we told him all about the picture—how there's this American saloon keeper in Morocco and his old girlfriend shows up, and the letters of transit, and the Germans are putting pressure on the Vichy officials and—"

"And not once does he look up from his soup, but he just keeps spooning it in as if we weren't there at all."

"So finally Phil said, 'Oh, it's just a lot of slick shit like *Algiers*—'"

"And he puts down his spoon and lifts up his head and says, 'Okay, you can have her. I want de Havilland in return.'"

"De Havilland?"

Once more Rydo went up on tip toes and—I should say there were no more pins in his mouth—whispered in his ear.

"Yeah. Right. Okay. He can have her."

"Great," said Julius J. "Now we know who to write Ilsa's lines for."

From the shadow that passed over the Chief's face, you'd have thought that some big cloud had moved over the sun. And from the way he grabbed Miss Kaiser's arm and tried to pull her away, you'd have thought it was about to rain.

But the actress stood her ground.

"Ilsa?" she said. "Isn't that my part? Weren't we going to make the test now?"

"Uh-oh," said Phil.

"You said it," said Julie.

The Chief turned on the two of them. "Now look what you've done!"

"*Loose quips*," said one of the twins.

"*Pink slips*," said the other.

Miss Kaiser yanked her arm from the Chief's grip. "Don't you touch me! 'The perfect face,' you said. 'The perfect accent.' It's no different here than the Third Reich. But at least Goebbels keeps his word. I could have been Annelie. The model of the German woman. I could have been the greatest star in Europe."

Rydo, the costume man, said, "You don't mean that, darling. You are in a free country now."

Suddenly the girl burst into tears. If it was an act, then in my opinion she deserved an Academy Award. They came spurting out of her. Rain after all.

The Chief put his arm, with the oak-leaf cluster on the sleeve, around her. "Stop it. I can't stand crying. If you don't stop I'll start crying, too."

But that seemed to make it worse.

"Look, there was a misunderstanding. I'll give that Wallis a real dressing down. The son of a bitch! Whose name is on the water tower? A *W* and a *A* and a-a-a—"

Julie or Phil: "*R*, J.L.?"

"Listen, you've got to stop crying. Didn't you hear there is a drought? Please. I'm on my knees. So to speak. Don't worry. Look how beautiful you are. And listen to you. What acting! What pathos! We'll get you another part. A great part."

That seemed to grab her attention. The Chief looked around desperately at the Epstein twins. "Right, boys?" Then, with what they call in the business sotto voce: "Right, goddammit?"

"Sure," said Julie. "Let's figure it out. How about there's a foreign refugee, see?"

Phil spoke up. "She's stuck in Casablanca, see?"

"A Romanian!"

"A Norwegian!"

Then they both shouted together: "No, no! We got it! A Bulgarian!"

"What the hell does it matter where she's from? As long as she's got an accent. This is perfect for KK. She's beautiful, okay? With a neck. And a figure. Not too big on top. Young, vivacious. Lost in a foreign land. Do you hear that, sweetheart? It's practically written for you. Here's how I see it. How you have suffered. Fleeing for your life. From Nazis! It's absolutely heartrending. Thank God this happened. I see the hand of providence. *Fräulein Karelena Kaiser*: she was going to be a model for all German women. But now, now—"

He paused. It was like the imaginary clouds had parted. You could see the sunbeams on his face and the way they bounced off all his oak leaves and his teeth. "She will be the symbol of all German *victims*. The persecuted. The nameless. The hunted. All right, cutie pie? Everything okay now? You are the hope. You are the dream. For all the wretched of the earth!"

Behind his back, the two writers pantomimed clapping their hands together, and to tell the truth at this performance I almost broke into applause myself.

6 } SCREEN TEST

Goebbels: First Day of May 1945, Berlin

At last the dentist knocks on this door. "I'd be grateful to you, Herr Doktor Kunz, if you would be so kind as to help my wife prepare the children. Nothing must wake them this night." I say this with no more emotion than if I had asked him to look at a troublesome tooth.

A troublesome tooth: for me, that is still Fräulein Kaiser, or Miss Charmaigne, or whatever name they chose for her in a depraved and Sybaritic America. The first time I saw her—I mean in the flesh and not on a screen—she stood before me wet and dripping, her hair in a tangle and her figure perfectly visible in what had become a transparent dress. Absurd, is it not, to be thinking of a Jewess's breasts while in my underground tomb? The resurgence of the life force, a philosopher might say. Or the Erektion of a man on the gallows. Lebenslust. But would I be in this tomb if she had not failed us?

JUNE 1941 BERLIN

In the afternoon Fräulein Kaiser arrives at the ministry, soaked through to the skin. Her light dress in a daisy pattern clings to her. Before I can utter a word she bursts out: "What have you done with him?" Her skin shines from the wetness and the energy of her fury. Her eyebrows—unusually dark in one so fair—seem barbed, like angry arrows. Her Brüste are loose beneath the silk and are small, firm, high, and pointed in the way often found among those of mixed heritage. The very portrait of health and vigor, which is what our scientific farming methods hope to achieve by breeding together two strains of corn. Irresistible.

"With whom, my dear Fräulein Kaiser?"

But of course I know. Her lover. The spy. Engelsing.

"Alex. We were to meet at the Anhalter Bahnhof. For the trip to Poland.

He did not come to the platform. The train left. I waited outside. An hour in the rain. Then your car came. Your Mercedes. They pushed me inside."

"No lady this beautiful should wait in the rain."

"Your famous bulletproof car. And now your famous endearments."

"But see: you are wet. And cold. I'll have a robe brought for you. And some tea. Would you like that?"

"No. Nothing. Oh, I felt such a fool on the platform. Everyone staring. And then in the rain—"

"Well, here we are, where it is nice and warm and dry. But you really are shivering. I hope you are not frightened. There is no reason to feel at all uneasy."

"I can't help but feel frightened. You can change so much about my life. On an impulse. On a whim."

"How people exaggerate! I can tell you that at times I feel powerless. Just as you say, subject to another person's fancy."

"You? The Reichsminister? When could you possibly feel powerless? Do you mean with the Führer?"

"Not with the Führer. I am certain you do not wish to suggest that he makes his decisions by caprice. Or by anything other than the iron laws of logic."

"Of course. By logic. But then, when—?"

"When, my dear lady? Well, at this very moment."

The girl does not have time to blush. In comes Semmler with tea and savories. I motion toward the sofa. She hesitates.

"Please do sit. Nothing so terrible can happen when sipping tea. Let me pour for you. Have pity on these leaves; they have come round the world from Japan."

"The terrible thing has already happened."

"And what can that be?"

I held out the cup, but—a juvenile gesture; I have to remind myself she is only a girl—she puts both hands under the pits of her arms and stares with her pale, wide eyes.

"Have you murdered him?"

"What an idea! Where do such thoughts come from? From what far-off planet?"

"Why didn't he come to the train? Everything was arranged. You must have taken him in your car. You must have put him in one of your camps."

"It astonishes me how people get these fantastic notions. That we murder people. Or throw them in prison for no reason. Listen to me, Fräulein. Herr Engelsing is a world-famous actor. If we harmed him there would be a reaction in a hundred different countries."

"I don't understand. Didn't you assign us our roles in *Heimkehr*? I memorized my part. So did Alex. We were about to leave. We were going to film the suffering of the German people in Poland. Nothing happens without your approval. Didn't you agree to all of that?"

"We decided that we had made a mistake. Paula Wessely is on that train at this very moment. Do you know her work? She was the voice of Snow White—until we banned that film. I know that some people, unfriendly people, say it was because I did not want to show the dwarves. Those same people like to say I am a dwarf. Grumpy and Sleepy and Sneezy. Do you share that opinion? That I am a dwarf? Limpy, perhaps?"

"I don't care why you replaced me. Or who takes my part. I only want to be with Alex. Can you at least tell me that he is alive?"

"You see, we had a discussion at the Reichsfilmkammer. About the art of film. Everyone agreed: the two of you do not work well together. The Eschnapur film, for example. When you took off the veil—"

"My first close-up."

"He hid your beauty. He made you into a Gypsy. With greased hair and sleepy eyes. He has no idea of how to bring you out on film."

"My eyes are open now. There was no discussion at the Reichsfilmkammer. Not about art. You want to separate the two of us. Heaven knows what you've done with him."

"I shall be frank with you, Fräulein Kaiser. You are correct: we have not taken you off the *Heimkehr* project for artistic reasons. You are valuable to us. We expect from you a brilliant future. We acted to stop you from committing—perhaps I should say, from continuing to commit—a serious crime."

"A crime? Everything now is a crime."

"Not everything. But some things. For instance, Section Two of the Nuremberg laws. No subject of the state of Germany may have sexual relations with a Jew."

"But Alex is not Jewish."

"But, my dear Fräulein Kaiser, you are."

"We have done nothing more than kiss in our films."

"You must not treat me as you would a child. Do you imagine we do not know you and Herr Engelsing have been living together? And that this arrangement began even before you returned from the Orient?"

"But why punish him? Punish me. I am guilty of being the Jew."

"Not so very guilty, Fräulein. Your mother is innocent. Which means that the Jews themselves do not want you. But, my pretty Karelena, we do. You do not have four or even three Jewish grandparents. You practice no faith. The eyes, the nose, the facial structure, the golden hair: all come from the maternal line. Yes, and your hips. Mathematics are on your side. I should say our side; we fully expect you to share in the artistic life of the Reich."

I think: she is going to rise. She is going to flee. Instead, she sinks deeper into the soft cushion. "Yes. My name in lights. 'Karelena Kaiser. Mischling of the First Degree.'"

"In the end, meine Liebe, it is I who decides who is and who is not a Jew. And I have decided that, indeed, your name will be written in lights. That is why you are sitting with me now. We intend to offer you another part. Far greater than Maria in *Heimkehr*."

"You did not answer my question, Doktor Goebbels."

"You must forgive my forgetfulness. What question was that?"

"About Alex. Is he alive? Or have you killed him?"

"I do not know any reason why he should not be alive."

"But you took him. You stopped him from getting on the train. You must know."

"You keep saying the same thing. It is becoming tiresome. Would you believe me if I told you we did not seize him? Have you not once considered the possibility that he did not join you on the platform of his own accord?"

"No! It's impossible. He wanted to play the part of Dr. Thomas. We—"

She stops herself. Perhaps from mouthing, *We are in love*. Or some such Quatsch. Instead, she says:

"Why would he not come?"

"This tea, in your nice porcelain cup. It's cold. May I—? No? Well, to answer your question: there are generally two reasons for a man to act as Herr Engelsing seems to have done. To run toward something that is pleasant or to flee from something that is not."

"Flee? What do you mean? Who would want to harm him? You said yourself, he is known throughout the world."

"And we know him, too. All too well. Perhaps he came to realize this and no longer felt comfortable in the Third Reich."

"I don't understand. It makes no sense. He—"

"Excuse me for interrupting, Fräulein. I have an engagement that I must attend upstairs. In just an hour. To answer your question: Is Herr Engelsing alive? I believe he is. And he seems to wish to remain so. Now let us discuss more agreeable things."

"And the other possibility? That he was not fleeing, but was going to something—or someone—more attractive to him?"

"We have only this hour. I would prefer to talk about someone who is more attractive to me."

FIRST DAY OF MAY 1945, BERLIN

Another knock at the door. The dentist has returned. I do not say a word. He nods.

"All are sleeping?"

He nods again, then says, "It is not too late, Herr Reichsminister. We can bring them to the hospital. Under Red Cross protection. The morphine will wear off. They are children. Innocent."

"They are guilty of being the children of Goebbels."

To this he does not reply. I thank him for his assistance in making the fate that awaits them easier. I wish him good luck in life. I escort him outside to the corridor. And so farewell to dentistry and the dentist. Through the open door to our room, I see that Magda is playing patience. Calmly, she lays down the cards. She waits for Stumpfegger. She wants what he will have in his pocket.

I, too, await Stumpfegger. For what he has in his other pocket. Cigarettes.

JUNE 1941, BERLIN

This conquest does not come easily. I move from my chair to the sofa. I mention the part we propose for her: *Annelie*, the mother and nurse of those who fought for the Fatherland in 1914. I describe how, in one scene, she will be the girl who, mud-stained and with a tear-streaked face—I must tell Von Bäky to put this in extreme close-up—crawls beneath the coils of fanged wire to tend to our men in the medical tent. There she finds her dying husband, who is too weak to inhale his last cigarette. She takes it from his lips, inhales for him, and blows the smoke into his mouth. What a magnificent gesture. He has only enough strength to utter the words, "Ah, Annelie, how thankful we must be for the gift of love."

This Jewess does not reply. Outside, the rain has stopped. A last shaft of sunlight breaks through the clouds and plays on the window glass. A perfect filmic effect. And now the sun itself goes down, and the room grows dim, as if Semmler has turned down the lights.

"All of Germany will see your tears. All of Germany will feel what you feel. Your sorrow. Your joy. You embrace the dying man. He raises his arms to you." I raise my own arm and put it around her. As I go on speaking, I see that her mouth has fallen open, as if she were an Adoleszent, watching this film, seeing herself, in the darkened theater. The tip of her tongue, the one tooth pushed against the other, like passengers in a crowded tram.

"Can you feel his breath, his last breath, on your lips? Do you want to give him a final kiss? Will you be the nurse for all our poor boys in all their beds? Will it be your face they will see? Your name that they call out? Yes! You will be their nurse. Their mother. Their beloved."

Still, no word from this girl. But I see her small, perfect breasts heave up against the summer silk. An odor from under her arms or from between her legs, which open a centimeter. I put my hand there.

"Are you that strong, meine liebe Karelena? Can you accept from all of Germany that gift of love?"

Her legs continue, microscopically, to open, and her breasts, the nipples of her breasts push against the damp silk cloth. At last I hear her murmur:

By a waterfall, I'm calling you-oo-oo-oo

"Did you speak? I cannot hear you."
She goes on, in what seems the voice of a child:

By a waterfall, he's dreaming, too—

"What is it that you wish to say, Fräulein?"

Now, in her own voice once more: "My father. He took me to those films. The Warner Bros. films. You killed him."

I find myself on my feet and in a sudden rage. I feel the blood steaming in the sockets of my eyes. "Your father! An insect. An ant. We could have eliminated him with the sole of a shoe. But we did not. He killed himself."

"I know that. It's why he wouldn't take me that night. The Gloria Palast. But you beat him. You threw him out of his job. He was in despair. It was you who drove him to it."

"It's a lie! I can prove it! I have evidence! The autopsy report. The letter your father wrote to his studio. And the answer they sent him. Your mother's letter in reply. Every letter that comes into or out of the Reich. Including the one Herr Engelsing left for you. Nothing escapes us."

"A letter from Alex? For me? Where is that?"

"Listen to me, Fräulein. The Hebräer von Hollywood are excellent at propaganda. We have much to learn from them. That Wonskolaser—that *Mister* Jack Warner: your father wrote to him, he begged for a job. His old friend wrote back saying he could not even sweep the floor of his studio. Yes, yes: we both know your father put a Mauser to his head. But it was the Jew in California who pulled the trigger."

"I heard what you said. About Alex. There was a letter—?"

I return to her. She does not pull back. I take one of her hands. "My dear. My Karelena. I have been trying to spare you. It has been hard work! But the truth is best. I see that. Don't you agree?"

I thought I saw the slightest nod. I went on:

"It seems that your Onkel Engel has received a better offer."

"'A better offer . . .'"

"Yes, from that man. Wonksolaser. A contract from Warner Bros."

"It can't be true! He would not vanish overnight. Without a word to me. The train. He, he—"

Her voice breaks off. I move to my desk, take out the letter—the fotokopie of the letter—and hand it to her. "Here," I say. "The contract for Herr Engelsing. You must decide for yourself. Would you be better off if we had killed him?"

I watch as her face turns as pale as the paper she holds in her hand. Her lips form the shape of each word, like a child learning to read. I know what those words say. Warner Bros. had offered the actor a two-year contract. At five hundred dollars a week. The rest was arrangements: money transfers, travel vouchers, and even a rented house on—odd how the memory seizes on this or that detail—a certain Argyle Avenue. In less than a minute the sheet falls from her fingers to the cream-colored carpet. I stoop to retrieve it. Such thin, pretty ankles. Also from her mother.

From my knees I address her.

"A strange thing, Fräulein. They all say that the Minister of Enlightenment and Propaganda is a tyrant. You said it, too: that I beat people and deprive them of work and throw them into camps. But what am I compared to this Wonksolaser? He kills your father. Then he steals away your—the man you love. *I* am the tyrant? Here you have with proof what it is like when a Jew rules his kingdom. That is why we are fighting this war: to make certain they do not rule the earth."

There is no reply. There is no sound. I look up at her. The color has returned to her face. More than returned. Two round blotches have formed on her cheeks, like those of a woman who walks the streets. Her full lip, the lower lip, is a dark red, a magenta, as if she had smeared it with dye. I do not think any force in all of conquered Europe could prevent me from kissing it and sucking the blood from it. One thing is certain: she will not.

Fräulein Kaiser: June 1941, Berlin

When my screen test was over, the Reichsminister took my arm and led me from the room. We went up the staircase. Of the Ordenspalais. On the Wilhelmstrasse. It was grand. The steps looked like melting marble. The kind that people in the films used to sing and dance on. All the lovely ladies. In their lovely gowns. Halfway up, I remembered my question. I asked it again:

"And Alex's letter? The one for me?"

"Oh," said Herr Goebbels, "We tore that up. It was only ein Liebesbrief. A silly love letter. Of no interest to the Reich."

Goebbels: June 1941, Berlin

I lead the Jewess upstairs; I grip her arm, so there will be no doubt she is my mistress. I see they have already turned off the lights. I sense the breathing of the crowd. More than thirty people. That was the invited number. But it seems each guest has invited another. From out of the darkness I address them. "Damen und Herren. You are about to see a new version of a film by the studio owned by die Brüder Warner." I can feel Fräulein Kaiser stiffen at my side. I can hear the little gasp. How many of these pictures has she seen in the past? Sitting with Kauffman? But she has not seen this one. I speak quite firmly. "It is their declaration of war against the Reich."

Then, as we take our seats, the film begins.

Confessions of a Nazi Spy
IT WAS OUR DUTY TO MAKE IT!
IT IS YOUR AMERICAN PRIVILEGE TO SEE IT!

I have seen, and much admired, this motion picture a dozen times. I know by heart its scenes and its lines. For example, how it depicts our comrades in the United States chanting their motto: *America is founded on German blood and German culture*. And how, at their Bund rallies, they declare over and over that only a band of subhumans stands in way of the German destiny of America. The film gives us more than words. We are shown how our saboteurs are at work in every great seaport, how they copy the timing mechanisms of the latest torpedoes and count the number of troops stationed near the city of New York and even steal the secret code by which planes in the air communicate with military personnel on the ground.

At each such exploit our small gathering on the Wilhelmplatz hoots and cheers. They fall silent, however, when the scene shifts to the high-windowed room in which at that moment they themselves are sitting. Suddenly they are watching an impersonation of myself: small-boned, thin-necked, with Brilliantine shining in my hair. I can sense how, as my double barks his orders or spreads his maps and diagrams across his desk, my guests strain forward to see me—or is it the beautiful young woman at my side?

Next they growl with indignation when the Jew, Goldenberg—reborn, I should say *Christened*, as Robinson—begins to round up our brethren and haul them into court. Guilty! All of them guilty! "In this country," says the judge to our blood brothers, "we do not spread sawdust on the surface of our prison yards." Again, the camps. Always the camps. The common touch, the common man, comes at the end, when two ordinary

Americans enter a breakfast shop for a cup of coffee. They have read the headlines. "The nerve of those Nazis, sending spies to this country," says the one fellow.

And the other: "We'll show them!"

At which point the sixteen-millimeter stock runs out and the lights in the chandelier and the sconces come on. Now the real Minister of Enlightenment and Propaganda gets to his feet.

"I wonder," I quite calmly say, "where they got that vulgar portrait of the Führer. I ask you to look around: here is only the bust of Friedrich der Grosse. Signed by Gladenbeck."

The tension breaks. The crowd talks over each other.

"Did you hear how they never once said the word *Jew*?"

"These people are cowards. They know if they condemn the way we deal with our Jews, we'll show them worse things about their own country. If we treated our chosen ones to the kind of lynchings they have in America, the Reich would soon be Judenrein."

"Yes, yes," I say, over their merriment. "But what is your opinion of Herr Dr. Goebbels? I mean, what did you think of the limping actor who depicted me?"

No one replies.

"Why do you suppose they did not ask me to play the part myself? I would have been happy to do it—and donated my fee to the Winter Relief. Look close: in real life this is how the Reichsminister walks. No limp at all. Do you see one, my dear Fräulein Kaiser? Look with care. What do you see?"

She shakes her head. She whispers the word, "Nichts."

"Really? Is it true? I give thanks to my shoemaker and to my special shoe."

Once again, silence in the room.

"Alas, they did not request my services. They cast instead the actor Kosleck. Born Yoshkin. In the town of Barkotzen."

"Undoubtedly a Jew!" someone calls out.

"They're all Jews! Every one! Did you see their faces?"

"I am ashamed to watch such dreck. I want to take a bath."

I hold up my hands. "No, no. We must be fair. This is a skilled work of persuasion, one from which we intend to learn and soon surpass. Indeed, it is so powerful that we could not expose the masses to it. Eighteen months ago, before any hostilities had broken out, we warned every nation: *Do not allow this film into your theaters.* The result was that even then it was shown in very few countries in Europe or South America. Now, of course, it is banned in every country under our control."

The room bursts into applause.

"Damen und Herren, I thank you for coming. You will find, in the entrance foyer below, a modest table of things to eat and a few things to drink. Just small aperitifs before you set out to enjoy, on what has become this fine Berlin evening, your nightly pleasures."

Everyone rises. Speaking of this and that, a mixture of comments and pleasantries, they head for the doors. I hold up my hands one last time.

"Oh, one thing I forgot to mention. Seven theaters in Warsaw ignored our request. I am pleased to inform you that every one of those managers has been hanged in his own picture house. This war will not be fought under the rules of the Geneva Convention."

There is a gasp from the crowd, then much laughter and even louder applause. In another moment, the room has emptied. I take out my cigarette case and offer Fräulein Kaiser a cigarette. Virginia tobacco. A Lucky Strike.

She shakes her head. "I'd like to go. You don't know me. I don't smoke."

She stands. I take her arm. "There is something, Fräulein, I failed to mention. One man escaped from Warsaw. His name was Jankolwicz. Boris Jankolwicz. He had to drag himself and drag himself and drag himself—" And here, not hiding my limp, exaggerating it, I haul myself back and forth between the blank white screen and the rows of chairs. There is, I have found, much pleasure in mocking oneself. "Yes, he had to drag himself five hundred kilometers until he reached safety."

Once more she turns to go, and once more I grip her arm. "Poor Herr Jankolwicz. More dead than alive. Do you happen, Fräulein Kaiser, to know who this man was?"

Before she can reply, I say, "Let me tell you. He was the manager of the Warner Bros. Corporation in Poland. If I am not mistaken, that is the post Herr Joseph Kauffman wished to secure for himself. The job that Herr Warner told him did not exist. Well, so now you know. It is important that you know: no place is safe from us."

"Why have you brought me up here? I thought, after—"

"Why? An innocent motive. I thought you enjoyed watching the films of this company. What a pity that Herr Powell did not appear. But these have been instructive moments, don't you think? Now you have seen the kind of filth that this Wonksolaser puts on the screen. Was that not worth climbing up all those stairs?"

She pulls away. "Will you allow me to bid you Auf Wiedersehen, Herr Reichsminister?"

"One more minute, bitte. There is another reason I have asked you to accompany me. We have here a special guest. He knows of your work and asks if he might make your acquaintance."

With these words, I escort Fräulein Kaiser to the back of the room. Of course she is astonished to see who is seated there—and even more astonished when he modestly rises, holds out his hand, and tells her he has been following her career with interest and so took the liberty of asking his Reichsminister if he would be so kind as to arrange for him to greet her.

I am amazed myself to see her response, which is no different from that of a thousand Bavarian peasant girls. Her mouth half opens, her eyes roll up just a little, and she performs a deep curtsy, almost to the ground. Next, in a trembling voice, she says, "Mein Führer."

FIRST DAY OF MAY 1945, BERLIN

Is there a single cigarette left in the bunker? In all of Berlin? The minute the Führer was gone everybody lit up. None would have dared one hour earlier. We are all swine. Did they think I did not hear their music? Dancing on the grave—before the corpses have been buried inside it. All that is forbidden returns.

I could not join their dancing, even if I had so wished. Some professor, in some university, should make a study—the role of the lame foot in history: Achilles, Tamerlane, Claudius, and the Englishman Byron and the Englishman Scott.

Tamerlane. I remember the story. From schoolbooks. When his tribe wished to choose a new leader they drove a stake into the ground and said, "We shall run thither and whoever is first to reach the stake will be our chief." All dashed forward, but because he was lame Timur lagged behind.

At the last moment, before the others reached the stake, he threw his cap on it and said, "Only your feet have arrived, but my head reached the goal before you." Thus was he made their prince. Clever lad—cleverer than the cripple, Oedipus, who answered the riddle of the Sphinx, *Mann*, but who could not solve the mystery within himself.

7 { UNION STATION

The Terrible Turk: December 1941, Los Angeles

Even though the world got turned upside down yesterday morning, I sat down to my usual breakfast: coffee, toast, and two eggs cooked in a pan so that they stayed sunny-side up. I do not eat bacon. What I am saying is that even though the country is now different than what it was before, I wanted the Terrible Turk to be in his personal habits exactly the same. That's why, as usual, and still in my pajamas, I picked up the *Los Angeles Times* from the doorstep on Camarillo Street and unfolded it to the column I always read first. *Then* the coffee, black and hot. Out clangs the toast like a cash-register drawer. Eggs? They are ready. That's when I put on the spectacles that reveal my age and start to read. And what do I discover but the very same advice about how to behave.

Hedda Hopper's Hollywood: December 1941, Los Angeles

Now I'm going to sign off by offering the one pearl of wisdom I possess. I'm certain all of us today are united by a single thought: how best to serve our country. May I, in all humility, suggest that the worst treachery to our Flag is hysteria and fear.

So let's continue to play golf, go to the movies, and keep on laughing!

The Terrible Turk: December 1941, Los Angeles

Those words jumped up at me from the bottom of her column. Miss Hedda Hopper is still a beautiful woman, with ankles so thin you could put your hand around both of them and snap them like matchsticks if you were ever angry enough to have such a terrible thought. Just take a look at her picture with that eye-catching smile.

When she was young she used to like the fights. She was a tourist in town when I lost to Dummy Jordan on points. What I remember is that Fireman Jim Flynn brought her up after the decision to introduce us. I am the one who helped train the Fireman for his big fight with Jack Johnson exactly two years before: 7/4/12. American Independence Day, which of course I think of now with a lot of extra feeling in my heart.

She had a big smile, that lady, and a big hat, and she was full of sympathy. But I just said *well you win some and you lose some* and *the important thing was to get up off the mat and go on fighting*—even though it came to me in a flash that very moment that I was not going to be in the ring anymore. Also, I noticed those ankles.

At the time she was named Elda and was just passing through. But she came back soon enough to act in the silent movies, which was the profession where I already had, as they say, a foot in the door. When I was an extra at First National, who should show up to play a big part in *Virtuous Wives* but the girl from the fight. I recognized her and she recognized me. This was an ironical title because in the picture she was a married woman who has practically a harem of gentlemen admirers.

In real life the situation was reversed because Elda had married this Hopper who was a womanizer with four or five wives already. Elda was not happy—and not so virtuous, as I can tell you from the horse's mouth. I do not wish to spread stories, which is also ironical, since that is what after her divorce and with her new name she has spent most of her time on the stage of life doing, but the plain fact is that for the next two years we were paramours. And later on, afterward, now and then my phone would ring when she was down in the dumps because she, like a number of ladies, knew that Abdul was something of a Turkish delight.

So it was a pleasure for me and for her, I think, when we saw each other twenty-four hours ago at Union Station.

Hedda Hopper's Hollywood: December 1941, Los Angeles

After that sneak Jap attack yesterday, Hollywood is mad as hell—pardon my French—and you can bet that half the town has already fired their buck-toothed gardeners. Everyone I talked to, and that means Joel McCrea and

Gary Cooper and that glamor girl Betty Field, is rolling up their sleeves and is absolutely certain their country will come out victorious. That doesn't include Brit Charlie Chaplin, who tried to stir up trouble between Germany and the U. S. of A. with that silly dictator picture. He'd have been a lot smarter if he'd listened to that other Charlie, and I do mean the greatest navigator of the century, about who our real enemies are.

There is not a single American from sea to shining sea who will not remember for quite some time what they were doing at eleven a.m. yesterday morning: Spencer Tracy, for instance, and Irene Dunne, who were at the christening of Pat O'Brien's newest. As for little old Hedda, you could have spotted me in the beautiful garden at Union station, waiting for the Super Chief to get in from Chicago. I was eager to take a gander at the mysterious new Warners star, Karelena Kaiser, who flew in to New York on the Lisbon Clipper just a few days ago. What a story she has to tell! Seems that her poppa was a big pal of Jack Warner, who has looked after her like a godfather ever since her dad's accidental death. You can believe there was plenty of intrigue in her hasty departure. Herr Goebbels, the dashing head of the film industry in prosperous new Germany, had big plans for this exciting headliner and had taken a personal interest in her career. But he graciously allowed her to fly away after a lot of pleading by the man she calls Uncle Jack—and maybe a bit of arm-twisting by FDR.

Speaking of "that man," I saw an old friend, Abdul Maljan, who I happen to know shows up in our nation's capital whenever the president's condition—don't you forget that he is stuck in a wheelchair—acts up on him. Abdul came to this country as a very young man and was a championship boxer and starred in silent films. I wouldn't know myself, but others claim he has magic in his fingers. Abdul was there to meet the same train, along with his boss, Jack Warner, who was holding a beautiful bunch of calla lilies.

Just as we were starting toward the platform, a gorgeous blonde came sprinting up to our little party and threw herself into the arms of the Warner Bros. chief. "Uncle Jack," she cried. "Oh, Uncle Jack!" Those lilies flew everywhere. There wasn't a dry eye in the house.

It was at that very moment, wouldn't you know it, that everybody began running this way and that and gathering wherever they could find a radio, and a voice came over the loudspeaker system to announce that the United States Navy had been attacked in Pearl Harbor by the Empire of Japan. You could have knocked over this girl from Hollidaysburg, Pa., with a feather. The whole room began to spin and the strangest thoughts popped into my mind, like the news that Claudette Colbert was given a toy French poodle named Lulu Belle by husband Joel Pressman. The announcer was saying that thousands of American sailors were treacherously murdered, a tragedy so enormous that a gal can only comprehend it by comparing it to the more inconsequential misfortunes of her own—such as how when I tried to shine up my brand-new copper kettle I foolishly took off all the lacquer that had been put on to preserve its pristine glory and, lo and behold, next day it was black as my hat. I said to Moli, "That will teach me to keep my nose out of your department!"

I was awakened from this sad reverie by a shout. The crowd was chasing a little yellow Jap who had been pretending to prune the roses in the garden. They had him against a wall and were giving him what for and in my opinion it served him right. Isn't it about time that we put America First?

Well, you've got to admit your correspondent had quite a day! And so did all of the U. S. of A. Now I'm going to sign off by offering the one pearl of wisdom—

The Terrible Turk: December 1941, Los Angeles

Play golf! You've heard that pearl already. And *Go to the movies.*

Some of what Hedda wrote was true. The Chief and the Terrible Turk were there to meet Miss Kaiser's train. And the Chief had flowers, but they were only a bouquet of daisies and pansies I bought in the station shop. He doesn't like to spend more than he has to. Also true: that we heard about the sneak attack over the public address system. But no one said anything about thousands of murdered sailors. That came later. The crowd did chase a man out of the garden. No one knew for sure he was Japanese. But they were kicking him and punching him as if he definitely was. I like a fair fight. So I was going to go over there and give him a hand and maybe a fist, but Hedda held onto my arm. I thought she was going to faint if I let her go. So the Americans had their way with that poor fellow.

What Hedda got wrong was the girl. She did come running toward us from the platform, but she went right by the Chief and into the arms of a man with curly hair and a shabby brown suit. That was the German, Engelsing, we'd brought over to make into a movie star earlier this year. He bent her over and kissed her, and she, like a scene in the movies, was kissing him back. That's when the loudspeakers came on and made their announcement. The Chief just stood there, still holding his flowers and saying, "Pearl Harbor? Sunday? But that's what I told FDR. I warned him. How come he didn't know?"

56

8 } THE FÜHRER'S DECISION

Goebbels: First Day of May 1945, Berlin

Here at last is Stumpfegger, mit Zigaretten und Zyanid. A handshake.
Then off he goes to the children, the little glass capsules rattling in his
pocket. How many cigarettes? Three. I thought I would pounce on them:
to light up, to inhale, to blow out the figures of smoke. No greater joy on
this earth. But here I sit staring at them as if they were wooden sticks. I
suppose I have become addicted, not so much to cigarettes themselves but
to Virginia tobacco. We had discussed how we might grow this strain in
Romania or in Morocco. *Morocco,* where we missed our chance to win the
war. On my desk: these three pieces of German Scheisse.

How many times did I tell the Führer that it was a mistake to deprive
the civilian population of its pleasures? Especially after Stalingrad. He
wanted to water the beer and not inform the people it was being done. I
talked him out of that mistake. Less luck with the anti-smoking campaign.
The Führer had come to hate tobacco. He said it was the red man's revenge
on the white man and that it damaged the ability of the German woman
to reproduce. What else can one expect from a man who never had a beer
and would not smoke? Who shoveled that mush down his gut?

I see that I, too, have joined the latest dance, leaping up to criticize the
Führer the minute he is no longer with us. I should pull out my Mauser
and shoot myself, the same way I would shoot anyone else I caught in such
an act. This remains true even when I consider him not as a god but as a
man made of bone and human flesh.

But he was a god. No woman has ever made me feel what I did, and
still do, for Adolf Hitler. I still remember what I wrote in my Tagebuch
when I first saw him:

Those large blue eyes! Like stars!

I thank Fate, which brought us the Führer. He gave us the gift of hate—both the hatred our enemies feel for us and the hatred we have for them: may it burn forever in our hearts.

But the man of bone? Of flesh?

No thought of that without this first cigarette. The smoke, so calm. Curling and curling. Contemplate it. Do not go mad. An axiom: the Führer is a human being. Human beings make mistakes. Ergo. . . . Ergo. I must draw this shit deep into my lungs. *Ergo*: the Führer made mistakes. One, above all others, has led to the destruction of a Reich that might have lasted a thousand years. Aborting the attack at Dunkirk? Allowing Göring to cripple the Luftwaffe? Delaying, delaying, delaying Sea Lion? These are nothing. In the end, the great mistake—

A tremendous blast. Right on top of our heads. Loud enough to wake the children, whether they are in this world or the next. Lights out. Silence. Dust falling on the back of my hands.

> *They gaze on me. I am filled with delight.*
> *Intoxication! Enslavement!*

Ah, the ventilators have started once more to hum. Come, come: now the electric lights.

Was it the Jews? Was that our mistake? Should we have smiled on them and caressed them and encouraged them to build us an atomic weapon? Never. For come what may, that is the war we have won. This victory alone allows me to leap laughing into my grave.

I know what history will say. That we were doomed on the night we invaded the Bolshevik lair. History will be wrong.

JUNE 1941, BERLIN

Like good doctors, we gather at the bedside of a sickly Europe. We are ready to insert the catheter that will drain the pestilence from the entire continent. Stalin knows it. He trembles, as if with palsy. His double game has come to its end. As the hour approaches, all in this room instinctively turn toward the east, the way the followers of Islam turn at the time of prayer. In our new Mecca, the age-old plague, and the rats that have carried it, are about to be exterminated.

The moment arrives. The Führer approaches and bestows on me a healthy, confident smile; in his eyes, which gaze into mine, there is nothing but steely determination and complete commitment. He says: "Right or wrong we must win. It is the only way. Victory is not only right, it is necessary. And once we have won, who is going to question our methods? In any case, we have so much to answer for already that we have no choice but to emerge victorious. If we do not, our nation—with us at its head—and all we hold dear, will be eradicated. So, to work!"

FIRST DAY OF MAY 1945, BERLIN

Not Dunkirk. Not Sea Lion. And not the Jews. Nor was it Barbarossa that brought on our defeat. We could have sustained the losses in the east if only we had avoided the catastrophe in the west. Why did we not? In 1941, during the heady days of July, August, even September, no one paid much attention to the increasing aggression of our Axis partner. If anything, the prevailing opinion in Ribbentrop's ministry was that an outright war between America and Japan would lead to a favorable outcome for the Reich. Even the Führer believed such a development would be a gift from heaven—that once the Americans became engaged in the Pacific, they would not be able to pursue hostilities with us. I confess I was not immune from such thinking. But as we moved from a triumphant summer to a more dubious fall, my thoughts began to change:

What if the United States should enter the war not only against Japan but against the Reich? That would force us to fight precisely the conflict that every German statesman, and above all Bismarck, has always dreaded: a war on two fronts.

Look what I have done: lit a second cigarette from the burning butt of the first. And I swore to Magda I would never perform that trick again. It's what the Faulenzer do, when lying in the gutter.

Well, I am in the gutter now.

Still I ask myself: How did what we most feared come to pass? It wasn't that we did not know the intentions of the Empire of Japan. In the month of November, the Sicherheitsdienst informed us of three key things: Naito, their naval attaché, had left Berlin for Taranto to study how British aircraft had destroyed half the Italian fleet with torpedoes; that shallow water maneuvers had taken place in Kagoshima Bay; and that our ally had developed a new airborne weapon with stabilizing fins. Obviously they were planning a harbor offensive. Then, toward the end of that month, the last straw: Ott cabled from Tokyo that Yamamoto and the Japanese fleet, with submarines, had either sailed or were about to sail from northern Japan. What no one at the Reichkanzlei or anywhere else in Germany knew was where that fleet was about to go: Manilla? Singapore? The Dutch East Indies?

No one, that is, save for the Reichsminister für Volksaufklärung und Propaganda. That was the fortunate result of my decision to take over our film industry. We had no choice but to interest ourselves in what our competitors were doing in Hollywood. Gyssling, our consul there, and a former Olympian, had many friendly contacts in Los Angeles, including the cartoonist Disney. But much of his information came from a certain Klatschkolumnistin who from the late thirties onward became more and more sympathetic to our cause. On the occasion of Frau Riefenstahl's visit to Hollywood, she was the only one to protest our filmmaker's treatment by the reigning fraternity of Jews.

Hedda Hopper's Hollywood: December 1938, Los Angeles

Young Doug Fairbanks has been rushing Zorlina in New York. Cafe society claims there was no problem when Marlene Dietrich arrived. He carried the torch for her a long time, but even torches go out.

Leni Riefenstahl, supposed to be Hitler's erstwhile girlfriend, can't even get a peek through the keyholes of our town. The studio execs have closed them tighter than a drum, especially since all that fuss a few weeks ago in Berlin when the shops of their co-religionists had some of their windows broken and a few beards got pulled. As if our guest in Hollywood had anything to do with that. I ask you: What price justice?

Goebbels: First Day of May 1945, Berlin

Yes, we pulled a few beards on that night. The masterstroke: the Jews had to pay for their own broken glass. A billion Reichsmarks. This will remain one of the great jokes of the century. But it was false to say that Riefenstahl was the Führer's mistress. A good thing for the Reich, or we would not have been able to give the world *Triumph of the Will* or *Olympia*. And a good thing for Riefenstahl, since all his actual mistresses have ended their lives—or had them ended.

Time for the third cigarette. The last for the condemned man. Can I put it off until the gallows? Let me make the attempt. This will be a true Triumph des Willens.

Gyssling was expelled from America after we stupidly sank that *Robin Moore* vessel. But our ministry kept a faithful eye on Frau Hopper's columns. Not only was she drawing closer and closer to the ideals of National Socialism, but it began to dawn on me that buried in her Klatschblatt were certain pieces of information she was well aware we might like to read.

Hedda Hopper's Hollywood: February 1941, Los Angeles

Hugh Herbert and Bob Cummings are trying to get even with Nancy Kelly. She borrowed their hankies and put lipstick stains on them. What a time they had explaining!

I was knocked for a loop last night when the new Academy Award nominations came out. That *Dictator* picture got five of them, including three for noncitizen Charlie Chaplin for best picture, and best writer, and best actor. Maybe I shouldn't be surprised, considering the people who have most influence in this town and what their goals are for the good-old U. S. of A.

They say people get a good laugh out of that movie, but this gal under the hat thought it was practically a call to arms. Nobody asked me but I don't see how anyone in their right mind would want America to get into this unnecessary European dust-up. I'm willing to fight and die for the little patch of Pennsylvania land that my great-great-aunt Furree got from William Penn, but not in far-off lands whose peoples share our values and way of life. Would the MAN whose resurrection we celebrate each spring want us to kill young, clean-cut boys and destroy great cities? I fear that our Christian nation is going to get dragged into a war by those who live and work among us but who are not even Christians themselves.

Here's a tip for the restless sex. Rudy Vallee is arriving in town girl-less. Line forms at the right!

I'm still in such a dither about that Chaplin picture that I've decided to tell a story I thought I had best put in a drawer. It seems that for years Charlie's Japanese chauffeur had to sit in his master's car, ready to whisk the little tramp wherever he wished to go. Only once did he drive him to the wrong address. The supposed friend of the working class went into a real snit and said, "Don't you dare start driving until you are sure exactly where I want to go." A few days later Charlie came rushing down to his car and said, "Take me to the ocean."

Kono, the chauffeur, sat looking at his employer. "Atlantic or Pacific?" he asked.

Isn't that a scream? And that little Japanese fellow had a lot more to tell me besides that.

The other day at Mike Romanoff's joint over on Rodeo Drive I heard someone give a cheery "Hello, Hedda!" and when I turned around there in the next booth was Bette Davis, wearing a neckline that plunged deeper than Bill Beebee's bathysphere. And we were only eating lunch!

Speaking of oceans, Bud Abbott and Lou Costello, together with all those Andrews Sisters and star Dick Powell, will be sailing to the Hawaii Theater for the premiere of *In the Navy*. Wait till you see the madcap maneuvers of the battleship *Alabama* at the end of the picture. I expect when fully commissioned, she'll make port in Hawaii, too—along with all those other big ships sitting there in Pearl Harbor.

Well, I've already given you my two cents on this subject, so I might as well make it three! The element in our industry so eager to reward a picture that makes such fun of the leader of a friendly and orderly country—as Molly says to Fibber, "T'ain't funny, McGee!"—ought to look over their shoulders to see where the real threat to our nation is coming from. It certainly isn't from the land of lederhosen! I'm looking into my crystal ball and predicting that when the awards come out, Mr. C. Chaplin won't win a single one. That's because everyone knows we go to our theaters for a little relief and amusement. Why not give us cheerful, happy romance and adventure? These leave us with a song in our hearts, which is the best way I know to get us back the next night—for more!

Goebbels: First Day of May 1945, Berlin

"Atlantic or Pacific?" Was that not the question the whole world was asking? Now I believed I had the answer: Japan was contemplating an attack on the naval facilities of the Hawaiian Islands. The question I could not answer was what the Führer's reaction would be, should that strike occur. Would he remain aloof, as wisdom dictated and the Tripartite Pact allowed? Or would his emotions and misplaced ideals of honor compel him to join forces with the Empire of the Rising Sun and so plunge us into the kind of two-front conflict that might well destroy us and that, during the Punic Wars, devastated the Empire of Rome?

NOVEMBER 1941, BERLIN

The Führer has called us to the Reichskanzlei. Urgent. Practically at dawn. Ribbentrop and Göring will be there. And probably Canaris for the Abwher and Schellenberg on behalf of Himmler and the Sicherheitsdienst. I shall sleep on the Wilhelmstrasse, so I can be the first to arrive.

But I do not sleep. I devote this anxious night to the problems of my beloved Berlin. What to do with the "bomb hobos?" They evoke sympathy in some quarters. But not in this German heart. The Gestapo must take certain measures. These parasites are doing tremendous harm to morale.

Even worse: the unendurable sight of Jews walking the streets of our city with smiles on their faces and their department-store purchases under their arms. One feels one is living in a fantastical world, like that of an American film in which all the criminals have been released from their jails and walk wherever they wish, pushing aside the good folk of the town. The Gestapo will solve that problem as well.

At last the dawn. The meeting at the Reichskanzlei. Much tension through the tea and pleasantries. Then, a surprise: the Japanese ambassador, Baron Oshima, arrives with a formal note from Prime Minister Tojo. *Will we or will we not in case of hostilities honor the terms of the Tripartite Pact and declare war on the enemies of the Japanese Empire?*

A small disturbance among us. For a moment no one speaks. I am the first to find my voice: "May I ask, Herr Ambassador, whether the Japanese nation expects to be attacked or is intending to attack itself?"

The only response is the enigmatic smile of the Asiatic. I continue, "I am sure you understand that the Tripartite Pact obliges its members to join forces only if one of them is assaulted, not if that signatory is the aggressor."

Alas, before the Oriental can respond, that dunce, Ribbentrop, steps forward. "You must understand, Baron, that the Reichsminister speaks only for himself and not for the Aüswärtigen. I believe you will appreciate it if I express my own view: a great nation does not allow others to declare war on it. A great nation declares war on others."

The ambassador, in his reply, seems to be speaking past the salesman of champagne and directly to me. "And why has your great nation not done so? Are not Germany and the United States in an undeclared war with each other? Your ships are being fired upon at sea. All your consulates have been closed. Your assets have been frozen. Those who support you are subject to arrest. As a response to such grievances, the German nation has every right to declare war on the United States. Can you doubt if it did so the Empire of Japan would not, in the spirit of mutual obligations, immediately engage the Americans at your side?"

"Just as that Empire now wishes us to engage the Americans at yours?"

"What we wish," says Oshima, "is that our two nations shall always be side by side."

With that the Führer thanks Oshima and tells him that he has called this meeting to discuss the prime minister's note and that if he would be so kind as to wait until after these deliberations—"they will not take more than an hour"—he will be given an answer. The Baron bows. He leaves the room.

FIRST DAY OF MAY 1945, BERLIN

I seem to have dozed off. The sound of artillery has awakened me. No—not artillery. The report of guns. Here, within the bunker. Who, I wonder. Krebs? Burgdorf? Schedle? Everyone with a shred of honor is following the path of the Führer. My own Mauser is fully loaded. But someone has to remain—let it be Schwägermann—to pour petrol on my body.

I lose the struggle. I light the third, most precious, cigarette. I hope it will keep me awake.

The first to speak after the Baron's departure is Göring. He does so with a sigh. "This means there will be no attack by the Asians on the Bolshevik eastern flank."

The Führer says he is neither surprised nor disappointed. Our first Panzer units are now within sight of the domes of Moscow: the city will fall long before Stalin can bring his Siberian units—"and you can imagine what specimens these Übermenschen must be"—across the vast expanse of his country. On the contrary, the Führer feels it will be the best possible thing for us to let loose the Japanese, whom he calls the "Prussians of the Pacific," upon our enemies.

But which enemies? About that he seeks our opinions. He requires only that we speak with frankness.

Naturally, we all turn to the chief of the Abwehr, who only repeats what has been said before: that the Japanese fleet will attack either Singapore or Manila—or possibly be split into two sections and strike both simultaneously.

Schellenberg says that based on what we have just heard, the attack must surely be against the territories of the United States.

"Manila then," says the Führer.

I find myself speaking by impulse, without prior thought. "I agree. Japan is ready to attack America. But not in the Philippines. Not at first. There is no opportunity there to strike a decisive blow."

"Then where might such a target be?" asks Canaris.

"Jew York!" exclaims Göring, to much merriment.

The Führer holds up his hand and his piercing gaze falls on me. "What is it you wish to tell us, Herr Reichsminister?"

So now the moment has come. I cannot ignore a direct request of the Führer. "We know the Japanese navy has been preparing a shallow harbor attack. Admiral Canaris can confirm that the American fleet has gathered at Pearl Harbor in the territory of Hawaii. Yamamoto will seek to destroy so much of it that America will not be able to retaliate—at least not for several years."

Among the ensuing tumult, the Führer remains calm. "Have you any evidence for this conclusion, beyond what we have heard here this morning?"

I then explain that to the intelligence of our various services I have added what Gyssling has told us and what we have learned from a friendly source at the *Los Angeles Times*.

The Führer asks, "If you have been able to make this deduction, would not the Americans be able to do the same?"

"We cannot be sure," I reply. "It is possible that they have this information and are keeping it from their citizens."

Schellenberg asks why Roosevelt and the Yids around him would do that.

Canaris says, "Perhaps they wish such an attack—if there in fact is such an attack—to occur. That way they can feign surprise."

Schellenberg: "And lose half their fleet? Why would they wish to risk that?"

I answer: "It is the ultimate provocation. At last the Jews will be able to go to war."

Canaris: "Against Japan?"

"Not Japan," I respond. "Does that race care about Japan? What they care about is the Reich."

Ribbentrop, as always, points out the obvious: an outraged American public will demand full mobilization against the attacking nation and pay no attention to us, "Which, as the Führer has said, would be a gift from the gods."

We all glance to where the Führer has remained seated, with a plate of pastries balanced on his knee. It is in truth the fate of the world that is balancing there. Because of that I dare the following:

"That is true, Herr Aussenminister, but only if we give Tojo what from the standpoint of the Reich can be the one correct answer. It is a fantastic thing to say, but at this moment the Empire of Japan and the Jewish cabal that runs America are allies: their desperate hope is that we shall give the wrong one."

Göring, in some agitation, breaks out: "There is only one answer. We have already given it by signing the Tripartite Pact. It makes clear that the signatories will assist each other by military means."

The Führer quite softly says: "But has not our gifted Doktor Goebbels already explained that the pact comes into play only if one of the signatories is attacked by a power not already engaged in either the European war or the Sino-Japanese conflict?"

Gifted Doktor Goebbels! I am so delighted by these words that I hurriedly add, "Should we not bear in mind that it was surely for just that reason that the Japanese did not leap to support us after we launched Barbarossa? If they did not join us in our struggle against the Bolsheviks, why should we join them in their adventure against the United States?"

"Because we have given our word," says Göring. "The Third Reich does not quibble. It acts with honor."

A cretin! Lost in his opium dreams. I rise to my feet to answer him. "I must repeat myself, my dear Göring. We are not obliged to join forces with either of the two signatories unless *it* is attacked. If, as seems inevitable, Japan fires the first shot, we are under no obligation whatsoever."

"The first and perhaps the last shot," says Schellenberger. "The American fleet will be crippled or destroyed. We shall have a free hand on the continent of Europe—and Africa, too. This entire discussion may well be moot."

Canaris: "Unless, as Herr Goebbels fears, the United States should enter the war against the Reich as well."

"Impossible," says Ribbentrop. "Have I not already explained that the American people will be obsessed with one thing only: revenge? Roosevelt's hands will at last be tied. We won't have to worry any longer about his compulsion to drag his country into war with the Reich."

I then state my deepest fear. "But what if the Reich declares war on the United States?"

Göring: "Are we writing the Talmud here with all this haggling?" Amusing to watch him attempt, and fail, to place one of his legs atop the other. "It is in my opinion shameful. Baron Oshima has made it clear that his nation will fight side by side with the Reich. Will the Reich fight side by side with its ally?"

In the aftermath of that question there is a pause. Then Canaris says, "As we all know, a decision of this magnitude can only be made by one man. We are here to seek his guidance."

At that, all in the room turn toward the sofa, where, still, the Führer has remained seated. He begins with the gracious remark that on the contrary he has asked us to come this morning to seek our guidance. Then he turns to the Reichsmarschall: "I am not, Göring, immune to the demands of honor. Who attacks whom is at this stage indeed hardly more than a trifle. We are all at war with each other, God knows. And in our world struggle we have a powerful ally, one that has not been defeated in three thousand years."

Can it be? I wonder. *Is the Führer really leaning toward joining the Japanese in their adventure?* I amaze myself with what I dare to say next: "Mein Führer. Kameraden. I should like to put before you a historical fact: never in our history has our nation won a war on two fronts. That is why our Führer so wisely delayed Barbarossa until the war in the west was won. From the tip of Italy to the Arctic Circle we are the masters of Europe. The situation there is not a front; it is an occupation. Moreover, Moscow is about to fall. We control the Atlantic. And Rommel has just entered Egypt without opposition. Yet all this will change, change in an instant, if we give General Tojo the answer he desires. The active engagement with the United States will reopen the western front before we have a Slavic dependency in the east. A two-front war. That alone can lead to our defeat."

Shocked silence. Not that I dared speak, but that I committed the sacrilege of uttering the word *defeat*.

The Führer, however, has heard a different word. "Why are you standing, dear Doktor? Please resume your seat. What you say is correct in every respect—except for one thing. The destiny of the Third Reich is not to repeat history but to write it."

It is as if, as in the old days, the Führer were speaking before the masses. I sense that those in the room are stirred to applaud. Göring actually puts his fat hands together. I turn my head away. I fear I shall break into tears. I have been stabbed in the heart—not because I have failed to persuade the Führer, but because, in that heart, for the first time, I feel the blade of doubt. I sit, as requested. "Very well, mein Führer."

But while I feel that all the bones in my body have turned to sand—How dare I doubt? Why this moment of distrust?—Göring is grinning like a cat with cream:

"Then, Führer, may we now recall the ambassador and tell him that when his nation attacks the United States we shall at once issue a declaration of war?"

"Yes, Herr Reichsmarschall," the Führer replies. "Our good Aussenminister may request him to return to us. But I do not think he will receive precisely the answer he desires."

In only a minute, Ribbentrop escorts the Baron back to where we await him. The Führer remains seated. There are no formalities. He speaks with all his old decisiveness. "Herr Ambassador Oshima. After consultation, I have decided not to give the prime minister either one answer or the other. The best course of action for the Reich is to wait and determine whether your planned attack is a success. If it achieves its goal, we shall do one thing; if it is a failure, we shall do something else."

I look closely at the Baron. Beads of perspiration have on the instant sprung up on his brow. Something like ink seems to come from the black roots of his combed-back hair. His thick lips grow thin. He makes the slightest of bows. "There can be no failure," he says. "Operation Z has been planned to succeed. Down to the last detail. The attack will be on a Sunday. The people will be sleeping. Sleeping or in their churches. And it will come out of the rising sun. Not only to blind them, but because that is the symbol of the Empire of Japan."

Without another word, and without escort, he turns his back on us and leaves the room.

Hosannas fill the air. Ribbentrop falls over himself in his exclamations of praise. "Is this not a wonderful thing to see? That our Führer, a man of action, of inspired daring, the master of the lightning attack, is also wise enough to know that at times decisiveness means it is best to wait? Yes, wait, watch, calculate, and not leap in the dark."

The others are no less fawning in their remarks. The Führer rises, which means our meeting is over. At the door, Linge pulls me to one side. He says the Führer desires a word with me. At once I am certain that he has read the mind of the traitor—for is not doubt treason? I try not to tremble as I approach him. But he only says, "That young Fräulein. Last June. When you were showing the American propaganda film—*Kaiser*, wasn't that her name? The daughter of the Jew Kauffman? Bring her to me tonight."

FIRST DAY OF MAY 1945, BERLIN

—Guten Abend, Vater Abraham.

—A gutn ovnt, Herr Reichsminister.

—What are you selling this fine evening?

— Shmate, old shoes, shoelaces. A pot and a pan.

— Tabak?

— A bisl tabak.

— Virginia Tabak?

— Virginia Tabak.

— Have you Zigaretten?

— Ikh hobn nor tsvey.

— Gut! Prima! Zwei! Will you sell both to me?

— A mekhaye! It would be the greatest pleasure of mayn leben.

— How much? I give you Gold! Silber! Anything in die Welt!

— Do forgive me. But this pretty one, so shlank! So bleykh! Like the mindster finger fun a printsesin: this one—

— I'll take it! I'll take it! Name your Preis!

— This one I am going to smoke myself. Do you have a shvebele? A little light?

— I do! I do! Bitte! Allow me!

— A sheynem dank. Ah! Azoyner aromat. Azoyner taam. Fayn Virginia.

— You have one left. I know you have one left.

— Indeed, I do. Here it is. Never in the history of the welt has there been one like this. A verk of kunst. A shaft of zunlikht.

— Wären Sie so freundlich, Vater Abraham, as to sell it to me?

— Just name a prayz, Herr Reichsminister. I'm sure we can do business.

— Einhundert Reichsmarks!

— A good offer. Very good. But it comes a bisl shpet. The Reichsmark has fallen in value.

— Keine Reichsmarks? Here, take this Zigarettenetui. Solid gold.

— Couldn't you go a little higher?

— My wristwatch! Once in the Rothschild family. Take it. That's a good fellow. Mein Kumpel. Mein besten Freund.

— Tsum badoyeren, mayn fraynd, but I have such a zeygerl already.

— Is there nothing I can give you? Why are you torturing me? Didn't I give you your life?

— Herr Reichsminister für Volksaufklärung und Propaganda: A piece of shit is worth more than that.

— Then tell me. I beg you. I am on my knees to you. Tell me what you want. For a single Zigarette.

—Oh, not much. Not gelt. Not a brilyant. Only a little thing.

—Was? Was?

—Bullets. Little bullets. The sheynen pitsink bullets from your pitsoyl.

—What? I can't give you that. They are the most precious thing I posess.

—Then, Josef, mayn fraynd, I must be going.

—Wait! I have in my Mauser zehn bullets. I can give you—fünf.

—Finf? For a Virginia? You are makhn a shpas. Ha. Ha. Ha.
Gezegenung, Herr Minister.

—Wait! Stay. Don't go, my Abraham. Six. Eh? What do you say?
Six bullets for eine Zigarette.

—Zeks? Nisht zeks? Nisht zibn?

—Ja, sieben. Acht! I can't do better than that.

—Farshemen zikh. I'm ashamed. You are such an important man.
Let's not haggle. Let's do takhles.

—Yes! Let's! What do you want? Tell me.

—Alts. Everything, mayn tayer bruder. Every bullet.

—I can't give you all! Abraham! Geliebt Abraham! Father of your
people! One bullet is for another. One is for myself.

—Zayt mir moykhl. You must pardon me. A gute nakht.

—We are not selling rugs! We are not selling rags! This is the
Reichsbunker, not a bazaar. Give me that Zigarette!

—I wish from the depths of my harts I could do so. Nothing I have
experienced—not riches, or the smell of perfumes, or the favors
of sheyn maydele could give me greater fargenign. Alas, I must
have every bullet.

—Then take them! Here! In your heart! And here! In your belly.
And here, between your eyes. And here! And here! And here!

—Fir iberblaybn, mayn gelibt Josefchik.

—Here! Here! Here! And the last one: here! Was ist ist das? Not dead?
Not yet dead?

—I can't be killed, my poor little fellow. I will always be alive.
Hashem-yisborekh!

—Nein! Nein!

Nein! Nein! No!

After all I have fallen asleep. What a hideous dream. A nightmare.

Mayn tayer bruder! On my knees to a Jew! Wait. Wait. My Mauser. Yes, every shell is here.

That was the last sweet nap I shall have in this life. Oh, that old Jew! Bargaining for a cigarette!

NOVEMBER 1941, BERLIN

The Führer has asked that I escort Fräulein Kaiser from the Ordenspalais to the Chancellery this very night. I spend the long afternoon going over and again over in my mind the meeting of the morning. I am haunted by my responsibility. I cannot allow the Reich to bring America into the war. The only sure way to prevent it is to make certain Yamamoto fails to achieve his objectives. But how to do so? And how much time is left? A Sunday. But which Sunday? And the submarines have sailed! I am a Herr Doktor Professor. A Herr Doktor Professor is capable of thought. So. I shall think.

Fräulein Kaiser arrives just before nine. I walk with her through the chill night. She wears the plain cloth coat of a good German citizen. But she trembles. I can smell, beneath her perfumes, the piquancy of her perspiration. As unique as a fingerprint. Is that why I am trembling, too?

A strange phenomenon. Dreamlike. As we approach the Reichskanzlei our pace slows. I find it difficult to put one foot before the other. I experience the impression that each paving stone is the grave marker of a woman or a young girl who has taken this journey before: little Mitzy; little Suzi; Inge Ley; Mitford, the Englishwoman; poor Geli. Renate! My Renate! Her songs!

Today I feel so happy! So happy! So happy!

I come to a stop. I see Linge step between the SS guards. He stands waiting, beneath the outspread eagle's wings. I remain rooted. Why do I stop here, with Linge's eyes full upon me? I know that each of those women died by her own hand—no, Mitzi survived the noose she put around her neck. She is for all I know alive even now. And Eva—she has tried twice. I imagine she will try again. *Why can't these women obey like Blondi?* A joke from the Führer. But dogs do not commit Selbstmord.

Walking on air.
Without a care.

Is it, my sudden Paralyse, because I once delivered Renate, arm in arm, just as I am at this moment escorting Fräulein Kaiser? *Reichsminister für Volksaufklärung, Propaganda, und Zühälterei*: Enlightenment, propaganda, and pimping.

"Huhu!" cries Fräulein Kaiser. She has seen Linge. She waves her free arm. She was not trembling from fear but from excitement.

My Mischling breaks from me. She runs to the steps. Skipping. Like a girl. A young girl. The guards hold out their arms in salute. Linge makes that special little bow of his. He leads her inside.

FIRST DAY OF MAY 1945, BERLIN

The game of patience has ended. Magda is at the door. She wears the silver mother's cross—well deserved!—and the Golden Party Badge that the Führer himself pinned on her blouse. She says, "It is all finished with the children."

"Helga, Hilde—"

"Do not, I beg you, mention their names."

"Because we have failed them—?"

"We did not fail them!" The words come out like an animal's howl. "We saved them from the worst: a life under the rule of world-Jewry."

"You have earned that golden badge."

"Now we must think of ourselves."

"Is Schwägermann ready? With the petrol?"

"Of course he is. Why are you waiting? Don't you hear the guns? We have to hurry."

"Yes. I am coming. Wait outside. I need a moment."

The look she gives me: Has any man survived such scorn? But she goes. She believes, she half-believes, in resurrection. She thinks the children will have other, better lives.

NOVEMBER 1941, BERLIN

Dawn. Schwägermann and I are waiting in the Mercedes as she, the Mischling, comes down the steps of the Reichskanzlei. I half expect to see one of the harlots from the Giesebrechtstrasse; yes, the celebrated Kitty herself, with her diamonds and her mink. But our Fraülein Kaiser looks no different. Her hair, down now to her shoulders, not wound up in a

Bavarian braid, is still combed. With her crowded teeth she manages her familiar smile. But there is a dot of color on each of her cheeks, like the double dots of a fever patient. Schwägermann opens a rear door and she steps in to sit beside me. I draw the curtains. My adjutant starts the engine. She is already speaking, without taking a single breath.

Fräulein Karelena Kaiser: November 1941, Berlin

The Doktor was up and waiting for me in a beautiful red- and cream-colored automobile. The minute I saw him I started babbling. I could not stop.

"Oh, what a time I had! Glorious! Like a dream. We had dinner, just the two of us, by candlelight. There was a soup, a beet soup, and there was veal, only the Führer—Wolf, that is what he asked me to call him: *Wolf* would have none because he thought it was cruel to raise animals only to kill them for our pleasure, but he did not mind as long as he could see that I was enjoying myself, and I was! All he had was spaghetti, can you believe it? The leader of the Reich, of the whole world, and he is eating spaghetti: and when they took the plates he clasped my hand in his and asked if I minded—as if that were possible!—and he said it was a beautiful hand and how happy he was that I was there with him, and then under the table you know I felt his foot press mine, and he gave such a shy smile, like a schoolboy, and it just melted my heart, and then there was a compote with a pastry crust, so very delicious, and he told me that—let's see if I remember, that because of the rain our army had for the longest time been bogged down in mud, Schlamm, Schlamm, he kept repeating that word; but now, you see, a freeze had come just as his scientists had predicted, so that the soldiers would soon move forward and take Moscow just the way Napoleon had done and did I know he had started our invasion on the same day in June that Napoleon had and that if I wanted it I could be—oh, Doktor Goebbels! Well, I am just going to say the exact words he said: *You could be my Josephine.*"

The Doktor turned his head. He was impatient. He said, "And when the meal was over?"

"What meal? What are you talking about? Oh! Our dinner! With the candles! Well, you know, it seemed to me that he had made a kind of proposal; it was a proposal, wasn't it, that I could be the Queen, no, the

Empress of the world, and I didn't know what to say, and he said, please do not be anxious, and that I should take my time and to think about what he had said, but that he had seen all my films—I think that must be thanks to you, Doktor Goebbels, I am sure of it—and that that was what had made him fall in love with me, and was it possible that he might be a person that at some time I could love in return: and then I stood up to thank him for the lovely dinner and that of course I would think carefully about what he had said, and then he said—and this was for some reason so heartbreaking, the way he said it, as if some mean grown-up person had taken away this bright and pale and charming little boy's treat: he said, *Oh, you aren't leaving?* And I said no, no, and he said that was good because he wanted to give me what he gave no one else, a tour of his private quarters, and so we went from one beautiful room to another—oh, the flowers, the sweet-smelling flowers, and the paintings, and the tapestries and the sculptures, it was like a museum, and the carpets, too, and then we came to a room that must have been his bedroom, because of the bed in it, and his personal things, and I didn't want to go in, well, *half* of me didn't want to go in, but he said, *Wolf* said, I want to show you something, and he took me by the hand up to where there was a statue of a woman, you know, a nude woman, up in a niche in the wall with lights on it, a lovely woman, all in marble, and he said to me, *Die Umwegen der Schönen Karl*, and I must have looked a dunce because he laughed and said *you don't remember? One of your early films? I can't tell you how many times I have watched it, alone, at night*, and that I was wearing a bathing costume—and as soon as he said that I *did* remember how Herr Froelich made me run in and out of the water, that *freezing* water, I shivered just thinking about it, but the Führer, Wolf, was saying how I was wearing a two-piece suit and how it made him feel when he saw me in it and—oh, my, he had gone behind me and was—my zipper, he was undoing my zipper, and he was saying that the statue was that of a goddess, of Minerva or Venus or I don't know I couldn't hear him my heart was beating, and he was saying something like he wondered how that young girl's body had developed and was it as bountiful, that was his word, *grosszügig*, as that of the Greek goddess and would I—that was the voice of the little boy again, the shy little boy—would I allow him to discover in real life what he had only seen on the screen, and then the straps of my gown were down and he was still behind me and he asked if please would I step out of it, completely out of it, and how beautiful my legs were and how he should have that cameraman punished for not doing me justice, for defaming me, and that because I was a goddess he would like to remove my underthings and when he took everything off my body he said *would I be so kind* as to pose with my arms over my head just the way Venus, Aphrodite, the goddess of love was standing, and so I stood with my arms over my head for a minute, for two minutes, for even more minutes and Wolfie said he knew it was hard but that he could hold his arm out in the Hitlergruss for hours at a time—it was a strength he had and that Göring could only do it for ten minutes—but my arms were starting to ache, and when I dropped them and turned around, he was naked but still shy with his hands in front of him and then he lay down, not on the bed but on the floor, on the carpet that was on the floor, he was lying on his back and his little man thing was quivering and, oh, it was so touching when he said *Do you love me just a little?* and so then I gave myself to him and let him do everything he wanted and it was of course the happiest moment of my life."

Goebbels: November 1941, Berlin

She stops. At last she stops. For a moment there is no sound but the growling of our diesel engine. "Fräulein," I begin. "I would like you now to listen to me. I have not slept this night. I paced through the halls of the Ordenspalais. Thinking. And making arrangements. I—"

But she does not hear me. Her eyes are closed. The early light filters through the curtain cracks. I see that there are no more dots on her cheeks. Her whole face, her neck, her throat, has turned red, even the hair on her head—surely this was a hallucination?—seems about to burst into flames. I dare not speak. I fear it would endanger her, the way it is said that it is fatal to wake a person who is walking in his sleep. Schwägermann rolls down a window and flicks away his cigarette. Simultaneously the color in her face drains away; it is as if all the blood has been pumped from her body. She opens her eyes. She smiles.

"You are an expert in cinema, Herr Doktor Goebbels. I cannot fool you. You see what a terrible actress I am."

"Will you permit me to help you?"

"My God! Nothing can help me!"

"I have a plan. Listen—"

"*Do you love me?* You don't love him. You catch him. Like an incurable disease. *Just a little?*"

I lift my attaché case to my lap and pull out the papers. "Look, Fräulein. Look here."

But she is doubled over on our leather bench. She clutches her bowels. I hear the moan.

"Are you in pain?" I ask.

Over the engine noise, over the hissing tires, I can barely make out her words. "The glass." That is what she says. "The pane of glass."

I know about that Glasplatte. Renate told me. What he did with it. Or almost told me. *The happiest moment of my life.*

So Glücklich, so Glücklich, so Glücklich

What happened to that singing girl? Through a different pane of glass: out the window.

"My dear Karelena. I want you to look at these letters. They are from California. I hope you are going to forgive me. Please forgive me. I did not show them to you."

She says one word: "Alex."

"Yes. No. From Wonskolaser. But he writes because of Engelsing, his employee, his actor. Look. Fräulein. You must look. Three, four, five letters. For almost a year. Engelsing has convinced Herr Jack Warner of how beautiful you are."

She only doubles over once more. "The filth," she mutters. "Auf die Oberlippe."

"Please. Raise your head, Fräulein Karelena. My dear. Look at this photo. This is what you look like."

I hold up the glossy image: mouth half open; hair parted; a bare shoulder; shadows, thick shadows, like a liquor, in the hollow of a collar bone.

"Tobis," she says, glancing up. "Publicity department. I've already aged."

"This photo will be sent to Warner. In California—no, not California. To the capital, to Washington. Our sources—well, we have learned that is where he is at this moment. We shall include a letter from Tobis that releases you from your contract. You are free to go to America."

At that she fully raises her head. "*Go to America?* That is impossible. I am not certain I am a citizen of that country. I was born in Berlin. My mother is German. My father—oh, they will never let me in. There are a hundred thousand names ahead of mine. Every Jew left in Germany has made an application. They will wait forever."

"*Forever*. We don't have forever. We have only until Sunday. I am not even certain about which Sunday. Perhaps we have a week. Perhaps we have two weeks. Then: Operation Z."

For the first time she seems to really open her eyes, to look about her. "I know where I am. In your beautiful automobile. The same one that picked me up at the Anhalter Bahnhof. Where are you taking me? This is my country. I shall stay here."

"Impossible! That cannot be allowed. Don't you understand? You now have a secret. The same secret that all those women possessed. The Führer's women. Do you know what happened to them? They all—it was knowledge they could not bear to live with. Or be allowed to live with. You must go. You are in danger. I ask for your sake and for the German Reich. You belong to both countries—they cannot go to war with each other. You will help make sure that does not happen. We have work for you. For this moment and for the future."

"*The future!* A cabaret joke."

"Listen to me, meine Liebe. I am not going to send only this photo. And not just your torn-up contract. There will also be a letter, over your name. It will say how much you wish to go to California. How you *must* go to California. It will contain some information. Crucial information. It will arrive before you do. Our only hope is that Wonskolaser brings it to his friend in the White House. He can save you—changing the quota is a matter of snapping his fingers; and he can save our nations from a disastrous war."

"No, no. I understand nothing. Don't you see, Doktor? Geliebt Doktor. I am not the same person. I am not even a different person. I am not any person. I have been erased."

"We had tea together. A warm rain in June. It seems, doesn't it, in a different geological era. You are the same beautiful woman now that you were then. I am making certain that you will be safe in California. Not only that: I am giving you a chance to take revenge on the man who killed your father. You will serve your country and yourself."

"No, no." She says this quietly, her eyes shut once more. "You speak to me as if I were alive. I am someone who has crawled out of her grave."

"Are you listening to me? Do you hear me?" She stares ahead, not blinking. I make my words the slap across her face. "Pay attention! I am giving you an order. An order to a German woman. You belong to our nation, and to me, and to our Führer. You said it yourself: he is in your bloodstream. And in the cells of your body. Do you hear what I am saying to you? Nod your head. Now."

She does as she is told. "Good. You are about to leave for Lisbon. In only hours. It is the first step of your journey. You will remain there while these papers and this photo make *their* journey: thousands of kilometers in less than a day. A feat worthy of Lindbergh, wouldn't you agree?"

She does not reply, but once more nods.

"I told you. I have been awake. I have been busy. Do you see this envelope?" I took the tan folder from the case. "It contains your passport and any other papers you will need. Your clothing, in two suitcases, is in the boot behind us. In Lisbon you will be met by a trusted member of my staff. He will escort you to your hotel room. If I am not mistaken, you will not be there long. A day or two. Then New York and then—your destination: Los Angeles. Hollywood. There you will be met by—undoubtedly by Wonskolaser. To this Jew you must cling, and cling, and cling until he persuades himself that he cannot live without you. A form of Symbiose. We shall see how long the ivy will remain on the oak. You will also be met by another person. A friend of the Reich. A woman you can learn to trust, just as we have. And, of course, your cherished Herr Alex."

Our Mercedes comes to a stop. Schwägermann turns off the engine. All we can hear is the sound of its ticking as it cools. I lean close to the girl.

"I do not think we shall see each other again. Well, nothing is certain. Perhaps after the war. My hope for you is that when you are in the air, above the clouds, you will look down on this stinking earth and recall that some things in it are lovely to see—the mountains, the rivers, the lakes—and that some people on its surface will—well, let's hope they will be able to help you forget. No—do not look at me. I am not looking at you. Do you see?

My excellent adjutant is getting out of our automobile. Such a gentleman: he is walking around it to open your door."

"Where are we?" she asks.

I draw back the window curtains. Men in uniform, eager and smiling, rush forward. They open the boot. The morning sun falls blindingly on the glass windows of Tempelhof.

"At the airport. The executive entrance."

Schwägermann indeed opens her door. But she does not move.

"Auf Wiedersehen, meine Karelena."

Still she sits, unmoving. I dare to turn my head to look. Her mouth is moving.

"What is it, Fräulein, that you wish to say?"

A brief pause. Then she repeats her words, this time so that I can hear them.

"Heil Hitler."

She gets out of the car and, without looking backward, walks away.

Hedda Hopper's Hollywood: November 1941, Los Angeles

The stork is preparing that package for delivery at Alice Faye's house between St. Valentine's Day and St. Patrick's Day. The Herbert Marshalls expect theirs in April.

Jack Warner canceled his tennis match with Bill Tilden for this Sunday because he took off for our nation's capital and is now holed up as usual on the ninth floor of the Mayflower Hotel. It's not the exec FDR wants to see. It's his personal assistant, that Terrible Turk, Abdul Maljan. It seems he does wonders for "that man." Well, this way Jack can claim he would have won in straight sets!

Since Ginger Rogers switched to drama, most people think she has gone too high-hat for dancing. "But, Hedda," Ginger told me, "it isn't true. I'd like nothing better than doing another film with Fred Astaire. But no one has offered me a script."

Goebbels: First Day of May 1945, Berlin

Another explosion. I feel, or imagine I feel, the ground shift beneath me. The lights flicker, but they do not go out. Magda. In the doorway.

NOVEMBER 1941, BERLIN

By now the Fräulein is in Lisbon. I am free to accept the Führer's invitation to join him at the Reichskanzlei. He is in a jovial mood. He says that with temperatures now at -7°C, our motored units are able once more to advance. A reconnaissance battalion will soon be at the suburb of Khimki. The domes of Moscow are in sight. I expect him to break into a jig, as in the forests of Compiègne.

After dinner we watch his favorite film. I think he has seen it a hundred times. Warner Bros. Wonskolaser. The plot: at the last minute a chorus member replaces the star. The girls in their little frilled skirts. The identical smiles. The synchronization of movement. This is the perfection of an ideal. Women as the cogs and spokes and gears of an intricate machine. All limbs interchangeable. Replaceable parts. Never a word from their mouths. They spread their legs. The camera moves through them. The Führer is in heaven. Six-inch heels.

Fräulein Karelena Kaiser: November 1941, Above the Atlantic

Sehr Geehrter Herr Dr. Goebbels:

I write you after taking off from the city of Lisbon. Already we are above the clouds. I tell you now the truth: my heart is beating and beating; my breath is like the panting of a dog; I have already scratched with the nails of one hand the wrist of the other—my handkerchief stopped the blood. Why did you send me away? Why did I listen to you? I feel I have been kidnapped. In America they say "shanghaied." But I was not drugged. No one dragged me aboard a ship. I correct myself. I *was* drugged. By your voice. Your eyes. Your hands, the way they move through the air. I was hypnotized.

In danger, you said. I am no longer the silly girl that crossed the Wilhelmstrasse with you. The girl who dashed in excitement up the Reichskanzlei steps. That is a role that life had taught me to play.

Do you remember? The little Bavarian Mädchen who curtsied before the Führer? You did not have to tell me I was in danger. I know what happened to the other women. *His* other women. When I was young, I saw all the films of Renate Müller. Not with my father. With Hannelore. My mother. I used to skip along the sidewalk. *Ich Bin ja Heut' So Glücklich*. All day long. I carried the song in my head: *So Glücklich. So Glücklich. So Glücklich*. They were like the words of my talking doll. Of course, half of Germany was singing, too. Also you, my dear Doktor, unless I am quite mistaken. She, too, flew through the air. On her own? Or did the Gestapo throw her through the frame? Because she had been with *him*. Because she knew what I know.

And so, the words of the hypnotist: *Safe in California*.

More magical words: that when I flew from Berlin I would look down on beautiful things, *lovely* things, like the lakes and rivers and mountains. They would lift my spirits, you said. They would help me forget.

Yes, I saw mountains. Yes, the rivers, the lakes, the ponds. For me they held no interest. Yet my face remained pressed to the window. What I wanted to see, what I did see, were the towns, the hamlets, the cities. A railway line. The roads, the crisscrossing roads. Automobiles, a tractor in a field. Smoke from chimneys. Smoke from fires. All the signs of human life, the hurrying human beings. Three times I jumped from my seat. Down the aisle. Not to the cabin door—though I admit that was a temptation: to hurl myself down. No, I ran to the door of the water closet. I wanted one thing in all the world: the pleasure of shitting on every man every woman every child beneath me. What joy at that thought. What pain, like a blade in my belly, twisting my bowels around it like the Führer's spaghetti around his fork.

The horror of that first flight, Berlin-Lisbon, remains with me now, when I am high above the clouds and the sea. Not because—or not so much because—I still wish to smash through these windows and cast myself down. No, Herr Doktor Reichsminister. The horror is that I want to make this huge flying machine turn around. The horror is that I want to go back. To where Wolf is waiting.

Miss Karelena Kaiser, December 1941, Los Angeles

Sehr Geehrter Herr Doktor Goebbels:

I am now in the city of Los Angeles after traveling across the broad country, first from New York to Chicago, and then from Chicago all the way to the Union Station, with no passengers permitted either to get off or to board the train. My mood with its dark thoughts slowly left me as the thousands of miles went by: the flat plains, the high mountains, and the desert, with American Indian villages and the teepees and the horses, the same as in the pages of Karl May or one of the Hollywood motion pictures. I wonder how you will feel if I tell you the Negro attendants were helpful and pleasant. They did not smell of anything besides the cologne they wore. One, with spectacles, was reading in his free time a novel by Thomas Mann.

You will think with these words I am becoming an American. But do you remember I told you I have caught the German disease? Imagine a scene from one of those novels or one of those films. The savages have tied down the white girl, with her limbs spread and as much of her clothing gone as the censors will allow. The hot desert sun beats down on her, hour after hour. They wish to force her to join their tribe. I could play that part. I could be that girl. But the infection is in my blood. Perhaps it is in my bones. The sun cannot bake it out of me. The dancing Indianer—is it the Navajo tribe? The Apaches? These young braves will be disappointed.

From nowhere, from somewhere, I remember another film, from when I was ten, perhaps eleven. With Joe-Joe beside me, taking his notes. I think it was called, in English—what was it called? Yes! *White Zombie.* The girl, Madeleine: she climbs from her tomb. She walks under a spell. She is capable of murder. Do not worry, Doktor. Am I not a reanimated corpse? I shall remain loyal. To you. To my only country. To him. I shall be capable of murder as well.

We arrived at Union Station at eleven a.m., Pacific Coast Time. I saw that a small group of people were waiting for me: a man with a little moustache and a bouquet of drooping flowers; next to him

a large, dark-skinned, hairless fellow; and off to one side a rather
attractive woman, with what looked like a Gugelhöpf on top of her
head. Then I was running down the platform and the man with the
bouquet stepped forward, grinning with what looked like five hundred white teeth and holding out the flowers, but I went right by him
and threw myself into the arms of Alex, my dearest Alex, standing
there in his old brown suit; and I kissed him there on the platform
and he kissed me, and every thought that had ever entered my head
flew away.

I do not know how much time went by—perhaps no more than a
minute; then others were running, too, and still others were standing
motionless, taking off their hats, and the voice from the loudspeakers was repeating something, and though my English is very good,
almost without an accent, they say, I could not understand, as if it
were speaking an unknown language. Alex stepped back and shook
his head, so serious, and said, "It is war. The Japanese have attacked.
They are bombing." But for a moment this did not for me sink in.
My happiness refused to disappear. But at the same time, Dr. Goebbels, I was thinking: that woman. The woman with the hat. Was
she the friend you said would be waiting? And, was this your Operation Z?

I am with Alex now. I mean, I am in his small bungalow house
on Argyle Avenue. It is two in the morning. He is in his bed. I am at
the kitchen table. Yes, writing, Herr Reichsminister, to you. Why?
This should be a night of joy. I should be thinking not of you, not of
anyone, not of anything. I should be the way I was for that moment
in his arms. Yes, another Hollywood ending. Or one from UFA. With
music playing.

There are two reasons why. First, America is now at war. I know
you did not want this to happen. I fear what you fear: that Germany
will join its ally. If that occurs, will this be the last letter I shall be
able to send you? Will you be able to read even these words? I do not
know. The other reason—it is a sad one, and one difficult for me to
say. Why am I not in Alex's bed? It is not only to write to you. It is
because in that bed and in his arms I felt nothing. I could have been
a patient. Under Anästhesie. Already it is over between us. He is my

Onkel Engel once more. Now I must stop. I hope this letter reaches you. Oh. That person on the platform. With the moustache. With the flowers. That is the man who killed my father.

Goebbels: First Day of May 1945, Berlin

I take my hat. My coat. My Mauser. My gloves. I join my wife and together we go up the flights of stairs until—ah, at last: here is the garden.

PART II

~~

FIGHTING

The Terrible Turk: December 1941, Los Angeles

Ring! Ring! Ring! The telephone. I had a prophecy about who it was even before I picked up and heard her voice. "Is that you, Abby?" Only one person ever called me by that name. Right away I felt a stirring below the belt, where the Little Turk makes his home.

"Hello, Hedda," I said, feeling all over again how the day before she had held onto my arm and pressed her body against mine. It did not matter that this was a woman of some age. I am not a spring chicken myself. "It was good to see you, even in the circumstances."

"You know I always enjoy seeing you, too, Abby. You look really smashing."

"Well, so do you." I pictured her to myself as Maida in *Battle of Hearts*, which she used to show from her projector against the bedroom wall. Long hair, dark hair, a white sailor suit. Half-bare arms. Just a girl.

"Keep talking and you'll get half a paragraph! Did you see today's column?"

"I always read it first. Ahead of the sports. Those weren't calla lilies."

"And you weren't a star in the silents. Sometimes the lily is gilded."

"What is that, Shakespeare or something?"

"Don't play the dope with me. You know, you *could* have been a star. I have a nose for that in people. As a matter of fact, I got a call this morning from the old gray Mayer. He saw my notice, and he says he's got a part for you. A big part."

"Did he call you or did you call him? It doesn't matter. I'm too old. Plus I'm happy here with the Chief. I don't need to look for more."

"Stuff and nonsense! I'm building you up so the whole country will want to see you. You've got your looks. I could feel those muscles under your jacket. The mature man of mystery."

"Okay, Hedda. What do you want?"

"Do I have to have an ulterior motive? What if I only wanted to tell you that I enjoyed seeing you yesterday and that it brought back a lot of memories and that I miss you and do you miss me?"

The Little Turk, now more a pasha, doesn't lie. "I guess I do, to tell you the truth."

"You know, this war scares me. They say there might be bombings. I've got no one. A maid! A cat! And more enemies than the Japs. I'd like to see you."

"I get off work at six. Would you like me to come over tonight?"

"Tonight? You are a fast worker! La! La! Oh, my dear, I'm a little hard of hearing in my dotage, and there was so much noise and tumult yesterday morning. Could you remind me? What was it that Jack said? Yesterday? At the station?"

Warning bells, a flashing red light. And may the gods laugh: a little shiver of disappointment. "What do you mean? The Chief? He didn't say anything."

"You'd better do a girl a favor, Mr. Maljan. That pretty German blonde ran right by him. I could have printed that. But I protected him."

"Then why not ask him? He owes you the favor."

"I protected you, too. I know you wanted to help that little Jap. Always the hero! The champion! They would have beaten you to a pulp. Knocked out again! I held you back."

"No, no, Hedda. I held you so you wouldn't fall."

"*I told him.* Jack said that much, I remember. Told who? Told him *what*? I've got my suspicions. *Sunday!* I remember that, too. Yesterday was a Sunday. What's going on, Abby? What's it all about? Don't play Mr. Numbskull. If you don't tell me, plenty of other people will."

"Hedda, listen. I *will* do you a favor. Forget it. You don't—"

"*Forget it!* I never heard such a thing in my life. Forget this? I told you I've got my suspicions. It's the scoop of the century!"

"Scoop? What scoop? Nothing happened."

"*Warned him!* I heard that, too! Now be a darling. Be the sweet man I care for so much. I always think of you. *Magic!* Didn't I always say it? Your hands. I am alone. Maybe we can talk tête à tête. Would you like that?"

Human beings. You have no choice except to shake your head when you think about them. Everybody is like two people. Upstairs, in my mind, I was appalled. She stung me like a wasp with every word. But the other part of me, which is the more primitive part, was at those words, *I am alone*, already a sultan. Head over heart: I told her I was late for work and that I had to go and if she knew what was good for her she would write about something else.

"You two are in this together!" I had to hold the receiver away from my ear, she was shouting so loud. "I know you and Jack and Harry and the whole Warners crowd have it in for the Germans. That's why you made that dreadful *Confessions* picture. I'm going to get to the bottom of this. I've got other sources. What about that Berlin blonde? What if I give her a call? And don't forget I can build you up or I can tear you down. One of my dearest friends is Mr. Hoover and all I have to do is snap my fingers and you'll be deported. Or put into a camp. *Snap!* Did you hear that? *Snap!*"

And with that the girl in the sailor suit hung up.

Hedda Hopper's Hollywood: December 1941, Los Angeles

Wouldn't you know Marlene Dietrich would take advantage of her little accident? She's wearing on the lapel of her tailored suit two crossed legs of gold, one done up in bandages. It's as cute as Christmas—

My old friend, Abdul Maljan, that oh-so-Terrible Turk, has overnight turned into one of the hot gents in town. Jack Warner has got his eye on him to play Bill Delaney, the manager for Gentleman Jim Corbett, who's going to be portrayed by Errol Flynn. That might be interesting, since Maljan has been strutting around Warners telling anybody who will listen he could knock out Flynn with a hand behind his back. Methinks this Turk had better watch his step, and that's no Instant Bull! He wasn't born in this country and he could get decked not by Mr. Flynn, who come to think of it wasn't born here either, but by Mr. Hoover. There's a fighter who never loses a bout!

Pat O'Brien had to spend a month growing a mustache because the first scene of *Trinidad* shows Pat shaving one and—

The Terrible Turk: December 1941, Los Angeles

I put down the paper. A right cross and a left hook. Build you up, tear you down. But heaven help me I still found myself waiting for the phone that did not ring. Not that day or the next. But she pulled no punches in her column.

Hedda Hopper's Hollywood: December 1941, Los Angeles

A little blond birdy who recently flew into town chirped in my ear that the last time super-masseur Abdul Maljan went east to get FDR "on his feet," he was accompanied by studio boss Jack Warner. That was only a week or so before the Japs pulled their fast one at Pearl Harbor. The smart money is that the two of them had come not for a massage but with a message. And just a few days later glamour girl Cheryl Charmaigne—which is the moniker a certain Fräulein Kaiser was given by Warner to make her more acceptable to American audiences—arrived on our shores from Berlin. A lot of strings had to be pulled to accomplish that trick. She was about a hundred thousand names down the list. This is a mystery for Bulldog Drummond or Miss Christie's Monsieur Poirot. Just because I haven't yet put two and two together doesn't mean that Mr. Jack L. Warner shouldn't take a word of advice from a friend. We're all better off when we folk in Hollywood concentrate on what we do best, namely creating wonderful pictures that make the whole world cry and laugh, and not meddle in international affairs. After Jack made that biased *Confessions of a Nazi Spy*, he had to hire people to dig up his backyard looking for bombs. That's nothing compared to the explosives he's tinkering with now. Shoemaker (that's the profession practiced by Papa Wonskolaser when he, too, came to this welcoming land), stick to your last!

The Terrible Turk: December 1941, Burbank

There wasn't a word in her column the next day. The only item about the war was that from now on there were to be no more world premieres, since all the spotlights would be needed for coast defense. Plus, a lot of stars like

Buster Keaton and Bob Young had rounded up station wagons and stood ready to drive off to any stricken areas. But my telephone did ring—not at home, not at breakfast, but when I was already in my office. She didn't let me get a word in edgewise:

"Is that you, Abby? I know it's you. I am so angry I could spit! Did you hear the news? Turn on the radio. Germany has declared war on the United States! I never dreamed such a thing could happen. Why that country and this county should be allies. Against the Communists! Charlie Chaplin must be dancing in the streets!"

"I am as surprised as you, Hedda. Why—"

"Oh, be quiet and listen. I've been thinking and thinking. Who wanted this war more than anyone else? *That man!* It's no secret. Everyone knows it. And now he's got it. *Why?* Because Germany had a treaty with the Japanese. Say what you want about Adolf Hitler, Abby, he's an honorable human being. But if Japan had not pulled off that sneak attack none of this would have happened. Could Franklin Roosevelt have wanted Pearl Harbor? Isn't *he* the one you two warned? Jack practically said so himself. I heard him with my own ears. Our elected president did nothing. What a scoop! And I put it all in today's column. But I couldn't print it. Not a word. For the first time in my life I've been censored. As if I were the enemy! And not born in Pennsylvania! They made me write instead some nonsense about how Abbott and Costello were exhausted doing a long dance routine with a dog, and when the director said *Cut*, Bud said, *Thank heaven!* and the director said, *Oh, it's not for you. The dog was tired.* Dog-tired! Ha, ha, ha. Oh, it's a cute story, but it's not what I wanted to say. I've got to have proof, that's what they told me. I need a source. Tell me, Abby. You were there. This isn't gossip. Not this time. This is a story about treason—"

I did not hear anything more. I dropped the phone and ran into the hallway and up the stairs, three flights to the Chief's suite. I barged into Minna's office and crossed the carpet to the locked door. I put my shoulder against it. It flew open, and I burst into the room.

"Chief!" I shouted. "Hedda knows something! And Germany has declar—"

What I saw before my eyes could not be in a picture. Joe Breen would never allow it.

Cheryl Charmaigne: December 1941, Burbank

I have been waiting for this. Up against his desk. He wanted to pull my legs up around him. But I turned around. Not for pleasure. There is no pleasure. But I can lean forward. I can look out the window. Though I don't have to. I know what is waiting there. A desert sun. As bright in the winter as in July. Inexhaustible. Round-faced. A drawing by a Mongoloid child. Between me and its rays: the pane of glass.

He wants me to stay with him. In my own flat. In the Hollywood Hills. Briarcliff Road. The other half of the bargain: I am to play a leading part, this Lois, even if they do not have now a word of the script. I think of Joe-Joe. In the dark. At the UFA Palast. He looks up and sees his daughter, with her terrible teeth, with the smooth skin of her neck, and he writes, *You've got a hit with this one, J.L.! You should have heard the audience. They were on their feet. What casting! A new German star.*

Mr. Jack Warner can do what he wants with me. Nothing can compare with what I have done to myself.

The Terrible Turk: December 1941, Burbank

"What the fuck are you doing in here? I thought that door was locked."

"It was, but this—"

"But nothing! But nothing!"

The Chief hopped around, trying to pull up his pants. The girl walked away and started to do some things with her hair. She wasn't even blushing.

"Here," said the Chief, as if nothing had happened. "Look at this." He picked up some typed sheets from his desk and held them out to me. "It's a new property. A synopsis. It came in a month ago."

I glanced at the sheaf of papers. It said *STAGE PLAY: Rec'd MS from NY. 11/8/41. Summary.*

The Chief flashed one of his smiles. You could have held a premiere with the light from his teeth. And what was that? With his eye? A wink? "There's a hell of a part for Miss Charmaigne. I was just showing her how I thought they ought to play one of the scenes." He snatched the papers out of my hand put his finger down on a couple of sentences:

Lois soon returns alone, and spends the night with him. In the morning, torn between unquenchable love and deep distrust, Rick challenges her motives.

"See that? *Spends the night.* That's the love scene for Miss Charmaigne. She's already got the perfect accent—" And then, under his breath to me: "and the perfect ass, too."

The girl stood in the light that was coming in from the window. The Chief called out to her:

"You've got the part, sweetheart! You can take it to the bank. Abdul is my witness. Only we'll change that name, *Lois.* To something more European. Ilka or Lisle or something like that. We'll need a new name for the picture, too. *Everybody Comes to Rick's.* Rick's? The sticks! For hicks! No wonder it was never produced. We're going to call it, let me see: *Letters of Transit!*" That's got sophistication. It's perfect! What do you say, Abdul? Isn't that perfect?"

"Yes, yes, *çok parlak!* Brilliant! Chief, you've done it again!"

10 } SNEAK PEAK

Jack L. Warner: December 1941/January 1942, Washington, DC

Okay, looks like we've got a hit. GLORIOUSLY UPROARIOUS! We're getting the same laughs at the White House we got in the Little Rock preview. We should make everybody fill out a card. Hell, it's not like we charged them admission. The president kept pestering us because he didn't get to see the play. He's like a kid, for Christ's sake, always wanting his sneak peek before anybody else gets a chance.

Here come's Banjo's entrance, where he picks up the nurse and then puts her down. Now he's playing the piano and doing the same thing with his hat—putting it on and taking it off:

> *Didja ever have the feeling that you wanted to go*
> *But still had the feeling you wanted to stay?*

I never got the point of Durante, even though he's doing okay business with *You're in the Army Now*. A NEW TEAM! YOU'LL SCREAM! But this crowd loves him. They're busting their goddamned guts. Funny how people laugh the same in every language. Got to remember that, in case I ever write a book. Abdul, right next to me, is doubled over, slapping his knee. FDR, he's the type who throws his head back, as if the laughs were up there on the ceiling. And his old lady, she doesn't make a lot of noise, only shows those choppers and squirms around like she's peeing in her pants.

What's so appealing about this picture, anyway? Everything depends on one gag. Woolley, he's the *Man Who Came to Dinner*, NOTHING COULD BE FUNNIER, breaks his hip and drives the local yokels nuts by staying all winter. And the laugh is that when he's finally about to leave, the phone rings and he turns and slips and then breaks his bones all over again.

I admit it, at first I didn't get the joke; I thought it was kind of mean, to tell you the truth. It took Wald, and Wallis, and both the writers to explain it. *Now he'll have to stay there six more months!* Ha! Ha! Ha! The trouble is, that gag was in the play, too. Why do I have to pay those Epstein bums a fortune when half their stuff is already written for them? I ought to hire George S. himself. *And* Hart! At least they wouldn't come strolling into the studio an hour after lunch.

Haw-Haw-Haw! There goes the president. He's lapping up this crap. Good thing, too: I was plenty nervous because of the wheelchairs, his and Woolley's. Another thing about this Woolley. People call him Sherry. What kind of name is that for a man? It sounds like a drink—or some kind of fruit. Speaking of fruits: the Broadway theater is full of them. I told Wallis and I told Wald: get Barrymore, get Grant, get maybe even Cagney. Why listen to me? Just because my name is on the water tower. So now we have this hambone and it's obvious he's some kind of nance. Men who don't love women—and vice versa. Maybe they go on stage to do it because they don't in real life. Another thought I could put in a book.

Hopper told me that Eleanor, with her horse-faced pal, is no different. Do you think FDR can't do it? Maybe his schlong got polio, too. I'll ask Abdul. He'll know.

Meanwhile, on the other side of me, sits my blondie. Nothing makes her laugh. And I've tried with feathers. The president made a big fuss that I should bring the Kaiser girl with me. Except she's not the Kaiser girl, or Karelena either, anymore. *Cheryl Charmaigne.* I thought of it myself. Has a touch of French class, halfway between Champagne, which I never touch myself, and Charle-somebody, who I know was a big shot over in Europe even if I never went to college. The lights are just dim enough for me to try the old crossed-arms maneuver, undetectable in church or synagogue or up in the balcony: you use your right hand to grab the mammy on the right, or vice versa, depending. Do I dare? I mean, the whole fucking cabinet is here. I'll start with—there, a grazing action, like a carom shot. It's not like there's a lot to get hold of. She's not exactly overdeveloped in the melon section.

Whoa, the whole joint is cracking up. They're rolling in the aisles. For a second I think, *maybe they've gotten wind of what is happening in row C, or wherever I'm sitting*; but instead I see it's because up on the screen Woolley's penguin has just taken a bite out of Nurse Preen. Now they're all breaking into applause. Hey, should I take a bow or something? Why not? I mean, the whole penguin bit was my idea. *Ladies and germs*—

Hey, wait a second. They aren't clapping for the picture; they're clapping because someone has just come into the room. It's Churchill. I don't like when people come in late. If I ran the theaters they wouldn't get in at all. The applause gets even louder. He's raising his hat. He's all smiles. Gee, that hat. The cigar. That suit that barely buttons in the front: hell if I'm not clapping too. I mean, the blitz, for Christ's sake.

He's got a crowd with him—that general, what's his name, something, something: Dill! And the other guy, looks like a corpse, no left hand. Halifax! The ambassador. And—

"Carry on, carry on," says the PM. He and his little group start to move toward some chairs at the back.

"No, no!" everybody starts to shout.

"We want to know what happened up north."

Then FDR pipes up. "Yes, Mr. Prime Minister: What did you have to tell our friends in Ottawa?"

Churchill pauses and takes the cigar out of his mouth. "What did I tell them? I told them what I wish to tell you: our ties are indissoluble. I intend with this visit to infect America, so that you will carry my antibodies in your system, a means of defense against all outside invaders; just as I carry the blood of George Washington's soldiers—Jerome and Ball—forever in my veins. Fighters at Valley Forge! Against the stout armies of Britain!"

"That's quite an irony, Mr. Prime Minister." This was some admiral or other, with fruit salad all over his chest.

"Yes, my dear Stark," Churchill replies. "But there was no irony in what I told them next: which was that, in spite of all, and in spite of our Declaration on the morrow, if our United Nations should become *dis*united, Britain will continue to fight on alone and fight on forever!"

Everybody bursts into applause. They stand and cheer. Okay. Okay. Including yours truly, even though I never stand up—it's my rule, except once for the elephants in *Aida*. But I know good acting when I see it. I'd like to get *him* under a seven-year contract. Maybe I could borrow Laughton to play the part.

FDR: "And I hear, Prime Minister, you have American Indian blood in you, too."

A Brit, Beaverbrook: "A red skin is harder to take off than a red coat."

This gets more laughs than the penguin. Or even the octopus.

Now this guy Dill: "We need have no fear of falling out. Our Declaration pledges that, against our common enemy, we shall never consider a separate armistice or a separate peace."

"Then we'd be in a pickle!" No one responds to this witty remark.

"Yes, Field Marshall," says Halifax. "Yet everyone in this room, and perhaps above all our friend Ambassador Litvinov, knows that even the most solemn pledges can be broken."

At this a jowly Russian, of the portly Hebrew type, looks up over his wireless glasses. "It is true," he begins, in a comical Yiddish accent, all the funnier because of his dreary expression, "a solemn treaty with my country was broken. Might I ask the prime minister a question? Since that terrible day has he had any approaches from the Nazi beast about just such a separate peace?"

"I think I must remind everyone that this is an informal gathering. We must not discuss matters of security or the war before our guests."

Here the speaker—Abdul whispers that it's a general named Marshall—seems to give me in particular the eye. Some nerve! When I made the picture that exposed all those Nazi spies.

"Oh, that's all right, General," Churchill says. "It will not endanger us if I say that we have had no such feelers. But then I believe the Third Reich must be pressed for materials of all kinds and would not wish to waste either the paper or the ink."

More laughter, though I've heard better cracks.

Now FDR turns to the Russian ambassador. "Maxim," he says. "We're here to celebrate: both the coming New Year and our Declaration. Why that long face?"

The gloomy Russian—is there any other kind?—mumbles an answer: "Leningrad." Right away his glasses seem covered by a mist. You can't see through them to his eyes. "The last link to land has been severed. It is minus 30, Celsius. Do you know what this means?"

"It means," says one of the Brits—*Who's that, Abdul? It's Wilson, Chief. Churchill's doctor*—"a damned hard winter."

"It means," Litvinov goes on, "they will soon start eating each other."

"I don't mean to be rude," says our admiral, Stark, "but this is the man who is holding up our Joint Declaration."

"Oh, no," says FDR, "it's not Maxim here who is at fault."

"If you mean Premier Stalin, I can inform you that I have heard from Moscow this afternoon."

FDR: "That's just grand, Maxim. I have every hope you will tell us that our wishes—and by that I mean the wishes of all our United Nations—have been granted."

"Premier Stalin has instructed me to inquire first whether you have in turn granted *his* wishes—and by that I mean a final commitment to a second front. He had hoped, from our allies, more support."

"More support, is it?" That's Stark again. "We, too, have been attacked without warning. By an Asian nation. Yet we now agree to make the liberation of Europe and the defeat of the Nazis our first priority. Do you think that was easy? To go on the offense on a continent that has not harmed us and to engage in only defensive actions throughout the Pacific? Would you like to explain that to the American people?"

FDR, with a laugh: "Sometimes I wish someone would explain it to *me*."

But Churchill does not join in the laughter. "You cannot deny, Mr. Ambassador, that from the very first day of the German invasion of your lands, I have labored to obtain all possible support for Soviet Russia in the United States. And you have received that support, human and material, in the most generous amounts."

"That is no substitute for the second front."

"About that there is no disagreement," says Churchill. "Her Majesty's government will open that front."

FDR: "As will America. We intend to fight together."

"Words," says Litvinov. "When? Where? With how many troops?"

Now Marshall cuts in. "Yes, words. Too many of them. Really, I must insist the discussion stop."

He's red in the face. So is Churchill. The Red is, too. I figure somebody's got to do something before this becomes an international incident. "Hey, look, everybody." I point up to the screen, where Durante and company are shoving Sheridan into a mummy case. They're going to ship her off to Nova Scotia. I'd like to ship her farther than that, the way she's always griping about her contract. "Isn't that hilarious? I thought up that mummy business myself. Ha, ha, ha!"

No one pays any attention. We sank eight hundred thousand into this baby and they're watching for free!

Wilson, the doctor, decides to horn in. "It's late. We have traveled. It's been a difficult day. I think the prime minister had best retire."

"Just a minute, Charlie," Churchill says. Then he turns to Litvinov. "Mr. Ambassador, I want you to know that His Majesty's government understands your dilemma. Let Comrade Stalin be assured. The military assault he desires will soon be launched."

The unhappy Russian stares for a minute. "How soon?"

The president leans toward the ambassador. "Help is coming, Maxim. I promise you. You shall have your second front."

"I do not want promises. You wish us to sign your Declaration? Then tell me: When will this front be opened?"

FDR: "Before this coming year—the year that begins in one half hour—is concluded."

"1942. May I tell Premier Stalin you have made a commitment?"

"You may."

"But a commitment by whom? All of the so-called United Nations?"

Churchill: "By Britain and America. We intend to fight side by side in this, our first joint battle."

"And in what numbers? Is this to be a true front? Or merely a feint—I don't mean to deceive the Germans. I mean to deceive us."

"In the hundreds of thousands," the prime minister answers.

"Very well. And now the key question: Where? In Holland? Across the Channel in France?"

"About that," says FDR, "there is some disagreement. Or I should say, some discussion. We Americans are indeed leaning toward a cross-Channel invasion, but our friends in London have a different plan."

"In either case," says the fancy admiral, "our navy will play the key role. Along, of course, with the navy of our great ally."

Here General Marshall pops off again. "We really should not say any more, Mr. Ambassador. You understand these matters are highly confidential. I must insist that we put off the discussion until a later time."

Litvinov doesn't have a chance to answer because there is a tinkling sound at the door. Prettyman and another darkie are wheeling in trays, one with bottles and the other with glasses.

"Ah," says Admiral Stark. "The champagne!"

All exclaim and applaud.

Eleanor laughs. "Not yet! Too soon! You can't drink for another—let's see: twenty-five minutes."

But Churchill is not inclined to wait. He walks over to one of the carts and pours what doesn't look like champagne but Scotch into a glass. "It's been a new year in Britain for hours." He drinks it down and pours another. "I drink to our great new adventure. With all deference to the navy men here—why, I like to think that I am a former naval person myself—and above all to you, Admiral Stark, and to the great fleets that you command: this war will not be won by ships but by a thousand tanks. We shall engage Rommel and his Afrika Korps on their own ground. We shall fight on seas of sand and not those of water."

All of a sudden an idea like a lightbulb in *Merrie Melodies* goes off in my mind. What did the PM mean, *seas of sand?* Why did he say not ships but a thousand tanks? *Rommel? Afrika Korps?* I clutch my noggin. It's throbbing like the gong in a J. Arthur Rank production. Wait, wait, wait: bingo!

"Hey, everybody! Guess what? We're going to invade Africa!"

"*Africa?*" echoes Litvinov, except it comes out *Hefreeka*, like Thomashefsky at the Grand. "You are opening the front in a desert?"

Dill: "Yes, by God! We're going to throw the Hun from that continent!"

"What a story! It's world-shattering news! Wait until I tell Hedda! And I figured it out myself!"

Across the room, I see General Marshall slam his fist down on a table. He turns to someone and says something. Because of all the silents we made, I'm pretty good at reading lips: *Arrest that man.* A couple of starkers—they're maybe secret service, maybe military police—trot forward on the double. They're making a beeline right for me but stop when all of a sudden there is a honking sound, like this, *HONK! HONK!,* and who should show up in the doorway but one of the Marx Brothers.

"Harpo!" I shout. "What the hell are you doing here?"

Of course he won't answer, just gives another honk, but Beaverbrook—there's a flower in his lapel they call a butt-in-the-air—cries out, "Why, it's Mr. Marx. Wasn't he your first ambassador to the Soviet Union?"

"Almost," says Eleanor, with a horsy flash of those teeth. "Mr. Bullitt was our first representative there, but we sent Harpo on a good-will tour. He was the true American Ambassador so now he is a guest of honor here."

"Given that choice," I remark, "I'll take the Bullitt."

"Welcome, welcome!" says FDR, but Harpo, fright wig and all, stomps right by him and makes for Litvinov. The sad sack of an ambassador doesn't even look up. So Harpo sticks out his hand to shake and—watch out! I see this coming—ten thousand knives pour out of his sleeve and fall clattering to the floor. Big laugh. Bigger than my *Bullitt* gag.

Then Harpo sees me and with a big goofy grin comes loping right to where I am sitting. Except it's Cheryl Charmaigne he comes up to and right away, *HONK! HONK!,*, lifts his leg up against her, which everybody in the whole world knows is a chubby. Blondie pulls back like she's seen some kind of snake. Then Harpo throws a gookie and reaches for both her breasts and makes like he's going to screw in lightbulbs—in this case, only forty watts. With a scream, my female companion jumps up and in maybe only three or four bounds leaps across the room and—with gasps all around—throws herself onto the president's lap.

HONK! HONK!, Gookie! Laughter! Applause!

FDR, he's beaming like its election night, calls out: "Jack, old boy! Come over here. Are you not going to introduce me to your lovely friend?"

Everybody is looking at the two of them. She's crushed up against him, and he's got his cigarette and his cigarette holder sticking up like he's got a chubby, too.

"Yeah, okay," I answer, and walk over myself. "This is Miss Cheryl Charmaigne, halfway between champagne and, and—"

"No, no," she says. Now she's got an arm all the way around his neck.

"What do you mean, *no, no*? You're under contract."

"I mean my name isn't Cheryl and it's not Charmaigne."

"Okay, okay. Stage name. Her real name is Kaiser, but not spelled the way Kay—"

"Kauffman," she says. "That is the name of my father. It's the name I was born with."

"Right," I say. "Joe. Great guy. Great member of the Warners family."

I'm laughing. I'm smiling. But inside my mind is reeling. That look she gives me. Those words. She's Kauffman's daughter, all right. Joe, not George S. Does she think I beat him up? The krauts, those bastards, did it. *They* smashed up his apartment. *They* burned his car. And *they* shot him in cold blood. When all he was doing was his job, watching one of our pictures. *Twenty Million Sweethearts.* THERE'S ROMANCE IN THE AIR. A money-maker. I paid for the funeral, for Christ's sake!

"Very pleased to meet you, Miss Kauffman," says FDR.

I grab her arm. I lean in close, so no one can hear me. "Are you nuts? Look, sooner or later, people are going to find out you're Jewish. Better later."

She yanks free. She turns to the president, "You can call me Miss Kaiser. I am close to my mother. She has hair like mine. They say I look like her. She is not a Jew."

Just then Mrs. R calls out—her voice is like chalk on a blackboard: "Over here, everyone! This way! It's time! We shall say good-bye to this unhappy old year and welcome the one that is about to begin. This way! This way!"

And everybody starts to move to where the two carts are set up by the front windows. Well, not everybody. The two gorillas from the Secret Service are heading again in my direction.

Cheryl—okay, okay, Karelena, maybe we can bill her as KK: she twists around so that her boobs, such as they may be, are practically jumping ship. "Please don't let those men bother Mr. Warner," she says. "He was so brave, so kind. He saved me from the Nazis and brought me to America. With your help of course."

Hearing those words—*brave! kind!*—I get a warm feeling, you know, down in South America.

"Oh, it was nothing," says FDR, and with his wrist he waves the agents away. "I'm always happy to do anything for a lovely young lady like you."

"Well, Mr. President," says KK—I like that: KK, "when I was in Germany I was offered a part in a film. A wonderful part. Annelie. A nurse finds her husband on the battlefield. Perhaps in a bed. Perhaps in a wheelchair. He is wounded. He is dying. He hasn't the strength to inhale his own cigarette."

I stand there, like I'm watching Grable or some other great star. Look at that: tears are running down her cheeks. And that ain't glycerin. "So she reaches out"—that's KK talking—"and takes the cigarette from the dear man; the dear, dear man." Believe it or not she takes FDR's Chesterfield right out of its holder and inhales it herself. It's an intimate moment! I'm thinking, *How do I get the rights to that picture?*

Now Annie lay, or whatever her name is, leans even farther back—mam overboard! Two mams overboard!—removes the holder and blows the smoke practically into the mouth of the commander in chief! Holy smoke! No pun intended. It's like what I saw in the rushes of *Now Voyager*, A

WOMAN FIGHTING FOR THE RIGHT TO LOVE, when Henreid does the two-cigarette bit with Davis.

"You see, she has given him the gift of love." She says this, with her lips in the neighborhood of his. I see I don't need to ask Abdul about the president's equipment, because—and I don't want to seem unpatriotic—everything is A-OK in that department. "Now what gift will he give to Annelie?"

FDR's nose-pinchers are completely fogged up. He says with a sort of gasp, "Anything she wishes. What would she like?"

"I know Germany and I know Germans. They are strong. They are ruthless. Do not open a second front in Europe. Not in France. Not in Holland. All your soldiers will be killed. Hitler and his army will throw them into the sea."

The president's face, which had been the color of a fire truck, now starts to go pale. "What would you have us do, then?" he asks.

"Mr. Churchill is right," she answers. "You must attack in Africa."

"Listen, K-K-K-Katy," I start to say. "You better leave politics to—"

But the president interrupts. "I can't do that. No, I can't." Now he's really white around the gills. His lips are white, too. "You have heard of the suffering of the Soviet Union. We have to do something for Stalin. I think, my girl, you had best join the others."

The *fille*, if I can practice my French, flinches backward, as if avoiding a blow.

Now I start to hear a kind of murmur. From the other side of the windows. There's a crowd out there. They want to celebrate the New Year. I check my watch: five minutes to twelve. In here, everybody has already got a drink in his hand. Blondie, as red in the face as if she had really been slapped, hurries over to a cart and grabs a glass.

"Be smart, Mr. President," I say, "and never listen to an actress. That Africa idea is nuts. If you want my—"

I stop. In the middle of a sentence. It's not characteristic.

"What's the matter, Jack-o? Cat got your tongue?"

But it isn't a cat. It's a tiger. All of a sudden a thousand of them are racing around in my head like the ones around Little Black Sambo. *Africa. Tanks. Desert. Sand.* Why couldn't we make a picture out of this invasion? Something like *Algiers*. That piece of crap. Come with me to the Canasta.

Wait! Hold on! We've got that picture already! *Letters of Transit!* I thought of that title myself.

I can't believe my luck! What a break! They invade Africa at the very moment we bring out the picture! Maybe around Thanksgiving. Maybe Christmas. Whenever the fighting begins. What a tie-in! Publicity is going to cream themselves! LANDING ON THE BEACHES AND LANDING IN YOUR HEART, or something like that. And not only do we have the picture, we've got the star! She's got blond hair—and not just on top, either, do I have to explain?—she's got an accent, she's got everything. Okay, not tits. I can't believe how the pieces are coming together. Maybe there is a God.

"Listen, Mr. President," I say, with what they call savoir faire. "We've just bought a property about a bunch of refugees, and if we start shooting soon, maybe we can have another sneak preview just for you."

"That's the spirit! And it sounds like it could be part of the war effort. The plight of the refugees. It's such a pity: half of Europe is trapped. There's no exit."

"Well, these chumps aren't in Europe, exactly."

"Oh? Then where are they?"

"It's a dicey situation. The French are in control, but they're more or less controlled themselves by the Germans. So—"

"I see. They are under the Vichy government. It must be Marseille."

"I only read the synopsis, Mr. President, and I read it fast. But they're not in Marseille. They're across the ocean. The . . . the, oh yeah: the Mediterranean! In Morocco. All in a café. Rick's, it's called. Good thing, too. We only have to build one set. And the café is in—what the hell is the name of that city? Biggest berg in the country. Starts with a C. Rhymes with kasha. Wait! Casablanca!"

Here the president's face does what is, in my professional opinion, a first-rate spit take. Except without any spit. The cigarette, still on fire, falls out of his mouth.

"*Casablanca?* Is that what you said?"

"Also rhymes with Sanka."

"Let's stop playing games, Warner. You knew about Operation Z. Now you know about Casablanca. About our plans for Gymnast."

"A gem heist, sir? We did that pict—"

"Don't play dumb. It's Churchill's nonsensical idea. That we land troops in Casablanca. It's top secret. There are thousands of lives at stake. I could turn you over to Hoover. I could have you locked up, old boy, for the duration."

I don't like the turn this conversation is taking. It occurs to me I better get the hell out of there and I'm about to tell him so, the words are on my lips, *Mr. President, you'll have to excuse me, but I've got to put a bet on a horse,* when a high voice—it's Mrs. Roosevelt's—cries out from across the room:

"Friends! Only one moment left of this terrible old year. Let's bid it farewell."

Everybody but me and FDR starts running over to where she's standing by the window. They all go *Hear! Hear!* and raise up their bubbling glasses. That Beaver with the butt-in-the air says, "But it *wasn't* a terrible year. Not on our side of the pond. Why? Because it brought a powerful nation to our side. With her we cannot help but achieve victory. So let us drink first to our great ally: the United States of America."

Once again everybody yells, *Hear! Hear!*, which when you think about it is a funny thing to say.

"But it *was* a terrible year."

Who shouted that? Goodness, it was the fellow with his name on the water tower. And why? I don't know why. A hand, that's what it felt like, came out of the sky and grabbed me by the throat and squeezed out the words. And it's still got me, it's squeezing even more until the tears are being pushed out of my eyes and what I'm thinking is: you bet it was a terrible year, all those Japs in Zeros and the bombs going off and our sailors with the water coming up over their heads—not to mention we took a real bath with *Singapore Woman*, YOU'VE NEVER THRILLED TO SUCH—oh, fuck it. Fire. Smoke. Drowning. The *Oklahoma*. The *Arizona*. A surprise attack. And then the hand, it gives another squeeze and out of my mouth pops the following sentence:

"*And you knew.*"

"Knew what, old bean?"

I lean over the wheelchair; now the words are coming out like spritz from a soda machine: "Operation Z. You knew! You knew it was Sunday! And you let it happen. Maybe you wanted it to happen. Those yellow bastards attack and the whole country wants to pay them back—in spades. We were ready to make horsemeat out of Hirohito. And that Tojo! I wanted personally to kick his ass down the stairs. So there'd be a little nip in the air, ha, ha, ha! But you want to attack Germany instead. Germany first! I see it now! I see it all!"Across the room the crowd is waving and making toasts. *To the president! To the president!* But the president just lowers his head and says:

"Even if I knew, and I don't say I did—I mean, who could have imagined it would be so savage? Those poor boys."

All of a sudden the hand lets go. I'm on my own. No one is forcing me. I take a breath. I go for broke.

"Listen to me, pal. You can't invade France. Churchill is right. So is the girl. You're going to invade Africa. The French part. Like, you know, Morocco. So we can make our picture. Forget *Letters of Transit*. That stinks. Whoever thought of that? I should fire the nogoodnik. I've got it! I've got it! Son of a bitch, I've got it: *Seas of Sand!*"

FDR: "Old boy, I haven't the slightest idea of what you are talking about."

"Now *you* are the one playing dumb. You said you would hand me over to Hoover. Maybe I'm the one to hand you over. How'd you like that? We could share our bread and water together."

The president doesn't answer. He just sits there, with his head hanging down.

Next comes a lot of laughing and even shouting—and for one crazy moment I think they heard what I was saying and maybe I should take a bow. But in the nick of time I see the reason. *The Man Who Came to Dinner*. It's finally ending. Woolley is outside the house, he's saying so long, and, uh-oh, the phone is ringing. It's long-distance. Woolley turns. It's for him. It's Mrs. Roosevelt.

What? Eleanor?

There he goes! Head over heels! Right on his ass! Ha! Ha! Ha! Great piece of business. I thought of it myself.

Ha! Ha! Ha! What consternation! The lady of the house, that's Billie Burke, faints dead away. And her husband is banging his head on the mantelpiece. Out come the penguins. The penguins! It's a touch of genius. WARNER BROS.' HAPPIEST HIT!

Hello? Hello? Hello?

Oh, dear! Something must have happened to Sherry. Operator! Operator!

Music up. Iris down. THE SCREEN'S BIGGEST HOWL.

But the howling doesn't stop. It's getting even louder. Listen! They're actually cheering. This may be our biggest hit ever! And it's not just in this room. It's coming from outside, where a thousand people are in the street. *Did they show the picture out there? Like a drive-in?* But now I hear cars sounding their horns and bells starting to ring and then I remember, oh, yeah: it's the New Year. It's 1942.

Roosevelt still hasn't moved. I lean down to him. "Listen. Africa. Not until Thanksgiving. Do we have a deal?"

He doesn't answer. Instead he reaches for the little table behind him and the next thing you know he's got a drink in his hand. He raises it up toward the ceiling and just before he gives his toast he gives me, and there is no mistake about it, a little nod.

"With God's help, victory!"

Now there's a tremendous commotion. A real brew-ha-ha! The president throws down his glass so hard it breaks into pieces. I am shouting like the little Philip Morris man, *Victory! Victory!* and the answering cry is loud enough, I think, to hear in L.A. and maybe even London and all over the world; and the bells are ringing, and the crowds are yelling, and now Harpo shows up again and he's squeezing his horn, *honk, honk, honk!* and giving everybody a gookie; and across the room KK, our Karelena Kauffman, or Cheryl Charmaigne, or Kaiser—it doesn't matter what the hell we call her as long as she's under contract—she gives me the kind of big fat smile that lets me know everything is going to be fine down Mexico way.

11 〉 GOOD PICTURE-MAKING, TAKE ONE *Black and Blue*

KK: June 1942, Los Angeles

In Hollywood I would be called a film brat. In German I do not believe there is such a word: *Wurstbrat*, Jack called me when I would not give him what he wanted during the premiere of *The Male Animal*. In the dark. People all around us. When I was two years old, Rin-Tin-Tin used to lick my face. He was a movie star, just like a man or a woman, and Joe-Joe was in charge of taking him from one German city to another so he could do his tricks. I do not remember the animal, not truly; but I remember the film, *Where the North Begins*. I think my father took me then for the first time to a movie theater. On his lap. The beam of light in the air. This was my introduction to Filmgeshäft.

We also saw the feature, over and over, on our home projector. The dog—raised in the wild by wolves—must choose between his pack and his new human friend. He chooses, the fool, the human. At the end I would always cry, not from sadness but from happiness. Because not only does the human hero get his sweetheart, but the true star, Rin-Tin-Tin, the Wolf-Dog, gets his own family of little pups. Careful, fool: you might cry like that dewy-eyed doll of a girl.

Alex was there from the earliest days. He always had his camera with the three lenses with him. Home movies. In these I was the main attraction. Running toward him, running away. Joe-Joe tossing his daughter into the air. Hannelore tying ribbons on both my—what is the word in English? I have lapses. *Haarzöpfe* in the mother tongue. In all these eight-millimeter clips not a word was spoken. Nor, in *Where the North Begins*, did the Wolf-Dog growl or whine or bark. A mistake, in my opinion, to introduce sound into film. Think: a hand points a gun. Pigeons fly from a roof. It is we who must work in our minds to hear the shot. And now? That stupid *bang!* Our minds drift off to sleep.

Pigtails!

Joe-Joe would not agree. He predicted the success of *The Jazz Singer* in Germany. Even if the hero was a Jew. Even if he sang as a black-faced Neger. Jack listened to him—and made him the manager of the Berlin office. The Sturmabteilung also listened. That is when they beat him. They let loose their dogs. At night. In front of our flat. They were silent, too, those Hunde. They went about their business with their teeth. The people on the street walked by. Or stayed to watch. They knew a Jew was on the ground.

"Nein, nein!" I cried. I was six years old. "Rin-Tin-Tin will come! Wolf-shund! Wolfshund! Schnell!"

But the Wolf-Dog did not come.

I might as well have been in silent films myself. I don't mean the home movies in which Alex urged me to make funny faces; I mean the motion pictures he made for German theaters, thirty-five millimeters, with sound, in which I did not say a word. *Zu Neuen Ufer*: a squinting girl in braids. *Andere Welt*: black hair under a cooly's hat, smiling with my bad teeth— one over the other to this day. *Die Umwege der Schönen Karl*: the bathing suit, in two pieces. The cold, curling waves. The Reichminister noticed the girl of sixteen. Then he noticed the girl with the smear of lipstick. And the girl with the cigarette in her hand. But the tongue of that girl was tied.

I am not allowed to tell that to the Sahib: my first words, like a child saying *Mama* or *Papa*. Wearing the veil of the maharaja's servant. And when the veil was pulled aside, when I felt the sun, like a giant klieg light, on my skin, when I saw the other actors, when I saw the crew—all of them looking at me—I knew what I would become. Herr Goebbels, in his screening room, knew it, too.

Here is a question to which I do not know the answer: Was I infatuated with Dick Powell, *I'm calling you-oo-oo-oo*, because he reminded me of Onkel Alex; or did I fall in love with Alex because he, with the wave in his hair, the spitzer haaransatz, the dimpled cheeks, resembled the actor fifteen meters high on the screen? If I dwell on it, I think his constant gaze, through the triple lenses of his camera, the gold flecks floating in the iris of his eyes, left a kind of varnish on me, so that in some fashion I was in love with an image of myself. Stardom.

I froze beneath his touch on Argyle Avenue. A stone statue of myself. He left today. Before dawn. On his way to Moscow to fight against my country in this war. But he fought for me on Sound Stage 1 yesterday. He knocked Jack to the ground. He might have broken his back. Oh, he was as fierce as Rin-Tin-Tin when he sank his fangs into the movie villain. And all for this absurd, pathetic part: Annina. A Bulgarian: *Monsieur Rick, what kind of man is Captain Renault?*

An example of the chaos of Hollywood. The madness of their picture-making. Here, with the great lights burning, giving off smoke and fumes; the heads of the microphones twitching; the tape measures reaching to one's nose—and wherever one looks, the faces of excitable Jews. Every word of it, just as I knew it would be, is in this morning's newspaper.

The Terrible Turk: June 1942, Burbank

"Okay, Chief, if you insist. Here goes." I start reading the column out loud:

HEDDA HOPPER'S HOLLYWOOD

Mary Martin, of all people, went temperamental—refused to kiss Dick Powell in the new Panama and Frank *Happy Go Lucky* because he had a cold, for which I don't blame her. But then she held up things another hour because she didn't like the way things were written.

Madeleine Lebeau's got a part in Warners' *Seas of Sand*, but she's pouting because her pal Michelle Morgan doesn't—or maybe it's because she's feuding with spouse Marcel Dalio, who's got a bit part himself. These days Madeline is sitting at the directors' table while her hubby has been seen gulping down the ham sandwiches that Dick Mosk, the old Lithuanian waiter, piles up in front of him at Pinky's. Ham? That sounds more like just-hired costar Paul Henreid. And I'd bet that Marcel, who was born with the moniker Israel Moses Blauschild and who hightailed it out of France a skip and a jump ahead of the invading Germans, was eating chicken!

The most popular dog in pictures hereafter will probably be a little cocker named Whiskey. A Great Dane was scheduled for scenes in *Girl Trouble*, but he got sulky, so Harold

Schuster sent for the cocker, whose nickname now is One-Take Whiskey.

But I don't want to talk about dogs. I've got more important things on my mind. Did you notice that all three of those people at work on *Seas of Sand* were not born in our U. S. of A? Two came from France and one from that scrambled egg of a land, Austria-Hungary. Just take a look at the rest of the cast that Warners has thrown together. Sidney Greenstreet and Claude Rains are Brits who decided not to go home and face the music the Nazi band is playing. There are others from all over the globe: Russians and Spaniards and Italians; a Dane—but he's not barking!; a Greek and a Scotchman and Cuddles Sakal from Budapest; a Norwegian, and a fellow from the wrong side of the Rio Grande, not to mention—oh, I've gone through this list with a fine-tooth comb!—a Syrian and a Swede (on loan from David Selznick) and an almond-eyed gal from China. Whew! I almost ran out of breath!

And of course there are more Germans than you can shake a stick at: Conrad Veidt; Curt Bois; Peter Lorre (why, hello there, Mr. Moto, or should I say Mr. Laszlo Loewenstein?); Louis Arco, who, I'm told, has only one line ("Waiting, waiting, waiting . . . I'll never get out of here . . . I'll die in Casablanca") and who once answered to the name Lutz Altschul; Ilka Gruning; the very pretty Trudy Berliner and the dashing Helmut Dantine, seen squiring actress Gwen Anderson at Ciro's and the Players; and that tongue twister, Hans Heinrich von Twardowski; and—well, I don't know how many more, but I do know who's shaking that stick at them and it's got a pretty sharp point at one end.

It's all well and good for Jack and Harry Warner to gather the oppressed of the earth and all those "huddled masses yearning to be free," but don't you think there's a limit before we turn—speaking of canines—into a mongrel nation? My goodness: a Scot and a Norwegian and who knows what all in the middle of the desert. What's next? Cuddles on a camel? Let's look at the other side of the coin: of all those playing major parts in this picture, only two were born in this country—and one of them is a singing Negro! Here's the question of the day: In times like these, when we are under attack and every patriot has his blood up, can't the folks in Burbank find more Americans to fill those roles?

If Paramount is intending to have Zobrina do a sensational ballet in *Star-Spangled Rhythm*, why don't they let her repeat the one she did with the elephants on opening night of the circus in Madison Square Garden?

Back to *Seas of Sand*, which I can't help chewing at the way Whiskey does a bone. A German I did not name is the highly touted Karelena Kaiser, briefly Cheryl Charmaigne, who came to America just days before the attack on Pearl Harbor, and under highly suspicious circumstances. The reason I didn't add her to my list is she's not going to be in the picture at all. Forlorn Fraulein!

First Jack Warner dangled the lead role of Ilsa before her, only to have it snatched away by Ingrid Bergman, who never has understood why people call her a "Cinderella Girl," since she never even heard of a glass slipper. Then she was in line for the smaller part of a newlywed refugee so eager to get out of Casablanca that she considers giving herself to the lecherous Captain Renault, played by one of my favorites, Claude Rains— who, not unlike that Vichy officer, is now on wife number four. Well, my pal Joe Breen—and he should be yours, too, if you worry about standards in our industry—wasn't going to stand for that. Imagine: a girl for sale in an American picture! So now Annina—that's the name of the desperate lass—is saved by Humphrey Bogart telling her to place her chips on twenty-one, which was the winning number played by the wife of one of the Epstein boys, who are in charge of the script. She hit it big and so does Annina. But poor Karelena didn't win a penny—or maybe it's a sou in French Morocco. That's because she just got bounced from that part, too. A little birdy told me that yesterday a jealous Ann Page, that's Mrs. Jack Warner, descended on the set of the gambling saloon with—

"*A little birdy! A little birdy!* Goddammit, Abdul! You better find out—Ouch! Ouch! Are you trying to kill me? That hurts!"

That was the Chief, and he was talking to me, the Terrible Turk. Here's what was going on. The Chief was laid out on the table, just like he was almost every day, except this was the first thing in the morning instead of, as usual, five o'clock in the afternoon. It was so early, as a matter of fact, that he had not read the papers, which was a job he gave to me. It wasn't easy. I had to keep both hands at work on his body and at the same time keep my eye on the columns—first Parsons in the *Examiner* and then Hedda in the *Times*. I thought I knew every muscle of the Chief's anatomy by heart, but he was especially sore that morning, in the physical and the mental meaning of the word.

"Sorry, Chief. I guess I'm all thumbs."

"You'll be thumbing a ride out of here if you aren't more careful."

"Ha! Ha! That's a good one!"

"You think I'm kidding? The butcher at Ralph's could do a better job than you."

"You want me to stop reading? Maybe that's—"

"No, no. Where the hell were you?"

"Let's see . . .'The most popular dog in pictures hereafter will—'"

"Goddammit! You read that already. *The birdy! The birdy!* And Ann!"

I picked up where I left off.

> . . . a jealous Ann Page, that's Mrs. Jack Warner, descended on the set of the gambling saloon with her latest horoscope in hand. Ann, thin as a splinter and with a cinnamon blouse to match her tan, must be one of those jealous Scorpios—

"*Scorpios!* Who knows what month she was born? I buy her a present every first just in case. Hell, I don't know the *year* she was born. She hides her passport and—Ouch!"

"Sorry, Chief. I guess I got, for hands, ha-ha, two left feet."

"Leave the jokes to me. It's not you that's killing me. It's that blouse. It cost me two hundred clams. Well, what are you waiting for? Keep reading."

"You sure you want me to? I could switch to the sports pages. There was a terrific fight at the arena last night—"

"Do what I tell you. Stick to the fight on the lot."

... must be one of those jealous Scorpios, because she walked right up to the young German actress and the green monster was in her eyes. We'll have to give Blanca Holmes, Ann's favorite astrologist, a call to find out what was in that horoscope, but I'd bet dollars to donuts it had less to do with the moon and the stars than a certain bungalow up in the Hollywood Hills. Did that birdy whisper Briarcliff Road?

"Jesus fucking Christ! Are you making this up? Give me that goddamn paper."

I wasn't making it up, as the Chief found out. He half sat, snatched the *Times* from where I had spread it out on the table, and began to read out loud:

Irene Dunne says no more screwball comedies for her.

"What the fuck? *Irene Dunne!* Wait a second. Wait—"

... whisper Briarcliff Road—

"Christ!"

Whatever the reason, Ann ordered Fraulein Kaiser off the set. *You aren't playing this part,* she told her, and right on cue who should walk into the saloon but Joy Page, Ann's daughter by ex Don Alvarado, that dark-hued star of *La Cucaracha.* Joy is just seventeen and cute as a new red scooter—

"She's got a red Plymouth *roadster.* Six thousand fucking bucks! Where was I? Oh, yeah":

She was dressed in Annina's costume—dark wool jacket over a white sweater. Not only that, she started to spout her lines: *Monsieur Rick, can I speak to you for just one minute, please?* Joy is one girl scout who is prepared! But Cheryl, I mean Karelena, knew her lines, too. And what she said is not printable in this family newspaper and anyway was mostly in German: it amounted to *I was promised this part and I am not going anywhere.* Gott im Himmel!

Now the fur really started to fly. Ann and her daughter went after their rival, who defended herself like the British at Dunkirk, though maybe that's a bad example, and everybody on the set came running up, with poor S. K. Sakal caught in the middle, tummy and all; no one could do a thing until my old friend Abdul Maljan raced through the sound stage door, Jack Warner puffing behind him, and with the powerful hands of a professional fighter separated the squabbling women. Then all three of the combatants descended on poor Jack, who—

"Who should have stayed in Youngstown!"

With a groan the Chief turned onto his stomach. I went back to work, pressing and kneading as carefully as I could. In about ten seconds he started to snore. I guess he didn't need to read the rest of Hedda's column since he already saw everything else that happened with his own eyes.

It's true, just the way the *Times* printed it: I did my best to keep those girls apart, but I couldn't stop them from screeching like *balicideas*—you say here I think banshees. Maybe fishwives.

First went Ann: "Get out of here. Off the set. Off the lot. Out of our lives."

"But, darling—" That was the Chief.

Then Miss Kaiser: "I am not going. Where do I go? You promised me Ilsa. You can't take this role from me, too."

"We'll get you another part. A bigger one. In a better picture."

"The hell you will," said Ann. "Do you think I was born yesterday? I know what's going on."

"But, sweetheart. Nothing's go—"

"*What* part?" Miss Kaiser demanded. "*What* picture?"

The Chief: "Huh? What picture? How should I know? Anything but this piece of shit."

"What about—?"

"Keep your trap shut, Abdul. Now *you're* telling me my business? I got it! *The Gorilla*! No, no, that was with the Ritz Brothers."

"Excuse me, J.L.," that was Ernie Glickman, one of the production assistants. "Do you mean *The Gorilla Man*? They're just starting production."

"Yeah! Yeah! *The Gorilla Man*. MAN ALIVE, JUST PICTURE THIS ENTERTAINMENT! Or was that for *Desperate Journey*?"

Miss Kaiser put her foot down: "I will not be in a film about a gorilla! I am right for this part. She is European? I am European. She is a refugee? I am a refugee." Then she turned with scorn toward the stepdaughter of the Chief. "Who is this girl? An American teen. Does she do the jitterbug dance? Has she acted before? Ha! I thought she had not."

Now Joy burst into tears. "Mama! You promised! You told me to learn all the lines."

"It's not about a gorilla," said Glickman. "Actually, it's about Nazi spies."

"Aha!" cried Ann, pointing a finger at Miss Kaiser. "Typecasting!"

"Papa! Let me do it. You never say no."

We all gasped as Miss Page dropped to the feet of the Chief. She actually threw her arms around his knees.

"No crying, dammit! You know I can't stand tears. When Momma chopped onions I—"

"Can't you ever stop joking?" Ann demanded. "This is serious. Do you want her? Or do you want me?"

"Darling! How can you ask? Light of my life!"

"One moment. One moment, please."

The man who spoke was Alan Castle, who had a German name, Alex something, before that. He had wavy hair and was wearing the white suit and the white Panama-type hat of the character he was supposed to play in the picture. Out of some leftover habit, he took the hat off his head when he came up to the Chief. What he said next was, "You cannot take this part from Miss Kaiser."

"And who the hell are you? You look like the milkman."

Mike Curtiz spoke up for the first time. "It's Mr. Cattle, J.L. You signed him to play Laszlo."

"Laszlo?"

"Victor Laszlo," said Glickman. "Leader of the antifascists. He looked great in the rushes."

"So did Moses. And what were *his* grosses? Okay, you: Where do you get off telling me what to do?"

"Karelena and I are old colleagues."

"So what?"

Castle, the actor, was standing chest to chest with the Chief. He said, "This Victor Laszlo: the man is brave, he fights for freedom, he wishes to defeat the Germans. Excellent. But I only accepted because I was told that Fräulein Kaiser was to play the role of his wife. Then, suddenly, you took that from her. I do not know why."

"I'll tell you why," said Ann. "He got what he wanted from her."

The Fritzie ignored her. "But you will not take this role from her also."

"I won't, eh? Not only is she fired. You're fired, too."

"No, no, J.L.," said Curtiz. "We need him. We have no one else to conduct *The Mayonnaise.*"

Everybody laughed out loud except for the director and the Chief, who turned his head in time to see Hal Wallis coming up at a trot.

"What's going on? Why is everybody standing around?"

"Good afternoon, Hal."

"Hello, Ann. What are you doing on the set?"

"I've brought Joy. Jack has decided she's to play Annina."

"*Jack* decided? Jack doesn't make these decisions."

"Whose name is on the water tower? A *W.* A *A.* And, and—and so forth. I'm putting Joy into the picture and that's that."

"Fine," said Wallis. "Then get the water tower to produce it."

"*Another* wise guy!"

Now Ann, thin and tan, like Hedda said, spoke again. "Be fair, Hal. You haven't seen Joy act. She's got her lines and rehearsed them with me." She waved what I guess was her horoscope in the air. "And I happen to know she will be a success."

"Then why this delay? We're already behind schedule."

Next came the Chief: "Because of this buttinsky—what's his name? I fired the son of a bitch."

"Are you out of your mind? That's Alexander Engelsing."

"The dental king? I'll knock his teeth out for him."

"Listen, Jack. You can't fire him. We don't have anyone else."

"There's always someone else."

"Sure, if you want to shut us down for six weeks. Or maybe two months."

"We can't do that! What about the landings? We've got to release the picture in the fall."

"What landings? What are you talking about?"

"In North Africa. In Casablanca. Oooops."

Engelsing or whatever his name was took a surprised step back. "What did you say? Are you talking about a second front? In Africa? Does Comrade Stalin know about this?"

"Comrade who?"

"This is shocking news. A second front. Why do—"

"Look, forget it. Never mind. You're hired again."

"Hired again? Only if Karelena has her part back."

"*What!*" That was Ann.

"*Papa!*" That was her daughter.

"All right. All right. I just thought of something. You know the movie business: A Jew can't play a Jew in a picture. The Kauffman kid is out. That's final. I knew her father."

"Then Joy is out, too," said Wallis. "Because Ann—"

"Why, you creep! I've been blessed by the pope!"

"Hold on. Hold on. I've got an idea. That guy, what's his name? Who lit two cigarettes in his mouth. The one in the *Voyager* dailies."

"You mean Paul Henreid?"

"Yeah, Hemorrhoid. He's European, right? Continental type. Perfecto! Why didn't I think of him before?"

"You did," said Wallis. "He wants twenty-five thousand and top billing."

Everyone was silent. You could count all the way to ten. Finally the Chief turned to the German:

"You're rehired."

"Not without Karelena."

Ann: "Ja-a-a-a-ck..."

"P-a-a-a-a-pa..."

"Make up your mind, J.L. We've already lost half the afternoon."

I looked at the Chief. His face was changing colors, like a lizard does when it moves from one place to another.

"Sign Henreid for the part. And get Sonny over here. I want this goddamn Nazi thrown out of here."

Wallis: "For heaven's sake, J.L. He's an *anti*-Nazi."

"I don't care what kind of Nazi he is, I want him and his whore off the lot."

At those words, the German took three steps toward the Chief, with his hands balled into fists. But he did not use them to strike; instead, he saluted.

"You have a uniform. You are a colonel—"

"*Lieutenant* colonel, dammit."

"—of the American Army Air Force. You are my ally in the great patriotic struggle. For that reason, I salute you. I salute you three times."

That is what he did.

"Well," said the Chief, "that's more like—"

"But you have insulted this woman. So now you must pay."

Without another word, Engelsing lowered his head and like a *koc*, a ram in the Anatolian mountains, he used it to butt the vice president for production square in the chest. The Chief flew backward like Gorgeous George after a flying tackle. He lay rolled up and twitching on the ground.

Everybody was yelling. The women were screaming. People started to run—some toward the Chief, others out of the sound-stage doors. I leaped forward and took hold of the Kraut, but to my surprise he knocked my arms away and pushed me aside. He was, if I can mention it, twenty years younger. Before I could recover, this Engelsing dropped with both bony knees onto the Chief, whose back made a loud cracking noise. Then he grasped his foe by his colonel's collar and pulled him to his feet. Next, to the astonishment of those who were still present, he threw his arms around him and kissed him three times: first on one cheek, then the other, then back to the first. His own cheeks, we saw, were wet with tears.

"Danke!" he cried. "All antifascist fighters thank you! Jack Warner! Jack L. Warner: you have given me back my life and my soul! All torment is over! Now I know my fate: I return to the struggle. Good-bye, America! Good-bye, this Hollywood life! I shall go to the struggling Russian people! To those starving in Leningrad. To those who are dying on the steppes. To those who are fighting to defend the sacred soil of the revolution. Danke! Dankeschön! I have once again my task before me! I have once again my honor. Now all is clear."

The actor seemed to be having a vision. He threw his arms skyward, as if to the gods. But the minute he did so, my boss, the executive producer at Warner Bros., fell in a heap to the ground.

He lay there, whimpering a little, as Sonny and three of his security cops led Engelsing away. But now, I mean *right* now, on the massage table, he wasn't making a sound: not snoring, not moving, still as a stone. For a terrible moment I thought his heart had stopped. Mine stopped, too. Somewhere, a mile overhead, an airplane was flying. LOCKHEED, THATAWAY! Closer by, a crow, I think, went caw-haw, as if enjoying some private joke. Then, while I was holding my breath, I heard these beautiful words:

"Murderer! Traitor! You're killing me!"

At once Abdul, The Terrible Turk, was filled with joy.

"Sorry, Chief. I'm trying to stay away from the bruises."

Impossible task: his whole torso, where it wasn't black, was blue.

"Stop! For Christ's sake, stop! Just finish the column. What does the bitch say at the end?"

I picked up the *Times* again and spread it out.

> Carmen Miranda promised me she'd sing "Chattanooga Choo-Choo" in Portuguese. Her tan is the envy of everyone and—

"Enough with the tans! Enough with the choo-choos! What does she say after that Nazi knocked me out cold?"

"Oh, nothing, Chief. It's not worth—"

"*Pardon me, boy!* Just read the damned thing."

"Okay. You're the boss."

> The most important thing about all that hullabaloo on the *Seas of Sand* set yesterday wasn't that Paul Henreid was brought into the cast in a leading role or even the physical fight that brought battling Jack Warner to his knees. It was something Jack said about an invasion of Casablanca. Was he just trying to stir up interest in this run-of-the-mill drama, which is set in Morocco? Or does he know something that the rest of the nation does not? In that case my old friend Mr. Hoover might like to ask this question: *Is this picture being timed to come out when there is a secret invasion—or is the secret invasion being timed to come out with the release of the picture?*
>
> I know all this sounds preposterous—can the tail of our little town wag the dog of our capital city?—but let's not forget that

funny business about how Jack Warner's new favorite, recently Cheryl Charmaigne, got into this country just hours before Pearl Harbor and how happy *that man* in the White House was when Germany declared war on the U. S. of A. There's something dodgy, as our cousins overseas would say, about this business, but you can be sure that the gal with the hats and Mr. Hoover will get to the bottom of it. One thing seems pretty obvious to me: that a certain type of person has too much influence in this White House. Hollywood was built by these folk and believe me some of them, like dear Louis B. Mayer, are among my best friends. But when a studio boss—

The Chief let out a pitiful moan. "Go back to Miranda."

... *tan is the envy of everyone and* she won't tell me what kind of oil she brought back with her from South America.

"That's all, Chief. There isn't any more. Released by the Chicago Tribune-New York News syndicate. Period."

He didn't say a word. Everything was quiet in the room. "Caw-haw," went that crow once again, like he thought the whole thing was funny.

"Is that her birdy?" mumbled the Chief. "Who do you think it is, Abdul? Is it you?"

What a terrible thing for Mr. Warner to say. For a moment I stood, unable to speak, while my chest filled with sorrow. At last, words came to me.

"You know, Chief. *Seas of Sand* isn't such a terrific title."

"Yeah. I know. That fucking Zanuck. People are going to mix it up with *Blood and Sand*. What a lot of bull!"

"I was thinking—"

"You aren't paid for thinking."

"What about *Casablanca*? Just the one word. The name of the city. All by itself."

"Naw. They already made *Algiers*. Forget it."

"If you say so, Chief."

Another moment went by. The crow had flown off. There wasn't a sound anywhere.

"Say," said the Chief, "I just got an idea."

"What's that?"

"I think it's fantastic. I think it's colossal. But tell me what you think."

"Sure."

"What if we call the picture *Casablanca*? Magnificent, right? Just the one word! It says everything! Right? Isn't that a brilliant idea?"

"Chief," I said. "Only you could have come up with that!"

12 } KROKODIL

Jack L. Warner: August 1942, Moscow

Do we have a deal? And FDR gives me the old nod. Six months later the phone rings right on the Stage 1 set and he's telling me that he's going to make me an ambassador to the Soviet Union, the way he did Harpo with his harp; but I know and he knows that the real reason is I'm supposed to pull the same kind of stunt on this guy Stalin that I did with him: go fight in Africa instead of France and not so toot sweet, either. *It will be up to you, old boy. I'll hold my end up. You've got to make Uncle Joe do his part.*

The next thing I know I'm flying over the ocean—not just one ocean, but after Cairo, where I didn't even get to see a belly dancer, another one; and then over half of Europe, when every minute we could have been shot down by a Mess-of-Shits. Ever try to sleep on a B-24? Churchill did, pj's and all. Not me. The cold. The noise. All four engines are still ringing in my ears. Even worse: when I tried to canoodle with KK on top of the bomb bay doors, it was no dice. Still hot under the challah about not getting those parts in the Casablanca picture.

Where is she, anyway? There, at the far end of the table, gazing away at that smart Alex, Castle we called him, who I kicked off the lot a couple of months ago. He's gazing, too, not at her but at some little freckle-faced redhead. What's he doing here? He said he was going to fight for the starving people of Leningrad. But we're in Moscow, right? Inside the Kremlin, right? Jesus, my head is spinning. It's because of all these goddamned toasts! I'd give half my Warners stock for a potted palm.

> *To our great leader, Stalin! Do Dna! Tost!*
> *To Winston Churchill! Do Dna! Tost! Tost! Tost!*
> *The gallant Red Army! The Red Air Force!*
> *Comrade Zhukov! Savior of Moscow! Do Dna!*

Now the Big Shot is getting out of his chair. He's going over to where Blondie is sitting. "We drink to your wife; then I will kiss her."

"Hey," I declare, "that's no wife, that's my lay—"

Uncle Joe gets the gag. All he does is kiss her on the cheek. *Do Dna!*

Finally—and not a moment too soon—everybody else is getting up, too, the Russians and Churchill and Overall Hairyman and all the generals and guests. Oh, boy, I'm thinking, at last we can grab forty winks. With an extra wink, if you know what I mean, for my Fräulein. Ever since we left Burbank she's been playing hard to get, which means I've been getting hard. Is it my fault I have to have a woman every eight hours—okay, okay, twelve hours in an emergency? I mean my balls feel like they're in a vise. Didn't I tell Loshak how to make these fucking pants? *On the left! Not on the right! They go on the left!*

Anyway, up we get from the table, and I'm half asleep on my feet; but we don't go to bed; we go down a hallway, all the windows painted over, a guard at every door, and into a movie theater, some kind of screening room, and we have to sit there and watch a picture, with the catchy title *The German Rout Before Moscow*. First the Heinies run their tanks left to right over a lot of people and smash their way up to the last station of the Metro; then everybody starts to shout, "Let's defend Moscow, Comrades!" and we see these close-ups of women with shovels and girls in factories and then a long shot of warriors in white pajamas, the *Sibiriskii soldats* someone explains, running like hell right to left. Next, nothing but corpses, dead Germans, buried in snow, arms frozen in the air, their bellies ripped and—

"Stop!" That's the Big Cheese, way down in the front row. "Turn off the machine. We have seen enough death for tonight."

So the lights come on and the picture stops. Naturally, I get up and start to look around for KK. But the People's Commissar goes, "Aha! Our friend from California. Excellent! You have brought us something to make us laugh. Laughter is what we need."

"Not so fast," I answer him. "We shot this picture in Death Valley."

The Bagel Ring, or Engelsing, or whatever his name is, gives a big guffaw, even though it's not all that funny, and then everybody else joins in.

That's when the Big Man on Campus makes a movement with his hand and instantly the whole crowd shuts up, as if their throats had been cut. "Now we enjoy ourselves with this Amerikanskiy film."

So the lights go down again and up comes *The Bride Came C.O.D.*
THE PICTURE THAT WILL HAVE YOU HOWLING FOR
MONTHS! It's this dumb comedy about two guys chasing one dame,
with an even dumber running gag where Cagney keeps pulling cactus
quills out of Davis's ass. Listen: everybody's snoring. I don't blame them.
Instant morphine.

What were those Epsteins thinking? I pay them top of the scale and
they stroll in for work an hour after lunch and write dreck like this. They
can't get away with those shenanigans with an Army Air Force officer! I
hauled them into the office and threw those pages on the carpet and told
them this was the worst crap I'd ever read in my life. So Phil, or maybe it
was Julie, looks up and says, "But Jack, how could that be? We wrote it at
nine." Wise guys. Think they're smarter than me. *Me!* Hell, I can make
money with a *good* picture!

"Ouch!" goes Davis.

"Ho! Ho! Ho!" goes Uncle Joe. "Kaktus!"

"Ha! Ha! Ha!" The whole audience wakes up and starts laughing, too.

Now, right in the middle of the picture, the Top Dog stands and makes
that motion with his hand again. Bingo! All the laughter stops—and so does
the film, as if the celluloid had been sliced in two.

"Grandiozno!" says the People's Commissar.

"Grandiozno! Grandiozno!" goes the crowd.

"Hey, is there an echo in here?"

I see that the Numero Uno is looking up at me. "Tovarich Warner,"
he starts to say.

"What are you talking about?" I answer, while getting to my feet. "I'm
not Tovarich. You should see the taxes in Beverly Hills."

"I mean you, Jacob Benjaminovich."

"Uh-oh."

"Minister Molotov has awakened from his map. What a man he is. He
says, 'I will nap for thirteen minutes,' and in thirteen minutes he wakes
up. Vyacheslav Mikhailovich—"

Up stands this guy with a moustache, glasses on his nose, and a glum
expression. He starts to speak.

"For this excellent example of moving-picture art, we declare Comrade
Warner a Hero of the Soviet Union."

"Huh? *This* example? You've got to be kidding. You must mean *Law of the Tropics.* LOVE'S TRAGIC LESSON. We were going to use Miriam Hopkins, but—"

The Unsurpassed Guide swipes that hand at me. My jaws clamp shut.

"Not at all, Comrade. You are too modest. The girl is wealthy. Her father, the industrialist, will pay the pilot ten dollars for each pound she weighs. I congratulate you on this penetrating analysis of inevitable class conflict. A hundred and ten pounds equals one thousand one hundred dollars. Thus we see how in the capitalist system human flesh becomes the basis for commercial transactions and how human beings themselves are reduced to a commodity to be traded like any other on the shelves. C.O.D. Bravo! Bravo, Hero Jack L. Warner!"

"Well," I say, "you know our motto: Combining Good Picture-Making with Good Citizenship." *And great pickled herring.*

The applause gets louder and louder, and now a girl, the same little redhead I saw before, stands up from her chair, holding a bunch of flowers.

"Ah," says Uncle Joe. "Here is my Little Housekeeper. Setanka, did you enjoy this excellent kino?"

"Oh, yes, Papochka," says the teenager. "I like all Hollywood kino. All!" *Papochka?* This is no housekeeper. This—

But already she's skipping up the aisle and holding out the lilies—at least that's what they look like, all white with those stems.

"Who died? Don't translate that."

The girl is smiling up at me. "I am pretty enough to be movie star?"

I take a look. Red hair and freckles. Milky blouse with something inside. Grass-colored eyes. Yeah, pretty. But not pretty enough.

"You bet!"

With that she goes up on tiptoe and says, "Oh, I am adoring you so much I must to give you this potselui." Then she grabs my lapels and plants a big one that does not completely miss my lips. Hmmm, maybe she *is* pretty enough.

The Papochka interrupts. "Comrade Litvinov has just arrived from Washington. Has he strength enough to stand?"

I look down to where this plump guy in a rumpled jacket is struggling to his feet. How do these Russkies keep those little glasses on their noses? Of course this nose is unmistakable—it belongs, like that thick lower lip, to a Jew. And not just any Jew. I remember him from last New Year's Eve at the White House. Always griping about a second front.

"Would you do the honors, Maxim Maximovich?"

So up the aisle comes the ambassador, limping a little. "Comrade Jacob Benjaminovich Warner," he begins.

"You oughta know," I reply, but mostly under my breath.

"On behalf of the Supreme Soviet of the USSR, for your Marxist/ Leninist photoplay, *The Bride Came C.O.D.*, I declare you—"

"So you really *did* like it, huh? The critics panned it, but they can go fuck themselves. DID WE SAY GLORIOUS? WE MEANT UP-ROARIOUS. The box office was terrific. We grossed—"

"*Hero of the Soviet Union.*"

"Ouch!" I yell, because the pin of this medal goes right through my tunic and maybe a half inch into my chest.

"Ho! Ho! Ho!" That's the Man of Steel, thinking I am doing the Bette Davis routine.

Ho! Ho! Ho! comes the usual echo.

I sink back into my chair, my arms full of flowers and the medal shining on my breast.

"Comrade Harriman," says the Muckety Muck. "Comrade Warner. Prime Minister Churchill, General Brooke, and all guests. Recreation period is over. Please follow me. Our real work now begins."

Everybody starts to get up and file out of the room. I try to stand, too, but I can't. It's as if that pin had gone right through my body and nailed me to the seat. Frankly, I don't feel so hot. In my head squirrels, it seems like, are running around. There's a funny feeling in my heart, kind of an ache, as if the pin had gone through that, too. Suddenly, in the eye of my mind, I am making a comparison. Davis, with those needles in her ass, going *Ouch!* That's in one part of my head; in the other, I see the tanks, the burning villages, the piles of corpses, and widows on the side of the road.

What the hell is the matter with me? Drunk, that's what. Exhausted, too. Didn't *C.O.D.* gross two million? That's nothing to sneeze at. But two million what? Bucks. Dollars. Simoleons. But the war: it's grossed two million, too—*bodies!* Bodies of human beings. Frozen in the snow! And in my life? Two million gags, jokes, wise cracks. That's what I've got to show for my fifty years.

Have I wasted my life?

Bullshit! You want to talk about millions? What about the millions, the tens of millions, that have laughed and cried at my pictures? What about *Captain Applejack*? What about *Misbehaving Ladies*? YOU'LL LAUGH AT THESE GALS UNTIL YOUR BELLY ACHES!

Who am I kidding? *Death Valley*. That's where I've been, all right, but I never knew it. Wandering there ever since I was a kid—and what a kid! I was smart. I made up rhymes in my head. I had a beautiful voice:

In the evening when I sit alone a-dreaming
Of days gone by, love, to me so dear—

A soprano. Like an angel. Like when you hit a crystal glass with your fork. And now? That boy? What happened to him?

"Hey, where is everybody?"

I jump up. The room is empty. I yank at my collar. All of a sudden I'm suffocating. I need air. Where are the windows? There. Covered with curtains. I stagger over, rip the cloth to the side, and stick out my head. It's dark, dark. What's that? The moon. In the black of the night. Like Ethel Waters, wearing an earring.

Your fair face beams

Oh, God! What's this? Something thick. Something gummy. It's wobbling, like a slab of Jell-O, up inside me. A sob. Push it down. I'm the vice president for production, for Christ's sake! Executive producer! Repeat after me: *he can make money from a good picture!* But it's still coming up, it's in my belly, it's in my chest, it's in my throat. Damn it: tears are in my eyes.

This moon. Won't everyone at Warners see it when it comes over the Hollywood hills? Won't it shine on the gravestones at the Home of Peace? On Benjamin! On Pearl! Oh, Sammy! And won't it rise over the little town of Krasnashiltz, on the graves of Schmul, who is Benjamin's father, and on *his* father, what's-his-name, and on all the ancestors I never knew? Everyone, everywhere can see how beautiful it is. Look. This Kremlin. How everything is silver and shining. The spires! The domes! My heart! It's breaking!

There's a picture that in fancy oft' appearing
Brings back the time, love, when you were near

"Tovarich Warner. Jacob Benjaminovich."

Someone is speaking my name. Different than the one on the water tower.

"I'm sorry!" I cry. "I'll do better!"

A man is standing before me: stocky, crop-haired, a zillion medals on his chest. "Please, Tovarich," he says. "The air raids. We must close these curtains."

I take a better look. "I know you. Aren't you the Savior of Moscow? Mr. Zhukov?"

He shakes his big head. "No one man has the power to perform such a thing. All he can do is not stand in the way of historical forces. That is how Kutuzov defeated Napoleon. You may discover this in *War and Peace.*"

I remember. Zanuck wanted to make that picture. He told me to read the book. *Read it?* I couldn't even lift it.

The general steps in front of me and closes the curtains. Then he does a double take: "Why, Tovarich Warner. What is it? You have tears in your eyes."

Not just in my eyes. At those words they come pouring out of me—down my cheeks and over my chin. *The moon,* I want to say, but maybe for the first time in my life I can't bring out a single word. The tears keep coming, soaking my tunic, falling on the floor.

The general puts both hands on my shoulders. "Do not be sad, I beg you. Our offensive will not stop until we have forced the invader from our soil. It will not stop even then. We shall push them back—to the west! To the west! I make you a personal promise, Tovarich. We shall liberate the town of your fathers, Krasnashiltz. We shall avenge the suffering of your people."

At last my lips start to part. But instead of the sob that had been dammed up behind them, this is what comes out: "*Krasnashiltz?* Just try to spell it. Just try to pronounce it. It can't be done unless you are gargling with— *Kruggh-nachuggsh-shpititz*—Listerine!"

Josef Vissarionovich: August 1942, Moscow

Here we are at the double doors. Two Kadets on guard. Well trained. Chins tucked in. Who's in charge of the corps these days? I'll ask Lavretiy Pavlovich to give him a commendation. Fine Soviet boys. They have learned not to blink their eyes. I nod and instantly, as if they were mechanical, they pull the doors wide. I motion everyone inside and touch one of the Kadets on the elbow. That is a thing he will remember the rest of his life. He'll tell his grandchildren. The other Kadet won't forget, either. Already he burns. That feeling will grow.

The billiard room. All is correct. The green table in the middle. The little vodka glasses lined up on all four rails. At least a hundred. The copper lamp makes them shine. What would Yesenin say? Or Mayakovsky? *Like an emerald in a diamond setting!* It's easy to be a poet. You compare one thing with another. No need to be sensitive. No need to torture yourself. See? The glasses dance, they *glow like little candles*. They should name a Moscow Metro station for me.

We'll drink these oafs under this table! They're trembling already. Because other Kadets stand against the walls. At attention. With rifles. Look at Churchill. He has a nose for vodka. Why wait for toasts? That's what he's thinking. Everyone here? Where is Zhukov? Where is Warner? What are those two cooking up? *The Savior of Moscow!* Who gave that toast? Poskrebyshev was there. With his notebook. The Director of the Special Section will tell me. Was it Litvinov? I think it was Litvinov. But he's only repeating what people are saying in the streets. *Georgy Konstantinovich! You saved us!* I should send him back to Leningrad. Let him starve with the children there: *A crust of bread! A crust of bread!* What scheme is he making with the Jew? Does he want to be in an American picture? Winning the war all by himself? I could not stand another moment of that *C.O.D.* so I stopped the projector. Selling a woman by the pound. Sleeping side by side in the desert. This California Yidiy: Does he think I am running a brothel?

Ah, here they come, practically holding hands. Look at Comrade Hollywood. His eyes are red. His cheeks are pale. He looks like he's been masturbating in the toilet.

"Georgy Konstantinovich. Where have you been? We want to drink the first toast to the Savior of Moscow. *Do Dna.*"

The glasses are no bigger than thimbles. Up in the air they go. *Do Dna!* And the Kadets, with their dry throats, call out, *Trost!*

"Not just Moscow," cries Litvinov. "All of Russia! December! That was the turning point of the war. Another toast! To—"

"One minute." So it *was* Maxim Maximovich. All freeze at my words. "Alexander Nikolaevich, are you here? Of course, you are here. Look at that head. It is shining like a lighthouse."

They laugh, Poskrebyhshev louder than anyone.

"Can you tell me what was just said?"

"It was a toast. To the savior of all of Russia."

"May an old Bolshevik ask a question?"

I do not hear an objection.

"Is it true that this was the turning point? The victory of our Siberians? Maxim Maximovich Litvinov, I am asking you."

"No, no. I did not mean that at all. I meant something else." Here our ambassador—yes, only five months in Washington and look what's happened to him: he sucks in his fat lips, as if he meant to swallow them, along with the tongue that uttered those words.

"If you will permit me, Josef Vissarionovich—"

Ah, here comes Molotov, on his John Wayne horse. He will save the day.

"I believe the turning point occurred before the battle in December— and in fact made December possible."

"Of course you are permitted. All are free to speak. It is in the Constitution. What month do you have in mind?"

"October!" Our foreign minister shouts the word. "Think back, comrades. Think back ten months. Do you remember the situation? How the train was waiting at the Kazan Station? How it was packed with our Wise Teacher's books and his papers? Other trains had already left with our government officials and all of the foreign diplomats. Yes, Prime Minister Churchill, your Ambassador Cripps went along, too."

"Against his wishes," Churchill grumbles.

"Five days and five nights they traveled—without either a dining or a sleeping car. Getting them on board: *that* was diplomacy."

Now Litvinov makes jokes. It's a whole new side of him. We should find out the cause.

"Comrade Litvinov," our foreign minister continues, "I am surprised that you have forgotten. People were fleeing any way they could: by automobile, by horse cart, by putting one foot in front of the other. Many in this room were already in far-off Kiubyshev. More than I can count on these fingers. So you did not see how our factories had been dismantled. How explosive packages had been placed everywhere. Practically under our beds Here's how bad it was: our merchants and shopkeepers threw open their doors. 'Come, Comrades!' They shouted these words in the streets. 'Help yourselves! Before the Germans can take it.'"

"I have forgotten nothing, Comrade Molotov," says Litvinov. "But why are you using so many words? What is your point?"

"My point? This is my point: *Comrade Stalin refused to leave Moscow!* Though the engines of his airplane were turning. *That* was the true counteroffensive. And it occurred two months before the Siberian troops could arrive. In October. *Octyabr!* Our blessed month: *Velikayha Octyhabr'skaya Revolyutsia.* The month when we made our revolution and the month when the personal bravery of J. V. Stalin saved it."

"Trost! Trost!"

Everyone has a glass. Everyone lifts it in the air. But my hands are empty.

"Do these words not require further thought? They do. Comrade Litvinov and Comrade Molotov are both incorrect, though no one questions their good intentions."

"Don't be modest, Josef Vissarionovich!"

"We want to drink to you!"

"To the October turning point! To the man who saved the revolution!"

"You are too eager to have your vodka. There has been no turning point. Our fascist foes have only been taking a nap. Now they have awakened and are gathering their forces at—where did you say we face the maximum threat, Georgy Konstantinovich?"

"At Stalingrad."

"Perhaps I *am* too modest. I did not wish to mention a city with such a name. The threat is grave. Soon the crisis will come. Thus the truth becomes clear: there has been no turning point and there will be no turning point until our allies—" See how Harriman looks at Churchill and

Churchill at Harriman, and then—since there is so much modesty in the air—they both look down at the wooden planks in the floor. "Not until our allies find the courage to open the second front."

"Who, me?" This comes from the clown from California. "I didn't know there was a first one."

The prime minister, the first to look up, responds. "That is what I have come to Moscow to discuss—and to do so frankly. And privately."

"Too much has been decided in secret, my dear Prime Minister. You have come to tell me something. There is no reason why all in this room cannot hear your words."

"Very well. I regret to say there can be no second front on the continent of Europe this year. It is impossible. It cannot be achieved."

I address our foreign minister: "Vyacheslav Mikhailovich, are you awake or are you napping?"

"Awake, Comrade."

"Then will you tell us whether President Roosevelt guaranteed there would be an invasion this year?"

"He did, Comrade Stalin."

"And was this guarantee not put in writing and was it not made public? Will you repeat for us the exact language?"

Look at Molotov! He throws his arms out. He throws them out again. He's thrashing like a swimmer in search of the life buoy. Bravo! He's found it.

"*Full understanding was reached with regard to creating a second front in Europe in 1942.*"

Slowly I turn to the American envoy. "Very well. And does the president wish to honor this commitment, Mr. Harriman?"

"I assure you, Premier Stalin, that the president made his declaration in good faith. It was his intention to engage the enemy in the greatest possible strength and at the earliest possible moment. He intends it still."

Now is the time to take out my pipe. Cold. Unfilled. Everyone knows what that means: *He is displeased.*

"And have we not arrived at such a moment? Why do you not wish to seize it?"

"Well, because our great friend and ally has pointed out difficulties that are apparently insurmountable."

The *great friend*, this plump sturgeon, turns to me. "My dear Premier Stalin, don't you think we would mount an invasion if we thought we could make a success of it? Do you imagine we do not appreciate your own desperate straits? But after September the Channel is untrustworthy at best. And even in good weather we haven't the landing craft; we haven't enough airplanes with the range; we—"

"*Range?* Are you saying that your aircraft cannot come and go over the Channel as they wish?"

"They can come, sir, and they can go, but they cannot fight. Nor do we have as yet the trained troops. To attempt such a venture would be folly. A disaster in France would not divert a single German division from your front."

"What you are saying is that the Soviet Union must continue to fight alone."

"I know I have not brought you good news. But next year the news will be better. I trust you will believe me when I say that even now we should be willing to place a hundred thousand or even two hundred thousand men on the beaches of France, if we thought that would draw a similar number of Germans away from Russia. But the likely result of such a sacrifice would not only be a defeat for us and a triumph for our foe, but would jeopardize our real chances in 1943."

I turn to the great capitalist. "Is this now the position of your government?"

Harriman replies: "Our position is immaterial. We cannot hope to fight without our ally by our side."

How tall this fellow is. A full head above everyone else. If he were in my government, we could make him the same size as everyone else. Behind the American are the windows. Of course, covered up. But why with black curtains? Are there no other colors in the Soviet Union? Why can't they be painted over, like the windows in the city? Who made this decision? I'll ask Lavrentiy Pavlovich. He should be more watchful. He knows what happens to comrades who get lazy. It is obvious that someone intends to send a message. Black curtains: you put them on a hearse. Who do they think is going to die?

"So it is England that has betrayed us."

Churchill takes the cigar from his mouth. "It breaks my heart to think there might be division among us. The three great nations must remain inseparable. We must continue, whatever our sufferings, whatever our toils, hand in hand. Let us fight on as comrades and brothers until the Nazi regime has been beaten into the ground."

Yes, he is famous for his speeches. You would think he was in Parliament, not in a room for billiards.

"Noble sentiments. But they are only sentiments. We are obliged to face the fact that we must resist by ourselves. Our friends in the British Isles have lost their will to fight. They are afraid."

The face of the bulldog, always pink, like a baby's, turns as red as our flag. "I am prepared to forgive this insult only because of the heroism of the Russian Army and the sufferings of the Russian people. You speak, Premier Stalin, of having to fight on alone. And what of Great Britain? Did you not abandon us when you joined your forces with Hitler's? Did you not look on with indifference at the threat of the obliteration of Britain as a nation? And did you not perhaps entertain the thought of joining your new ally in the invasion of our soil?"

"We have much to forgive on both sides, perhaps," I reply. I look round at the Kadets. These boys have never heard anyone speak this way to their leader. Better for them if they had not. Let us hope they instead remember what I say next to Mr. Churchill.

"But what cannot be forgiven is cowardice. We shoot those who withdraw from the fight. In the Red Army, it takes more courage to retreat than to advance."

"And we have every intention of advancing. But not in Europe."

I look for a moment into the empty bowl of my pipe. "I have a thought that I cannot remove from my mind. It flies about in my skull the way a bat flies in its cave. You cannot hear it. It is inaudible to human beings. But I can. It makes a cry that echoes and echoes. Allow me to express what it is: *That the capitalist powers, always hostile, now enjoy the spectacle of the communist state bleeding to death.* You stand back, your arms folded, your promises broken, your convoys suspended, and you talk of 1943 or 1944 or 1945, it does not matter when: you will wait until the last Russian kills the last German, and the last German kills the last Russian. Then you will make a feast of the world for yourselves. This is the unspeakable cry of the bat."

I have uttered these words even more softly than usual. Everyone knows I do not shout. I do not rave. They think it's because I want to hide my accent. I am proud of my accent. I like people to lean toward me, to wonder whether I have really said what they heard. They are leaning now. "On the soil of my nation ten thousand comrades are dying each day. Three hundred thousand each month. While we have been standing here, talking calmly to one another, more thousands have died. And while we were in our seats, watching that idiotic film of Hollywood, five thousand more."

"Hey," says the latest Hero of the Soviet Union. "Everybody's a critic."

Brooke, Chief of the Imperial General Staff, speaks next. "Might I say that I regret you do not feel we have given you sufficient support. I trust you have not overlooked our bombing campaign? One thousand aircraft were sent over the city of Cologne. It has been reduced to ashes."

"That is only the beginning," says Churchill. "We regard the morale of the German population as a legitimate military target. We sought no mercy, and we shall show no mercy."

"That is a word that no longer exists in the Russian language. I expect that you will not leave a single building standing in all of Hitler's Reich."

"The General Secretary may be assured, that is our goal. You see what we have accomplished with a two-ton bomb. We now possess bombs of four tons, and we believe that by the end of the winter we shall double even that. One such weapon, properly deployed, could destroy the center of Berlin."

"May an old fighter make a suggestion? You must drop that bomb with parachutes. And in daylight. People will come out of their houses and out of the factories and out of their beer halls to see what is floating down from the sky. You don't want a gift of the gods to bury itself in the earth. That is a waste. Everyone should see such a beautiful explosion. Like the opening of a flower."

Why have they all fallen silent? For what reason do they look again at the floor? Is not a flower something beautiful, natural, and also given by God? If no one speaks, I will: "Where is Tovarich Warner? Ah, there is our friend. Did you not hear what I just described? Would it not be possible to film this scene? First put your cameras in an airplane. Then show the ground on fire and the death throes of the enemy—not a boy kissing a girl with an invisible orchestra playing behind them."

"Didn't you see *Dive Bomber?* A NEW HIGH IN SCREEN

ADVENTURE. TOP ENTERTAINMENT. Get it? *High? Top?* And it's in Technicolor!"

"*Each to his own taste* is an expression of bourgeois France. Herr Hitler tells us he has seen the opera *Tristan and Isolde* by Wagner three hundred times. We need to know nothing more than this to be confident in our ultimate victory. A Jüngling and a Mädchen. A love potion. A fairy tale.

"I, too, have seen an opera three hundred times. *Ivan Susanin*. By Glinka. What a joy to sit in a private box and eat boiled eggs while this simple Russian lad leads the Poles into the depths of the forest where, one after the other, they freeze to death. My dear Jacob Benjaminovich, why not make a film of *that*? The snow-laden branches. The deepening darkness. The white breath, the chattering teeth, the whimpers of these Poles as the tentacles of ice close round their hearts."

"Yeah, well, we tried to borrow Henje from Fox, but Zanuck didn't feel like doing me any favors. Have you actually sat through *Nanook of the North*? You've seen one walrus, you've seen them all. Take my word for it, your highness: There's no business in snow business."

"Then permit me to make a different proposal. A film about Shah Abbas, the Persian Emperor. He would make an excellent subject. Think of the scene in which he blinds both of his sons. Or when a father receives from Abbas the heads of his own children. There is a wise saying from that Oriental land: *The Persians are but women compared to the Afghans, and the Afghans but women compared to the Georgians.*"

I note with interest how Litvinov whispers into this Ivan Warner's ear: "Josef Vissarionovich is a Georgian."

"Yeah? Big deal. So's Butterfly McQueen."

"You don't like this kino idea? It has no appeal?"

"I didn't say that, J.V.! It's stupendous! It's fabulous! It's colossal! But is it any good? I mean, the theaters these days are filled with women. I'm not sure they'll go for blinding the kids and putting their heads on a tray. I mean, is it family entertainment?"

"Ah, you want an example of true Soviet parents. Very well. I invite you tomorrow morning to the Moscow Zoo. Oh, yes, our Russian animals are true patriots. They did not run off to Kuibyshev—eh, Vyacheslav Mikhailovich? No, they remained at their stations, even when our foes were advancing, and do so now, when the bombs rain down."

"We should give them the Order of Lenin."

Who said that? I look into every face. But every face is once more looking down. What is so interesting about these floorboards? Does someone want to pull them up? To make a pine box? Yes, the same person who hung these curtains.

"Ho, ho, ho! I am human. I like a good joke."

Ho, ho, ho! comes the chorus.

I slap the Hollywood Jew on the back. "Tomorrow morning! Ten o'clock! At the zoo. In our special lagoon you shall see a loving mother and father. Krokodily! Such beauties. They lie half in sun and half in water. Please watch as their young move about in their mouths. Happy children! Flitting in and out, over teeth, over tongue. Here are true Soviet parents. At any instant those jaws can snap shut."

"I get the picture."

"Good! Grandioso! You will make the kino and I will make a toast!"

I lift my arm. As if wires run from it to all four walls of the room, the Kadets jerk forward. They don't carry their rifles. They carry bottles. Vodka. Sovetskoye shampankoye. Ruby wine. They fill all the little glasses. To the top. "But what shall we drink to, Comrades? What are your suggestions?"

"Why, there is only one toast," says Molotov, raising his glass. "To our Wise Teacher! *Do Dna!*"

"I regret to tell you, Vyacheslav Mikhailovich, I have heard that before."

Maxmim Maximovich steps forward. "To the Bright Sun of Humanity. *Do—*"

I feel something strange. A stab of sadness. "I think I have heard everything that can be said."

Molotov has broken into a sweat. Who can blame him? "What's left?" he asks. "The Brest-Litovsk Canal?"

Now everyone is sweating. They are thinking and thinking. I'll put them out of their misery. "Pick up your glasses, Comrades. Lift them in the air. *To family entertainment!*"

Trost! comes the cry, not just from the Bolsheviks and capitalists but from our handsome young soldiers all about the room.

I narrow my eyes. I see better that way. For instance, this Jacob Benjaminovich is only pretending to drink. Why? Is he planning something? See how he pours his glass into one of the billiard pockets. Ruining our good Soviet leather. He keeps as close as he can to his mistress, the German girl with the neck. It's white, it's long, like a swan's. You see? Anyone can make poetry. Why do we give them medals? And then they kill themselves. And the woman? She prefers Comrade Engelsing. Yes, *Comrade*. He did good work for us in Berlin. Look, her hand is in another kind of pocket. And Alexander Wilhelmovich himself? He keeps looking over at Svetlana. And what about the Little Housekeeper? It's unmistakable: she wants to be in pictures. That's why she keeps smiling with the gap in her teeth at the Warner brother. It's a French farce. With slamming bedroom doors. With sweat and perfume. That is the film we should be making. Box office number one.

"Jacob Benjaminovich, everyone is making a toast. What about you? Do you have a reason for remaining silent?"

"Who, me? You guys have said it all. Great dialogue. There's nothing left."

"Come, Comrade. Here is a glass. Filled with our vodka. Our peasants suffered to grow the grain. Many died so that you might drink. Do not insult their sacrifice. Give us a toast."

Trapped. He looks left. He looks right. He can't escape.

"Ha! Ha! Ha! I once saw a picture where Keaton or Chaplin or one of those Three Stooges drank from a glass without using his hands. Wait. Maybe it was Martha Raye."

"Comrade, we are waiting. Somewhere a clock is ticking."

"Okay, okay. But what the hell am I supposed to drink to? There's always world peace. What about the United Nations? The struggle for a better world. I've got it: Liberty, equality, and, and—what is it? A fraternity? Wait! I've got it! I'm ready!"

Here's to the girl with eyes of brown
Ha! Ha! Ha!
Who makes her living upside down
Twenty dollars is her regular price
Give her thirty and she'll do it twice

All fall silent. All pull back in dismay.

"Hey, what did you expect in a pool hall? George Jessel?"

Now the People's Commissar for Foreign Affairs stumbles forward to where the last of the glasses sits on the rail of the table. He plucks it up, spilling the liquor over the rim. It seems that all this time he has been trying to discover something original. Something that no one has heard before. Up goes his glass.

"Comrades! To the animals in the zoo! *Da Dno!*"

Trost!

"To the krokodil!"

"The jaws of the krokodil!"

But at this moment Churchill, who has not said a word, holds up a roll of paper. "There is no need to drink such a toast. Nor need you visit the zoological gardens. I have the reptile here. Brooksie, will you give me a hand?"

"What have you got there?"

"What is it?"

But I see what he has done. While we have been drinking, he has been at work. The amateur artist. With his charcoal stick. He has made a drawing of the armor-plated beast.

"What is it?" the prime minister repeats, as he and his general unroll the paper across the felt surface of the table. "Why, it is a portrait of the future. Of our second front. And, just as promised, it will take place this year, 1942."

The drawing is spread wide, held down by a four ball and a number six. Everyone comes crowding around, leaning over the railing. They think they are strategists, studying a map. The reptile stares back at them, with its half-lidded eye. The artist—we should put his works in the Hermitage—holds forth:

"This second front will be launched not on the continent of Europe, but in North Africa. We'll land in the west and catch Rommel in our pincers— the Eighth Army and Montgomery on one side, the Anglo-American force on the other. We'll drive the Germans out of the Mediterranean. We'll have control of the sea and control of the air. Once that is achieved, we'll take a visit to the zoo of Europe, where friend crocodile resides. Our plan is to kill him by attacking through his soft underbelly—Sicily, Italy, the south of France—rather than swatting him, here, on his snout."

Litvinov gives a snort of derision. "This is what you offer us? Such pinpricks? The reptile is armored; it will not feel a thing."

"On the contrary," says Churchill. "A wound to the abdomen is always fatal."

"This is no second front," Molotov declares. "It will not draw a single German soldier or airplane or tank from Russian soil."

Zhukov, after one victory, thinks he's Hannibal the Great. With elephants. Who does he want to conquer next? Just listen to him. One big idea after the other. "For centuries the path to Berlin has been through the low countries and France. You wish to pull at the limbs of the beast instead of driving"—and here our good general brings the butt end of a pool cue down upon the middle of the reptile—"a stake through its heart."

At this concussion, people scatter from the table like so many billiard balls broken from the rack.

But Brooks, of the Imperial General Staff, does not budge. He rolls the drawing back into a scroll and returns it to the prime minister. "Perhaps you will permit me," he begins, "to make the case for Operation Torch."

"Torch?" says the slick-haired Californian. "What is this? A picture by Columbia? The germ of the ocean?"

The Britisher ignores him. "Our landings will take place within months, well before this year is over, and not at some unknown date in the future. It will engage American troops for the first time—green troops, undoubtedly; but after the success of this operation they will be green no more."

"And might I add," puts in Harriman, "that with American troops fighting in this hemisphere, the pressure from Admiral King and many other of our fine patriots to turn to the east, to put the Japanese within range of their guns, will be appreciably lessened."

"There is a further advantage of bringing in the Americans," Brook continues. "When they land under their own flag at Algiers and at Oran, the French are as likely to welcome them as to fight. We think we possess near-even odds of luring Vichy over to us."

"Algiers?" Jacob Benjaminovich shouts out that word. And the next one, too. "Oran? What happened to Casablanca?"

Churchill has the same trick as I. His mouth had been empty. Suddenly there is a cigar in it. By magic, the cigar is lit. "Casablanca is on the Atlantic. This must be a Mediterranean operation. If we attack North Africa we shall have—and this cannot be said of any landing in Europe—a real chance of success. That's the chief thing: a victory. A victory at last, instead of the prospect of yet another defeat. Mr. General Secretary, we have not come here to dictate terms. These are our plans. We know full well we cannot execute them without the approval of our great ally."

Everybody, Maxim Maximovich, Georgy Konstantinovich, Vayacheslav Mikhailovich—all of them, and the foreigners, too, wait for my reply. The eyes of the Kadets slide toward me as well. Let them wait. I shall also be a magician. My pipe had been empty. Now it is full. How did I do it? Ho, ho! In my pocket! Opened the tin of Herzogovina Flor, shredded the cylinders of tobacco, and packed the bowl full. All with one hand. And let them wonder about this: it, too, is lit and smoking! The cloud forms around my head. A sign of fair weather? Or is lightning about to strike?

"So many explanations. Vichy. Admiral King. The friendly French. Herr Rommel. The training of troops."

No one says a word. I pause. I puff. The cloud thickens. It flattens, into the shape of a thunderhead. "Why so many reasons? Experience teaches us that when one wishes to conceal a real motive he will attempt to distract his listeners with many false ones. What, then, is the real reason? That is what we must determine."

Now it is time for the lightning bolt. All the more effective, more thunderous, because I speak in little more than a whisper. "The Middle East, North Africa, Egypt. This is your sphere of interest, Mr. Prime Minister. It belongs to you. It is your empire—and you wish to retain it."

Now we hear from the Chief of the General Staff: "Premier Stalin, I can assure you—"

"You are capitalists. Good merchants. Your goal is to trade Russian blood for British oil."

No one dares a reply. I turn now to the plutocrat, Harriman. "What of our American comrades? Do you, too, fight for the British empire?"

"No," answers the special envoy. "Our goal is to put our men into action as quickly as possible. The president wants the landings to take place by September. By October at the latest."

"No! No! No! No!" These explosions come from the Howitzer of Hollywood. "Not before Thanksgiving! We've still got problems with the script. I can't believe what I pay those two bald-headed—"

"And who," interrupts Molotov, as if he has seen this Yidiy Amerikanskiy for the first time, "are you? What are you doing here? Who let you in?"

"Who am I? Maybe you never saw our water tower."

Litvinov raises his hand to speak. I give permission. "It's a good question, Vyacheslav Mikhailovich. A month ago I met with the Americans. All, including the president, were full of enthusiasm for the second front. The front across the Channel. No one spoke of this foolish venture. Who was it that changed the president's mind. Who—?"

"Well, I don't want to brag, boys, but—"

Harriman speaks up for his compatriot. "Mr. Warner is a confidant of President Roosevelt, with considerable influence on his opinions. It was he who insisted that his good friend come with us to our meetings."

Molotov: "But why? It wasn't to bring us a film. Anyone could have done that. *Why*, is the question."

"My dear Jacob Benjaminovich," I begin. "Would you be good enough to answer it? Why have you come here?"

Harriman: "But I told you. The president—"

"Excuse me, Averell Eduardovich, but I was addressing myself to the Jew."

"Only on my parents' side, ha, ha, ha, though I give plenty to Bnai Br—"

"Take care." Maxim Maximovich whispers this to his co-religionist. "We are only temporarily alive."

"What's the big tsimis? I'll tell you *why*. I've got a million bucks tied up in this production. I'm making sure where and when this landing takes place."

"The answer has come to me," says our foreign minister. His glasses flash as if they were indeed receiving a signal. "Isn't it obvious? He was sent here to spy. Well, we shorten spies by the size of one head."

What exclamations! What an outcry! I see that the Kadets, already at attention, grow a little stiffer. Zhukov reaches for his holster, even though we have taken his gun. The whole room takes a step away from—what shall we call him? *The man who would not join us in a drink.* No one else noticed this. They were too busy drinking themselves. But nothing escapes my eye. I take a puff or two of my oriental tobacco. I let the cloud thicken around my head. Then I speak.

"No, no, Vyacheslav Mikhailovich. Those are barbaric methods. Like the ancient Persians. Our friend from Hollywood does not wish to make a film about such primitive folk. He is sensitive. He thinks of the women, with handkerchiefs to their eyes.

"We are modern people. We have up-to-date methods. There is a bomb crater on Malaya Dmitrov Street. What if a car should accidently slip into it? Or Vorovsky Boulevard. It is known to have a dangerous intersection. What if something goes wrong when inspecting the Kalyusha rockets? Such things have been known to happen. But why be so subtle? We have here a room full of fine Soviet lads. They have rifles. They know how to use them. What would they do if they saw a spy? A spy in holy Moscow? Would they ask questions? They would not ask questions. They'd put their cheeks to the good wood of our Russian stocks. They would aim down the polished metal of their Russian barrels. Kadets! Do you see the target? Kadets! For the fatherland! Fire!"

Crack! There is a loud percussion. A percussion followed by a rumbling sound. Is it a gunshot? Is it the lightning bolt, followed by thunder? A German bombardment? Ho, ho, ho! Nothing of the sort. It's the billiard table. Where the balls are now spinning and whirling and bouncing about. "Hurrah!" I shout. "Russky piramida!"

Jack L. Warner: August 1942, Moscow

Jesus H. Christ! I almost had a heart attack. I thought I'd been shot by a firing squad. For being a spy. Like Stroheim in *Three Faces East*. DID THE BUTLER DO IT? SUSPENSE LIKE YOU YOU'VE NEVER SEEN BEFORE! Didn't make a dime. Better get up off the floor. Did I mess up my hair? It's getting a little thin. Well, I got a long way to go before I get to Stroheim. Anyway, who wants fat hair?

"Four ball in the corner pocket."

It's K-K-K KATY! BEAUTIFUL KATY! She's the one at the table. She's the one who made the break. She saved my ass from the K-K-K Kadets. She's still got the stick in her hands and is leaning so far over the felt that her boobs—nothing to write home about, but nothing to sneeze at either—are taking a bow. She might as well be posing for one of our publicity stills. It's a hell of a tough shot. Bam! Down goes the four ball.

I throw up my hands. "I'll take on all comers! Twenty bucks a ball! Ha, ha, ha! They used to call me the *Yid from Youngstown!* Come on, suckers! Who wants to take on the Champ of Chalky's?"

The answer was: *more people than you could shake a cue stick at.* They all came crowding around. The Americans were waving twenty-dollar bills and the Brits five-pound notes. Any Russkies? Here they come, with fistfuls of rubles.

Now Blondie stands up. "I was thinking of higher stakes, Mr. Warner."

"Yeah? No kidding? Okay. I once dropped a hundred grand at Monte Carlo."

"You don't want to bet against me. We're on the same side."

"Huh? I don't get it? Are we playing doubles?"

"I think I understand this blond-haired devushka." That was the Head Honcho. He comes cruising through the crowd and right up to KK. "You wish to play not for cash but for continents, am I not correct?"

"Yes. If I win, you'll agree to what the prime minister and the others are asking. You'll give your approval. The invasion will be in Africa."

I could kiss her! To use a euphemism. She was going to save the whole production! A million-buck bet! And there I was, disparaging her breasts! Hey, wait a minute: What if our side lost?

"And if you lose?" says the Muckety-Muck, like he was practically reading my mind. "Then the president will keep his word. Or at least this gentleman—"

Does he mean me? Well, I've been called a lot worse.

"—this gentleman will agree to use his *considerable influence* to make him do so."

"Hey, we go fishing now and then, but—"

KK, to me, puts her fingers to her lips. And what does she do to the Mentor of Millions? She hands him the stick.

In ten seconds flat he has racked up the balls—which are all white, by the way, except for the cue ball, which is red, and in ten seconds more he lets fly. There is a tremendous *crack!*, louder even than before, and all the balls go racing around like lunatics escaping from an asylum, and—*holy shit!*—it looks like half of them go in the pockets!

The room bursts into cheers. *Hurrah! Hurrah! Hurrah!* go all the Kadets. The Russian toadies clap their hands and the Brits, even though they are rooting for my good friend Miss Kaiser, say *Well done* and *Good show*, and other corny understatements.

Stalin holds up his hand for silence, and gets it. "Before we continue," he says, "I shall explain two rules of Russky piramida. Rule one: when the eighth ball goes into the pocket, the game is won. Rule two—a Kremlin tradition: loser goes under the table."

All of a sudden the One Pathfinder, as he was known, has like magic a pipe in his hand, and he takes a couple of puffs. Then out of the cloud he says, "Who would like to challenge the Chairman of the Council of Ministers? Is there someone who would like to put him on his hands and knees? Come, Comrades, a friendly game."

What a madhouse! All of the Russkies are pushing and shoving and trying to get under the table. It's as crowded down there as the stateroom in *A Night at the Opera*. The Brilliant Genius of Humanity only shakes his head. "It is difficult to find a partner. I remember the old days. I used to play with Grigory Yevseyevich. I didn't care that he was a Jew. One evening I was playing with his daughter. She sank the first four balls, ho-ho-ho; the next thing you know her father yanks the pool cue from her and starts beating her with it on her back and on her head and crying *Fool! Fool! Fool!* She was girl of eleven."

With that all the Brits and the Amerikanskiys also make a dash for the table legs. Even Churchill, though before he crouches down with the others he lays a note on the table. "Ten pounds on the lady." In a moment only the three of us—I mean, the present speaker, the Light of All Nations, and the former Cheryl Charmaigne—are left. I say, as a venture, "Gee, maybe we ought to go back to twenty bucks."

KK takes the stick from the Creator of Joy. But instead of racking the balls, she looks up into the light from the long copper lamp and says, "Do you know who taught me how to play?"

"How should I know?" I say. "I'm cue-less." From under the table, from that whole crowd of losers, not one laugh.

"My father. Joe-Joe. His father was Abraham, my Grandpa Abe. He taught little Joe, in Cincinnati, how to play."

"Yeah? Well all the way across the state, I was teaching myself."

"Every Sunday morning, from when I was eight, my father took me to a place called Zylinderhut Billard. That is a funny name for a pool hall: Top Hat Billiards. It sounds more like a nightclub, wouldn't you say? Every Sunday morning, like going to church."

I notice that, while she's talking, the Delight of All Children, so-called, is one by one putting the balls back into the rack.

"And then, one day, they would not let us in. Everybody knew me. I had a three-quarter-sized cue. I could beat any German in the room. The manager was polite. 'Bitte, Fräulein,' he said. 'Would you be so kind as to not return?' Because, you know, the Abraham in my father's name.

"So then on Sundays we went to the movies. *Your* movies, Jacob Benjaminovich. The Mercedes-Palast. *Fashions of 1934.*"

"LET'S GO TO GAY PAREE!" I shout, like a rubber hammer had hit my knee. "OUT-FOLLIES THE FOLIES-BERGÈRE!"

"I had just turned twelve. Can you imagine? The wonderful clothes. The girls! Dancing with feathers! With harps! And Paris! You never forget when you are twelve years old."

"I never forgot, either. Davis was a pain in the neck. Always complaining. We turned her into a Garbo. The wig. The eyelashes. The goddamn gown. You'd never know we were doing her a favor!"

"He was a wonderful pool player, Joseph Abramovich Kauffman. That four ball? An easy shot. He taught me well. He asked for the job in Warsaw. You said there was no job in Warsaw. Oh, he would have shined your shoes anywhere in the world. He would have poured the cream into your coffee. Don't worry: it does not matter. If he had gone to Warsaw, they would have hunted him down. Anywhere in the world. Even in beautiful Paris:

Play your broken melody
Upon the strings of fantasy."

For a moment, it was as quiet as the audience at *Gold Dust Gertie*. A HIT! A WOW! A SMASH! Yeah, if only: we had to cut out all the musical numbers. Then, from under the table comes a voice. I recognize it. The foreign minister. Mazeltov or something like that. With the moustache and the glasses. He says, "Beware, Josef Vissarionovich"—Christ, all these guys are sons of viches—"She was born in Berlin. She is a German citizen. She wants Roosevelt to break his word to us. It is a possibility that *she* is the spy."

But KK is still looking into the copper light:

"Forget about your rainbow schemes
Spin a little web of dreams.

"I think the trouble with me is that I have seen too many movies."

Then she puts the stick on the felt and, without another note from Sammy Fain, gets down under the table with everyone else. Now it's just me and the Fountain of All Wisdom mano a mano, like they say in France.

I see that the Big Panjandrum—actually, he wouldn't be much more than five feet in curled-up slippers—has already put all those white balls back in the rack. He looks over at me. "Perhaps our guest will permit me, with all my infirmities, to play?"

"Infirmities, huh? What are you looking for? Two balls on the break?"

"No advantage. We shall play one game. And the stakes? Everything. What is meant by this word, *everything*? Must I explain it to you?"

"Maybe a hint? Animal, mineral, or—"

Here he takes the rolled-up crocodile from the edge of the table. "Here are the stakes. The continent of Europe. Or the continent of Africa. Would you care to hold them, Comrade?"

He hands me the drawing. Right away I get a funny feeling in the kishkes. It's like the paper is burning. I stretch up on my toes and stick it on top of the metal lamp. "That's how we did it at Chalky's," I say, meaning whoever holds it at the end wins the match. "By the way, if you ever happen to be in Youngstown—"

I can barely get the words out. The Friend of All People, that's a nickname of his, snaps his fingers and one of the Kadets comes running up with a cue case in his arms. There's a real beauty inside: a two-piece made out of maple. The private screws it together and hands it to Uncle Joe.

"I am a poor player," he says. "Out of practice. With many cares and disadvantages."

"Hey, you wouldn't hustle me, would you?"

He only smiles. I see, with a shudder, that his teeth go inward, like the ones on a snake. "You are a guest in our country. A Hero of the Soviet Union. Would you care to break?"

"After you, Gaston," I reply.

And then, without further ado, which is a line from Shakespeare, the Kingpin puts down his pipe, leans over the table and gets ready to shoot.

"Three cheers for Comrade Stalin!" go all the soldiers.

"Okay, okay, we don't need to hear from the peanut gallery."

I watch the Hope of Mankind, another moniker. His neck is swelling over his collar like an amphibian's. And it's turning the color of corned beef. Back and forth goes his shining cue, over the claw of what I now see is a half-paralyzed hand. By now his neck is like an eggplant. I figure his temperature must be up around a hundred and four. And like a fever patient, he's even started to mutter:

"Look at them. Pale. Frightened. Huddling together. They think that way they are safe. That I don't see them. Watch out. Watch out, traitors. Beware, wreckers. Nothing can save you."

The stick is going back and forth over the fingers, the temperature of the patient is going higher and higher, until—this is amazing, it's like some kind of magic trick—the pipe he set on the rail by contagion begins to smoke.

"Kulaks!"

It's a war cry—and with it the Gardener of Human Happiness sends the cue ball screaming across the felt and into a perfect break. The balls go flying like a mob being chased by a bull, until one of them falls into a side pocket—"Kazakhstan," murmurs the shooter, and another goes into the far-left corner: "Siberia."

"Hurrah!" go the soldiers. Like they have nothing better to do.

The slaughter has only begun. The Master of the Age, another handle, is eyeing a nine ball that I swear to God starts to tremble. He's going to knock it off with a six.

"Hey," I say. "That's not the cue ball."

A voice, Litvinov's, comes up from under the table. "Amerikanskiy piramida. Any ball hits any ball."

But the Protector of the People is muttering again, just like before:

"He wants to be King of Leningrad. To show off by walking around like a proletarian. He thinks he will win the hearts of the people. Does he think we don't notice? That we'll just sit back and smile?"

Back and forth goes the cue, like the pendulum in that story—was it by Irving Washington, maybe?—that gets closer and closer to the condemned man's heart.

Crack!

"Kirov!"

The number nine drops into the waiting pit.

The next victim, it's going to be the three ball, is a really tough shot. To deal with it the Genius of Geniuses, what the Frenchies call a nom de plume, has to use a bridge. He places it on the felt, lowers his cue into the metal groove, and now leans so far forward that both feet leave the ground.

"Foul!" I declare. "Joe Breen won't allow it."

The Commissar swings his head around. I see that his eyes are yellow. Jaundice? Is that his disease? "I once had some oysters that—"

But he cuts me off. "Perhaps you have noticed that Josef Vissarionovich is not a tall man. Neither was his father. A simple shoemaker. Why do you draw attention to this? Do you think it is amusing?"

"No, no, some of my best friends—"

"It is my fate. I starved as a child. Like so many of the Russian people. Now let us use logic. I cannot be made taller. But you might be shortened a bit. By a head. Then we shall have an even match."

"Ha! Ha! Good one, Joe! Listen to this: Confucius say, *Short man who dance with tall woman get bust in mouth!*"

But the Great Helmsman, so to speak, isn't laughing. Instead, he's moving his cue back and forth through the slot of the bridge. Here comes the chant:

"Listen to him. Just listen. *Don't shoot! Don't shoot me! Call Comrade Stalin! He won't let anyone shoot me. Didn't I confess? It's a dream. It can't be happening. Mamele! Mamele. A Yidiy wants to live!*"

Crack!

"*Zinoviev!*"

So much for the number three. Now what? The thirteen. The Leader of Progressive Peoples, that's his screen name, gets ready to shoot:

"What? Another of our Hebrew friends? How many there are! Crush them and smash them and cut them to pieces: still they grow. Like worms. *Mercy, mercy!* The cry of the worm. *I love our Brilliant Genius of Humanity! I killed for you, so don't kill me!* A pornographer. A pervert. A garden of two thousand orchids."

Crack!

"*Yagoda!*"

I watch while the thirteen goes from one cushion and then to another, before dropping into the grave that has already been dug.

Holey moley! Is this guy going to run the table? He only needs three more to get to eight. It's dawning on me: I've been snookered. I'll lose my shirt. They're going to invade France!

Now he's talking to the number two ball:

"Confess. Why won't you confess? You think you can take back your words? We have written them down. You want to send me a letter? *Koba, why do you need me to die?* Letter returned. Addressee unknown."

Crack!

"*Bukharin!*"

Uh-oh: the two wasn't hit hard enough. It's slowing down, slowing to a crawl, and now it stops right at the edge of the pocket. Is this my chance? Am I going to get my turn?

The Big Wheel stands up, squints his eyes, and glares at the hanger. It's shaking, it's shuddering, and now it slips into the hole.

"A suicide," says the Paragon of the Party and turns to—I'm counting on my fingers—the next-to-last ball. Two more and I'm toast.

"Now our great marshal. Our military genius. Our own little Napoleon. A plotter. Fifth columnist. Give us names! More names! Or we are going to kill your wife. Ah, that is good. These lovely names. Music to my ears. That is what I like to hear."

Crack!

"*Tukhachevsky!*"

With a hop and a skip, the ten ball plunges into the depths.

"Ho! Ho!" laughs Stalin. "We killed Nina Yefgenyevna anyway."

Vosem! Vosem! Vosem! go the Kadets.

You don't have to tell me what that means. It means *eight*. In other words, The High Man on the Totem Pole has sunk seven of the fifteen balls and there's only one more to go. Was this guy really going to beat the Yid from Youngstown? All he has to do is tap in the twelve and it's *I see England, I see France, I see Hitler's underpants!* And I've lost a million bucks. There he goes, muttering through those backward teeth. Think! Think, J.L.! Do something!

"Bronshtein. Another one. There is no end to them. They breed under the rocks. In the soil. Out of thin air."

"Excuse me, Holy Father, but have you heard this one? In Hollywood, a groom carries his bride over the threshold, ha, ha, ha, and she looks around and says, *Gee, this looks familiar. Have we been married before?* See, in the film business, there are—"

"He wanted a Fourth International. We showed that scum the door.

Buenas dias, señor! Do you enjoy sitting in the Mexico sun? Watch out for the kaktus! You might get a needle in your ass. Or, ho, ho, ho, an ice pick in your skull!"

"Good one! Ha, ha, ha. What happens to a grape when an elephant steps on it? *It lets out a little whine!* Speaking of wine, why don't you and me, just the two of us, let's take a break and have a snort. We could—"

But he doesn't look up from where he is aiming to knock in ball number twelve.

"I'll tell you what flows like wine. The blood of the traitor. It flew out the window and onto the street. L'Avenida Viena: filled with red Russian wine!"

"Great pun, J.V.! Outstanding! Here's another one! Do you know why a bicycle can't stand on its own? Give up? *Because it's two-tired!* Okay, okay. I don't like it either. *When the smog lifts in Los Angeles, UCLA.* Well, it's kind of an inside joke, because—"

"Ice pick. Skull. Blood. Brains. This makes Josef Vissarionovich laugh."

Vosem! Vosem! Vosem! go the Kadets.

"T-T-T-T—" stutters Stalin.

But the stick doesn't move. It just goes back and forth, as if it's stuttering, too. Time for me to get a move on.

"What kind of shoes are made from banana skins? *Slippers!*"

"T-T-T-T-T—"

Sweat is shooting off of the Uplifter of Mankind's brow, like the fountain at Wilshire and Santa Monica. His moustache, it's wet as a sponge. Now he stands up.

"It seems, Comrades, I must subject myself to self-criticism. Why do I hesitate? Is this not our Soviet Union's greatest foe? Before me I see his little glasses. His little goatee. I could eat his heart! Yet I must ask: Is it possible I am having second thoughts? A moment of regret? About Comrade Bronshtein? About Kirov? Zinoviev? Yagoda? The seas of blood? The mountains of human bones? Was all this a mistake?"

"Listen, Joe, apropos: Why do cemeteries have fences around them? *Because people are dying to get in.* What? No cigar? Okay, did you hear the one about—"

"Niet!"

It's a blood-curdling scream. But it can't muffle the sound of what happens next:

Crack!

"T-T-T-Trot-Trots-Trotsky!"

Hoorah! Hoorah! Hoo . . .

This time the soldiers have to swallow their words. The number twelve got slammed all right, but too hard. It bounces around like it's trapped in a pinball machine, from cushion to cushion, until it ends up, still spinning, in the middle of the table.

"Thank you, Jesus," I mutter, without crossing myself, and I pick up my cue.

Snap!

Smithereens: that's what's left of Uncle Joe's stick after he breaks it over his knee. I know I've got to act fast. Already one of those infantrymen is hustling up with a new case. The Champ of Chalky's bends over the table, he runs his stick through the loop of his finger, Ohio style. And in his mind's eye—oh, the hell with this—in *my* mind's eye, I paint a pair of thick eyebrows and a patch of thinning hair on the surface of the little globe. *Fuck you!*

Crack!

"Cohn!"

Voila! The first ball of my run drops in.

Take a gander at that: they're screwing the two halves of the new cue stick together. Get a move on, J.L.! I take a bead on the number six.

"Just because you're my brother, you think you can order me around? Tell me what pictures to make? How much to spend? You got another think coming. Fuck you, too!"

Crack!

"Harry!"

Bingo. In the pocket. How come no one is yelling *Hoorah*? I give the soldiers the eye. Fine, you don't want to cheer for me, I'll cheer for myself: "Sis-Boom-Bah! Princeton!"

I line up the five. "No one walks out on Jack L. Warner, head of production. Fuck you, Daryl!"

Crack!

"Zanuck!"

"Bulldog! Bulldog! Bow-wow-wow!" Hey, I should have thought of this years ago. *"Hal is making trouble. Wants to run the whole show. Grabbing all the credit. Eli Yale!"*

Crack!

"Wallis!"

And good-bye and good-night, ball number fifteen. I'm halfway home. But out of the corner of my eye I see the Big Wig chalking up his new cue. I trot to the other side of the table. "Davis! Bellyaching about her contract. And that goes for Cagney and de Havilland, too. Fuck 'em all!"

Crack!

Curtains for number eleven.

"Pardon my intrusion, Tovarich." Uh-oh, it's the Prince of Putzes, which is one I just made up. "This shot is mine."

"Huh? What about the rules? You missed your shot."

"That was a temporary interruption. Please step aside."

This might be the greatest challenge ever for the Youngstown Yid. Got to work ASAP. Without a word, without even looking, I smack the nearest ball, which crashes into the eight and caroms off the fourteen and then—faster than shit goes through a goose—those two identical spheres, smooth as shaved scalps, fall simultaneously into the corner pockets.

"Epsteins!" I yell. "That'll teach them to show up halfway through the afternoon! *Annassa, kata, kalo, kale. Bryn Mawr!"*

Silence in the poolroom. Silence in the Kremlin. Everyone's as quiet as a church mouse. "Hey, you know what Confucius said: *Man who fart in church sit in pew.*"

Still no one speaks. But I can hear something—like a hum, like a buzz, like bees maybe—way off in the distance. Inside the room, everybody is holding his breath. Now I hold mine. The fate of the world, millions and millions of lives: that's what the stakes are. Not to mention our A-level budget.

The guy with the big moustache has sunk seven balls. So has the guy with the little one. Two remain on the table, the cue ball and the leftover number twelve. Neither shot is all that tough. I take a look at Uncle Joe. He's sweating buckets. He's staring at the ball he missed, so plump, so white, like one of those eggs he used to eat in his private box. He wants to gulp it down. But it's my run, and I'm going to sink this baby!

Outside, the bees, the cicadas, some kind of insects, are humming louder—and lower, too, like the bass notes in a barbershop quartet. I go ahead and chalk up my cue. I can knock off this shot. I can do it in my sleep. I bend over. I stare at the shiny white surface of the ball. Time to draw a moustache on it. That little Fuller brush on the lip of the world's number one Heinie. And that hairdo that drops peekaboo-style over one eye. But I don't see a lip. I don't see a forehead. What I see is that round pearl of the moon, the same one I saw before, out of that window. It has moved on. I can feel it. It's right over my head. It's pulling on me, on the juices inside my brain, just like it's pulling on all of the oceans.

"Well, my dear Alphonse," says—it's a kind of pet name—the Idol of all Workers. "Please proceed. Or have you lost your nerve?"

I pay no attention. I'm looking up now, at the beams of wood that run across the ceiling. All of a sudden, they pull back, like a trick shot, and I can see all the stars like dancing girls up in the sky. There it is! That moon! My moon! It's shaking, it's throbbing, like a cymbal on a bandstand, and I can hear the song the band is playing:

In the evening when I sit alone a-dreaming
Of days gone by, love, to me so dear—

Days gone by. The moon, it's still there. But the boy, the one with a voice so sweet and high and pure: Where did *he* go? Has anyone seen him? Does anyone know where he is?

In all my dreams
Your fair face beams

I do. He is a prisoner inside the man I have become.
"Don't do it!"
Someone is screaming. Someone is holding on to my shooting arm.
"Do not shoot! Go under the table! You don't know him! He missed on purpose! He *wants* you to win! He'll do something terrible. Something unspeakable!"

Is it KK? Does she want to protect me? Maybe she loves me? *Niet*, as they say around here. It's the Little Housekeeper. His majesty's daughter. She's still yelling, she's shouting, but I don't hear her. That's because the humming sound, the barbershop quartet, has swollen into a chorus of basses and baritones and tenors, all of them howling right over my head. I yank my arm free from the carrottop.

"What the hell?" I say to her and to the others and to the whole world. "It's just green cheese. Fuck it, too!"

Crack!

The cue ball clobbers the twelve with a tremendous concussion, but whether it went in or not I can't tell because just then the walls start to shake and dust pours down from the ceiling and the howling from the sky is drowned out by the howling inside the room.

That's when I figure out what's going on. Those are planes above us. *German* planes. That damned moon is turning everything into a perfect target. All of Moscow is lit up for them, so bombs are tumbling down not just over the city but inside our Kremlin walls.

Who won the match? Who the hell knows? But just then a piece of paper comes fluttering down from the swaying copper lamp. I grab it and hold it up. "I've got the crocodile!" I shout. "We're going to land in Casablanca! I won the Amerikanskiy piramida! It's all because of me! Me! Come on, you guys! Let's hear it! Come on, *Flim flam, Bim bam,* OLE MISS BY DAMN!"

There's a tug on the cuff of my pants. Zhukov, the big general, is pulling at me. He's covered head to toe with splinters and plaster dust. "Comrade, Comrade." He's calling to me. I bend down to the floor, so I can hear him.

"Do you remember our discussion? About Tolstoy? About *War and Peace?*"

"Yeah, sure. Helluva read."

"Then you know the truth, which is that great events are shaped by a thousand or ten thousand causes and that no single man—not you, dear Comrade Warner, and not I, and not even *he*—can determine the course of history."

13 } GOOD PICTURE-MAKING, TAKE TWO *A Poodle*

KK: *July 1942, Los Angeles*

I knew about Blondi. Everyone knew about Blondi. A true germanischen Urhund. Cousin to the wolf. When I skipped down the Wilhelmstrasse, when I ran up the steps of the Reichskanzlei, how old was I? Almost twenty. Then why did my heart beat like a schoolgirl's at the sight of the SS guards: tall, strong, in sable and silver? And why did I long to see the Führer's new dog? Because I told myself that she must be the descendant of one of Rin-Tin-Tin's lovable pups. That is how the mind of a child works: you sit on your father's lap, the beam of light flickers over your head, an animal in black and white saves the hero. You are saved, too. On those steps, in the cool Berlin evening: the last day of my life as a kleines Mädchen. No: the last day of my life.

A Chinese fire drill: that's what Jack called this morning's work on Sound Stage 1. I was not there to see it. I spent those hours here in the trailer, squirming into my bathing suit: one piece, with my hinterbacken coming out at the rear and a bullseye over my left breast. Jack rushed in, so enraged that he did not notice the target. "We've got no ending! Those goddamn Epstein twins! They want to shoot Strasser, but they don't have a line for anyone to say. It's a Chinese fire drill. Everybody running around in their bathrobes. With that bitch from the L.A. *Times* writing all of it down. And they don't even know which guy gets the girl!"

Then he did what we call a double take: "Who the hell do you think you are? Esther Williams? Never mind: come here."

"No, no. I have to go to the rally. So do you."

"What rally? What are you—?"

"Look." I pointed out of the grime-covered window. Abdul, he really did have a bathrobe on, was leading half the cast down Third Street. The crew was with them, and a fire truck with people waving on the fenders, along with an oversized stuffed rabbit. Bogart was there, and Bergman and Madeleine Lebeau, flank on flank with her director.

"Jesus H. Christ!" Jack shouted, bounding down the steps of the trailer and running after the crowd. "Hey, you! Curtiz! And the rest of you! Where the hell do you think you are going?"

I shuddered, but not because, in my scrap of a suit, I felt any chill. July. The valley. Over ninety degrees. It was Curtiz, the Hungarian. The first day I met him he kissed my hand, with the top of his head shining; then he put his own hand under the hem of my May Company outfit, the one with the zigzags and the little girl puffs at the sleeves. Naturlich! I knew his reputation. I tried to laugh. But my head whirled and the bones in my body seemed to collapse as if a puppeteer had dropped his strings; it was all I could do not to scream.

I did scream when his picture, *Doctor X*, played at the Mercedes-Palast. Joe-Joe had talked the studio into sending over the new two-tone negatives; it was the first time I had seen a film in anything but black and white. The corpses were like chalk in the moonlight, and so were their ribs where the Moon Killer had eaten away the flesh. The Berliners laughed at my high-pitched wail. Joe-Joe patted my knee. He patted my head.

"It's only a movie, Karelena. Light and shadows. Das ist nicht das Wahre."

"No, no! It's real! It's real! The blood is red!"

My dreams were in the Technicolor process as well. Joe-Joe tried to comfort me. He waved the bedsheet over my head: it was an angel, a white angel, carrying everything bad away. An impossible task. At the end the Moon Killer, on fire from kerosene, hurls to his death through the glass of a window. I saw the bright flames. I saw his melting face. Out loud I cried: *The poor man!* Over and over: *The poor man.* You see? What was bad was already inside me.

Yes, Frau Hopper, Hedda, was on the set. She saw all the craziness, the way she always does. Everything is in this morning's paper. She has also learned that next month, in August, Jack will travel to the USSR. She will get to the bottom of that, as well. Jack flashed his usual smile, all ten thousand teeth, when I told him that I would go with him. He does not know that Alex is already in Moscow or that I have no choice but, like the poisoned vine, to remain at his side.

One thing about this picture: it is in black and white. Adding color is like adding sound. Another invasion by the troops of reality. A further retreat by art. Now they are talking about stereoscopic images, because they cannot conceive of a world that is not in the round. What next? Smells? Touch? The taste of lips during a kiss? A camera on a tripod: a medium shot, a close-up, a little girl running with pigtails toward the lens. The rest must be in the imagination.

I looked for Blondi. I asked where she was. But he said never mind. He said to call him *Wolf*. Because *Adolf* meant *noble wolf*. And I thought it cute. *Wolf, Wolfie*. Like the way he ate his spaghetti. Dragging the pieces across his chin. For a moment everything was adorable. I was a goddess, Minerva, Aphrodite, with my arms over my head. I waited. I was aching. But Blondi did not come. The Wolf-Dog did not come. Nothing and no one could rescue me. Without a word, as if in a silent movie, I moved obediently above the pale body; like a squatting dog I performed for my master.

161

Hedda Hopper's Hollywood: July 1942, Los Angeles

Hollywood stars, who have set the fashion for the world in homes, motor cars, entertainment, and dress, are now being asked to deglamorize themselves for the duration. *Farewell to allure*, that's the new call, and *Hail to good sense*. Well, this gal who likes her nylon stockings and rubies on her hairpins objects! Really, do they think unless they make Roz Russell a dowdy dowager—as if such a thing were possible!—or the beautiful Ingrid Bergman some kind of frump, that American women will balk at necessary sacrifices? That paints a pretty dismal picture of American patriotism for our enemies to gloat over.

Speaking of Ingrid, I ran into the sexy Swede on the set of *Seas of Sand*—I should say *Casablanca*, since that is the new name for this Warners picture. If you want my opinion—and you know you'll get it anyway!—the old title was far more poetic. There she was on Sound Stage 1 clad in a stodgy suit with pockets that a kangaroo would have felt at home in and a schoolmarm's white collar. "Oh, Hedda," she declared. "I am so angry!" "I don't blame you, Ingrid, having to wear an outfit like that." "Oh, it's not my clothes, though of course they are not glamorous," she replied. "It's because no one will tell me my lines. How can I act when I do not know who I am supposed to be in love with—Rick or Victor?" She meant Humphrey Bogart or Paul Henreid, who were playing the men in her life. "I am supposed to be flying off in that plane, but I don't know whether it's with my husband or with my lover!"

That's when I noticed for the first time how the set had been transformed into an airport. The plane Ingrid mentioned was a cardboard cutout, complete with the Air France flying horse on its tail and a bunch of white-clothed mechanics—why, they were midgets, as cute as munchkins!—gathered around it. That's the magic of our business! In the pea soup that the fog machines were pumping out, it all looked so real. Incidentally, Paul was born Paul Georg Julius Freiherr von Ritter von Wassel-Waldingau. What that tongue twister means is that he comes from an aristocratic family, not at all like those of dubious descent who play so many parts in this Hungarian goulash of a picture.

"Look, Hedda. Just look at this!" The actress reached into one of her outsized pockets—you could get half the UCLA Bruins football team in there—and pulled out a handful of papers, all of them in different colors: brown and blue and salmon and pink and a bright magenta. "See? Each color has a different ending. As soon as I memorize one line, they come up with another. It's driving me crazy! Until they make up their minds, there's nothing for us to do but sit on our hands."

I took another look around the set. Those dwarfs were indeed dawdling under the fake wings of their DC-3. Over to one side, Bogie was playing chess with Conrad Veidt, who is the heavy in this rather run-of-the-mill drama. Art Edelson, who runs the cameras, was circling horse after horse on the Santa Anita form, while Hal Wallis paced back and forth with the steam coming out of his ears—and can you blame him at twelve thousand dollars an hour?

Just then I saw the pretty Madeleine Lebeau—her name means "the beautiful"—come out from behind the front end of a fancy German car. Mike Curtiz came out from around the back, adjusting his trousers and shouting, "Where is poodle? I asked for a poodle!" Ernie Glickman, the plump PA, said that there was no such thing in the script. Then Mike practically turned purple. "You dumdum. Big bas**** dumdum. I go nuts! Where is poodle?" Hal Wallis said, "For C*****'s sake, Glickman. Don't stand there: go get him the dog."

"Dog? What dog? Idiot! Headknuckle idiot! I want *poodle*! On the runway! Poodle of water! Mr. Rick! Mr. Renault! They must go splash-splash-splash when they take the walk."

Everyone laughed. But I was sad because it looked like the rumors about M. Dalio divorcing his little French poo—I mean filly—were true.

At that moment Jack Warner in his handsome Army Air Force uniform came striding through the Stage 1 door. Right away everybody pretended to be busy. The darling Lilliputians began hammering away at their aircraft; Claude Rains put on the kepi of a Vichy capitain; and Mike Curtiz cried out over the hubbub, "Anybody who has some talking to do, shut up!"

"You can't con me," Jack said. "I heard all of you laughing. What's the big joke? And why aren't you shooting? I heard you let that old bag of a gossip columnist for the *Times* on the set. You know the rules. No one except—Oh, *there* you are! Hedda, *darling*! Maybe you can let me know what's so d***** funny?"

But Ingrid spoke before I could get in a word. "It is the writers. We don't know the ending. How can I act if I don't know who I am in love with?"

"I knew it! Abdul! Go get the Epsteins. Abdul!" He meant my old pal, Abdul Maljan, who was nowhere to be found.

"What the f***?" Jack exclaimed. "Where is everybody?"

"I'll get him, J.L.," said Ernie. "I'll get the Epsteins, too."

At last your faithful correspondent was able to get a word in. "You don't need the writers, Jack. I can tell you right now that Joe Breen will never allow Ingrid to leave her husband to fly off with another man. And even if he did, I'd set up a howl. There's enough for young people to worry about without our industry corrupting their morals. There! You've got your ending. And I'm not even on your payroll!"

"Hmmm," said the vice president for production. "I do believe you are right."

"And while this old bag of a gossip columnist is at it," I continued, "I want a word with you about these costumes—"

But that's when Hal Wallis elbowed his way in. "Don't worry, J.L.," he said. "Everything's under control. The boys promised to give us the lines any minute, and we're going to shoot around them until then. We're just setting up the last scene now. Look—"

He pointed to where one of the grips had run up with a bucket of water and was spreading its contents onto the make-believe macadam of the runway. "Okay," he shouted. "Let's have some more fog! Plenty of it!"

He got what he asked for, though I couldn't help wondering how the weather in London had moved into the desert. I was just about to ask that very question when out of the mist came Julius J. and Philip G., the bald-domed Epstein twins. The moment I saw them I had to look away, because they were dressed in nothing but their bathrobes. Jack saw them, too.

"What's going on here? Did we wake you from your naps? No wonder you can't come up with the lines after Strasser is shot. How can the president fly me off to Moscow next month when no one knows how the picture ends? It's intolerable! It's, it's—disloyal!"

"Then why don't you ask Joe Stalin to finish it?" said Julie. Or maybe it was Phil.

"What?" I cried. "Moscow? What? What? What?"

"Ooops," said Jack Warner.

"You tell me. Tell me now!"

But the studio executive, hands on his hips, was glaring at the two writers. "G******! This time you sons of b****** have gone too far."

"What is it, Jack?"

"Did we forget to salute?"

"Salute? I don't want you to salute. I want you to come up with the lines you've been paid for. It's not too late to take you off this picture. If you don't have them in two minutes, *two minutes*, that's just what I'll do."

Wallis stepped between his boss and his writers. "Come on, Jack. You know you don't mean it. We can't do a thing without the boys."

"Oh, yeah? That's what you think. And don't call me *Jack*. There's a war on, in case you didn't notice. I'm a lieutenant colonel."

"Excuse me, Colonel. I only wanted to say this is no time for a court-martial. The boys will have an ending in just a minute."

"And one minute is all they have left. I'm looking at my watch. Well? I thought so. These bums don't have a clue about who says what to who."

"Not a clue?" echoed Julie. "What a terrible thing to say."

"Scandalous," said his brother.

"Perhaps libelous."

"You'll be lucky if we don't sue you for a statement like that."

"Yeah?" said the lieutenant colonel. He slapped his olive-colored trousers as if there were an invisible swagger stick in his hand. "Go ahead. Tell me. Tell everybody. I'm counting. *Forty-seven. Forty-six.* Er, er, *forty-five!*

Just then that portly PA, who, if he knew what was good for him, would Reach for a Lucky instead of a Sweet, came onto the set with the still-dashing Abdul Maljan in tow. *Heavens to Betsy!* That's what I said to myself, because he was wearing a bathrobe, too!

"What is this?" said Jack. "A pajama party?"

"Sorry, Chief. I was just—"

"Never mind, never mind," said Jack Warner. "I'm about to fire these two jokers. You don't think I'll do it? Just watch. *Eleven. Ten. Nine.* Hmmm: *Eight!*"

Julie looked up, Philip looked down. Then Philip looked up and Julie looked down. Both bit their lips.

"*Four. Three—*"

Off to one side Mike Curtiz had been busily rehearsing Major von Strasser for a gunshot scene. He was showing him how he wanted him to fall after he'd been hit. "Lunge!" he shouted. "Like this. *Lunge!*"

"Okay," said Julius Epstein.

"If you insist," said his brother Phil.

And before you knew it the entire company broke for lunch.

14 } SEAS OF SAND

Hedda Hopper's Hollywood: November 1942, Los Angeles

When Veronica Lake was in New York, she decided to make her first visit to an automat. As she was deciding between a ham sandwich and a piece of cake, a well-dressed older woman nudged her and said, "What's the matter with you youngsters—always trying to look like movie stars. You're a pretty girl. Why don't you just look like yourself?"

Here's a head-scratcher for you: some of our top studio brass have gone AWOL. Yes, I mean you, Daryl F. Zanuck. And you, too, Jack L. Warner. Where are you off to? No one has seen hide nor hair of you—and my friend Jack may have a plenty thick hide but awfully thin hair—for the last three weeks. I haven't laid eyes on the top Warners' exec since that first sunny Sunday in October. He was in his tennis whites and bragging to everyone how he'd just taken a set from Bill Tilden. Tell that to the marines! Well, maybe that's just what he is doing. Dollars to donuts, these fighting filmmakers are off on a secret mission on behalf of our country's armed forces. Where could it be? I've got a hunch, but I can't print it here without revealing state secrets. Here's a hint: Don't take your Luckys, boys; where you're going you'll need a camel!

Jack L. Warner: November 1942, Off the Coast of Morocco

"Wake up, Chief! It's 0400 hours."

Abdul. I don't say a word. If I open my mouth I'll lose my dinner. My stomach! It's flipping around like a flapjack. *Don't think about food!* Two weeks and I still can't keep down anything but these goddamn biscuits. Sea biscuits, ha ha! That's a good one. Oh! I get even sicker at the thought of that nag. Ten thousand bucks down the drain at the Hundred-Grander. And don't talk to me about the Match of the Century. I put a bundle on War Admiral at 1–5. And he lost by four lengths. *Seabiscuit!* They put up a statue of that dog at Santa Anita.

I wouldn't bet a nickel on this war admiral, either. Hewitt or Screwit or whatever his name is. Keeps chuckling whenever he sees me: *What ho, my hearty!* Who does he think he is, *Captain Blood?* ONCE AGAIN THE SEA ECHOES TO THE THUNDER OF HISTORY'S MOST DARING PIRATE! Two million gross.

"Chief! It's 0410. We go over the side in half an hour."

"Beat it, will ya? Or someone else is going over the side. And can't you speak English? What the hell time *is* it? What's going on?"

All of a sudden somebody else starts in, but he isn't speaking English, either. *Allô, Maroc. Allô, Maroc—*

"Hey, wait a minute! I know that voice. It's—"

> *Le Président des Etats Unis, M. Franklin Delano Roosevelt, s'est addressé cette nuit au peuple Française. Mes amis . . .*

"It's the president, Chief."

"I *know* it's the president. What's he saying? What's going on in the mezzanine?"

"He's telling the French that we're coming in peace, as friends, and that we want to fight the Germans together, and—wait a second, my French isn't all that hot—"

> *Vive La France Éternal!*

"Long live France. Do you know what that means? The invasion is on!"

"Invasion? What invasion?"

"The one you're here to photograph. The invasion of Casablanca!"

"*Casablanca!* Why didn't you say so? Zanuck, that son of a bitch, pulled every string in the book. He came over on a plane. He's probably already landed. Don't just stand there, you dumb Turkish towel. Where is my helmet? Where are my boots?"

George S. Patton, Jr.: November 1942, Off the Coast of Morocco

Woke at 0200, dressed, and went on deck. Fedala lights and lights at Casa burning, also lights on shore. Sea dead calm. No swell: God is with me on the ladder of destiny. At 0410 every ship began to broadcast Roosevelt's message. Too soon. If the enemy was sleeping before, they are wide awake now. *Mes amis. Mes amis.* Where did he get that God-awful French? At Groton? Too late to do anything about it, so Hewitt and all the others began to broadcast Ike's message, which basically came down to *don't fight your friends* and *switch your searchlights to vertical as a sign of welcome.*

The troops were given my letter when they woke this morning.

Soldiers:

You are to be congratulated because you have been chosen as the units of the United States Army best trained to take part in this great American venture.

It is not known whether the French African Army, composed of both white and colored troops, will contest our landing. It is regrettable to contemplate the necessity of fighting the gallant French, who are at heart sympathetic toward us, but all resistance by whomever offered must be destroyed.

The eyes of the world are watching us; the heart of America beats for us; God is with us. On our victory depends the freedom or slavery of the human race. We shall surely win.

In other words, Blood and Guts, speech number 32. But better than *Mes amis.*

At 0500 the first of our landing craft set out for the beaches at Fedala, and a few minutes later who should show up on deck but the Kike. Green around the gills. Phosphorescent, almost. Stuck his thumb in his eye, it looked like, when he tried to salute.

First I heard of him was right before sailing, when Hewitt and I reported to the president. "Come in, Skipper and Old Cavalryman, and give me the good news." Then he proceeded to lecture the admiral about how to moor a ship to keep it head to wind by a stern rudder. It's what he does with his yacht. And that was pretty much that, except I managed to get in my line that, "The admiral and I feel that we must get ashore regardless of cost, as the fate of the world hinges on our success." Naturally the admiral felt no such thing, but before he could say a word, the president answered, "Of course you must."

Then, just as we were leaving, he told me he arranged for a friend of his, a lieutenant colonel, to cover Operation Torch for the Signal Corps, and would I keep an eye on him as he had never been in combat before. With that we shook hands and said our familiars. A great politician is not of necessity a great military leader.

And who did this lieutenant colonel turn out to be? Our Kike, which is to say a man who is not prepared to die for his country—or for any other reason.

"Where is your Bell & Howell?" I asked him.

"Yell and Howl? To scare the Frogs?" That's his idea of a joke.

"You've got a camera, soldier. That's what you're here to shoot. Lord knows it's not a gun."

"Abdul," this son of Abraham shouted to his orderly. "You forgot the camera. Go back and get it."

Just then—it was 0530—a searchlight on shore went vertical. "Goddamn it to hell! The signal! They're not going to let us have our fight."

Jack L. Warner: November 1942, Off the Coast of Morocco

Up on deck. Either the boat is rocking or I am. Patton reminds me to get my Bull—and How! I haven't been behind a camera for thirty years, not since Sam and I made *Raiders on the Mexican Border*. WE PUT THE DARING IN DERRING DO! And if you want to know the truth, it was me, not Griffith, who invented the close-up: not on Dot Farley's face but on her boobs. We zeroed right in after Pancho Villa with a fake moustache and a shoeshine tan ripped off half her blouse and hauled her up on top of his rented horse.

> Now, Señorita, you will come with me to my
> hacienda.

Harry made us cut the footage, which in my opinion was a terrible mistake and solely responsible for turning a sensational box-office hit into a turkey. Now we're stuck with Joe Breen, who wouldn't let Bergman into bed with Bogart, though even a two-year-old would know they were schtupping all night. So we shot a searchlight going left and going right. That's your meshuganah highbrow art!

"Look! Will you look at that?"

The general, he's pointing toward the Moroccan coast, where a searchlight—what a coincidence, huh? It could be the same one we showed in *Casablanca*—was now aiming down toward the beaches.

"We're going to get our fight after all!"

Just then all hell breaks loose, so I hit the deck, and from down there I see red sparks flying through the air, and in spite of the fact I haven't set foot in schul since I was kicked out for pulling the rabbi's nose, I start to shout, "Sh'ma Yisrael!" and cross myself to boot. Now Abdul comes up with the camera and wants to know what I am doing lying flat on my back, and I say, "Some schmuck dropped a banana peel." Then I get up just in time to see that all those sparks are coming from the boats in our fleet and going in the direction of that far-off searchlight, which—presto—goes out.

"Got the son of a bitch!" says Patton.

Now the sun is starting to come up, and I can see the white wake of the landing boats pushing through the water, and the geysers shooting up all around them, and the flashing of the guns on the ships and on the shore, and I've got my thumbs in my ears it's so loud, and our ship—what's it called? Oh, yeah, the *Augusta*—is zigging and zagging, which isn't doing my kishkes any good, especially when I see Old Faithful erupt on one side of us and we get a good spritzing on the other, and some planes from our carrier are zooming about ten feet over our heads to attack this big Frog battleship in the harbor; it's like the scenes with the Spanish Armada in the *The Sea Hawk*, with Flynn playing the same role as ever, and the cannons going off and hand-to-hand fighting, NEVER BEFORE SO MANY GIANT THRILLS IN ONE PICTURE. Yeah, never before in one picture, and I hope never again, so many giant dollars, one point seven million, you could build two of these *Aghastas* for that kind of money; but thank you, Jesus, we ended up netting more than two, because we had a happy ending with Flynn getting the girl. Really, there's only one plot when you come right down to it, even *Hamlet* by—wait! Don't tell me! Shakespeare! Boy meets girl, boy loses girl, boy gets girl: then why did those Epstein wise-acres change the *Casablanca* script so that the boy loses the girl again and then walks off with Rains, which is more than a little fruity if you ask me? We can't have that, no, no, no—so we'll release the picture in a couple of weeks on Thanksgiving and that way it will be eligible for an Academy Award, though my personal favorite this year is *Murder in the Big House*, IT'S THE CRIME OF YOUR LIFE!, with

Van Johnson over the titles, speaking of fruits. Then we'll withdraw the Bogart picture and reshoot the ending, with the footage from this very invasion, maybe shot by this same Bowl of Chow—don't mention food to me! Sometimes, when I think of how all this came together—I mean how I thought up the name of the picture, and the timing, and the talk with Roosevelt and billiards with the Russians, and now this searchlight and the army landing right on cue: well, I think okay, maybe Somebody Up There is looking out for this Yid from Youngstown, even if I did give a good yank on that rabbi's beard and—

"Hey! Hold on! What's going on? You can't do that!" The reason I start yelling is I see where the city of Casablanca was one minute white in the light of dawn and now the next minute I can't see it at all because of clouds of smoke and leaping flames, with the airplanes going in and out of the clouds and the flashing guns from that Frenchie warship. I don't think with all the boom-booming Patton heard a word I was saying, so I grab his arm and pull him closer and shout, "The city! Don't hit the city! What a tragedy!"

"Don't worry, Leonard—" For some reason he likes to use my middle name, or sometimes he calls me Jacob. "That's just the harbor. We've got to put the *Jean Bart* and those other ships out of action."

And no sooner do the words come from his mouth than those same boats come steaming out of the harbor—who said Cheese-Eaters can't fight? With all their guns blazing and the big battleship, what did he call it—a Bean Fart?—is shooting, too, and the next thing I know Abdul is yelling, "Watch out, Chief! Duck!" and I see something coming right at us, well: not the thing itself, but something screwy in the sky, like what you get when you're about to experience a migraine, or maybe, in winter, the way the empty space above a radiator seems to go all wavy. It's a disturbance in the air, and then I hear a screaming, real high pitched, like Stanwyck has made a sort of a specialty, and all of a sudden there is a thump I can't compare to anything, and half the Atlantic Ocean shoots sky-high and our ship—now it seems no bigger than a canoe some schmendrick has stood up in—gives a shudder and a lurch, and something like a fist slams into my chest and now it's curtains for the son of Pearl Leah Eichelbaum, *Mama! Mama!*, yep, he's a goner.

"I'm hit, boys!"

"Chief! Oh, Chief!" That's Abdul.

"Where? Where?" Patton wants to know.

"In the heart! Right in the heart!" though some people claim I don't have one. The ship, still shaking, rights itself, but I go down, first on one knee, then on both, then backward on my ass. I am cold, and getting colder. Oooooo, and now it's dark.

That song. I hear it. The boy soprano. More beautiful than the voice of any girl.

Of days gone by, Love, to me so dear

Oh! Colder! Colder! Darker! Yes, I know the sun is rising. For me, it is the black of night. California: that's where the moon is up. Shining on the Home of Peace. *Take my body there.* My lips form the words but not a sound comes out. *But not too close to Laemmle!* Weeping? Why are these people weeping? For me? Tears for me? Yes, the middle of the night: in Burbank. At the studio. "Schmucks! Turn off the fucking lights!"

"Don't talk, Chief."

"Lay back. Lay still." That's the general. "The medics are on their way." But it's too late. My blood is seeping out. It's all over my chest. It covers my clothing. It's oozing through my fingers. Warm, sticky, and—I open my eyes to take one last look: yellow. *Yellow?*

G. S. P., Jr.: *November 1942, Off the Coast of Morocco*

Off to starboard the *Mississippi* batteries had been shelling the *Jean Bart* for about thirty minutes when six enemy destroyers came out of Casa at 0715. A hell of a racket with French bombers going after our transports and our ships opening up on the destroyers and a light cruiser that came out to join them and they throwing whatever they had at us, at ranges from 18,000 to 27,000 yards.

I was on the main deck, just back of the number two turret, when two huge shells from that damned stubborn battleship bracketed us. One of them landed so close that it splashed me from head to toe and made the whole ship tremble. The Kike wasn't so lucky. He went down with a piece of shrapnel in his chest—or so I thought with him yelling *Mama! Mama!* and *They got me in the heart!* Anyone would have thought he was hit in the head from the way he kept babbling about the moon and singing snatches from old barbershop quartets and telling us that Edison didn't need the money and would we turn out the goddamned lights.

The medic came up and burst out laughing. It turns out he hadn't been hit at all and what he thought was blood was the yellow dye the French gunners used for spotting their shells. It was the right color for this Nickel Nose. I remembered the old West Point story of how Napoleon went into battle wearing a red tunic in order to hide his wounds. I imagine this specimen was wearing brown drawers.

"Stand up, soldier!" I told him. "On your feet!"

"Close," he said, with a laugh, "but no seagull."

"Get moving! We're going over the side."

I pointed to where the Higgins boat, with all my gear stowed, was hanging on davits against the hull. "Take hold of that netting and climb aboard." At that he practically jumped into the arms of his swarthy Turk.

"What? In that little rowboat? You're kidding, right?"

"It isn't a joke, Colonel. It's an order."

"*Lieutenant* colonel. But I can't get into that boat. I've got a ringing in my ears. And spots in front of my eyes. Besides, I've got a phobia about water. I never take a bath. I don't even drink the stuff: fish fuck in it. Hey! Let go, will ya?"

I took him by the collar and yanked him away from his orderly, but he grabbed hold of a stanchion, dug in his heels, and started calling on his god and Abraham and Isaac to save him. Then up comes Hewitt, who gives a belly laugh at the sight of the Kike, with all of his shirtfront covered with yellow paint.

"Ahoy, there, Colonel: What did you have for breakfast? Scrambled eggs?"

Ikey-Mo gave a groan. "More like General Custard."

The admiral turned to me. "Good news, George. French resistance has collapsed at Pte. Pescade and at Beer and Beer Red Beaches. And we're about to launch an attack on the Casbah."

"*The Casbah?*" echoed the sheenie.

"Yes. I doubt we'll have much of a fight there. The French have no stomach for it. I think by midafternoon or a bit later General Juin will raise the white flag over all of Algiers."

"*Algiers?*"

"That's right, matey!" And here the admiral gave the cringing Kike a slap on the back. "And your pal Zanuck is filming every minute of it. They say he's right in the middle of the action. He'll bring home a medal for valor."

"*Filming! Algiers!* So that's his game!"

In the blink of an eye the Jew snatched his camera from the arms of the Turk and took two bounding steps toward the rail. "Come on, men! Don't you know there's a war on? We don't have a moment to lose. Action! Action! Zanuck's making a sequel!"

Jack L. Warner: November 1942, Off the Shores of Morocco

This is our new closing scene. Terrific! Colossal! And I'm getting every bit on film. The rest are all huddled down: Abdul behind the big ramp in the front, next to Meeks—good name for him—the General's colored servant. Everyone else, the armed guards and a couple of navy big shots are squatting on their butts; they must be rear admirals. Who can blame them? Bullets are buzzing, shells are—whoops! A big one just landed, maybe ten feet away. The wave swamps half our boat. But I stand tall at my spot, one hand on the railing, the other with my Bail and Now! What the hell: I figure I kicked the bucket back on the ship. I even had a kind of vision: Down I go, next to Ben, next to Pearl, in the ground. Hello there, my dear Sam! Harry shedding crocodile tears. Ann shedding real ones. Well, maybe. So now everything else is gravy. Hmmm. What about my little Heinie? A good name for her: that's how she likes it. What is she shedding? Her clothes? How many hours, how many days, without her? Or anyone! Better think about how tonight I'm going to climb in bed with a little French filly. *Ooooo, monsieur, mon Dieu! Mon Dieu! C'est formidable!*

I lean out. I see we are getting close to shore. Fedala, they call it. Smoke. Lots of smoke. Fire. Men running. Men lying down. Holy crap! Are they dead? But they won't get yours truly! It's this yellow paint. Maybe it's got magical powers. Bullets whistle and whine. They bounce off me. I've got nine lives. *Two minutes!* someone shouts. Two minutes before we hit the beach. Okay: music up. Faces of the soldiers. Cut to waving flag. Roll credits: Jack L. Warner, Camera. Live Footage. Academy Award. For courage under fire: Medal of Honor. Don't believe it? I've got witnesses!

A thud. The ramp goes down. Welcome to Africa. We all jump out and, son of a bitch, I'm up to my tits in water. Half the Atlantic Ocean pours into my pants. "Sandbar!" somebody shouts. Everyone starts to wade forward, except for old Two Stars, who's yelling, "Get back here. You! And, yes, you! On the double! Put your shoulders into it! You, too, Jacob Leonard! Okay, everybody: heave ho!" And our boat breaks free. We push it forward, we pull on it, too; but there's something blocking our way. A reef or something. Uh-oh. Uh-oh. It's not a reef. It's not a sandbar. It's four, it's five—"Six of them, sir," Meeks reports. Six dead soldiers are floating together. No blood. No wounds. "Drowned," says one of the admirals. "Pack's too heavy." They are all in a bunch. Practically holding hands. The skin on their faces: it's blue. To tell you the truth, I'm pretty blue myself.

"Gee, General, sir, your majesty: Do you think maybe we ought to call it a day?"

He pays no attention. He's getting our crew to lug the poor guys up the ramp and into the boat. We get back in, too. Somebody starts the engine. We go forward, nobody saying a word, not even me, until with a bump we land at—hats off! Fedora.

What a hullabaloo! Guns going off and everything on fire and people running in one direction and then the other, smoke everywhere; it's like the opening night of *Hellzapoppin'*. We start to tear up the beach, but all of a sudden a bunch of schwartzers appear on a ridge in front of us, and they've got swords and horses and funny hats; it's like a negative print of a Shriners' parade, except all of a sudden they jump down from their horses, take aim at our position, and start shooting. "Hey!" I yell. "I give to the NAACP!" A soldier right next to me goes down. So does another one close enough to touch. Down goes somebody else, squirting like from a hose. Blood!

I stand there in a daze. Everything is slowing down, like action at forty-eight frames per second, and all the noise of guns and human screaming goes far away and then stops completely, as if this really were a silent film, like our *Peril of the Plains*, when the West was wild and the girls even wilder, and where we hired the Missouri National Guard to pick off Indians like fish in a barrel, except that, holy shit!, this time the Indians are shooting at me!

"Get down, you damned fool!" That is the general, who yanks me to the ground, where the bullets are hitting close enough to kick sand in my face like the tough guy in the Charles Atlas ads. Holy mackerel! They're coming right at me!

Just then, with my life hanging in the balance, I get a kind of brainstorm. Why did my old pal, Franklin D., send me off to Moscow in a plane that could have been shot down any minute by the Mess of Shits? Why did he want me inside the Kremlin just when the Germans were going to bomb it? And why did he send me on this cockamamie mission to get bombarded by half the French Navy and my head shot off by this bunch of tar babies? Because I had the goods on him, that's why. He wants me out of the way! So I don't spill the beans about—what was it called? Operation Z? What a sap you are, J. W. We even made a movie where the blackmailer at the end goes over a balcony. *The Keyhole.* WAS HIS LOVE SINCERE? OR WAS IT PART OF HIS GAME? To think I voted three times for that son of a bitch!

Boom! Boom! Boom! It's a cannonade. It's coming from our ships. Already the shells are whistling over our heads and the big ridge above us is going through the roof. *Boom! Boom! Boom!* So much for those African Cheese-Eaters who had us pinned down. We can hear the neighing of their horses and the screams of the riders. A fez, complete with tassel, comes flying through the air and wobbles down beside me. The Shriners are racing away to their shrine.

"Up! Up on your feet! Goddammit! Get up and go after them!" That's General P. He's kicking at one soldier and hauling up another by the back of his shirt. "Attack! Attack! Come on you, sons of bitches! Attack!"

We all run up to what's left of the hill. But there's no one to shoot at. Only the dead, the wounded, and a single horse that manages to lift up its head. The rest are galloping off well out of range.

I look around. I suddenly realize I haven't seen Abdul. Not since we reached land. My heart starts to beat fast. If you want to know the truth, this is on earth my only friend. I start to go back toward the water. Could he be this corpse? Could he be that one?

All of a sudden the beach is full of Arabs, who have come up out of nowhere and are wandering around among the stranded boats and the burning equipment. They pluck up whatever they can and hide it in their robes. "Bon bons?" That's what they keep saying. "You give me bon bons?" It's quiet now. I guess this is a victory. One old guy selling pistachio nuts comes up to me. "Jew? Jewish army?" Is it that obvious? Even with my dapper moustache? Then I see he is pointing at one of our tanks. At the star on the turret. "That's right," I tell him. "The Jews have landed. You don't have a chance."

G. S. P., Jr.: November 1942, Fedala

After getting stuck on a sandbar, and pulling some drowned men into our craft, we hit the beach at 1320. Quite a fight was going on, with Spahis in front of us and planes overhead. A bombardment from the *Massachusetts* and the *Augusta* scattered the foe. Then no difficulty making our way into Fedala. All the French soldiers we encountered except the marines saluted and grinned. Inspected the port and the town and put on mixed military police: half American, half French. Will this be a cake walk? No: I can hear the gun duel still going on between our ships and the defenses at Casablanca. They've got plenty of fight left in them.

Take what blessings we can. A clean bed in the Hotel Miramar. No water in the pipes and no light. Cheese and fish to eat and champagne to drink. The Kike is sleeping in the room vacated by the head of the German Armistice Commission. The first revenge of the Jews in a war they believe we are fighting for them. If they think I'm about to restore the rights of their people in Morocco or give them back their property, they've got another think coming. The Jews won't be voting in any elections, and they won't be practicing law or medicine or any other profession in numbers beyond their percentage in the North African population. It's for their own good. Thus they will avoid the understandable resentment they faced in Germany. Hell, we ought to arrange things that way in our country.

Well, let this member of the tribe have his celebration now, which is what he is doing. His bedsprings have been singing Hallelujah all night long.

God has been good to me on this day.

NOVEMBER 1942, FEDALA

Harder fight today. More strafing on the beach. On the whole our men are poor. No drive. French troops willing to give up, but the navy is a different story. Their sailors have no ships left, but they've given them five cartridges each and they are causing mischief on the skirmish lines. Beach as chaotic as ever. Half the landing craft crippled or sunk to the bottom. Shore parties without forklifts, pallet rope, torches. Guns arriving without sights and no ammunition and no gunners. Medical supplies stuck on ships. No vehicles to remove the dead. I shot an Arab who was going through the pockets of a soldier. I'm paying others a cigarette an hour to be our stevedores, but this just gives them a chance to steal more.

Eighty percent of my job is to raise morale: flay the idle, rebuke the incompetent, and drive the timid. In other words, kick their asses, which I did. Sent out the 3rd Infantry to take Casablanca, but no sooner had they begun to push south than they had to stop for lack of supplies. The motor pool of the 15th Infantry Regiment has got nothing but a bunch of donkeys, a couple of camels, and five jeeps. The fourth battalion's attack has been called off. No munitions. No transport. We'll make an all-out assault on Casa tomorrow, and we'll conquer, though the costs on both sides will be great.

Still, the Christian in me calls out with a small voice. So I am sending a message to the sultan, who on paper is the ruler of this place. Doubt it will do any good. From the same Christian motives I dispatched Wilbur after dark with a white flag on his jeep and a black man, Meeks, at the wheel. He'll try to get through to the Admiralty, which is the fountainhead of all the opposition. Also doubt that will succeed, and if I am honest with myself I'd admit I don't want it to. I would rather beat them than barter.

Tomorrow will be a better day. And I look forward to a better night. No bedsprings. I have been told the Kike jumped aboard Wilbur's jeep. I suppose he wants to film the capitulation of the French.

Again God has been good.

Jack L. Warner: November 1942, Morocco

Where the hell is Marie Antoinette? It's already two in the morning! Can it be she isn't coming back for more? Last night she ate a lot more than cake. I'm no monk! I made up for lost time. Every which way, including backward—which has become the specialty of the house. Cherchez la femme! So what if Marie's a little sore. So am I. Say la guerre! What's that? Somebody is starting up an engine. Right below my window. It's a jeep, Patton's jeep, with the two stars. Isn't that Meeks behind the wheel? It is! And a couple colonels in the back.

Hey! Let me in on that! There's only one place they're going this time of night. I grab my Boil and Towel and half-dressed as I am run down the steps and out the Miramar's front door. They are already moving. "Room for one more?" I shout. But they only speed up and are about to drive right by me when one of the guys in back grabs Meeks by the shoulder. "Stop!" And the jeep stops. "It's a historic moment. We ought to have it recorded." Before the words are out, I'm aboard.

"Good thinking, Colonel," I yell over the roar of the engine. "As a matter of fact, we made this picture before. *Open Your Eyes.* A FLAMING DRAMATIC THUNDERBOLT OF YOUTH DISILLUSIONED AND LOVE BETRAYED! Sodom and Gonorrhea, ha, ha, ha! The evils of the brothel. Say, can any of you boys lend me a jimmy hat? You can't be too careful. I already found out these French girls are everything they're cracked up to be. Croissant my heart! By the way, have any of you ever had a German? I mean, before the war? Did you notice anything funny? Do they all do it backward? We made this *Open Your Eyes* picture under the supervision of the Public Health Service. In 1917. I was in the Signal Corps then, just like now. Funny about history. How everything seems to come back around. One of those Marx Brothers, maybe Groucho, said the first time things happen it's tragedy and the next time it's farce. But what if it's farce to start with? That's a pretty deep thought. I'm going to write a book and—"

"Arretez!"

Meeks jams on the brakes. We come to a swerving stop in front of a red-and-white striped barricade that lies across the road. All of a sudden we are surrounded by Frogs. They're yelling and parlez-vousing and waving their arms. Wilbur, behind me, says, "How's your French, Colonel Gay?"

"Not so great."

One of the Frenchies comes walking up to our jeep. "I'll handle it," I say, and begin to exercise my vocabulary. "À la carte! Bon voyage! Crème brûlée!"

"Quoi?"

Now he's pointing his gun in my direction.

"Mal de mer!"

Oh, shit. He's cocking it, too. In a panic I go back to my casting session with Lebeau, who we put in the film to play Bogart's mistress. Dimples. Curls. Double-breasted. "Monsieur!" I say. "Voulay voos cuchay aveck Moy?"

Instantly, the whole Frog squadron comes running up on the double.

"With your permission, Colonel," says Meeks, a little cheekily if you ask me.

"Carry on, Sergeant. That's what you're here for."

With that, out comes a stream of what I guess is the language of Lafayette, which gives me a start. It's like hearing a doberman pinscher give the Gettysburg Address. No offense.

"Ça va?" says he at the end of his speech.

"D'accord!" says one of the Frenchmen.

"Bonne chance!" says another.

Up goes the barricade and off we go again, bouncing down the road. It's pitch black and when I look up I see the stars are out by the shovelful. There's my pal, the moon. That means it's lunchtime in Burbank. Those fucking Epsteins are just showing up. I'll fix them.

After maybe another ten minutes, blackout or no blackout, we start to see what have to be the lights of an enormous city.

"There's Casablanca," says this guy, Wilbur.

"*Casablanca?*" I say. "We're going to Casablanca? That's where they've got the Bousbir! Everybody knows about that joint. I heard they've got women there who can rotate their breasts counterclockwise! Drive on, James!"

But that's when Gay taps Meeks on the shoulder and yells for him to pull over. We sit at the side of the road, with the engine tick-ticking; now first Gay and then Wilbur and then Sergeant Meeks get out.

"Cold feet?" I ask, just a tad worried.

"Come on yourself, Warner. We want to be dignified with the French. Let's do our business now."

Business? Then I see, up against a sand dune, the three of them taking a leak.

"Good idea," I say. "You boys are no amateurs."

I jump down, pull out Mr. J, and send forth a stream of my own. Always a pleasure.

"Say," that's me, turning to Meeks and keeping my eyes straight ahead. "What did you say to those Frogs? Whatever it was, why, they practically saluted."

"He told them the truth." That's Wilbur, standing to my left. "That we're on our way to the Admiralty."

"*The Admiralty*! Ha! Ha! Ha! What a name for it. It's where the sailors go, huh? I once knew a place in Pittsburgh called The Pipe Fitters. That's because—"

"What's so funny, Warner? I'm talking about the headquarters of Admiral Michelier."

"*Admiral*? I get it. What's she—this Michelle—call her girls? *Boat Swains*? Ha! Ha! Ha! *First Pretty Officers*? Do we have to dress up in sailor suits? What a drag! Pun intended."

"You'd better stop playing the clown, soldier. This is a serious mission. Admiral Michelier commands the entire French Fleet and for all intents and purposes is the head of the armed resistance. If we can't persuade him to surrender, there's going to be tremendous bloodshed. Not on our side. On theirs. I know George. He'll level the town. By sea and air. In eight more hours there won't be any Casablanca."

"*What?*" And just like that I drench my shoes. "No more Casablanca? There has to be a Casablanca! We don't open until January!"

"Well, of course, we want to save the city, too. That's why—wait! Warner! Where are you going?"

But I'm already racing across the desert, with my camera banging against my ribs. Here's the jeep. The engine is on. The lights are on. I step on the gas. Off I go, kicking up a sandstorm behind me. I yank the wheel to the left, make a half circle, and I'm back on the road, heading the way we came. I'm going twice the speed as before, so in only five minutes I see the barricade and the sentries: they are waving their arms and yelling, "Arretez! Arretez!"

I air it out, all right. I mean, I floor it and the jeep leaps forward and goes through the barricade as if it were made of peppermint sticks.

Now what? A fork in the road. To the left? No, no: to the right. Wait a second. The ocean's on the left. Fedala, and our army, are on the ocean. Ergo, as the fancy pants like to say: hold on, is it really on the left? What to do? Let's go right. I'm all turned around. I've always had a lousy sense of direction. Once I got lost on my own lot. In broad daylight. I mean, all those buildings look exactly alike. What was I supposed to do, go up to some phony pirate and ask, "Where the fuck is Sound Stage 2?" Where's Abdul? Poor Abdul. Missing in action. How I need him now!

Uh-oh, another fork. Which way? Eenie, meenie, miney, moe: catch a—what's that up ahead? It *is* one! A whole bunch of oversized boogers!

On horses! And with guns! I turn off the headlights. I turn off the motor. I sit there, huddled over, hoping they didn't notice anything. No such luck. I see the flash of their teeth, the whites of their eyes. Mother of God! Here they come! One of them, two of them, all of them. I'm surrounded!

"Well, if it isn't the Ink Spots! Ha! Ha! Ha!

If I didn't care—dum, de dum—more
　　　More than words can say
If I didn't care—doodle, de, do—
　　　　　　would I feel this way?"

One of the giants turns a flashlight on me. Another one leans down from his horse.

"You are the famed General Patton?"

But before I can tell them I'm not, they all burst out laughing. What's so funny? Okay, okay. So my fly is open.

"Dear General, you must now come with us."

And so I must. Wait till I tell this one at that hotshot writers' table. Jack L. Warner: a prisoner of war!

G. S. P., Jr.: *November 1942, Fedala*

Today has been bad. No real progress to report, except that the Shermans are moving up from Safi and are nearing the southern suburbs of Casa. Here, the logistical nightmare continues on the beach. French forces either welcome us with smiles and salutes, or fight fiercely and gallantly, especially the navy. *Jean Bart*, silenced for a time, has now resumed firing. My hat's off to them. As for our men, and their *esprit de guerre*, I put it back on again. Suppose I should not have expected more from troops this green. Speech 32 wasted on them. Well, they'll learn how to be soldiers or they'll die.

This afternoon a galling telegram from Ike. He talks of great success all across the front, except in our sector.

Dear Georgie,
　　Algiers has been ours for two days. Oran defense crumbling rapidly. The only tough nut left is in your hands. Crack it open quickly. I want no more delays in Casablanca.

He won't have to wait long. I've prepared an all-out assault by the navy. At this hour the *Augusta*, the *New York*, and the *Cleveland* have arrived at their designated fire support positions, along with a number of destroyers. The *Ranger* is ready to launch her planes. I have sent an ultimatum to the sultan and to Admiral Michelier. They know I shall give the order to attack at 0700. If they don't surrender, there won't be a Casablanca by 0730. I do not intend to spare anything or anyone. The nut must be cracked.

We've received the admiral's response already. I sent Wilbur into the city with no more than a jeep and a white flag. Brave man. Fine Point man. Meeks was the driver. Gay went, too. They went right through the French barricades. In town, most of the population cheered them on. They met Michelier at the Admiralty and offered him the choice of peace or getting the hell knocked out of them. Wilbur reports that at that very instant that cussed *Jean Bart* let go with a tremendous salvo. "Voilà votre réponse," said the admiral. A brave man, too. He's determined to slug it out with us. No word yet from the sultan.

Meeks told me how the Kike hopped in with them. It seems he wanted to film the surrender. I wouldn't have thought he had it in him. At the last minute, as they were approaching the city, he turned tail and took off in the jeep, so that Wilbur and the others had to enter the town in a commandeered Citroën sedan. I sent out a search party this morning. They found the jeep, but no sign of the man. Officially he's AWOL, though I have no doubt he's a deserter. I should have expected as much from this specimen of the Hebrew race. I've never known a Jew to be a good soldier, and I do not exempt from this stricture General Clark. Always pushing into the spotlight. Well, hell, so do I. We'll hunt down our sheeny, and when we find him we won't waste time or money on a court-martial. I shall be more than happy to shoot him like a dog.

This morning we shall have victory, either by peaceful means or the terrible swift sword. God favors the bold; victory is to the audacious.

15 } GOOD PICTURE-MAKING, TAKE THREE *Sucker Punch*

KK: *July 1942, Los Angeles*

I left the trailer in my bathing suit. Jack and the rest of the company who had poured out of Sound Stage 1 had already moved past the London Street and were heading toward Lot H. What madness! Instead of shooting the end of the picture, they were rushing off to a rally with cartoon characters and fire trucks. American Schlamperei! In our Alexander Engelsing productions there were hardly any multiple takes; and when he was in front of the camera, never more than one. Oh: except for *Die Umwege der Shönoen Karl.* I had to run in and out of those ice-cold waves. You can see, if you look, the goosebumps on my skin. That was because they wanted the transparent cloth to reveal, over and over, the body of the sixteen-year-old girl.

Alex! Dear Onkel Engel! Are you my enemy now?

I trotted down 3rd Street, past the facades meant to look like New York. Wasn't I the maddest one of all? Helping to raise money so that the bombs will fall faster on the actual buildings of Berlin? On the head of my own mother, perhaps? Or on my father, for that matter. The Weissensee Cemetery is not immune from the RAF.

Jack sent a huge wreath to the funeral, red flowers and white flowers. In a horseshoe shape, as if poor Joe-Joe had won an important race. No one came from the studio, not even his old colleagues from the Berlin office. Fear, of course. I was frightened, too: the mosses, the ivy, the giant trees that blocked the rays of the sun. The leaning black tombstones. No one came from the city of Cincinnati, either. The only person there, except for my mother and Onkel Alex and myself, was a stout, red-faced man with a bowler hat. He winked at me, then with his right hand made the motion of pushing an invisible pool cue through the crook of a left-hand finger. It was the manager of Zylinderhut Billard. It is not so easy in this world to tell what is good in people from what is bad. What I did, at the funeral of my father, was wink back.

And the day after? I begged Hannelore to take me to the Gloria Palast, where *Twenty Million Sweethearts* was still playing. When she refused, I stole money from her bag and saw it myself.

All my life I've waited for an angel.

I was herzlos. Unfeeling. I didn't wonder whether I was sitting in Joe-Joe's seat. What mattered was that Dick Powell was singing to me.

Hannelore did not want me to go to India, either. She said that if I went I should not come back. She meant to the new Germany. But I went. I rode on an elephant's back. I saw tigers and women dancing in the temples and cobras coming out of baskets, swaying. I dipped a toe in the Ganges. How could I not come back? To our shining Führer and the Reich, that I knew would last a thousand years. I would star in an industry that was disciplined, precise, and I was already falling in love with Alex Engelsing, and even the Reichsminister für Voksaufklärung und Propaganda would notice me and make me a star.

Meine Mutter! What a fight we had! But afterward she brought me my Schokokuss, just like every other night. The kind with the foam in the center. Of course everything comes from her. The hair, blond. The classic nose, the classic brow, a swan's neck, this bow in the lip. Like a goddess, they said. Minerva. Nothing from Joe-Joe. A Schnauze like an elk. Why don't they put those Jews in a zoo? Poor man: from him these teeth.

The rally was what Americans call a three-ring circus: no tigers, no elephants, but actresses selling kisses and autographs and their old silk stockings. In my tank suit, with my Arsch hanging out, I pushed my way through the crowd to the edge of the platform. I picked up my placards. A bell rang and rang again. I saw Jack up above me. He was waving his arms and yelling for everybody to get off the lot and get back to work. No one listened, so he yelled for the bell to ring again.

Clang. Clang. Clang.

I looked around to see who had followed Jack's order. There, with his moon face and his little hammer, was the actor Lorre. He, too, had given me nightmares when I was nine years old. *M.* He would whistle his little song for me. I was the one he would give the balloon. I would follow him with my bouncing ball. But now the sight of the squat, pudgy man only made me laugh. I was creating my own horror film. The bombs falling onto the graves of Weissensee. The earth flying into the air. The tombstones tottering, including the one we see, in close up,

Joseph Abraham Kauffman

Now in my mind the bleached skeleton climbs out of the ground and with the clatter of its rib bones and arm bones and the long bones in its legs begins to dance in front of Jack L. Warner. *What the hell?* says its old boss. *What the fuck do you think you are doing? Get back to work!* But the skeleton puts one arm around Jack's waist and another around his neck. *But J.L., I said I'd do anything. I said I'd sweep the writers' bungalow. The bottom of the ladder, right? The bottom of the barrel. And you said—may I quote you—"Where did you get the idea that we had any openings?"* And of course Jack screams as the skeleton of my father pulls him inch by inch into the blackness of the tomb.

The bell rang again. The Warner Bros. Studio was about to discover how its new picture would end.

The Terrible Turk: July 1942, Burbank

So we all poured out of Sound Stage 1 for lunch—except we didn't head for the commissary; instead, Hedda and I and everyone else started walking down Third Street toward the far side of the studio. As we moved forward, people came pouring out of Stage 5 and Stage 10. An old fire truck, with firemen clinging to the sides, drove from its station and rolled along with the crowd, ringing its bell. Pretty soon the street was filled, mostly with actors and actresses: you could see them in their evening gowns and tiaras and Indian headdresses; miners tramped along with lamps on their heads and the pilots had helmets and goggles on theirs.

After ten minutes or so, and from up ahead, past the London and the New York Streets, we could hear music and shouting and singing. Hedda grabbed my arm. "What's going on? Tell me, Abby! Are they making a picture? What's that music? What are they singing?"

We've got a job to do
So let's all see it through
And very soon there's bound to be
A V for Victory!

We came round the corner and could clearly see, standing at the back of the open Lot H, the chorus of grips and gaffers and construction men.

"Oh, my goodness gracious!" said Hedda at the sight of what must have been a thousand people. "It's a war-bond rally!"

And so it was, though it seemed more like a carnival to me. Over on one side Rita Hayworth was selling kisses, and on the other Harpo was playing his harp. Jimmy Cagney and Francis Langford were doing the "Over There" number from *Yankee Doodle Dandy*, and mobs of people were shouting out bids for Betty Grable's stockings and Jack Benny's violin. Signs were everywhere:

If you can't GO across
COME across!

You buy 'em
We'll fly 'em!

You've got a date with a BOND!

But I wasn't paying much attention to all that, because in the middle of everything was the raised platform with ropes all around it, where I knew that at any moment I was going to have to perform. Meanwhile, Bugs Bunny—he must have been nine feet tall—was dancing around in the ring:

The tall man with the high hat
And the whiskers on his chin
Will soon be knocking on your door
And you ought to be in.

"Abby! Abby!" That was Hedda. She was pulling on the sleeve of my robe. "Did I hear right? Did Jack just say he was going to *Moscow*? Why, that's the capital of the Soviet Union! It's full of Communists! Is *that man* sending him there? He's practically a card-carrying member himself. I've got more questions for that boss of yours. Plenty of them."

Any bonds today?
Bonds of freedom
That's what I'm selling
Any bonds today?

"For example, something *else* Jack said. Just six months ago. About how he warned him. Warned who? The president? Pearl Harbor?" I felt my arm was about to come out of its socket, the way she was yanking at me. "Don't you clam up on me. You were there. At Union Station."

Just then, and luckily, a bell sounded, and a man in a white shirt and a little black bow tie climbed through the elasticized ropes into what I knew was a boxing ring. I looked closer. Broken nose, cauliflower ears. Ridge of bone above the eyes.

"Why," said Hedda, "that's Slapsie Maxie Rosenbloom. Look at him. You can see the animal side."

The bell rang three more times. "Ladeeeeze and gentlemen! Ladeeeeze and gentlemen! Welcome to our championship bout!"

"What championship bout?" asked Hedda. "Why am I always the last person to know what—Oh, *there* he is! You-hoo! Jack! Yoo-hoo! Jack Warner!"

It was the Chief, all right. He had jumped up at one corner of the ring and was waving his arms at the crowd. "All right, everybody! All right! Goddammit! They can't hear me. Rosenbloom! Ring that fucking bell!"

But it wasn't the ex-champ who operated the bell; it was Lorre, the actor, who had a little hammer that he brought down on the brass gong. *Clang! Clang! Clang!*

"Listen, everybody! Lunch hour is over—and so is this rally. We've got pictures to make. Let's get back to work!"

Before anyone could react, Miss Kaiser, who was mostly on the outside of her skimpy swimming suit, climbed up on the platform and began to parade around the ropes; she was holding a placard with a big number one on it. The crowd broke into whistles and catcalls, as if they were infantrymen at a base. She smiled with red lips and waved.

"I know who that is," said Hedda. "And she's no dumb blonde. Believe me, she knows plenty."

The Chief turned to that card girl. "Get out of here and get out of here now," he commanded. "Or you're on suspension. That goes for the rest of you. You've had your fun. War or no war, this isn't a charity."

Slapsie, who was under contract at another studio, motioned to little Lorre, who struck the bell three more times. "Your attention, ladeeeze and gentlemen! In this corner, wearing green trunks, a former contender and local favorite, Abdul the Terrible Turk Maljan!"

I find it difficult to describe my emotions at that moment. It had been almost thirty years since I was last introduced in that manner, with the clang of the bell and the roar of the crowd. And it *was* a roar, louder by far than when I had stepped into the ring against Dummy Jordan, a fight I should have won but lost on points. I have a lot of friends in the Warner Bros. community.

"Are you really wearing green trunks?" That was Hedda.

But I was already pushing through the crowd and making my way to the ring. I was touched because the musicians were playing the "Istiklâl Marsi," our national anthem:

> *Fear not, the crimson banner that waves*
> *In this glorious dawn—*

"Where do you think you're going?" said the Chief as I started to climb onto the platform. "Go put your clothes on and get back to the office."

"But Chief—"

"No buts—or you'll be out on yours. Get moving."

Slapsie Maxie once more cupped his hands to his mouth. "And in this corner, wearing blue-and-white trunks, the NCAA Intercollegiate Champion of 1929, the Battling Bantamweight, Julius Julius Epstein!"

"You're the boss, Chief," I said, while I started to climb back to the ground. "I guess I'll just lose by default."

"Like hell you will!" he shouted. "It's one of *them*! You're going to beat that Epstein bastard's brains out—and not only that, I'm going to be your second."

The studio orchestra struck up another tune, to which a few people in the crowd sang along:

Fight on, State
Strike your gait
And win!
Fight on, on on on on,
Fight on
Penn State!

Julius J. climbed into the ring, slipped off his robe, and began to dance around on his matchstick legs. He was indeed wearing blue-and-white trunks. Philip G., his twin, slipped between the ropes as well. But he kept his robe on and went to sit down on the stool opposite me.

Once more Karelena Kaiser, with a bullseye on her breast, pranced around the four sides of the enclosure, holding up the sign for round one.

"I admit it," said the Chief. "This is good publicity for the girl. I had to promise her a part in *Edge of Darkness*. A STORY INCOMPARABLE OF A PEOPLE UNCONQUERABLE. She plays a Norwegian. German, Norwegian. What's the difference?"

The referee beckoned to Julius J. and the Terrible Turk.

"Take his head off," growled the Chief. "Chew up his liver. That'll teach them to come in at noon."

We walked up to Slapsie in the center of the ring. "I want a good, clean match between you two. No shlogn in the kichkes or the beytsim. Or in back of the kop. When I say tsebrekn, don't give me any tsuris: break. In case of a untergeyn—"

"*Untergeyn?*" I inquired.

"Knockdown, shmegege: go to a neutral corner. Most important, oyshitn zikh at all times. Farsheteyn? Did I make myself clear? Any questions?"

We shook our heads.

"Okay, touch gloves and come out at the bell."

We went back to our corners. Then at the same moment we both turned around and said, "What gloves?"

A thousand people broke into laughter. That was followed by a loud *Honk!* and who should climb into the ring but Harpo Marx. He had two sets of gloves around his neck and he went first over to J. J. E. and put them on him. Then he started over to my corner, where, instead of the Terrible Turk giving a massage to the executive producer of Warner Bros., the executive producer of Warner Bros. was giving a massage to me. He was chopping away at my legs with the edge of his hands like a butcher tenderizing a rump roast. *Kill him, murder him, slaughter him, crucify him*: that was what he was saying with each whack of his hand.

Up came Harpo and tied on the mitts. Then he reached out to shake hands with the Chief, and what came out of his sleeve was a fifth glove, followed by a waterfall of nuts and bolts and springs and sprockets and at last a big horseshoe made out of steel. Harpo plucked it up and stuffed it inside the glove. Gookie.

"Hey!" cried the Chief from where he was squatting. "We haven't got all day. Let's get this show on the road."

With that, Julius J. stood up and so did the Terrible T. Miss Kaiser held up the sign once more and made a sort of bow to all four directions of the compass. Then Lorre, grinning like the murderer in *M*, struck the bell with his hammer.

Clang!

This is what happened next. The Battling Bantamweight, though he looked more like a flyweight to me, came buzzing out of his corner and rotating his gloves in the air. I stood there awhile and let him flick at my abdomen and my arms and the old iron chin. But I knew the Chief was in a hurry so I wound up to deliver the haymaker, at which J. J. E. began to backpedal and hide behind Slapsie Maxie, who I have a lot of respect for as a former world champ of my division. This was a frustrating moment. No matter which way the referee turned, Epstein stayed right behind him. Left. Right. Forward. Back. He stuck to Maxie just like a shadow—or, and suddenly this came to me, like the little tramp in *City Lights*. I'll put it a different way: the whole thing had been scripted, like by a choreographer, but no one had given the lines to me.

"Kill him! Murder him! Wipe him off the face of the earth!"

Everybody—first Maxie and then Julius Julius—turned toward my corner to see who had uttered such terrible words. But I already knew, which gave me the opportunity to lash out like lightning and land my knockout punch.

Down went the Nittany Lion, flat on his back. What a shout from the crowd. But none louder than the one from my trainer or cut man or whatever.

"Drinks for everybody!"

In an instant Slapsie Maxie motioned me to a neutral corner and began the count.

"Eyns! Tsvey! Dray! Fir!"

At just that moment Lorre consulted his stopwatch and raised his hammer to ring the bell.

"Don't you dare!" came that same voice from the corner of the Terrible Turk. "I'm warning you! Suspension!"

Mr. Moto had to think fast. He put down his hammer.

Just then, while everyone, including me, was distracted, somebody came up behind me and tapped my shoulder. Who should appear before me but Julius Julius Epstein, back on his feet and rotating his gloves like a fighting kangaroo.

"Foul! Foul! Foul!" That was the Chief. "It isn't Julie. It's the other one!"

What he meant was that he saw how Harpo, the corner of my fallen foe, J.J.E., had dragged him off to his stool and how his brother, P.G.E., had thrown off his robe and skipped to where I thought, as the winner, I was going to start blowing kisses.

"Forfeit! Low blow! Disqualification!"

But no one in the crowd paid any attention to my corner, whether he was the vice president for production or the executive producer or anything else. That was because—*Clang!*—the bell rang once more and the fight continued. What happened next was no different than what happened before: the jabbing, the hiding, the running, and then what in France they call the coup de grace. Down went Philip G., with his face full of a knuckle sandwich.

"Drop that hammer!" cried the Chief as little Lorre was about to hit the gong, and Slapsie Maxie continued the count.

"Finef! Zeks! Zibn!"

I started waving to the crowd and began my victory trot, when all of a sudden somebody tapped my shoulder again, and there stood what could only have been the fully recovered Julius J. I put up my dukes and so did he, and it looked like this fight was going to go on for all fifteen rounds, and maybe even more, when from my corner there echoed a spine-chilling cry:

"Enough of this crap! It's my studio! It's my lot! And I'm declaring the winner!"

Right through the ropes came Jack L. Warner. He marched up to where

Maxie and me and whichever Epstein it was were standing. "Give me that arm," he shouted, and grabbed hold of me by the wrist.

"Just a minute, please." That was the other twin, I guess it was P. unless it was J. "Who do you think you are? The Marquess of Queensberry?"

"I'll put you on a mattress, you queen, if you don't get out of the ring and back to work."

But the Epsteins did not move. Neither did I or Slapsie Maxie. We were all standing there in a row, wondering what to do next, when there was a loud honk and Harpo, who I always thought was my friend, came running right at me, winding up with that extra mitt on his fist to hit me with a roundhouse right.

My old reflexes kicked in. I ducked. One after the other, all the former fighters did the same thing: Slapsie Maxie, Julius J., and Philip G. That's why, with a really terrible crunching sound, the blow landed right on the chin of the man who was the boss of the studio and the employer of all the men and women in the crowd. The horseshoe went flying off in one direction and the Chief flew backward in the other.

S. M. Rosenbloom went over to where he was lying, half in and half out of the ring.

"Eyns! Tsvey! Dray!"

The whole of Lot H was in turmoil. People were running this way and that. The fire engine was sounding its siren. From the corner of my eye I saw Hedda pushing her way toward the victim of the punch.

"Akht," cried Slapsie Maxie. "Nayn!"

Clang! Clang! Clang!

Too late: the referee, in his white shirt and black bow tie, had just shouted, "Tsen!"

The fight was over.

Oh, the cheering! The hubbub! The hue and the cry! In the middle of the ring, the referee was raising not the right hand of the Terrible Turk but a hand each of the twins.

"The winners by a knockout," he shouted, "the Epstein Boys!"

I turned to where Harpo was standing, even more silent than usual. "That blow was suspect," I told him.

Slapsie stared down to where the defeated fighter lay dead to the world. He shook his head. "Dos Jackie, er geyt tzu dem letzn round up."

Then a strange thing happened. While they were standing there, with their arms held high, the brothers turned to each other. "We've got it!" they both at the same time cried. "The words for the ending! *Round up the usual suspects!*"

"Jack! You! Jack L. Warner!" That was Hedda. She had pushed up to the side of the ring. She was lifting the Chief's head and shouting right in his face. "*Moscow?* Next month you're going to Moscow? And what about Pearl Harbor? You better tell me. You said you warned him. Warned who? About what? You can't fool me. I already know plenty. *Operation Z.* Open your eyes! What is the meaning of that?"

Amazingly, the Chief did open his eyes. He even blinked them. Then he said, "Huh? I don't get it. Round up the usual suspects? Round them up for what?"

16 } LOST IN A HAREM

Jack L. Warner: November 1942, Morocco

Those Ink Spots put a blindfold on me and stuck me on a horse! Don't they cover the eyes of a condemned man just before they shoot him? I thought of a great gag. Two Jews are put in front of a firing squad. The Gestapo guy asks if they want a blindfold. The one Jew says, "Yes, please." The other Jew gives him the elbow and says, "Shhhhah! Don't make waves." Didn't I see in some picture how somebody—maybe it was the Emperor of Peru—was torn apart by horses? Is that to be my fate? Anyhow, we've been going for at least an hour and my ass is so sore I am starting to wish they'd take one of their sabers and chop off my head and get it over with. I've had enough.

"Listen, Leroy—" I begin, but just then a couple of these Pullman porters lift me up like a piece of luggage and set me on the ground. *This is it, J.L. Say your prayers.* "Dear Lord, don't let Harry get his hands on production, or—"

Off goes the cloth that's been covering my eyes. Cor blimey! I'm standing on what looks like a set by DeMille. There's a big palace in front of me, three stories high, with funny-shaped windows, and a tower in the center, and columns everywhere; it's all lit up by torches, and there are hundreds more of these caddies, all of them on horseback and dressed in red tunics and white turbans, and all of a sudden a brass band with horns and drums and cymbals starts playing—and it ain't Duke Ellington, not by a long shot, but in its way it's not so bad. I mean, if I were a snake I might come out of my basket. Now, as suddenly as they started they come to a halt, there's a bang of a cymbal, but instead of a gun going off like in that Hitchcock picture with Lorre, all of the cotton pickers raise up their bright curving sabers and shout:

"Salut à le grand Général Patton!"

It all seems like a dream, right? As if I've been whisked off on some magic carpet, like in one of those pictures with Sabu. Plus, everybody is making a big mistake. But no one listens when I try to tell them who I really am. They lead me through this big courtyard to meet what they call the grand vizier, and he's dressed in a white robe with a white hood, like a bigshot in the Ku Klux Klan: I'm not about to explain to him about the cemetery in Krasnashiltz! He gives me a smile with these huge gold choppers, a four-thousand-dollar job in Beverly Hills, and waves his arm that I should follow him.

Up the stairs we go, three flights, and the band follows right behind me playing what sounds like "The Whiffenpoof Song"; they keep tootling and drumming until we come to this long, narrow room, where the rest of the Klan, with those pointed hoods on their heads and gym socks on their feet, are sitting.

In the middle of the room I see another one of these fellows, dressed like the others, sitting on top of a throne.

The GV gives me a poke in the ribs. "You must bow to the sultan."

So I give a bow, even though I remember from school somewhere that Americans are not supposed to do that before kings and queens and, I guess, sultans. His Highness beckons me forward and I cross all these thick red rugs with the band, like in a Mexican restaurant, coming right behind me, playing "A Tisket, a Tasket" and other hit tunes. Then they stop and so do I, and the Grand Dragon or whoever he is puts his hand out of his robe, and I don't know whether to kiss it or shake it or give it a manicure. He says, "We are very pleased to meet the illustrious General Patton," which comes out in perfect English, like the guy's been to Oxford, and he looks a bit, with his little moustache above his stiff upper lip, like a Brit, except with a sul-tan, ha, ha! Casting department: Ronald Colman.

"Pleased to meet you, too, Your Excellency," I say, sticking out my own hand, and all the pashas inside their stockings begin to mutter and murmur, and I look around to make sure they aren't raising a cross or something, and the grand vizier says, "Do not touch."

The sultan only smiles and says, with this BBC accent, "I have received your message, General."

"What message? And I'm no general. I'm a colonel. A lieutenant col—"

"Why, this message." So saying, he digs a piece of paper out of his bath-robe, puts on a pair of specs—now he's Clifton Webb—and starts to look it over. "You say that this coming morning if there is no surrender you will destroy my city of Casablanca."

"Right! That's why I was racing back in the jeep. I've got a fortune tied up in this production. We've got to save the city."

"Ah, General, about that we entirely agree—"

"Now you're talking turkey!"

The grand viz flashes his choppers, but without the smile. "Your letter presents us with a dilemma, General."

The sultan leans close. I can tell he's been chewing mints. "On the one hand, we must save our beloved city. It goes back two thousand years and was built, as you see it, in its modern form by my ancestor, Sultan Mohammed ben Abdallah. It was under his rule that the Kingdom of Morocco became the first nation to recognize the newly independent United States of America. So you see, General, we are your oldest ally; and we hope to become, in the current conflict, your newest ally as well. Inshallah."

"Gesundheit!"

"Yes, we must find a way to save our great ed-Dar el-Bida. But on the other hand, the grand vizier has spoken of a dilemma. It is this: no Sultan of Morocco has ever surrendered and no sultan ever will. It would be a stain on the throne, which he must then abdicate. Thus our quandary."

"Yeah, you're in a tough spot, but what's that got to do with me? You've nabbed the wrong guy. I've been trying to tell you: I'm not Patton or any other general. I'm Jack L. Warner. I made up the L. For Vaudeville. My parents were from Poland. All we spoke was Yiddish. Yiddish! Verhshtain? A pish un a fortz iz vi a khasene un a klezmer."

"This is no time for joking, General," the Grand V. replies. "We know you are a devout Christian and that you believe your God is your protector and that you thank that deity each day. You see? Our eyes are everywhere. From us there are no secrets. You will fail if you attempt to trick us."

"Oy vey, di ir un schlemiel mit un putz foist klas. Okay? They don't teach that at West Point."

"What they do teach," the GV goes on, "are the skills to become a two-star general. You cleverly went out without your uniform. But you forgot that those same two stars are on the fender of your jeep. The same vehicle you were driving when you were captured by the Nubian Guard."

"Uh-oh."

The sultan: "With the help of Allah, all difficulties are overcome and all questions find an answer. Thus we have discovered a solution to our dilemma."

"Oh, yeah?" I say, playing the straight man. "What's that?"

"You will remain here as our guest. Admittedly, this does not solve our puzzle, but it will serve, as you say in English, to buy us time until we can devise a strategy that will be more enduring. But for the moment, if you cannot order the attack, the attack will not come."

"Are you nuts? Are you crazy? Patton has already given the order! The attack's going to happen whether I'm here or not. You've got to believe me. I'm on my knees! I'm a full-time member of B'nai B'rith. I wasn't even born in America! You should try my recipe for latkes. Why won't you believe me? You've got to believe me. The trick is to fry the onions first. Gevalt geshrign! Five hundred thousand people! Innocent people! A million-dollar budget!"

The GV: "Rise, General. This is most undignified."

"But my name's on the water tower!"

The sultan, smiling, says, "Please put your mind at rest about your personal safety. We have many pleasures prepared for you."

"You don't get it! The boats! The planes! Artillery! Bombs! What? Huh? Pleasures? Really?"

The sultan must have given some kind of signal, because the next thing you know I'm being lifted to my feet and led out of the room, and with the band playing "Georgia on My Mind" we go down one corridor and then another and after that a winding staircase, until we finally come to two huge doors with two enormous guards standing in front of it. They're stripped to the waist and have these bulging muscles like Weissmuller and Atlas, plus drooping moustaches and arms crossed over their chests.

"Hello, boys," I start to say, but they stand aside and pull open the doors and the GV gives me a little shove and we step inside.

For a second I just stand and blink. There's nothing to see except wisps of smoke or steam that slowly rise from a little below me and travel up toward the ceiling. A gas chamber, I think, and I wonder if I should ask for a ham sandwich. Last meal is on them. And a Pepsi, please. I lift my eyes, not to pray but to follow the rising mists to where they drift out of the row of open windows; there I see something more frightening than the idea of dying in this African Alcatraz. What's that? The sky! It's getting lighter! Dawn! It's dawn! Only an hour or two hours or at the most three hours before the attack.

"Dive bombers! TNT!" I yell, the way I did a moment before. "Howitzer shells!" Now I'm jumping up and down and waving my arms. "Listen to me! I'm not Patton! I'm a Yid from Youngstown! We've got to act! Now! Now! There's not a minute to lose!"

But at this there is only the sound of laughter—not from the GV, not from the members of the marching band, and not from those two muscle-bound heavyweights. No, this laughter is light, lilting, and when the mists begin to part before my whirling arms, what do I see but a shallow pool, all turquoise and pearl, with vapors rising from its surface and, sitting all around it, or frolicking in the waters, ten, fifteen, count 'em, twenty dark-haired babes! Ladies and gentlemen: the harem!

Thump! The doors close behind me. No grand vizier. No out-of-date musicians. And no Strangler Lewis or Bronco Nagurski. Just me and these half-clad dazzlers, with haunches and rear ends and necks! *Hmmmm*, I say to myself, *the war can wait.*

"Monsieur le général! Monsieur le général!"

This time I accept the promotion. I go down the steps and one of these doxies, she's wearing nothing but a veil over her face and a see-through skirt around her hips, comes up and takes my hand and draws me down to the water. Then another hottie floats by and takes off my shoes. Now the others, giggling and tittering—never mind the pun—swim up to where I'm dangling my feet in the water, which is the same temperature as my bath on Angelo Drive. I swing round my camera and start to film the way their rear ends are going up and down in the water like dolphins, so I'll have some footage for the boys when we get together on Sunday nights. Zanuck not invited!

Through the viewfinder I see the last of these concubines coming toward me with her head held high; she's doing the breast stroke, and how, and it's obvious she's wearing exactly what Lamarr did in that stag picture, the one where she's swimming and running around in the woods.

"What's the name, toots?" I shout down to her.

"Oumaima," she replies, with a flash of her chicklets.

"Your Mama? We got to do something about that. What about Cindy? That has a ring to it."

Now this starlet, because already I'm thinking of signing her up, begins to haul herself out of the water, slowly, like a strip tease, and she's got a part in her hair like Lamarr and the eyelashes and the pouting mouth and now she's halfway out and these breasts, with nipples on them, are dangling right in front of my eyes, and all of a sudden she lets out a shriek—Mon Dieu! Quelle Horreur!—and all the floozies start screaming, and the doors burst open and I hear the band playing "Jeepers Creepers," and the two beefcakes are rushing in, along with the grand vizier and the sultan, too, who starts to speak like some Oxford don.

"I see, chum, we have made an error. General Patton is a Christian. It is evident you are not."

That's when I realize that he and everyone else is staring down at where by an involuntary action my Jewish-style member has burst through my unbuttoned fly and stands filled with happiness in the air.

G. S. P., Jr.: *November 1942, Fedala*

Meeks woke me at 0300; shortly after, Gay came in with the news that a French officer had arrived at the Miramar on a motorcycle. I dressed with all deliberation and went to our headquarters in the smoking room, where a few candles were burning in upright bottles of champagne. There I was greeted by a major in goggles, a leather helmet, and a uniform that once was khaki but had now turned white with dust. He saluted readily enough and handed me a ragged piece of onionskin. I pretended there was not enough light to read it, because I feared what it said. Those fears were confirmed by Gay, who told me that negotiations between Clark, Petain, and Darlan had resulted in a cease-fire across the entire North African front. Wilbur said, "Shall I inform Admiral Hewitt? There's time to call off the attack."

I remained silent. Wilbur then added, "We have to remember General Eisenhower's order."

As if I could forget it. At that moment it was burning a hole in my pocket.

> *No Casablanca bombardment will be executed without prior authority from me.*

Just like Ike. He wants to crack the nut, but he doesn't want to use a nutcracker. I'd like to tear that cable in two, because I intend to raze this city without informing Gibralter, much less asking for permission. I tore up the onionskin instead.

"Qu'est que c'est cela!" exclaimed the Frenchie.

"It means this isn't worth the paper it was written on. A cease-fire is not a surrender. Moreover, it applies to the French army and its auxiliaries. But it's the French navy that is doing the fighting. I gave the sultan and Admiral Michelier my ultimatum. You'd best put on those goggles and give the latter a reminder. At this moment my engineers are preparing to blow up your aqueducts and power lines. My pilots are studying the photographs of their targets. Sherman tanks are lined up to your south. Our ships have their guns trained on the city. Keep your ears open as you drive; you'll hear the pleasant sound of our infantry sharpening their bayonets."

Meeks, on hearing this, went as white as my two colonels, who were pretty pale themselves. When Gay started to speak, I cut him off. "It's too late, Colonel. Besides, it's never a good idea to change plans."

So we waited to hear what the admiral had to say.

0430: pas de réponse.

0510: pas de réponse.

Dawn was breaking. Soon it really would be too late. So be it. The responsibility lay with our foes. We had given them every chance.

Jack L. Warner: November 1942, Morocco

How does Pearl's baby boy get out of this one? I wish I could dissolve my whole body, including this damned pecker, which, all things considered, has gotten me into more trouble than it's been worth—yes, dissolve and turn into this steam that is going up, up, and out the window, into the blue sky, into the rising sun and become, isn't it pretty, look at it: that rainbow. And while my thoughts have flown away, leaving this earth behind, I get what someone inclined this way—Rabbi Magnin, for instance—would call a divine inspiration. To me, it's the pot of gold.

"I've got it!" I shout. "Your Majesty! Mr. Vizier! I know how to solve your problem: how to save the city without your having to surrender!"

The GV is a skeptic. "Impossible. How can you accomplish that?"

"You get somebody else to surrender!"

"And whom do you propose for such a task?"

"The admiral. At the Admiralty! Michelle! I mean Michelier! Look! The sun is up! It's getting higher! It's—Jesus H. Christ! It's already after six o'clock!"

The sultan gives a clap of his hands. "Call up the Bentley. At once. We have not a moment to lose."

Fade out and fade in and we're all aboard that black limousine, with the little flags on both sides, trying to squeeze through the palace gate without scratching the fenders. And after a close call we manage it, and all the Shriners are lined up on their horses on either side of the road and shouting with what I guess is a huzzah and holding up their swords, and we pick up speed and leave them behind us in a cloud of dust.

I should have been a diplomat after all: that's what I'm thinking, because this isn't the only problem I've solved by being quick on my feet and keeping my wits about me. Why, only a couple of months ago I'm walking around on the lot, staring down at the ground in search of stray nails in order to help the war effort, and when I look up who should I see coming around the corner of the writers' bungalow than one of those Epstein twins, and I do a double take because you never, and I mean never, see one of them without the other, and I don't have a clue: Is this Julie or is this Phil? I mean, they look so much alike that I don't think they can tell themselves apart. Anyway, I'm breaking into a sweat because whichever one it is has seen me and we're getting closer and closer, and what am I going to do, what am I going to say? Take a stab when the odds are only fifty-fifty? So again I get one of my inspirations, who knows if it's divine, and when we are practically face to face, I say "Hello, boys!" and walk briskly on my way.

Now *that* is tact! *That* is diplomacy.

I remember another time, when I opened the door of Flynn's trailer and inside the bathtub there was this babe, covered with soapsuds and I couldn't help but get an eyeful, and she was just opening her mouth to scream when—

"Ed-Dar el Biba," says the driver.

Yeah, it's Casablanca, all right, and we're barreling through stop signs and traffic signals while the police stand there saluting. From my spot in the back seat I venture a thought: "Do we have time for a minute or two at the Bousbir? I mean, just to see if they really go counterclockwise?"

But the Bentley plows on, twisting through the narrow streets, and then roaring down a boulevard, and now we pull up in front of a large whitewashed building. Wounded sailors, lots of them, are lying on the ground all around it, it's like Atlanta in *Gone with the Wind*, with bandages, and blood, and nurses, and by the front door, standing on end, there is this enormous unexploded artillery shell—I have this funny feeling it might have come from the *Augusta*—and next to it a wag has put up a sign that says, *We come in peace.*

Somebody opens the Bentley door and we get out and all the Frogs give a salute to the sultan and we go up the steps and into the Admiralty, though I don't want to forget what I told that bathing beauty in Flynn's trailer: I just said, "Oh, excuse me, sir," and turned around and went out. That's what the French call savoir faire.

Inside a lot of people are standing around. The sultan goes up to one fellow—he's got a bunch of stars on his hat and more scrambled eggs on his uniform than anyone else, so I figure this is the admiral. I watch while the two of them talk back and forth, parlez-vous this and parlez-vous that, and their voices are getting louder and louder and the admiral is getting red in the face and saying, "Non! Aboultement non!" I figure this means no dice.

My Bulova now reads 6:41; in other words, only nineteen minutes to go and—what's that? That buzzing? That humming? Everybody stops talking. Everybody stands like a statue. Then one of the Cheese-Eaters runs to the window and looks out and begins yelling, "Les avions! Les avions!" Yep, it's the Wildcats and dive bombers, all the planes from the *Ranger*. They're circling overhead. They're picking out their targets. And it doesn't take Einstein to figure out what must be the number one bulls-eye: the Admiralty. With all the wounded sailors. With the sultan. With the admiral and all the French high command. Not to mention the vice president for production at Warner Bros. Pictures. Speaking of Einstein, I've got my own theory of relativity: Don't hire 'em!

"Hey!" I shout, and step between where the sultan and the admiral are hollering face to face. "I'll handle this."

Then I turn to this Admiral Michelier and say, in excellent patois, "Rendez-vous! Rendez-vous!"

"Quoi?" says the Frenchman.

"Rendez-vous! Rendez-vous! For Christ's sake, don't you know your own language? Rendez-vous! It means *Surrender!*"

The next thing I know a couple of sailors have grabbed me by the arms and are starting to hustle me out of the room.

The admiral says something, and I hear the sultan reply with my name: Jack L. Warner. L. for Leonard.

"Quoi?" goes the admiral again. "Jack L. Warner? De les Frères Warner? De Hollywood?"

"Oui."

Now this Michelier makes some kind of motion with his arm and the Frogs let me go, and I don't go to him, he comes over to me, and he says, sounding a bit like Boyer, "Monsieur Warner? Can it be true? The maker of *Three Cheers for the Irish?*"

"That's me," I reply. "IT'S THE HAPPIEST, SCRAPPIEST SHIN-DIG EVER SCREENED!"

G. S. P., Jr.: November 1942, Fedala

Meeks had charge of the walkie-talkie.

0625: Pas de réponse.

0637: More of the same.

I realized there was not going to be a response. I looked over at Wilbur. His face was twitching. His eyes were moist. I had thought of giving him a promotion when he came back from Michelier. Damned audacious thing to do. Rode into the heart of the foe. People have gotten the Congressional Medal for less. But at the crucial moment he revealed his pansy side. And he let the Kike run off with the jeep.

At 0640 we heard the planes overhead: on their way to their targets at Casa. Perfect flying weather.

At that sound Gay turned tail as well. "Five hundred thousand people, General."

I told him that the Russians had already lost millions. "Do you know what Stalingrad looks like? There's not a building left standing. Or Leningrad? People are eating each other. Our men, including these pilots, have seen nothing worse than a slaughtered pig on their farms. They've got to get used to it. It has to get in their bloodstream. Before the fighting is over, there are going to be millions, maybe tens of millions more. This Arab town is only a down payment. It is now 0640. In this war, these will not be your hardest twenty minutes. I guarantee you that."

But they might have been the longest.

Jack L. Warner: November 11, 1942, Casablanca

"Do you know what was my favorite moment in this superb Irish picture?" That's Michelier, also speaking perfect English. Did *all* these guys go to Oxford? "When Mademoiselle Ann Sheridan sings 'Mi Caballero.'"

Huh? What's he talking about? Ten minutes to live and he's yapping about this back-of-the-lot feature? "'Mi Caballero?' Mi ass! That bitch wasn't even in it." Okay, maybe that's a little harsh, but last year she tried to hold me up for a big jump in salary, and I had to suspend her for six weeks. "You're mixing her up with Priscilla Lane, another blonde from the sticks."

"This is not so. True, she does not appear on the screen, but we hear her voice, that marvelous voice, off it. With piano. In the bar. Do you not recall?"

"Of course, I recall. I pay the salaries, don't I?" But I'm working my brain. Did we really pay a star for a bit like that when we could have gotten anybody, a chorus girl, for scale? Memo to Bischoff: *What the hell were you—*

"Pardon me, Monsieur Warner, but I assure you I am not mistaken. I would recognize her voice anywhere. It is not enough appreciated, this quality in her of the chanteuse."

Here the sultan comes up. Beads of sweat are running down his forehead. They're dripping off his nose. "Monsieur l'Admiral," he says, and points to the ticker on his wrist. I look at mine: 6:52! Eight minutes to go! We both start talking at once, but the admiral ignores us. "Par exemple," he says, which I guess means *For example*, and to the astonishment of everyone in the room he actually, and in a pretty good baritone, breaks into song.

You're just an angel in disguise
      —Who wandered down from up above
You're just a heavenly surprise
      —Who came to earth for me to—

"What the hell? What the hell? Has everybody lost his mind? In a couple of minutes we're going to be blown sky-high! That's your heavenly surprise."

"But, Monsieur Warner: She sings this in your own motion picture, *It All Came True*."

"TEMPTING! TEMPESTUOUS! THE GIRL WHO—Oh, I'm in a nuthouse!"

"I wrote her. She wrote back. I have, at home, a signed photo—"

"Listen. Listen, you crack-brained Frog. Don't you hear those airplanes? They're circling! They're about to drop bombs on top of our heads!"

"Calm. Always the calm. On this photo she writes, 'To Félix, my number one fan.' There is exposure of the chest. In the cleavage, much suggestion. Thus we discover the meaning of The Ooomph Girl."

"Well, ooomph you, you nitwit. We send out those pictures by the—"

"Wait. I will show you more. Regardez."

Here he takes out of his wallet a folded piece of paper.

"You see? Are you not making, with this actress, and with Monsieur Reagan, a film about the city of Casablanca? Is it not true? What I would give to see it!"

"What? What are you talking about? Let me—"

I snatch the sheet of newsprint. It's from the *LA Times*. An old column of Hopper's:

> I hear that Warners is planning to make a romantic spy adventure set in the Moroccan City of Casablanca. Shades of *Algiers*! They've already assigned the beautiful and busy Ann Sheridan for the sultry leading lady and Ronnie Reagan, who is rapidly becoming one of my favorites, to play—

"Ha! Ha! Ha! You sucker! We planted that phony press release. We—"

I bite my tongue at the sight of his stricken face. A thought comes to me. How many times, in the last couple of days, did I approach the cliff? The final cliff. You know the one I mean. On the ship, with the yellow paint. On the beach, being strafed by fez-headed Frogs. By a firing squad in the sultan's court. I'm on the brink again. But I don't want to jump off! Too young! I'm too young! Oh, to see Burbank! Beautiful Burbank. The Bousbir! Boobs! Buttocks! Blossoms, even. Little spring blossoms. *Get me out of this spot, Holy Mother of Jesus, and I'll never put another actor on suspension again.* Christ! Bulova watch time: 6:54! While I look the hands give a little shudder: 6:55! A Jew wants to live!

I turn to the Frenchman. "That's right. Sheridan and Reagan. She's great in the part. And you think you saw cleavage! Why, there's even a love scene in Paris. Maybe we can have the premiere right here in Casablanca. *Casablanca!* Wouldn't that be a terrific name for the picture?"

"Formidable! Merveilleux! And perhaps Mademoiselle Sheridan, she—"

"Sure! She'll come herself. Wait! What am I saying? There won't *be* a Casablanca. It's about to be bombed. Hey, hold on! Hold on! No city, no picture! No picture, no premiere. No premiere, no—"

"Attention! Attention! Garde-à-vous!" The Admiral is yelling to the whole room, where everybody is already diving under the tables and rolling into little balls on the floor. "Appelez le Général Patton! Immédiatement! Capitulation! Capitulation sans conditions!"

And for the first time in my life, and I hope the last time, too, I find myself kissing a grown man on one cheek and then, as if that were not enough, on the other. And the grown man is doing the same thing to me.

G.S.P., Jr.: November 1942, Fedala

At literally the last moment the French navy surrendered. I could not believe my ears when Meeks told me what he had heard. I asked who had surrendered and he said the Admiralty and without conditions.

"Too late," I started to say, but Wilbur and Gay jumped to their feet.

"Quick, Sergeant," cried the former. "Contact Admiral Hewitt. Tell him to call off the attack. *Salad Bowl* is the code."

Meeks looked over at me.

"For God's sake, Meeks!" shouted Gay.

I nodded. Our troops would suffer as a result. They would not get their inoculation. But there was no resisting what was clearly the hand of God.

Meeks, talking fast, got the word out. The question was: Would that word reach the *Ranger,* and then the pilots, in time? Meeks fell silent. None of us said a word. Then, after a moment or two, we heard the whine of the Wildcats and the deeper throb of the bombers in the sky over Fedala. Gay was grinning and wiping his brow.

"They're returning," he said. "They're—"

The smile disappeared. We all heard the sound, and I imagined we could feel the concussion of a dozen, then dozens, then surely hundreds of explosions. Wilbur was the one who figured things out. "The blasts are coming from over there," he said, pointing off to the west. "It's the planes. They're dropping their bombs into the sea."

I gave the order for Gay to go on into the town and if anyone stopped him begin the attack.

Then I said, aloud, "Well, I told Ike I'd take Casablanca by D plus 3, and I did. A nice birthday present to myself."

Meeks, his black face beaming, wished me happy returns. Hell of an irony. November 11th. Armistice day.

Gay encountered no opposition whatsoever.

At 1400 Admiral Michelier, the sultan, and the civil authorities arrived to discuss terms. I put out an honor guard. No use kicking a man when he is down. When you have been up against a gallant foe—and the French navy was that and more, though the army basically quit—it is best to tell them so, which I did, complimenting them on the valor and effectiveness of their resistance.

At the end of the talks, when the French and the sultan had agreed to all terms, I played a nasty trick on them. I rose and declared, "Gentlemen, we have now settled everything, but there is one disagreeable formality we must still go through."

I've got to write to Beatrice later tonight about the look on their faces. You'd have thought I was about to put them in chains. Instead I produced about forty dollars' worth of champagne and suggested a toast to the happy termination of fratricidal strife and to the resumption of the age-old friendship between France and America. The admiral held out his hand and I took it.

"You had your orders and you carried them out," he declared. "I had mine and I carried them out. Now I am ready to cooperate in every way possible."

We all drank to that, and to forty dollars more, and finally the sultan got to his feet and raised his glass and said, "A toast to the man who made this moment possible. To the man who saved the city of Casablanca! To the hero of the day!"

"Salud! Salud!" they all start to shout. "C'est un véritable héros! Jacques L. Warner!"

Speak of the devil, who should walk through the open door of the Hotel Miramar smoking room, and grinning happily ear to ear, but the Kike. The others all raised their glasses. But I reached for my gun.

Jacques L. Warner: November 1942, Fedala

So I walk up to the Miramar and ask where everybody is and they tell me in the smoking room. I figure I'll make a brief appearance for what is bound to be a hero's welcome. What a day! And not just because I saved a whole city and an expensive picture. The grateful sultan offered to take me with him to Fedala in the Bentley, but as a special favor dropped me off at the Bousbir, which let me tell you is just as nifty as Palm Springs, with its arcades and foliage and a stunning geyser that outdoes that Electric Fountain in Beverly, and there is a knockout standing under every arch, and my eyes are popping out, and not just my eyes, and I dallied there with those charming ladies and got some footage Zanuck would kill for, and after a couple of hours of this refreshment I grabbed a taxi and so here I am, at the smoking room door.

What's this? Do I hear my name? I throw back my shoulders and walk right in, and the next thing you know everybody, including my pal the sultan is hitting the deck and Patton is standing there and his nose is red like he's had a couple more than too many, and in his hand is a pistol with a fancy pearl handle, and he's calling me names, like a Kike and a deserter, and he's going to save the armed forces a lot of time and bother by finishing me off on the spot. I throw up both hands and yell, "Innocent, your honor!" or something like that, but old Two-Star, he's raising the revolver and squinting down the barrel, which is aimed at what some people laughably call my heart, and at that instant we all hear a voice shout out the word, "*Shoot!*"

I whirl around and who is now in the door but a big Arab with a turban on top of his head. Then I do a double take and let out a shout of joy because it isn't an Arab, I mean not exactly: it's in fact my only friend in the world, and it isn't a turban, it's a bandage because obviously during the landing or on the beach afterward he got shot by a bullet in his head.

"Abdul!" I cry.

"Chief!" he replies, and for the second time in a single day I'm in a man's arms and we are kissing each other, not just on the cheeks but, right in front of everybody, because after all I thought he was a goner, on the lips.

"Hey!" I say, pulling back from the clinch. "What do you mean, *shoot*? I don't regard that as very helpful."

"I don't mean with a gun," says the Turk. "I mean with your camera. You're making peace for all of North Africa. It's historical."

"Mais oui," says the admiral, getting off the floor. "We should all appear in this production."

And right away he's adjusting his tie and adjusting his hat and practicing a smile, and everybody else is doing the same, smoothing their moustaches and striking this pose or that pose and even Patton, though he doesn't put his gun back in his holster, is deciding which profile to present to the camera.

The camera. I've got it around my neck. The Bellow and Holler. So I lift it up and look through the viewfinder and compose a pretty good shot, and tell everybody to say *cheese*, and start to film, but after a minute Abdul comes up and whispers something in my ear.

"What are you talking about?" I reply.

"Chief, you forgot to take off the lens cap."

"*Men's clap*? Already? I've only been back for twenty minutes."

"Here. You see? You have to pull this off. Has it been on there all along?"

And he grabs this rubber thingamabob at the front of the camera, and from my toes up to the top of my head I feel the cold hand of dread, squeezing and squeezing; and now Patton, who has heard every word, drops his gun, that's because he's doubled over laughing, and slapping his knees, and pretty soon the admiral is doing the same thing, and then the sultan, and the colonels, and everyone else in the room, even Meeks, which is a little bit much, and I'm thinking: Oh, no, all the footage, it's wasted—not wasted, I didn't get it in the first place, how come nobody gave me any instructions, and so there won't be any combat scenes, no new invasion shots for the end of the picture, no attack on the beach, no royal court of the sultan, and not a thing from the Admiralty building, and not even—this is a blow, I'll tell you that: not even those incredible shots I took just an hour ago, something you wouldn't even see in Ripley's "Believe it or Not."

Now who in Burbank or anywhere else is going to believe me, never mind Ripley, that they went clockwise, and on request counterclockwise, to the left or to the right?

G.S.P., Jr.: November 1942, Fedala

A good day's work.
    To God be the praise.

17 } GOOD PICTURE-MAKING,
TAKE FOUR *Thanksgiving*

Hedda Hopper's Hollywood: November 1942, Los Angeles

Joan Crawford is really mad now. Her little daughter, Christina, managed to get hold of her collection of perfume and dumped the whole batch of sweet-smelling stuff into the bathtub. Why, I believe I can smell the results all the way over here in my humble abode. Watch out, Christina! Mommy's on the warpath.

Humphrey Bogart solved the golf problem since rationing by installing a putting green on his lawn. Speaking of Bogie, something has held up the release of his latest film, *Casablanca*, which has been "in the can" for months. Why, I wonder, is it coming out now? Could it have anything to do with the recent invasion of North Africa, where our fighting men at last were able to get into action after sitting around for all of last year? You have to wonder whether certain people might be profiteering from the suffering of our boys on the battlefield by releasing or not releasing motion pictures until the box office tells them the time is right. There oughta be a law.

Word around town is that Daryl Zanuck brought back spectacular shots of the conquest of Algiers, where he was wounded in action and received the Purple Heart. But Jack Warner came back to Burbank without any of the footage he took for the Signal Corps—according to him it included some of the most exciting documentary work ever done. Unfortunately all the reels were destroyed when the empty troop ship that was bringing it back to this country was torpedoed in the open Atlantic and went down with all hands. But all was not lost: Jack is telling everyone he made a great find in the war zone—a poor native waif who he is going to turn into the next Hedy Lamarr!

A real mystery is why the Warners exec, after returning from overseas to Argyle Avenue and the loving arms of his beautiful wife Ann (though some say he might have been birdwatching up on Briarcliff Road) less than a week ago, up and packed his bags and disappeared once again. And that pretty little Karelena Kaiser seems to have flown out of town as well. The last time this happened, he invaded North Africa. And to hear him tell it, he single-handedly brought the French to their knees. This time, though, methinks he's only gone to New York City to grab a bag of popcorn and sit through the long-delayed premiere of that interminable romance between Bogart and the Swedish nighty gal, Ingrid Bergman. Stay away from this one, boys and girls, if like me you are a fan of happy endings.

KK: November 1942, New York City

"Goddammit! That stupid bitch!" Jack threw down the newspaper. "She never gets anything right."

"What are you upset about, Jack? Briarcliff Road?"

"Who gives a fuck about that? It's the picture."

"But you know she never liked it. And it doesn't have what you'd call a happy ending."

"So what? I don't like it, either. And we're going to reshoot the last reel. Maybe we could have Patton landing on the beach. Maybe he's the one to get the girl. He's a personal friend of mine."

"Then why—?"

"Because it's not a premiere. It's not even a regular showing. What it is, is a technicality. We've got to open for a couple of days to be eligible for the Academy Awards. I've got plans for the real premiere. Big plans. You'll see. The whole world's going to see. Not that this dog is going to win anything. Fat chance! My money is on *Murder in the Big House*. BORN FOR TROUBLE! Or this terrific new *The Mysterious Doctor* picture. Even I got the heebie-jeebies at the rushes. There's this guy, see, in the tin mines, and I swear to God he's got no head. *No head!* How do they do that? It's genius. It's what I call movie-making. MURDER STALKS THE MOORS! This Nazi guy scares the Brits from mining the tin. Isn't that a magnificent idea? For the war effort? I thought of it myself. THE HEADLESS GHOST STRIKES AGAIN!

"Not only that, it's under budget. Hey, what's the matter, Blondie? What are you staring at? You look like you've seen a ghost yourself. Hell, it's only a movie. And hurry up, throw some clothes on. We came all the way across the country, right? We might as well see this phony premiere.

No, no, wait a minute. Stay the way you are. You're sure you can't make them move? Just a little one way or the other? It's definitely possible. I saw it with my own eyes."

Ten minutes later Jack was dragging me through the lobby of the St. Regis Hotel. "Hey, taxi!" he yelled, and as if he were on the Burbank lot, three yellow cabs came to a halt at the same time. He pushed me through the door of the first one and leaned toward the driver: "Get us to Avenue A!"

We pulled up in front of the Hollywood Theater. There were no searchlights. There were no crowds. The *b* in the word *Casablanca* was placed backward on the marquee. A redhead sat in the ticket booth. Jack looked through the glass at her pale, freckled skin.

"Guess what?" said Jack. "You ought to be in the movies."

"Guess what?" said the girl. "I already am. That will be six dollars."

"*Six dollars!* American money? You've got to be kidding. That's um, er; that's, wait a second—"

"Three dollars each."

"Highway robbery! Do you know who I am? My name is on the water tower!"

"And my name is on a two-dollar bill."

"Who writes your material, the Epstein boys? You wouldn't be free later on to—"

"Look, mister, do you want to see the picture or don't you? Other people are waiting."

So they were: four or five men and women now stood behind us. Jack pulled me out of the line. "Don't waste your money," he told them. "Bogart goes off with Rains. Hemorrhoid—don't ask me why—gets the girl."

Behind us, from inside the booth, the redhead cried out, "Happy Thanksgiving!"

"What did she say?" I asked.

"You got here last December, right? You poor kid, you don't know about our beloved holiday. Come with me. You're going to have the biggest feast of your life. And it's going to be on me."

We walked over to the Second Avenue automat, where we got rolls and desserts from little glass windows and hot turkey specials from the steam table. Coffee came out of dolphins' mouths. "Okay," said Jack, as we took our seats. "You've got to have turkey. It's a tradition. By the way, Maxim's has nothing on Horn and Hardart. There were these pilgrims, see. You know, these guys with buckles and funny-looking hats. They were the victims of religious prejudice, which went on in those days just like now. So after a lot of persecution, like frogs and hail, they went forty days in the desert with nothing to eat but stale bread, and finally crossed the Red Sea on the Mayflower—speaking of which, that's where we're going, not back to LA but to that hotel in Washington because the president wants me and Abdul to be on call. Anyway, where was I? The turkey—delicious, in my opinion. With these mashed potatoes. Hey, I forgot the cranberry sauce! Well, the reason we eat turkey is because the pilgrims were starving, the way I said, and they had barely escaped from the pharaoh and it was the Indians who showed them how to plant corn with fish, which wasn't so digestible, they were like bitter herbs; so then they brought them these turkeys, the breast meat, the drumsticks, the works, and everybody was so happy they danced around the golden calf and bought the whole island of Manhattan for bupkis, and that is why we ask *Why is this day so special?* and don't mix milk with meat—notice there isn't any cream in that coffee—and count our blessings and to grandmother's house we must go."

He finished his plate and started to mop up the gravy on mine. His mouth was full, but he kept on talking: "That's Americana, as you Krauts are going to find out when we get to Berlin. And I'll tell you something else. There was this guy, John Smith, if you can believe a name like that, in love with a lovely Indian maiden. Think Lena Horne. And if it weren't for the color line—are you going to finish that pumpkin pie?—which someday I have the dream to challenge once I can talk Harry into it: well, then we're going to make this tremendous vehicle, a colossal picture all about it. HE DARED TO LOVE AS NO MAN HAD BEFORE! SHE LEFT HER TRIBE TO FOLLOW HER HEART! Forget about all that crap that's playing at the Hollywood Theater. A LOVE STORY AS OLD AS AMERICA ITSELF!"

18 } PIPE. CIGARETTE. CIGAR.

Hedda Hopper's Hollywood: January 1943, Los Angeles

Judy Garland, dressed in an outfit of white doeskin on the *Girl Crazy* set, met Mickey Rooney wearing a flaming-red cowboy suit. Said Mickey, "Judy, you look like an ice-cream soda." "And you look like a bottle of ketchup," she replied.

It's been over a month since Jack Warner took himself off to spend Thanksgiving in New York City and no one in town has seen hide nor hair of him since. Everyone over in Burbank is keeping tight lips. And guess who else has gone AWOL? Abdul Maljan, who was so heroically wounded on the beaches of North Africa.

Well, a little birdy who has never steered me wrong before has been chirping in my ear once again—and believe it or not, it seems that Jack has taken his moustache, his masseur, and his sixteen-millimeter camera back to the field of battle. That's bravery for you. While some people, like Charles Spencer Chaplin, who made that foolish film in which he played both a Jew and Adolph Hitler—a bit prematurely, for my money—won't return to their own country in her time of greatest need, though of course with him or without him there'll always be an England.

The odd thing is that the fighting in Casablanca has been over for a month. Something is afoot, boys and girls. Something big. I can't say more—there's a Red Cross bandage over my mouth!—because of national security. But it wouldn't hurt to keep an eye on old FDR, just in case he pulls a disappearing act, too! They always say he's gone fishing. Well, there's something fishy, all right: Are Mr. Winston Churchill and old Uncle Joe, which is what people have taken to calling that out-and-out Red in the Kremlin, cooking up something? There will be plenty of smoke if that crooked pipe and that cigarette in its fancy holder and the fat cigar ever get puffing together. What a powwow! Well, these lips are sealed.

Joan Crawford is over her conniption about the spilled perfume. They're starting to call her the sweater girl again—not because she's wearing them but because she's knitting them for the army.

Goebbels: January 1943, Wolfsschanze

Semmler woke me with the article from the *Times* of Los Angeles at two in the morning. I was at Tempelhof by three and have been waiting here at the Führerhauptquartiere since half past six for the Führer himself to arise. I now give great weight to whatever Frau Hopper chooses to tell us. She has been a valuable resource—invaluable, really, since the departure of Gyssling and the declaration of war. It was from one of her articles that we first learned that the Jew Wonkskolaser had taken part in the North African invasion, a piece of information that we put to good use by targeting the troop ship *Joseph Hewes* and sinking her with all the reels of Herr Warner's lying propaganda. And where is that little Scharfmaker off to this time? Does he think he can film another defeat of our forces? We won't allow it. We'll sink his ship again. When the war is over we shall make sure Frau Hopper receives a medal.

The mood here at GHQ is grim. Out of respect for the sufferings of the Sixth Army at Stalingrad, the Führer has forbidden the consumption of cognac and champagne throughout the compound. The young secretaries walk about with long faces. Much of the good fellowship, the banter and card games and even dancing, no longer exists. In addition, these girls have had to copy sample letters from the front and know what the average German on the street has begun to suspect: that the Sixth Army is encircled and can no longer be supplied by air. Troops are not getting enough to eat. Once more Göring has promised more than he can deliver. He grows fatter as our men in the snow begin to wither away.

Nor is the situation in French Africa exactly rosy. Rommel can pull many rabbits from his hat, but he is not an Israelite magician: he cannot turn seawater into a single liter of gas. The enemy has deployed fifteen submarines in the Mediterranean; our supply ships are sunk one after the other. Mussolini's troops are worse than useless. Well, the Americans, whose forces are made up of criminals and jailbirds and drunken Neger will discover that the Afrika Korps are a bit different than the half-hearted French. The British will soon realize that they, too, have their Italians. The real problem is Stalingrad.

Midmorning. This ersatz sun is already thinking of turning tail and slinking away. And where is the Führer? Sleeping. Still sleeping. I shall continue to wait on *pins and needles*, as our foes, the English, say.

Josef Vissarionovich: December 1942, Moscow

A cable from Churchill. Roosevelt has received one, too. Do they think I can be fooled? The capitalists talk among themselves. Then they allow the Bolshevik to listen in.

> *My dear Premier Stalin,*
>
> Now that we have secured most of French North Africa and have every prospect of catching Rommel in our pincers, we can contemplate a time, not far off, at which the whole of that continent will be free of the Nazi tyrants. I trust that you will agree with me that it is vital that we convene a three-power conference between yourself, President Roosevelt, and the Prime Minister of Great Britain. It will be of more than symbolic importance if we meet somewhere in Africa and most ideally on recently liberated land. As to date, the president agrees with me: the sooner the better—either by the end of this month or during the first week of the new year. If we busy ourselves, that should allow sufficient time to arrange our separate flights, complete all security arrangements, and hold whatever preliminary talks among ourselves and our staffs that we think necessary. Would it not be a good thing for each of us, mired in the mud and our weak winter light, to meet together in the sunshine of Africa? There is a special spot there, truly the Paris of the Sahara, that I should like to show you. It is, and for the moment must remain, my great secret.
>
> I believe I speak for the president as well as myself when I say that the chief item on the agenda should be the opening of a second—or perhaps now, after our achievements in Africa, we can speak of a third—front on our own continent. It will be no small pleasure, Premier Stalin, to determine at your side the earliest moment at which

we can attack Germany in Europe with all possible force. It shall be in 1943. We know already it must occur before July, or, if need be, August.

Might I close with a note of congratulation on the recent meeting of your armies at Kalach. You have the Germans and their allies in your grasp. The iron ring about Stalingrad is now being welded. This may be the turning point for all of us. It certainly is the most heartening event of the entire war. The world of free peoples owes you and your marvelous fighting forces our undying gratitude.

And he puts down his name.

He wants to meet in Africa, probably in liberated Morocco. In a month. I cannot fight my way through the enemy. I must go by air. If I were a bird this would be easily accomplished. But I must go by plane. Not so easy. Vyacheslav Mikhailovich has been attacked twice in the skies. He barely escaped with his life. You have to go high. Thousands of kilometers. Where the fighters can't find you. But then you can't breathe. You are fed oxygen, like a man undergoing surgery. When you're unconscious, God in heaven can't see what they are doing to you. But does not Churchill fly to many places? Yes, he drinks himself into a coma. He might as well be asleep in his bed. And what about his own Eighth Army general? Crashed in flames. Before he could issue a single command. Well, it's fate. What is one life when millions are dying? If I fail to attend, I will be like a soldier who holds back at the front. I am having such traitors shot. If you fight in our Red Army, you are better off facing the Germans than my firing squads.

The bats are flying again. Inside their cave. The General Secretary hears their cry: the capitalists will wait in safety until the last Bolshevik kills the last fascist—or, perhaps more to their liking, the other way around. Even a schoolchild can make this deduction: these English speakers are putting the Russian at risk, so that when his aircraft crashes they will be left with the spoils. Dialectical materialism can see into the heart of man. Premier Stalin is congratulated on the coming victory of Stalingrad. What is meant by this? *Thank you for defeating the Germans for us.* Yes. And that schoolchild can complete the equation: *Then the only enemy left is you.*

The General Secretary must ignore the bats. Or he will lose himself in the cave. What danger does he face? What does he fear? A fat old drunk in pajamas. A cripple who must be wheeled about in a chair.

Let us turn things a different way. In the heat of Africa I shall be offered the second front. We have heard that before. The invasion should already have taken place. In the summer of this year. Litvinov had their word. Well, they can lie to Maxim Maximovich but not to me. *Not to my face.* And what conclusion can we draw from such a fact? That I must make this journey. And when I am in the sky? What mischief will my comrades be up to, down on the ground?

Back to the darkness, the cave, the flying bats: What do their radar waves tell us? *Remain, Josef Vissarionovich, in your capital.* Here is a puzzle. I am forced to go and I am forced to stay. That is the dilemma those tricksters have put me in. It is a scheme to drive a man mad. Or to drink, if I took more than thimbles of vodka and half a glass of Kindzmarauli. Watered. And tasted by others.

Pen now. And now paper.

To the Prime Minister, Mr. Winston Churchill, London:

I thank you for your message and congratulate you and President Roosevelt on your successful landings in French North Africa. I have every hope that you will soon, as you predict, catch Rommel in your pincers and expel him and the Afrika Korps from the continent.

I agree we should meet. I am heartened by your commitment to open a new front in Europe. This must take place in the next six months. No later than seven months, as you say. Our conference, with our military experts, can work out the details, since we are already in full harmony about the main goal.

The battle for Stalingrad, like that for Africa, is not yet won. A beast is most dangerous when it is trapped. I have every hope that by the time of our conference we shall have put the stake through its heart. Then, in a fresh and promising springtime, we can move west as your forces move east, until all join together in Berlin, that bandits' lair of the Hitlerites. Let it be by the end of this happier new year. Our own meeting will be the precursor to that of our armies. We shall clasp hands in Africa as in a short time our generals will clasp theirs in Europe.

I shall have Minister of Foreign Affairs Molotov contact you about arrangements.

I put down my name.

That will do for the moment. What a vision! *A fresh and promising springtime.* I should have broken into song. Yes, about how the swans arrive at Lake Lagoda. And the meadow warbler. Except that every bird stupid enough to fly near Leningrad has been eaten, digested, and shat out on the ground. Along with the rats and the mice and Olya the cat and Nika the dog; then the shit is picked over for a kernel of corn. That is springtime in the Soviet Union. But the plutocrat dreams of sunshine in Africa.

A knock. Poskrebyshev. He wants to know if I have a reply to Churchill's cable. I do not answer. I stare at his gleaming scalp.

"Do you know, Alexander Nikolaevich, that you have a peculiar head? It is shaped exactly like an incandescent bulb."

"You have told me this before, Comrade Stalin. Many times."

"And the light that comes from it! At least twelve volts. One hundred watts. When you come into the room I need smoked glasses."

"This, too, you have said before."

"Oh? And are you growing tired of my little joke? You do not find it amusing? Is that the meaning of your words?"

"Not at all, Comrade. See? I am smiling."

"Here's the thing, Alexander Nikolaevich. A lightbulb burns out. It has to be replaced. Even if it has been awarded the Order of Lenin."

He does not answer. After all, what can he say? He's undoubtedly thinking about his wife. He got on his knees for that Jew-bitch. Bronislava Solomonovna. But he could not save her. And why did he want to? That is the unanswered question. He should have thanked us for relieving the world of one more Trotskyite. And one more Jew. Instead, what did we see? The Director of the Special Section, Central Committee on his knees, with tears coming out of his eyes: *I am the father of two daughters!* Well, we gave him the opportunity to become father and mother to both of them. We didn't touch either one. For that he is grateful. For that he is loyal. Give them a crust after you have taken the loaf. Is that in Machiavelli? No, it is an original thought by the son of the shoemaker. That is what binds Alexander Nikolaevich to Josef Vissarionovich and Josef Vissarionovich to Alexander Nikolaevich: shoemaker sons. Besides, he married again soon enough. Now a third daughter. And I with only one. And such a one. Well, to hell with all of them!

"Is that your reply to Churchill?" he asks, and reaches for the words I have written. I snatch the paper away.

"Yes, but I have not yet decided to send it. Perhaps I shall compose a quite different response."

"May I cable him that a reply will soon be sent?"

Again, I do not answer. Silence is superior to speech. The citizen fills the vacuum with his own black thoughts and in seconds has convinced himself that he is bound for the Lubyanka and can already feel the bullet entering the back of his neck. Then, when I actually do say a word or two, even if it is a criticism or a rebuke, the man is so overcome with joy that if you allowed such a thing he would kiss your boots. Yes, this concept is definitely related to the example of the loaf and the crust. Thus does the thinking process reveal to us not only a means of governing but the full depths of human nature, such as only Dostoyevsky or Pushkin, but not that clown Gorky, have—

But I see that a film of sweat has broken out on the vast steppes of the Poskrebyshev brow.

"Tell me, Alexander Nikolaevich, have you flown in an airplane?"

"Of course. Often. Do you remember how I went back and forth to Kuibishev? The trains were too slow."

"Did you take oxygen? Did you wear a mask?"

"The Urals are not that high. We never went over two thousand meters."

"And how high must one be before the oxygen runs out? This high? Higher? Higher still?"

It is of interest how the actions we take in childhood are never truly forgotten, but wait, as in the case of hibernation, for warm weather. Thus without thought, but with the same skills I had perfected as a boy, I have folded my written words into the shape of an aircraft. With a blunt nose and a tail that sticks up over the fuselage. A little crease at the edge of both wings. In other words, the exact replica of the model I made as a youth, long before the actual airplane was invented by—I think by some Frenchman. Is this not a demonstration of intuitive genius? Is it not the same impulse we see in the work of a Lomonosov or a da Vinci?

"Take care, Josef Vissarionovich. Do not fall."

I do take care. I stand on the chair and now stand on my desk. I am responsible for all of the Soviet Union and for the people's revolution worldwide. The desk is reinforced. I hold the paper toy over my head.

"You see, Comrade Poskrebyshev? I am far higher than the Urals, relatively speaking. The passengers on board must have oxygen. Or else? They turn blue, ha, ha, ha! Like an old piece of cheese!"

"Come down, Comrade Stalin. Vyacheslav Mikhailovich is on his way. What if he should come in? What if he saw you at this childish game?"

"A game? This is no game, Alexander Nikolaeovich. It is life and it is death."

"I am slow-witted. It's a known fact. Could you explain your meaning?"

"No, you are a clever man. You are alive and you will go on living. With daughters. An explanation? This is how I shall make my decision. I shall launch the airship. If it lands on the carpet, it is one thing. If it lands on our good Russian floorboards, another. In the former instance, you will take the paper and burn it and say no further word about it. In the latter, please give it to Comrade Molotov. I assure you it is still legible. Then assist him in making arrangements for my journey abroad. Is what I have said clear to the slow-witted comrade?"

He nods and I throw my paper plane into the air. With the tail bent a little to the left, it makes a wide circle to the right—"Splendid! Splendid!" cries the Director of the Special Section—and almost completes a full orbit. For a split second, I was once more that lad in Tiflis who threw his glider from the rooftop of the seminary and watched it sail over the green tops of the trees.

"It has come down on the carpet, Comrade Stalin. I shall carry out your instructions. I understand completely. You wished to make the decision by chance. In that there is wisdom, for though we think we are choosing one thing or another and shaping our path in life, it is really the hand of fate that makes the final decision."

After all, a simpleton. He's supposed to be a student of Marx and Lenin. He has a law degree. And he's written books on our constitution and our Bolshevik history. Yet he talks about destiny. What's next? Will he read my palm? Or a horoscope?

"Here, Comrade Stalin. Do you see? Here is the paper airplane. And here is a match. And now: into the flame!"

"Stop, fool!" I manage to issue this command in the nick of time, while the match is still burning. And then, in a softer, more pleasant voice: "You are mistaken, Alexander Nikolaevich. The airplane did not land on the carpet. It landed on the floor."

He looks at me. The fire runs down the wooden stick. "You are correct, Comrade Stalin. The light here is dim. I did not see correctly."

"Take the cable to Vyacheslav Mikhailovich. He should send it at once."

"I shall do so, Comrade."

"Send for Svetlana Alliluyeva. I have something to tell her."

My jester pauses at the door. "At once, Comrade Stalin."

"And blow out that match. You will burn your fingers."

Goebbels: January 1943, Wolfsschanze

Finally, at noon, the Führer appeared in Casino 1. I tried not to gasp at the sight. Striding in haste, he was still, with his left hand, buttoning his tunic. His right hand clutched a group of dispatches and rolled-up maps. His hair was not combed. One legging remained outside his boot. His eye fell where I stood. I felt as if he were looking through me, as if peering through a mist. Then, the light kindles in the depths. For me, as always, the same sensation: the stars have come out.

"Mein Führer—"

"Ah, Goebbels. Will you forgive me? I am on my way to the bunker. To Keitel. To Jodl. To Göring. For this pack of Idioten I must interpret the most basic intelligence: like teaching children how to read."

He started to move away but stopped. The circles beneath those eyes. The hair, like a wisp of black straw, sticking up at the back of his head. He could not, with his hand, push the button through its loop. I looked away, so as not to confirm what I had seen: it was shaking.

"Why have you come?" he asked me. "Are you on the schedule?"

"No, mein Führer. I flew up this morning. I have information. From California. I hope—"

"Can't it wait, my dear Doktor? The circus performers expect my arrival. They have no net to fall in without me."

"I cannot stress enough how vital—"

"Yes. I understand. Your voice is now at the pitch you use with a crowd. Come, please follow me."

We went outside, where snow dust was whirling in the wind. I followed his steps—visible in the sucking mud—to the New Tea House. We sat at a table already piled with pastries, with cakes. An orderly brought tea. I could not help but marvel when he began our discussion with pleasantries. I knew full well what was in those dispatches and maps. The Bolsheviks had sent two emissaries under a white flag and with a trumpet player to Paulus's headquarters. They had the effrontery to offer terms of surrender. Of course there was only one answer our Führer would give—and he gave it: the Sixth Army will fight until the last bullet and the last man. Yet in the midst of this Napoleonic rout, the most serious crisis of the Third Reich, what did our leader find the strength to talk about? Magda! My health! And the little babe he held in his arms at the moment of her baptism.

"What of Helga?" he asked. "How is she doing in school? Still a problem with her maths? I hope she liked the bear I sent her for Christmas. She isn't too old for such things? It is my wish that she never grow old. The child, *this* child, must remain alive deep inside the mature and beautiful woman she will become."

Helga! Who cannot add together a five and a two! No wonder we have chosen such a figure to guide the nation. No wonder so many are willing to die for him, as I, at that instant, wished I could die myself. For the whole Reich senses in him the calm, the determination, and the necessary ruthlessness that the German folk must now find in themselves in order to survive. I yearned at that instant to express these thoughts—or at the very least to convey my heart's gratitude for the example he was setting. But I only said, in a voice that trembled, "Yes, mein Führer. Did you not receive her little note? In her own handwriting? She liked the bear very much."

A change came over our Führer. He looked at me like a man who has just awakened from deep slumber. Or a man who has received such a blow that for a moment he does not know where he is or how he arrived there. He kept staring, as if his eyelids were frozen, or as if his eyes had no lids at all, like those of that stuffed Christmas bear. Then, in a high voice, a strained voice, a voice that was almost a shout, he addressed me:

"What are you talking about, Herr Goebbels? Does the Führer und Reichskanzler des deutchen Volkes concern himself with the pleasures of a child? What of the Sixth Army? Their fate is not tolerable. Hundreds and thousands of our best German men are about to be sacrificed on the altar of National Socialism. And we, powerless to do anything about it. Hundreds of thousands. To the Schlachthaus!"

"Perhaps there is something, mein Führer . . ." As I said this, I brought out, from my vest, the article from California.

"These generals! They are the ones who should be shot! With the Romanians! The Italians! The Hungarians, they are the worst of all. Our German bakers units. Our baggage-formations. They fight harder than these allies. With their elite troops!"

I placed the newsprint flat on the table.

"What is this here?"

"A valuable source from America. A thing that might yet change the course of the war. It is from the film columnist from Hollywood. She reports that the Jew Wonskolaser has disappeared from his studio and has gone back to the front. That means to North Africa. To Morocco, where we upset his plans to film propaganda."

"Yes? And what has this to do with the tragedy on the eastern front? Is he a Romanian? I am concerned with Romanians. We should put them up on their sausage hooks. And let the rats eat the sausages."

"This woman, Frau Hopper, is trying to help us make that connection. But she must be careful. Churchill: do you know his movements? Where he is today? Where he plans to be tomorrow?"

"Schellenberger is investigating the whereabouts of this Schwindler—and of the others. I am going to the bunker to receive his report."

"Schellenberger should read the *Times* of Los Angeles. What of the cripple? Where is he? Today? Where will he be tomorrow?"

"Strapped in his chair. And may it roll into the sea."

"And Stalin?"

"What about Stalin?"

"Nothing is certain. But if I interpret the words here, the code hidden in the words—the columnist is telling us that our enemies—here, you see? The pipe, the cigarette in its holder, the cigar: they plan to meet together. Where? She practically shouts the word out loud: *Casablanca*. 'The city, not the picture.' But which city? *Casa blanca*. That means *white house*. The White House. Thus the rendezvous must be in in one of two places: the city across the Atlantic or the city across the Mediterranean. If the conference is in America—well, there we cannot act. But in Morocco. Ah, in Morocco. Think, mein Führer, of our great folk heritage. The Brothers Grimm. *Das tapfere Schneiderlein.*"

He looked at me over the rim of his cup. His blue eyes, as blue as a summer sky, sparkled. "*Drei!*" he declared. "Three with one blow!"

Josef Vissarionovich: December 1942, Moscow

Winter light. It is rationed, like eggs or gasoline. Look at this sun, dropping behind the Kremlin wall. How pale its face, as if it had been summoned to my office. Like that of Molotov, for instance, who stands in the doorway pretending to clear his throat. I can see him with the eyes in the back of my head. The sun sinks a centimeter. I stare. It sinks, the coward, another two. Soon it will be groveling on the ground. I should let our Minister of Foreign Affairs do the same, the way the sultans of our Soviet Republics, in Tashkent, in Alma-Alta, made their servants crawl on their bellies to bring them a glass of water.

"What do you think, Vyacheslav Mikhailovich?" I say, still with my back toward him. "Should I remove this carpet? I prefer the wood of our forests. That way you can hear the footsteps of anyone who comes up behind you."

I turn. Our comrade is in the doorway, clutching my cable instead of a glass of water.

"Comrade Stalin, have I been informed correctly? You wish me to send this message? To Churchill? You intend to fly to Morocco for this conference?"

"I have no choice, Comrade. I have thought it through. I cannot let these schemers meet without me. The prime minister is waiting for my reply. Send it."

"At once, Josef Vissarionovich. And I'll see to all preparations."

"Good. It seems, as the price for a second front, we must *clasp hands*. Go. Don't waste time. No. Wait. I want three airplanes at Vnukovo. Three identical airplanes. Make sure they are American. Understand?"

"I understand, Comrade Stalin."

"I do, too. I won't be in the same one as you."

He turns to go, and does go, but not before giving a mock military salute to the Little Housekeeper, the *former* Little Housekeeper, who laughs and returns the salute on her way in. Are they so friendly? This is new

227

information. But there is nothing new about her face, which is no pale sun. She has paint on it. Unbecoming. Like ripe fruit in the middle of winter.

"Did you want to see me, Papochka? Mikhail Nikiforovich received a telephone call and—"

"Did he? I hope it did not wake him from his nap."

"You always make fun of him. Such a kind, good man. And this time he wasn't sleeping."

"No? And not with his nose in his newspaper?"

"No. He was performing the task you have given him. But it's true? You wanted to see me?"

"It is true. And I am seeing you. Would the Little Housekeeper tell her old father whether she went to her very special and exclusive Model School Number 25 wearing on her face what she is wearing now? And if she did, was it to make the boys on Pimenovsky Street whistle? Or trail her, like a pack of wolves?"

"Of course not, Papochka. You know I wore my uniform. No makeup allowed."

"So you put it on to do your homework? To assist you in your studies? Perhaps to create in you the spirit of Pushkin. When Tatyana Lariniskaya writes Onegin her shameless letter."

"It is not a shameless letter. It is an expression of love, written from the soul. It is vulgar to say otherwise."

"Written from the soul. Where did you learn that? Not at Model School 25. In no school of the Soviet Union. Never mind: I know your teacher."

"In any case today's lesson was geometry. We did valuable work on Euclid's Fifth Postulate. It is so very difficult to understand."

"Then why did you not come home and—what does one do with this geometry? Count up the angles?"

"I did come home. And I completed my work. Here is proof: If the sum of the interior angles is less than 180 degrees—what is it, Papochka? Why are you doing that with your hand? Are you—are you crying?"

"Am I a man who possesses tears? No, I am shading my eyes so that I will not see the one person dearer to me than any other as she tells me a lie."

"A lie? What—?"

"You did not come home. He met you at the school door. He took you, first for sweets. Sweets! When whole cities are starving! And then to the

Tretyakov Gallery. Three hours and thirty-three minutes. What is the fascination of such a place?"

"The War Exhibition. In my opinion, it is every Soviet citizen's duty to—"

"Wearing paint? Should our soldiers rouge their cheeks, too? To hide their blood? It's coquetry! And I know where you are going tonight. And why you are wearing a dress that shows your knees. What is next? A wide-open skirt, like on a Chinese whore? No, do not speak! You are wearing it to go to the conservatory. With him. To listen to German music. Is that patriotic? We should have every note banned. Why are you laughing? Have I amused you?"

"I'm sorry, Papochka, darling Papochka. But you sound just like Mikhail Nikiforovich. He sleeps through all the concerts and then wakes up and cries for everyone to hear: *Just listen! They are sawing up the firewood!* Ha, ha, ha!"

"He is not sleeping. Comrade Klimov, your dear, sweet, most wonderful man on earth: he is pretending to sleep. Pretending to read his newspapers. Those are his orders. Thus I know everything. After the concert, it's off to dance the foxtrot. Eagerness. Restlessness.

"And last night? Like most nights: to the Cinema Artists Club. Garbo: Queen Christina. You think you are the Queen of Sweden? You think your companion is Don Antonio? Sharing a bed? And be exiled for love? Daydreams! Daydreams! He is the one to be exiled!"

"Papochka, Papochka. There is no bed. It's all so innocent. He is a fine, noble, and wise human being."

"You mean your Alexander Wilhelmovich. A fine man? A wise man? A German. And probably a Jew."

"He is not a Jew."

"Oh, and how do you know this? Is it from direct observation?"

"Papa! He is only my mentor. He—"

"I want your silence, Svetlana. I want you to think someone has cut out your tongue. And after the conservatory? To the Savoy. His room at the Savoy. And what happens there? The theorums of Pythagoras? Archimedes in his tub?"

"What happens? He reads me poetry. Heine and Kleist and our Russians, too. It is all so beautiful that—"

"What did I say about your tongue? The Tartars have cut it out of your mouth. Silence, Svetlana Alliluyeva. That is what we need from you now. Yes, I know about your poetry. Look. Here. In my desk. In my drawer. The very book he read from. Love poetry. Let us look further in my magical drawer. What's this? What do we find? Not love poems. Love letters!"

"They are not—"

"That tongue! That wagging tongue! Not love letters? Are they advertisements from newspapers? A list for shopping?"

"Stop! You must stop! He is my teacher! My guide!"

"Pimenovsky Street has no teachers? Geometry is not enough? Now you want to be a wise man yourself? A philosopher? I will tell you what an educated woman is: a herring that thinks!"

"That is the attitude I am trying to escape. Alex—"

"Let us see here what lessons you have learned. *I felt so warm and peaceful beside you. I trust every word you tell me. I want to put my head on your shoulder. I want to quietly close my eyes.* Listen to that filth! We have every letter. We have the transcripts of every phone call. Every word you have exchanged with this seducer, this Casanova. Who learned his lines in Hollywood!"

"You don't have—"

"Silence! Millions are dying! The whole world is at war. And you spend your time fucking an actor! Take a look at yourself, Svetanka. Your freckles. Your hair. That chin. Who would want you? Fool! You are a fool! He has all the women in Moscow around him. What a daughter! She wants to fuck and she can't even find herself a Russian."

"I am leaving, Papa."

"No, you are not leaving."

"Is this what you wanted to talk to me about? If it is, then I—"

"No! It is not what I wanted to talk to you about. But I cannot help myself. Sveta! Svetanka! How you make me suffer. What would your mother think, looking down from heaven? A schoolgirl and a man of forty!"

"My mother? Poor woman! Didn't Nadezhda Alliluyeva fall in love with a man twenty years older? And wasn't that man you?"

"Hush. Hush, Little Sparrow. You did not know her."

"I know what I know. And I remember what I remember. Her perfume. Every night. When she leaned over my bed. That is why I love flowers. You have no tears? I can't stop mine. When I think of those dear, sweet things, no stronger than paper, closing up in the darkness. Opening up in the sun. Oh, the darlings! Oh, Papochka! My mother!"

"Paper flowers. More poetry. You know nothing of her. I forbid you to speak of her. I forbid anyone to speak of her. Not another word."

"Nothing? I know everything! How could you treat her that way? *Hey, you!* In front of others. At the dinner table. Flicking orange peels. Flicking cigarettes. Flirting with dancers. And you lecture me about behavior? Our Great Teacher! You'll never be my teacher. I know what happened. You might just as well have killed her yourself."

"Beware, Svetlana Alliluyeva. I tell you quite calmly you might become an enemy of our Bolshevik republic."

"And then? You'll murder me! And put the pistol by my side. Unhappy girl. A suicide! Depressed over a love affair! Oh! What are you doing? You're hurting me! Help! He's pulling my hair!"

"Scream, you slut! Scream, you whore! This is a padded room."

"Papochka! Don't kill me!"

"No, no. No, no." I stagger back. The red curtain of blood lifts from my eyes. "Don't tremble. Don't worry. Forgive your poor father. It's Nadya. Nadya. When she—when she left us, my heart turned to stone. It is something I cannot explain. Something I do not understand. Little Sparrow, this is your lesson: that sort of goodness can be worse than any evil. I beg you, do not speak of her."

"Papochka. I was wrong. I am the one to be forgiven."

"Ah, Little Housekeeper: we should appoint someone else to be your father."

"No. It's over. All over. I am calm. And peaceful. Now you can tell me. Why did you call for me?"

"To tell you—something happy. Something you will like. I am taking a trip. A real journey. To the sun. To real warmth. And I want to take you with me."

"To Sochi? But it's the wrong time of year."

"Not Sochi. To hell with Sochi. To Morocco. To the desert and the sea."

"But you know I can't go now. The school. My exams."

"More geometry! It is not Euclid who keeps you. It is Comrade Engelsing. Take care, Sveta. In two seconds I could send him to the front. Let him write love letters from Stalingrad. Let him do the foxtrot in the trenches."

"He knows what you can do to him. He expects it. And so do I. Listen to me, Papochka. I swear on the grave of my mother—You see? I dare to mention her. I swear: Alex, Sasha—he is only my teacher. He pities me. He—he makes me think noble thoughts. Don't laugh. Pity me yourself. Do you know what is it like for me in the model school? Where my desk is the only one polished? Let me have these last days with him. Mikhail Nikiforovich doesn't have to go to sleep. Let him watch us and listen. He will be enobled, too. Just three days. A week. Two weeks. All our sun, all our warmth will be in Moscow if you would just give us that. Then send him away. To Stalingrad. To Siberia. Send me away. To America! To an island. Papochka. I am an innocent girl!"

"Two weeks? You can have your two-week idyll. Mikhail Nikiforovich will be with you. No Hotel Savoy. No dancing. No putting your head on his shoulder and closing your eyes. Be a proper Bolshevik woman."

"I always have been, Papa."

"When the two weeks are up you will join me on my journey. The father and the daughter in the sun. And his journey? Things will be cooler for Comrade Engelsing."

"He understands. He owns an overcoat."

"One thing, my one, my only daughter. Not a word of this to a soul. Not your schoolmates. Not Mikhail Nikiforovich. And above all, not to your actor, your playboy and—yes, if you want to know: your German spy."

"How can you say that? He risked his life for the Soviet Union. For the revolution."

"If he spied for us, he can spy for them."

"What nonsense! It is madness."

"Then you tell me: What other reason does a man like that have to take up with a girl like you?"

"I'm staying calm, Papochka. Our struggle is over. I am your Little Housekeeper. That Housekeeper agrees to her Lord and Master's demands."

"Will you swear it? I do not ask on your mother's grave. But as a citizen of our Soviet republic. About our journey, not a word?"

"Of course I do, little father."

"Then go. To Beethoven, is it? Let them saw their firewood. About this, Mikhail Nikiforovich has the proper opinion."

She goes. I should say she exits, because this has been a stage production and our scene is now completed. I want to laugh out loud. Why not? Isn't the room padded? Ho! Ho-ho! I am a better actor than Comrade Alexander Engelsing or Engelstein or Engelberg, the handsome leading man. And Svetlana will play her part. She will go right to her lover and whisper instead of sweet nothings the news of our trip abroad. And then? I am not a schoolboy. I know that bastard Goebbels. Reason tells us he would not allow a Russian spy to leave Berlin if he had not first turned him into a German one. It might take a few days, it might take those two weeks, but the Hitlerites will hear of my journey. Nor will it take the Fifth Postulate of Euclid for them to determine where the lines of the angles meet. Casablanca. And the three sides of the triangle? Comrades Roosevelt, Churchill, Stalin. Hurry, Little Sparrow. Fly, fly. And you, too, Comrade Engelsing. Betray me. Betray Eternal Russia. And do it at once.

Goebbels: January 1943, Wolfsschanze

With great sangfroid the Führer finished his cup of tea. His hand was no longer shaking. He finished his Franzbrötchen, too. Then he stood. He said, "Come, Doktor Goebbels. I invite you to join me at the circus."

As I followed him back through the half-frozen mud, I thought of the task before me—which was to present this defeat to our people. But I could not use the word *defeat*. I had to instruct the press to speak of *sacrifice*. The great and stirring heroic sacrifice that our encircled troops at Stalingrad are offering—perhaps this must be changed to *offered*—the German nation. Play the funeral march. Night and day. Our great, solemn Beethoven.

Why such pessimism, Herr Doktor Goebbels? Was not the gossip of Frau Hopper etched on the surface of my brain? "That pretty little Karelena Kaiser," thus wrote the Klatschkolumnist, "is missing from the Warners' lot as well." That could only mean she was still bound to the Jew—and to us. Were they together in Morocco? If so, the sands of hope had not run from the hourglass.

Pretty little Karelena Kaiser still has the name she used the night I gave her the screen test. Her girl's breasts beneath the wet cloth of her blouse. Did I not create her, just as certainly as I created Helga—too old now, I thank the good God, to sit on the Führer's lap? How that half-Jewess trembled, she was fluttering like ein Espenblatt, eine Feder, before her assignation with the Führer. *Huhu!* And off she went, a schoolgirl, leaving her pimp, der Reichsminister für Volksaufklärung und Propaganda, behind. Shaking like an aspen leaf himself.

If that same good God wills it, she will save us before, like all the others, she destroys herself.

Josef Vissarionovich: January 1943, Moscow

Comrade Churchill is in the air. Wearing his pajamas. Drinking his whiskey. But forbidden his addiction to cigars. Comrade Roosevelt is in the air. Between Brazil and the continent of Africa. He will need much oxygen. And that prick, de Gaulle? Also in the air? How the fuck am I supposed to know? Maybe on a boat. Maybe in a submarine. Ask him. He will tell you he can walk on water.

My airplane is waiting. The motors are turning. Any minute now Poskrebyhshev will knock on the door. Soft. Two knuckles. Then he will poke in his bulging bald head and before he has a chance to say, "Time to go, Comrade Stalin," Comrade Stalin will say, "Put on a helmet, Alexander Nikolaevich. Do you want to blind the pilots?"

How many planes at Vnukovo? I ordered three. All identical. All American. They don't fall out of the air when they fly through a cloud. Or when a little bird, a pipolinski, touches the wing. Which one should the General Secretary board? Answer: whichever one Molotov does not get on. The Germans always end up shooting at him. What a way to travel. It's unnatural. With a train, I can post a Red Army man every quarter kilometer. I can send railway workers to hammer on the rails. Even at the Moscow Circus they use nets to keep the performers from crashing to the ground.

Very well. Let my double get on the second plane. He has been practicing: stop at the door, turn, wave. Let the saboteurs stare all they wish. *Look at our Comrade Stalin! How he waves to his people! A Sun! The Source of Light! Safe travels to Our Teacher!* That's right. Give them a smile. Photographers: perform your duties. Tyelegrafnoye workers: to your keyboards. Inform the world, and the Messerschmitt pilots, that the Bringer of Happiness is on the Amerikaskiy aircraft number 2.

Which means that the real General Secretary is on number 3? In a disguise? Comrade Beria urges me to wear a soldier's uniform. Or pretend

I am a mechanic. What next? He will want me to dress like a woman. Then he can rape me, right in the cabin, and hand me a flower when he is done. Where the fuck is Alexander Nikolaevich? Tying his shoes? So he can walk to Casablanca? So: plane number 3. But really, should it not it be the first plane after all? It's like roulette. It's like rolling dice. I will let Setanka choose. *Cover your eyes, Little Housekeeper. Point to a plane.* God will not let an innocent girl kill her Papochka. He will have mercy. Churchill! Roosevelt! Those sons of bitches. Why have they called this fucking conference?

Why? I know why. Because we are about to win the Battle of Stalingrad. And if we win Stalingrad, we win all of Europe. The table is set for our feast. Paulus and his troops are surrounded. Göring thought he could fly in supplies. He failed even when they had the airfield at Tatskinsaya. Now they have only the single runway at Pitomnik, where the soldiers care more about the empty planes going out than the pitiful rations coming in. German discipline: they shove the wounded out of the way, throw themselves onto the floor of the cargo hold, and ten minutes later our gunners bring them back to earth.

Which is what Mr. Churchill and Mr. Roosevelt desire for me. They do not wish to share the meal. They hope I shall fall like a duck out of the air. We shall see. Little Housekeeper! The fate of the World's Bright Light is in your hands. Choose well!

KK: *January 1943, Washington, DC*

To my dear Onkel Engel,

I am writing to you from my room in the Mayflower Hotel, Washington, DC, before dawn on this first day of the new year. I have only a small hope that what I write will ever reach you. They say the courier flights to Moscow leave only once a week. They say the last one was shot down over Königsberg. The poor flyers lost. I have even smaller hope, my darling Alex, that I shall see you again. There is a glass window in my suite. There are windows everywhere. Do you know what I think of now? When I was five? You threw me into the air, almost to the ceiling, and Joe-Joe caught me and threw me up again. The happiest moment of my life. Or was it when I was acting for you? I act every minute now. But not in front of a camera.

Think of this as a letter of farewell. And also, perhaps, an explanation. In June of 1941—oh, does it not seem as if geologic ages have passed? That mountain ranges have erupted and that old species have been replaced by new ones? But it has been only eighteen months! I waited that day at the Anhalter Bahnhof. I waited in the rain. You did not come. The Reichsminister, the Reichsminister's car, came instead. He told me you had an offer from Hollywood. He showed me the contract. Five hundred dollars a week, is that not right? And a house. The little house we shared. Argyle Avenue.

Here is my shame. Here is my guilt. For a moment, for more than a moment I believed him. When I ran into your arms at Union Station, when I saw you in that old brown suit, I knew you were the same person. But I was not. This you discovered on that first night. What did you think, my own, dear Alex? I know: that I had turned into a stone. You held me in your arms, but you knew I was far away. Where? In the Reichskanzlei. With the wolf. My arms over my head like Venus, he said, like Minerva, and the goddess Aphrodite. He saw me in a bathing suit. Coming out of the water. In your silly film. There was a glass tabletop.

I am seeking words. I almost ran, that first night, from you. Leaving you alone in that pretty little bungalow. Thoughts, images: they are always in my mind; they circulate like a permanent infection of the blood. Every day is a struggle against impulses. I do not always win. Two attempts, Alex. Clumsy. Girlish. Unsuccessful. But not half-hearted. I walk through the streets with a constant fever. I mean by this an actual fever. You would feel my skin hot to the touch. On an American thermometer: minimum of 101. I tremble at every pane of glass. *This time? Will it be this time?*

Earlier this night I attended my second New Year's Eve party at the White House. Oh, Alex, you would have liked my blue dress. The president did. He laughed with me. Such a lovely laugh. The whole man is in it. I did not on this occasion sit on his lap. But for a moment, while I crouched beside him, he grasped my hand. I made a toast to victory. Of course he did not know my meaning. We are on different sides. As are you and I, my dear old Onkel Alex. I do not mean, of course, of the Atlantic Ocean. In any case, I shall be crossing that great sea soon. In ten days. The president insists that Mr. Warner's masseuse—how foolish of me! You know our Terrible Turk. How could you forget him? He wants Abdul and also

Mr. Warner to join him on that flight. And of course I must accompany Jack. The president will not object.

Jack Warner. At this moment he is in the suite next to mine. I must write hurriedly because at any moment he will come through the unlocked door and put his lips against my neck and his skin against my skin. When he was in North Africa during the invasion I had six weeks of peace. I did not know if he were alive or dead. No, in truth, I did know. He is the kind of man who cannot be killed. Not by a bullet and not by a bus. Always he comes back with a smile that will not leave his face and a joke I do not understand.

My confession is that I did not want him to die. It is not love that has grown between us. I do not think, either, it is Zärtlichkeit, which the Americans call fondness. I cannot help but respond to the life force in him, even if that is what makes it a necessity to be touched and submit not once a day but before eight hours, eight hours by the clock, go by. Not the way I want. The way he wants. He lasts. Lasts and lasts. And all the time I have to smile and laugh at what he is saying, because without my laughter, loud laughter, he will not and I believe cannot bring the act to an end.

Oh, I am laughing now! Alex! My protector! And hero! Alan Castle: Do you remember? How like a ram you knocked him to the ground. How you made the bones in his back crack and crack. The executive producer! Vice president for production! When I think of that: well, just for a moment, I forget that I am on the ninth floor and that behind the thick drapery there is the window glass.

Another memory, my darling. At the Weissensee Cemetery, so dark, so mysterious, the vines hanging down and reaching up: you were the only one crying. This is the thought that came to me: *now my Onkel will marry Hannelore and be my Vater.* Can you imagine the bewilderment in that child? With so many fathers—you; and of course the Führer, our Führer, my love for him filled my heart; and always, always poor Joe-Joe. How wonderful to his daughter. The Nappo he gave me, the kind with the nougat inside, before every movie began. I smeared his lapels black with chocolate; I smeared his tie. The trick shot he taught me: behind the back, my eyes closed, with the crowd of nice men, the men at the Zylinderhut Billard, laughing, clap-clapping their hands. I was a star. Now the man who helped kill him pours his yellow Samen inside me. And on my belly. Do you see why it is best I turned to stone? If I were warm, if I were breathing, if I were a woman: the milk from my breasts would poison my children. I will tell you what else I thought on that day. About the men who were shoveling the dirt on my father. *Hurry up! Hurry up! Dick Powell is waiting.* I am a Medusa.

Morocco, that is where the president will take us. Mr. Churchill will be there. Also, your own hero, Comrade Stalin. Perhaps also M. de Gaulle. There will be pleasures. The president said there is a secret place that Mr. Churchill wishes to take us. Even he does not know where it is. I dream of some spot with minarets and gardens and secret springs, like a tale from Sheherazade. An oasis from this life. I only hope the Führer has learned of this adventurous flight: then he could send his air force with its attack planes and shoot this half-Jewess, black and defiled, into the waves below her. *A letter of farewell*, I said. *Of explanation.* Or have I, like Joe-Joe, written a suicide note?

The door. Mr. Warner. I love my Alan Castle. I love my Onkel Alex. Do you know that there are bits of gold in your eyes?

Goebbels: January 1943, Wolfsschanze

We arrived at the Führer bunker. Here there were neither pleasantries nor formalities. The common chord was one of solemnity but with no hint of panic. First we heard the latest radio reports from Stalingrad. Nothing had changed since this morning. The two Russian envoys, with their trumpet player, were sent back to their headquarters under a white flag. Paulus's defeatism—imagine, he had dared to contemplate their terms of surrender—was overcome by Schmit, who, having received the Führer's directive, declared that the Sixth Army would remain steadfast no matter what fate befell them.

Generaloberst Zeitzler declared that the Bolshevik attack would begin sometime within the next two days. The opening barrage, he added, would utilize at least five thousand guns. "The Sixth Army will be decimated." *Decimated*: that meant the elimination of one tenth of the Roman legions. But we shall lose all.

Jodl, pale, thin-lipped, shook his head. "We shall experience the greatest defeat of German arms since Jena."

Göring, whose failure to bring in supplies brought on this catastrophe, was not pale. He was tanned from his Italian vacation. "No," he declared. "The greatest tragedy ever to befall the German folk."

Keitel, barely audible, echoed the Chief of Staff: "*Five thousand guns.*"

After that, all remained silent, silent and still, as if we too were soldiers waiting, in stoic fashion, the coming onslaught.

Then, one by one, we turned toward our leader, sitting calm and resolute among us. I thought at that moment what I have thought many times before: the more furious the storm, the more determined the Führer to face it. Under our gaze, he looked off, as if seeing through the walls of this underground shelter, through the thick, dark, surrounding earth, and through space to some distant vista:

"Can you imagine, gentlemen, how eager I am to exchange this gray uniform for a suit of blue or black or brown? Nothing will make me happier than to be once more a common citizen of the Reich, to visit theaters and museums and go to the cinema. Yes, I look forward to a future when I can drop in at our beloved Kameradschaft der deutschen Kuenstler, as an artist among artists and as a human being again among human beings."

"Mein Führer—" That was Keitel again. But at a single glance from his commander he fell silent.

"I know, Keitel. I know. You wish to speak to me of the situation at Stalingrad. But haven't I already given my orders? To the last bullet. To the last man. Jodl, you say we are faced with the greatest defeat since Jena. I heard you, too, Göring. The greatest of all misfortunes to befall the German folk. But if those German folk are weak, do they not deserve to be exterminated by a stronger people? Nature is just. We need feel no pity for them. No—save your words. There is no need of pity for me, either. What is life? Life is the Nation. The individual must die anyway, and the Nation lives on. How can one be afraid at the moment of death? It is death that allows a man to free himself from this misery and from the stupidity, the weakness, the cowardice of these people that surround me! You ask, but what if the Nation—? No, I shall not allow such a thing to happen. It cannot be allowed. Out of the question! I promise you all: when the war is over we shall go together to the Wintergarten. Listen to me, Jodl. The defeat at Jena? I shall turn Stalingrad into a victory more glorious than Frederick the Great's at Hohenfriedberg."

For the first time, Bormann allowed himself a word. "According to Schmit, and to the Generaloberst, the opening barrage will begin within forty-eight hours."

Keitel: "Thirty hours if they begin at dawn."

Zeitzler, the Chief of Staff, looked down at the sheaf of papers before him. "Rokossovsky has at his disposal forty-seven divisions and three hundred aircraft. The Romanian salient will break and run. Our own men—our own men cannot fit their frozen fingers around the triggers of their guns."

At this moment Speer—delayed, he said, on the road from Rastenburg—slipped into the bunker.

Göring greeted him: "The Führer promises us a victory. The equal of Rossbach. Of Luethen. Of Hohen—"

"Yes," broke in Zeitzler. "And all within thirty hours."

The Führer held up a hand and turned toward where I was sitting. "The Reichsminister has something to tell us. Listen closely. Doktor Goebbels, if you will be so kind—?"

At last! I had sat through the entire discussion, *cooling my heels*: another English expression. "We have received new information," I began, "crucial information." Then, in no more than two minutes, I told those in the bunker about the column by Frau Hopper and all the clues it contained.

Keitel: "A gossip columnist? From *Hollywood*?"

Jodl: "With this weapon we shall duplicate the charge of Seddlitz's cavalry? It was horses, not newspapers, that won the battle of Rossbach."

"What matters," said Speer, "is not whether the words are in a newspaper but whether they are true."

The Führer nodded. "Our task, my dear Speer, is to determine precisely that. Herr Standartenführer, will you kindly give us your report?"

"Jawohl, mein Führer," said Schellenberg as he rose from his seat. "We have made through SS Intelligence a crash effort. Churchill is still in London. He has been joined there by the American, Harriman. A Liberator bomber has been taken from the fleet and equipped with hammocks and a special petrol heater. Further, we have noted for some weeks that the Jew, Jacob, with the rank of Assistant Secretary to the War Cabinet, always at Churchill's side, departed for destinations unknown. Now, this afternoon, at 4:00 p.m., through the intense efforts of the Sicherheitsdientst SS, we have discovered his whereabouts. He is—"

I interrupted the report. "Allow me to hazard a guess, Schellenberg. Africa. He is in Africa."

"That is correct, Herr Reichsminister."

"In the city of Casablanca."

"Also correct. You would make an excellent member of our service."

Speer: "It is likely that he is making preparations for his superior's arrival."

Schellenberg: "That is a fair assumption."

Zeitzler: "And Stalin? And Roosevelt?"

Schellenberg: "In our modern age it is more important to pay attention to aircraft than to personnel. Stalin, too, is in his capital. But he has arranged for three American B-47s to be flown to the aerodrome of Vnukovo, where they are being kept under special guard. We know that unlike our own leaders, daring in their personal endeavors and forward-looking in their outlook on life, the Russian bear prefers to remain in his den. He has a peasant's fear of flying. It is our assessment that for the first time in his life he will enter an airplane, one of these three bombers, and that his own staff and his military aides will occupy the other two. These aircraft are capable of a direct flight to—perhaps the Reichsminister für Volksufklärung und Propaganda would like to supply the destination—?"

"Casablanca."

"Ja—or the aerodrome at Médiouna, quite nearby."

Zeitzler again: "You do not mention Roosevelt."

"With the cripple, too, we begin with aircraft, this time two Boeing clippers that arrived early this morning at the Pan American water terminal in the city of Miami. They are being held in isolation. None of our people can get near them."

"And what," asked Keitel, "is the significance of that?"

"In the case of this gentleman we can learn more from his train. Also this morning—I should say yesterday morning in America, in particular in Washington—a five-car train was assembled in the Naval Gun Factory, and one of these cars has glass windows that can stop a fusillade of machine-gun bullets."

"Yes, we know all about the *Ferdinand Magellan*. It is old news. What has this to do with the Boeings in Miami?"

"Well, Herr Reichsmarschall, we believe the president has on this same train already begun his travels. This is confirmed by the fact that the Negro

Pullman porters were replaced by navy stewards from Roosevelt's yacht. A real man of the people, no?"

"Again, Herr Standartenführer, you repeat what you have already told us: the president is taking a trip."

"We know something else. Something crucial. At 10:00 p.m., local time, the *Ferdinand Magellan* departed Washington and headed north—"

"North! Of what use is that to us? The Jew is heading to Jew-land. New York City. Or to his house on the river Hudson. The lazy swine spends more time there than at the White House."

"Permit me to finish, Reichsleiter Bormann: the train traveled as far north as Fort Meade, Maryland. Then it began moving south. This was a deliberate attempt to mislead the American press and the American people. But it did not mislead our agents. By our calculations, this secret train should be arriving in the city of Miami even as we speak. Its occupant might take off as early as tomorrow morning."

At this, Bormann's tongue flicked out, like an amphibian's when it wishes to reel in an insect. "Reichsmarschall Göring, this is a God-sent opportunity. Do you possess the resources to bring down all six of these aircraft? Can you send them into the sea?"

"Of course. The Luftwaffe will fall on them with claws out, like eagles onto a flock of pigeons."

"Is this the same Luftwaffe," Jodl remarked, "that cannot deliver a single loaf of bread to our surrounded troops?"

Speer: "Why have a meaningless discussion? We don't know when, precisely, the aircraft are leaving or what route they will take; nor does the Reichsmarschall control the air over the Mediterranean or any part of Morocco."

"Mein lieber Albert," said the Führer, "this discussion is not entirely meaningless. I have every intention of allowing our enemies to land safely in Casablanca. But they might find it a bit more difficult to leave than to arrive."

The Chief of Staff was the first to respond, though you could hardly hear the single word he uttered under his breath: "*Meuchelmord.*"

Then everyone began to cry out together.

"Of course!"

"Assassination! We'll kill them all!"

"A slaughter. A slaughter in the desert."

Zeitzler: "But, mein Führer, without control of the air. Without control of the sea. Our forces retreating to the east. How can such an operation be mounted?"

"How many fisherman does it take, Generaloberst Zeitzler, to draw the strings of the net? For this task we do not need an army or a navy or what is left of Herr Göring's air force. All we need is a single agent on the ground."

"Only now, mein Führer," said Keitel, "do I grasp the full depths of your genius. Stalingrad is only a decoy. The men must fight to the last bullet to keep the world's attention focused on the Volga. Meanwhile, we behead our foes and seize the world itself."

Jodl: "We lose Stalingrad but we gain Rossbach, Leuthen, Hohenfried-berg—that is to say, London, Washington, Moscow. Here is Frederick reborn among us: the art of the feint, of the oblique attack."

"*Lose Stalingrad?* Did I hear you correctly, Herr Oberkommando? Or perhaps you did not hear your Führer. The fall of Stalingrad is unthinkable. I will not allow it to happen. I declare it out of the question!"

Göring: "But thirty hours. Forty hours. The planes. The guns."

"Much can happen in thirty hours. For a man on the gallows it is a lifetime. Schellenberg: Can you contact the Russian embassy in Sweden? Within an hour?"

"Within minutes, if you command it. Semyonov, their agent there, never leaves the grounds in Stockholm."

"Then your Führer does command it: you are to make contact and offer the Soviet Union a separate peace. Make sure they understand we know about Casablanca. *Everything* about Casablanca. The travel. The conference. All. Stalin will grasp at once that we have offered him the gift of his life. And a second gift: all of the territory he possessed on June 21st. He will then rule more of Europe and Asia than Ghengiz Khan."

Zeitzler: "And the price of this gift?"

"Stalingrad."

Bormann: "Why must we give up Moscow? Is this not a war on Bolshe-vism and international Jewry?"

Speer laughed out loud. "There will be plenty of Jews left for us in Washington, DC, and London."

"But we must think further. What if—"

"No time, Bormann, for further thought. Schellenberg? Still here? Why are you not on your radio?"

The Standartenführer, already on his feet, clicked his heels and trotted toward the door, which the sentries were holding open.

Bormann was not done: "But why will he give up what he already has grasped in his hand?"

"Because," replied the Führer, with great calm, "he values his own life more than the quarter of a million lives he can take from us. Goebbels—" And here the eyes of our leader fell on me. "You are a Doktor of Philosophy. A learned man. Perhaps you can explain the situation more clearly to our friend."

"Don't you understand, Bormann? This is a great moment. A world historical moment. It is the end of the two-front war."

Still, the chief of the Parteikanzliei insisted on digging his grave deeper: "How can we count on Stalin? What stops him from warning the others? If he does, we will have gained nothing—and lost the Baltic states, the Caucasus, and half of Poland."

"Warn them?" echoed the Führer. "Warn Churchill? Warn Roosevelt? Does that sound like Ghengiz Khan?"

At that moment, a breathless Schellenberg returned. He struggled to speak. "Semyonov was at the embassy. Perfect conditions. Crystal-clear reception. Mein Führer, message transmitted."

I felt within me the full import of these brief words. Even more, I felt, even deeper within, the warmth of what the Führer had said: *A Doktor of Philosophy. A learned man.* Those words glowed in me like vacuum tubes. Now he turned one more time to his secretary:

"You need not worry, Bormann, about the Baltic States or about Poland. There will be only one victor in this war. We shall deal with Comrade Stalin later. Even the great Khan was brought down by a single poisoned arrow. And where is he now? In the earth. In an unmarked grave. You should read more, Herr Parteikkanzlieiführer, like our Goebbels, whose nose is always in a book. Follow his example and you, too, will discover the fate of kings and queens: it is all in the works of Marco Polo."

Josef Vissarionovich: January 1943, Moscow

The soft knock. Two knuckles. And Poskrebyshev pokes his bulletproof head through the door.

"Well, Alexander Nikolaevich, have you brought me my flying suit? And my leather helmet?"

"No, Comrade Stalin. I just wanted to alert you that Vyacheslav Mikhailovich is about—"

He doesn't get the chance to finish. Comrade Molotov comes rushing by him into the room.

"What is it? What is happening here? Vyacheslav Mikhailovich, why aren't you at Vnukovo? We'll be taking off in less than an hour."

I see that he is panting. His chest goes up and down, as if it were pumping out his flow of words.

"It's Semyonov. In Stockholm. I mean, I was at Vnukovo. But then the embassy in Stockholm. The telephone. Comrade Stalin, they know everything. The Germans. Everything about the conference. About Roosevelt and about Churchill. And about the General Secretary's flight!"

"I knew it! Engelsing *is* a spy. Svetlana ran to him. To his love poems, and he whispered the news into the ear of the German, the woman he really—"

Molotov doesn't hear me. He just goes on speaking as if I weren't even in the room. Such a thing has never happened before. It sets a precedent.

"They are offering a separate peace. All the boundaries of 1941. Immediate cease-fire in Stalingrad and withdrawal of their troops. Josef Vissarionovich! What an achievement! It's the end of the war! They want an immediate reply. What should I tell them? My God! Think of it. Only a year ago we were about to lose Moscow. We were going to blow up our own buildings. Now we have everything!"

"Alexander Nikolaevich," I say, speaking right through my foreign minister. Now *he* is the one who does not exist. "No need for flying suits. Please have the pilots at Vnukovo switch off their engines. And if you happen to see Svetlana Allilueva, tell the bitch that she won't be enjoying herself on the beaches of Morocco and that she had better run to Alexander Wilhelmovich as fast as she can because he is going to spend the next five years digging coal on the Vakuta River. He has an overcoat? Good. The temperature is on average minus twenty degrees."

Molotov looked at me as if he were in a state of bliss. "Then I am to tell Berlin we accept the terms they have proposed to us in their message?"

"Message, Vyacheslav Mikhailovich? What are you talking about? I have received no message."

The color drains from his face like a dirty bath from a tub. "Excuse me, Josef Vissarionovich. I have mixed things up. Ha! Ha! Perhaps I was dreaming."

"You should drink more steamed tea. It is good for the nerves."

"I thank the People's Commissar for his advice and his concern."

"I do want to send a message, however. To Rokossovsky. He has at his disposal seven thousand rockets and twenty-five hundred tanks. So please ask Konstantin Konstantinovich why the fuck he is delaying and tell him that Operation Koltso must begin tomorrow at dawn. With all five thousand guns."

"At once, Comrade Stalin. And may I send a message to Churchill? To President Roosevelt? To warn them of the danger? Otherwise, they will be assassinated."

"Yes, of course. Write them at once. Here is what you are to say, after the *Dear Mister Prime Minister* and the *Dear Mister President* and all of that crap:

> Final battle of Stalingrad to begin tomorrow. Cannot leave Moscow at such a crucial hour. I wish you success at your important conference and also a relaxing time in the warmth of the African sun.
>
> *Yours Very Sincerely,*
> *Stalin*

PART III

~

CASABLANCA

19 ⸾ DIXIE CLIPPER

The Terrible Turk: January 1943, Trinidad Harbor

It wasn't a bullet that got me at Fedala, though if everybody—I mean, everybody from the Chief all the way up to General Patton—wanted to say so, it wasn't hard to keep my mouth shut. What really happened was that I was the last one off our landing craft; I slipped on the ramp and went head over heels into the drink. That wasn't so bad. I got to my feet all right, but by then the others were nowhere around. When I turned to see where the Chief had gone, another boat, lifted up on a wave and coming sideways, hit me as hard as the punch I took from Billy Morris—that was at McCarey's Pavilion in 1908. Knockout. Fourth round. No excuses.

Well, this was no different, except that I was underwater instead of on the canvas. My own helmet, I think, sliced open my head. It looked like I was down for the count. You know what count that was and who was the referee. But some of the boys from that same Higgins boat dragged me up on the beach and left me in the shadow of a half-track that was already burnt and smoking. I kept seeing stars all that day and then everything went black until the next day, when I woke up in the field hospital.

What a terrible moment that was in the country of Morocco! I thought the Chief must be dead and he thought I must be dead. That is the definition of a tragedy. So when I got out of the hospital bed and saw him at the Miramar Hotel, the next thing you know we were in each other's arms. Even though he is a man's man, let me tell you. And I like to think the same of myself. To which Hedda can testify, though maybe not in print. Still, there is something about the love between two men that is—I don't know what to call it, exactly. Maybe more pure.

For example, when I got shipped out of the war zone and got back to Camarillo Street Hedda came over and didn't want pleasure as much as she wanted information. She is cold. Not me. I am the type that is hot. Anyway, what she wanted to know and kept asking over and over was why were they holding up the release of *Casablanca*. All I could tell her is that the Chief wanted a new ending, with shots of the invasion. We'll have to fake it. Maybe with Bogart looking out of a porthole on a boat and stock footage of ships at sea and a close-up of the flag. It won't cost more than a nickel. But it's hard to get anything out of the Chief right now. He's beside himself because with his camera he got nothing and Zanuck with his got everything, including a medal.

One thing I didn't tell Hedda, but somehow she knew it anyway, was that no sooner did I arrive back in LA than I got a summons from FDR to come back to the White House. Even though my head still hurt and I had a ringing in my ears.

"He's going to give you the Purple Heart," she told me.

"Naw, it's just a massage," I said. "The usual."

But I knew that wasn't true—because if that was all the president wanted, he would not have insisted that the Chief come, too.

We checked into the Mayflower. Three rooms: for the Terrible Turk, for the Chief, and for Miss Kaiser. Connected. On the last day of the year we were scheduled to go over to Pennsylvania Avenue for dinner, but first I had to show up at the White House for a hands-on session with the commander in chief. Almost an hour. He kept saying what he always said, things like, "Oh! Ouch! Keep going! This is marvelous! Don't stop!" But I knew better. I'll make a confession. I played a trick on the president. I folded my arms and stood like a cigar-store Indian. And he just kept on, saying, "I feel it. I feel it. Wonderful! A wonderful sensation!" The navy lieutenant stared straight ahead. Also made out of wood. But I caught the colored's eye and he caught mine. Almost invisibly, he shook his head. Then I went back to work on those gray sticks that had no more strength to them, I thought, than soda straws.

When I finished, I wiped him down. He didn't want to be dressed. He wanted to try out the braces. Prettyman strapped them on. The lieutenant stepped forward but was waved away. Prettyman, too. Now I really was turned into petrified stone.

"You see? You see? You have worked your magic, Abdul. This is progress. Real progress!"

He was lurching around like the monster of Dr. Frankenstein, with the braces clanking like chains.

"Wait until the admiral sees this. Can't you wait to see his face? Thinks he is an expert. A man of science. We'll show him!"

Just then Mr. Roosevelt, with the braces locked, began to tilt, like that leaning tower of Pisa. Prettyman caught him on one side, the navy man on the other.

"Well, McIntire," that's what I'm going to tell him. "Well, McIntire, what have you got to say now?" The president was grinning and his head was thrown back in that happy way of his. "Still think I am not fit to make that trip?"

I returned to the hotel and got into my monkey suit. Then the three of us—Abdul the Terrible Turk; Karelena in a blue gown, a little low in the front considering the occasion; and the Chief, yanking at his bow tie—drove in a limousine back to the White House in time for cocktails. The president made old-fashioneds for the whole crowd. I took a mental note to remember the guests, so I could tell Hedda when I got back. She was no fan of Mr. Roosevelt. She used to say that Hitler was God's gift to his country while the president was doing the devil's work in ours. Not in print, of course. And only before the war. Well, let's see: Hopkins and Morgenthau and their wives; the speechwriters Sherwood and Rosenman and theirs; and a prince and princess from the country of Norway, who like common people went by Olav and Martha. And some friends and relatives with names I never caught, plus Eleanor. After the cocktails, dinner. I wasn't surprised to see the Chief leave most of the food on his plate; it wasn't any better than the rations we had in Africa. He had animal crackers, an old trick of his, in his pocket.

Then we all went to the same room where they played *The Man who Came to Dinner* exactly one year ago. The lights went out and instead of the Warners shield we all saw the Paramount mountain. Next to me I heard the Chief grumble, like always, "Instant morphine." Then we all sat back and watched the latest of that studio's road pictures—this time it was to Morocco. Same old stuff: Hope and Crosby and Lamour. Arabs and camels. Whoopee pads and hotfoots or maybe hot feet and exploding cigars. "Splendid! First class! How charming!" That was FDR, who I could see was doubled up with laughter, especially when two of the camels started talking.

When the lights came back up, the president turned to the Chief and said, "Well, Jack-o, what did you think? Wasn't that the most uproarious comedy? And isn't that Lamour one pretty lass?" The Chief was fast asleep with his head on KK's bosoms, and I am afraid drool was coming out of his mouth. I gave him an elbow and he sat right up, "Lamour? Hell, I thought up that wraparound outfit. What sarong about that?"

By then it was almost midnight. Champagne came in on a cart. The president made the same toast as the year before:

"With God's help, victory!"

But this time he didn't throw down his glass.

Mrs. Roosevelt: "To our friends and family who are far off in the world and cannot be with us tonight."

Then everybody drank a toast to the president.

That was supposed to be the end, but Miss Kaiser—was she, I wondered, a little tipsy?—stood up from where she had been kneeling down and chatting with the president. I have an observant eye and saw how he had been holding her hand. Now she raised an empty glass. Her skin was pale, almost white against the blue color of what she was wearing. "I want to drink to something," she said. "I want to drink to victory, too."

Suddenly it *was* midnight. Shouts and cheers came up from the street outside, and bells rang because at last things were looking up for America and for her allies.

With that the evening broke up. People went for their coats. The Hopkins couple climbed the stairs to their bedroom. Mrs. Roosevelt wished everyone a good night and went upstairs as well. One of the coloreds was just handing the Chief his camel hair when the president came rolling up in his bicycle chair and asked the three of us if we would stay behind. Actually, he meant the two of us; to Karelena, whose hand he kissed and held on to, he said, "We need your kind of fighting spirit. Would you mind waiting here for just a few minutes?" Then the Chief and I followed him down the hall and into a little room with nothing in it but two chairs and a table. On the table was a phone. With a nod of his head FDR motioned for us to sit down. He lit a cigarette. Then, grinning around the stem of the holder, he said, "I wish you two gentlemen a happy new year. And I think I can promise that is what it is going to be."

We wished him the same.

"Jack-o, I know we were supposed to show your picture tonight. But I've got a more appropriate place for its world premiere."

"That's okay," said the Chief. "That will give us time to shoot the new ending. Bogart comes back to Casablanca and lands on the beach. With bombs bursting in air! I wish I thought of that line."

"Ha, ha, ha! Well, they tell me you did magnificent work. That you even got both the landing and the surrender on film. It's a shame it was lost. It went down with—what was that poor ship? The *Joseph Hewes*?"

The Chief nodded. "Yes, Mr. President. A German submarine got her. We lost every foot I shot."

"And the captain," said Mr. Roosevelt. "And a hundred of the crew."

"Yeah, them too," my boss declared. "What a tragedy."

"Well," said the president, brightening up again. "At least you'll have a second chance."

"Huh?" said the Chief, and he pulled at the tie, where its wings were digging into his throat. "What second chance?"

"Listen, old boy. I chose this Morocco film tonight on purpose. Actually, it's a kind of joke that I played on them all—even Eleanor, who is completely in the dark."

"A joke? I don't get it. You ask me, there wasn't a good gag in that picture. Those guys at Paramount—"

The president waved his hand. "So what I am going to tell you now has to be and must remain top secret. Is that understood? The whole course of the war may depend on it. And that in turn may mean the fate of mankind."

"*The Fate of Mankind?* I saw that script. By some French guy. We took an option, but it turned out it was full of Chinamen. We'd have to shoot the whole damned film inside a laundry. Or maybe you're talking about something else?"

"The time for jokes is over, Jack. Even if I did play one tonight. In ten days I shall be going on a little trip. An airplane flight. I'm greatly looking forward to it. Haven't been in the air since I flew to Chicago in '32 to accept my party's nomination. Well, here is the punch line: I am going to Morocco. I'll be meeting at Casablanca with Prime Minister Churchill and Premier Stalin, and I hope with General de Gaulle."

It was a cold night. That's why the window was shut. The room, I already said this, was small. Now it was filling with smoke. That didn't stop the president from lighting up again. He threw his head back to take the first puff. Then he swung forward and said, "What I want you to know is that the entire venture, with its consequences for all the world, depends on you."

Now the amazing thing was that when he said that, the president wasn't looking at the vice president for production, he was looking at Abdul the Terrible Turk! At first I thought this was an illusion caused by the haze. But no: his eyes, behind those little nose glasses, were on me.

"Me?" I said.

"Him?" echoed the Chief.

"Correct. Admiral McIntire doesn't think I'm up to such a long flight. Over the ocean. In an unpressurized cabin. And then the rigors of a foreign country. But I have no doubt, my good Turk, that with your magic, all will be well. I've convinced the admiral that what you do for me with your hands is the best tonic available. Will you come? I've inquired. We'll be able to set up a table in the Boeing. If all goes well, and I think it will, these old limbs of mine will be doing a jig ten thousand feet in the air."

My own brain was doing a sort of dance already. It was whirling around. "You want me to go to Africa? To Casablanca? But I've just got back. Practically. Everything, all of my stuff, is in California."

"Excellent! Send for your bags. Have them shipped to Miami. We'll be leaving from there."

"But Mr. President—" Without meaning to, I reached for my head, where the wound had started to throb. And the ringing, like cicadas in a treetop, began again in my ears. "My head," I said. "My ears."

"Nonsense! We're the same age, are we not? If I can do it, so can you!"

"But on the beach. On the boat. I almost died."

Mr. Roosevelt took the cigarette holder out of his mouth. "I am sorry, my friend. I don't like to pull rank. But we've made you a captain of the Signal Corps. You're still on active duty. I'm afraid I have to make this an order."

"Yes, sir," I said, and gave him a salute.

He smiled, a big one, and turned to the Chief. "As for you, Colonel—"

"*Lieutenant* Colonel," he almost shouted. Then he did shout. "I resign! I resign my commission. Goddammit, I quit!"

Here he started clawing at first one shoulder of his shiny black tux and then the other; then he ripped off the bow tie that had been annoying him the whole night and threw that down, instead of the silver stars.

"Well, it's entirely up to you, Jack-o, old pal. I need Abdul's services more than you. But if you do decide to come—and I hope you do; my reports say that you got along famously with the sultan and with Admiral Michelier. That could help our conference run smoothly. And of course you'll bring your camera—oh, and that fiery young lady. I like the way she drank to victory. I'm glad we could find a way to bring her to this country. We'll find something over there for her to do."

"Okay, okay," said the Chief, which didn't really mean much, one way or the other. And he didn't say anything else—not when we rejoined Miss Kaiser and not when he got into his camel hair or into his limousine, and not when he went back into his room at the hotel. But the next day he had the studio cancel our reservations on the Super Chief home. We stayed in Washington for another week and a half and then took the secret train to Miami and got aboard the *Dixie Clipper* later that morning. It wasn't until we were above the clouds, thousands of feet in the air, that the Chief leaned close to me.

"It's a good thing we're going back together," he said. I wasn't surprised. The president was wrong. He didn't need me more than the boss. In my opinion he didn't need me at all. Or put it this way: he did, but more in the head than in the legs. Psychologically. I treated J.L. every single day. But it turned out that wasn't what the Chief had in mind. "There's a girl there," he said—and in a real low voice, so that Miss Kaiser, two rows behind, couldn't hear.

I laughed. "I heard about that Bousbir. Everybody's heard about it. I don't mean the fountain."

The Chief didn't reply. We must have covered a couple of hundred miles, with only those four engines roaring and roaring, before he said, "Not the Bousbir. The harem. Wavy hair. With a part. The lips: they're, you know, bee-stung. In a pout. And you have never seen knockers like that in your life. My eyes were coming out of my head. What I'm saying is, she's another Lamarr. I'm going to get her under contract if it's the last thing I do. This is a business trip. I can write it off."

One more thing. There were copies of all the papers inside the cabin. Our turn to look at them didn't come up until we had already started our descent. The Chief was asleep, dreaming something, because his moustache kept twitching. The way you can tell a sleeping dog is chasing a squirrel. The harem girl? I got a three-day-old copy of the *LA Times*. Of course I went right to Hedda's column. Judy Garland at the top. Crawford at the bottom. But how she found out what was in between I had no idea. I didn't talk to her once since we went east. The Chief didn't call her, either. Our trip was a government secret. But she seemed to be talking about a get-together—a powwow, she called it—between the pipe and the cigarette and the cigar: even a barbarous Turk like me could figure that one out. She's a kind of genius, I guess. She's got this birdy, that's what she calls it: a birdy.

Suddenly a huge white spray flashed by the window and our flying boat came down in the waters of Trinidad Harbor. The landing was so smooth that the Chief went right on sleeping. With that smile on his face. Pleasant dreams!

20 } A SHIFT IN THE WIND

Goebbels: January 1943, Berlin

Churchill, code-named Admiral P, also Emperor of the East, also Air
Commander Frankland—we know all their childish disguises—landed
at Médiouna Airfield at 10:45 a.m. local time after a ten-hour flight in
his Liberator 405. A sixteen-kilometer journey dropped him at his villa
above Casablanca. Security at the airport: nonexistent. We have a Neger
in place at Casablanca. If that agent had a weapon, he could have shot
the jokester down as he pranced about the tarmac, shaking hands with
everyone and smoking his cigar. Drunk in the middle of the morning. We
shall be ready for him next time. When our enemies are together, our black
man will have his gun.

The Terrible Turk: January 1943, Casablanca

A better way to arrive: high above the water instead of underneath it. No
seasickness. No sea biscuits for the Chief, who has his nose pressed to the
window glass. I do, too. We're both watching the pie plate of the sun sink
into the horizon. Jam seems to be spilling out of it. Well, before it was my
blood. My head still hurts, two months later. I am beginning to think it
will for the rest of my life. Just one more punch-drunk fighter. Now we're
swinging back over the land. I can hear the wheels go down. I never wanted
to see this place again.

KK: January 1943, Casablanca

We arrived at the compound a little after 8:00 p.m. The soldiers took me
aside. Some officers asked a hundred questions. They knew about the films
I had appeared in for Tobis. They knew about Herr Goebbels. They did not
know about the Reichskanzler. I said my father was a citizen of America,

wasn't I a citizen too? This did not interest them. After an hour someone came in and whispered something. Then they took me to the villa where my companion was waiting.

Herr Wonskolaser, Jacob Leonard. He did not say a word. I wanted to unpack. To wash my face or wash my hands in the beautiful green-marble sink. But he put his fingers in my hair. Standing. With the windows wide open and guards, the boys, the soldier boys, walking by. All around was wire, barbed wire, hung with tin cans filled with pebbles. Just enough light in the sky to see the big muzzles of the guns. They all point upward. It will be impossible to attack from the air. The president's villa is close by. If I cried out, he would hear me. Except for the steel shutters over his windows.

Not just steel shutters. A tall, skinny boy from the state of Minnesota, "As far from the desert as a fellow can get," he said, told me how they had converted the swimming pool into an air-raid shelter. He boasted about how the steel plates came from the *Jean Bart*. That was a French warship destroyed in the harbor. All I had to do was smile and he said more: Metal detectors and Geiger counters and all the food and all the water is tested by medical doctors. Our task will be difficult. They have thought of everything.

Why wasn't our plane shot down? I begged for that. To fall from the sky. Over the ocean. Does Germany not have majesty in the air? Does it not rule all of Europe? How sweet to drop to my death next to the man who killed my father.

Hedda Hopper's Hollywood: January 1943, Los Angeles

I wish I could type out on my trusty Remington all the things that are on my mind. But almost everything these days is top secret. Well, it's no secret that Ginger Rogers is leading a write-in campaign to protest the government decree limiting everyone's compensation to 25,000. That girl worked so hard to get her salary up to 175,000 a picture, which if you ask me is the American way and not what they practice in Russia. Oh, Hedda! No one is asking you! The world has bigger fish to fry and what I really want to say is one whale of a story! Except that I can't put it in print—not unless I get the stamp of approval from my pal J. Edgar, and he won't give it, I'm almost sure of that. By the way, you could have knocked me over with a feather when Ginger told me that number three was going to be young actor Jack Briggs.

I guess no one can point a finger at yours truly if I say that Warners Exec Jack Warner is still missing. He has dropped off the face of the earth. And where is the president? The last time I asked they said, "Gone fishing." In January? By cutting a hole in the ice? I haven't seen that one since *Nanook of the North*. And Winnie Churchill, that dear old PM of jolly old you-know-where, hasn't been seen at Downing Street or playing chess up at Checkers (I couldn't resist that one). For that matter, is Uncle Joe in the Kremlin? Here's a word of advice: *if* those gents have taken the *Road to Morocco*, which is what that little birdy once told me, and *if* they are doing so at that super-modern Hotel Anfa with its lovely villas—Linda Darnell, who remained so loyal to Ty Power in *Blood and Sand*, stayed there with a French friend and raved about the sunken bathtubs and the flower gardens with their morning glories and the quail cooing at dawn—well, *if* that's all true they had best keep their wits about them because they are pretty big fish in a pretty small barrel, and I wouldn't be surprised if there was more than one plot afoot to do them in.

Lucky for them Georgie Patton, who doesn't take any guff from anybody, is on the job. That two-star general—and there ought to be a congressional investigation about why it isn't already three!—won't let anybody put a bomb under wherever our leaders are staying, whether it's the Villa Annette, for instance, or, to give another example, the luxurious Dar es Saada. Of course G. S. P. is itching to get back into action, as his "darling B" tells me, instead of playing the role of a glorified bodyguard.

Overheard at Mike Romanoff's the other night from Jack Benny: "I wonder if the ban on pleasure driving will stop the critics from taking my next picture for a ride." That's funny.

Josef Vissarionovich: January 1943, Moscow

The airfield at Pitomnik is now in our hands. The one at Gumdak can't hold out more than thirty hours. After that, only a few more days, a week, two weeks, until Paulus surrenders or has his throat cut with all his remaining men. The battle of Stalingrad is over.

No reports from Africa. No action by Luftwaffe forces, though they staged a raid on Casablanca only three weeks ago. Plenty of casualties. Meanwhile the plutocrats drink their cocktails and smoke their American tobacco and divide up the spoils. Won by the blood of our armies. We cannot depend on the Hitlerites to complete this operation. We have an agent of our own. In November, during the invasion, she made herself agreeable to that clown we made a Hero of the Soviet Union. She will become agreeable once more. If Goebbels and Rommel fail to act, she will complete the operation on her own.

Goebbels: January 1943, Berlin

No word from Rommel. No word from Skorzeny. Nothing from our friends in the sultan's palace. The paratroopers sit. But the Führer wants a report every four hours. I have to tell him something. I invent fantastic plots at night and in the morning light I see that I have been thinking like a child. Poisoned darts. Radioactive rays. A servant with a piece of rope. *Yes, yes, mein Führer: ice cubes filled with glass.*

Stalingrad is lost. My speech is ready. But I won't have to give it if we succeed with Operation Oasis. No Beethoven. Dancing in the streets instead. I can have any girl in Berlin. Yes, yes, yes: the dreams of a child.

G. S. P., Jr.: January 1943, Casablanca

The Secret Service ran things at Médiouna. All I had to do was make sure of air cover. We had fighters stacked up over the president's C-54, which had taken off from Gambia in time for him to arrive before the sun had completely set. For some reason the pilot swept well out to sea to make his approach. A surprise when there can't be surprises. I'd have put a navy ship out there, just in case. Christ, they thought of everything else. Snowshoes in case they went down in the Atlas range. Mosquito nets and malaria pills for a landing in the jungle. And for all I know a goddamned camel to get them out of the desert. But they forgot the last leg. Reilly had his men smearing mud over the windows of the limousines. Not sure that was to keep the natives from peering in or those inside from seeing our pathetic natives. A subhuman tribe if there ever was one.

We got the president off the plane and into his Daimler and he gave me the old thumbs-up. The transfer of the others went as planned. I'd arranged to maintain air cover and we had mine sweepers go over all ten miles of the road. Armed soldiers stood every fifty yards. Worst that could happen was a flat tire.

Then the last group got out of the plane. I did a double take. The Kike! With the same camera around his neck and the same smile on his puss. That big Turk was with him. And some woman, which surprised me because the way I saw those two going at in the Miramar, I figured no one else was in the picture, least of all a female. Kissing—and not those double pecks on the cheek like the Froggies do it. She wasn't on the manifest. I sent word to hold the car at the compound until we could check her out.

Jack L. Warner: January 1943, *Casablanca*

Date: January 15, 1943
Subject: Casablanca publicity
To: William Schaeffer
From: Jack L. Warner

Bill,

What I tell you you have to keep strictly under your hat. I'm not even supposed to let you know where I am. But where I am is Casablanca, the same as the name of the picture, which is why I'm writing this memo. Forget about the new ending, even though I like the idea. I mean, didn't I think of it myself? Robert or Rick or whatever his name is—you know, Bogart's part—is standing up in a landing craft with bullets zipping all around and the flag waving behind his head and the spray on his face and why not have Bergman waiting for him? She's dumped that stiff she was with, see, and joined the WACS, or she's a nurse tending the wounded right there on the beach, and then she looks up—cut to Bogie, cut back to her, and in my book that's a happy ending, which I begged the Epstein boys on my knees to give us. Whoever heard of a love story where the girl goes off with the second lead and Bogart, who we are paying 37,000, goes off with Rains? Like a couple of faggelahs arm practically in arm. I see I am talking myself back into it, especially if we could use all the great action I took that was blown up by a Nazi submarine.

No, no, forget it. All of it. There's no time for that now. We've got the greatest scoop in history on our hands, and I want to ship our negatives and positives immediately all across the country and everywhere overseas. I want to open no later than the end of this month and even sooner than that if possible. Tell Enfield that I want an all-out campaign. Drop the stuff you've already got, FIGHTING THE FASCINATION THAT DRAWS HER CLOSE and TORN BETWEEN TWO MEN and all that crap. We've got to hit the RIPPED FROM THE HEADLINES angle, but even bigger: THE CITY AND THE MEETING THAT CHANGED THE WORLD! Something like that. How about, THE PICTURE THAT WILL TAKE THE NATION THE WAY OUR BOYS TOOK CASABLANCA? Run that by Silver for the trailers and also Charlie, since I want to go all out with national publicity. I can't say much more at this particular moment, though just between you and me and the US Army censor we are going to have a Command Performance for a commander in chief and a certain bulldog of British extraction, if you are smart enough to read between the lines.

Get Enfield on this right away. And no reason to involve Harry, understand? And not Wallis, either. If he doesn't like the new campaign he can buy all the Warner holdings for 38 million in cash exclusive of tax. Then he can advertise the way he wants. He's taking much too much credit for this picture anyway. If he asks or Harry asks just tell them when the news breaks, they'll know why. It's the greatest story of the twentieth century.

Wait a second: THEY HAD A DATE WITH FATE. ISN'T THAT GREAT? A DATE WITH FATE—IN THE CITY THAT ROCKED THE WORLD! I want Silver to put that in all the trailers.

Another thing: Tell Trilling to hold off signing Michelle Morgan for the *Marseille* project. I'm going to bring back a sensational new find. A second Lamarr. With better bulbs.

KK: January 1943, Casablanca

Over and over. Until two in the morning.

Jack L. Warner: January 1943, *Casablanca*

They put Abdul in Roosevelt's villa, so he can work on him any time day or night. But what about the guy who pays his salary, which happens to be me? Even worse, they pulled KK out of the limo and marched her off some place I couldn't see. Seems they found out she was born in Berlin and that even if Joe was her father and born himself in Cincinnati, a fellow Buckeye, which is maybe why I went way out of my way to help him out, and sent flowers to his funeral, her mother was a Kraut and quite the fury and the hellion, which I know from personal experience, and I guess that makes her a Kraut, too. Like a Jew with a mother: same deal. I had to pace up and down in this joint for almost two hours. A man could go nuts. *In* the nuts. Even I know that's a lousy gag.

Anyhow, and I guess with the help of FDR, who has an eye for her and always had, she came out Glat Kosher, and when she stepped through the door I stopped in my tracks and gave her a five-star fucking, front door, my way, and back door, her way, so that my sacroiliac is out of kilter and I need Abdul more than Franklin D., because to tell you the truth it's all a fiasco, that massaging, and isn't doing him any good at all.

The Terrible Turk: January 1943, *Casablanca*

I am at Mr. FDR's villa and not with the Chief. I am sharing a bedroom with the navy man who I got to know during the White House sessions. Name of Rafael. That's how you spell it, I believe. The two Negroes, Prettyman and Fields, are right next door. The first thing the president said to me was how we must have that pretty actress over for cocktails. Not a word about the boss. I wonder if he knows we wouldn't be in Casablanca—there wouldn't even *be* a Casablanca—if Jack L. Warner didn't get that admiral to surrender. General Patton would not have left a stick standing.

We had a session first thing in the villa. The results were lousy. The president tried to stand up in the braces and couldn't take a step. He stumbled right away against a wall. He tried to put the best face on it. Grinned as usual and said, "Oh, spinach!" But he didn't try a second time. Maybe it was because of so many hours in the air. I was dead tired myself. But we didn't go to bed. Churchill came to dinner. After dinner they began to talk. I wanted to sneak out to the Chief's place, but all of a sudden the lights went out, sirens went off, and General Patton came bursting through the door—at least that is who he said he was: in the blackness you could not see a thing.

"Mr. President, it's an air raid. Mr. Prime Minister, sir, I know you're here, too. So does the enemy. No way to keep anything secret from these Arabs. They know, no disrespect, gentlemen, the color of your underwear and, down to the bottle, your inventory of scotch."

Churchill's voice came out of the dark: "Then we must guard both very well."

"Have you a flashlight? A match? A lighter? I am going to take you both to the shelter."

And just like that, as if this were a magic act, two lights appeared, floating in the air, all by themselves. For a second I thought these were the fuses of bombs and that we were goners, every one of us; but then I saw that the coloreds, Prettyman and Fields, were carrying candles. But before they could set them down, the room filled up with soldiers and Secret Service agents and even two men from Scotland Yard. They had flashlights and the beams were crisscrossing crazily all over the room. Mr. Churchill has a big voice, and he made sure we heard it:

"Oh, I'm an old hand at this kind of thing. I've long since learned that when the bombs start falling I prefer to stand beneath the iron arch of probability."

"Well," said Mr. FDR, "I'm new at it myself, but I'll take my chances with the prime minister."

The general walked toward the window. "I don't hear any ack-ack. I'm pretty sure this was a false alarm. Or maybe Mr. Reilly here would like to smear some mud on these?" He meant the metal shutters. He bent and raised one of them all the way up. Outside, everything was still. The only light came from the jeeps that had drawn up outside the compound.

Reilly said, "I'd like my men to remain here for another few minutes, just in case. I'm kicking myself. I should have thought of a generator. I should have thought of lanterns."

"Can't think of everything, Mike!" said the jovial president.

"That's what's wrong with people like Hitler," Churchill replied. "They think they can."

The general was right. No planes showed up. When everyone had gone, the president and the prime minister picked up where they had left off. They were having a big argument. About what to do after Rommel and his troops had been thrown out of Africa. The president was all for invading France and going right for Berlin, and Churchill was against it. He wanted to attack Sardinia or maybe Sicily. He gave me a look and said that he had every intention of bringing Turkey in on the side of the allies and what did I think. I said I thought it was a swell idea and that the Turks were tremendous fighters in spite of the impression I had created with my record in the ring. Ha. Ha. The president said if we didn't create a second front in France we were going to stir things up with Uncle Joe. I knew he meant Stalin. And on and on and around and around they went for hours, with the president smoking one cigarette after another and Sawyers, Churchill's man, filling his glass with drink after drink and resupplying him with black, fat cigars.

It got to be two in the morning. Then two-thirty. The lights were still out. No one had lowered the shutter, and when I looked out I saw the shape of somebody, the shadow of somebody, bent double and on the double running away from us toward the coiled wire at the edge of the compound. When you have touched the muscles in a man for year after year, you get to know him pretty well. I knew that shadow and that shape. It was the Chief! At three o'clock in the morning!

I held my breath. Behind me, Mr. Roosevelt and Mr. Churchill were still going on, but I wasn't listening. Instead, I heard, from far off, the rattle of the pebbles that were in the tin cans. J.L. was going over the fence! I strained toward the window. I thought I heard a kind of rip-ripping. Maybe I only imagined it. But I knew the voice that said *Goddammit!* and saw the white patch of his boxers bouncing like a bunny tail behind him as he raced toward the line of motor cars. Then a bunch of dogs started barking, and I saw them running after the Chief; they almost had him by the ankles before he managed to jump into one of the jeeps and drive away.

The two great men didn't notice anything. They were still discussing the affairs of the world when I snuck off to bed. For all I know they talked through the rest of the night.

Josef Vissarionovich: January 1943, Moscow

They don't send me dispatches. Vyacheslav Mikhailovich has heard nothing. What does this silence mean? Only one thing: another betrayal. They won't open a second front. They'll unbutton their flies and piddle into the Mediterranean. Or the Balkans. Churchill made a fool of himself there before. It is human nature to want to do so again. Or they will peck away at Sicily. What good will that do? An easy question to answer: the emperor wishes to keep his empire. He is not fighting against the Germans. He is fighting for Egypt, Suez, India, and Singapore. *Singapore!* He calls *that* the worst disaster in human history. Or British history: for him, the same. He could give a fuck about the bleeding of the Red Army. It's more of his crocodiles!

When is Hitler going to strike? He has his assassins. You want Churchill? There he is, in a dacha. Not as luxurious as he had hoped. What? No hot water for the bath! The Arabs in the desert could hear his howls. When he came to the Soviet Union, he marveled at our technology. The hot water and the cold water combined in a single tap. Those Arabskiys: they love Herr Hitler. He put their Jews into camps. What will the Americans do? Let them out.

You want Roosevelt? He is a cripple. He doesn't leave his dacha. It's protected like the Kremlin. All the servants have been replaced by Amerikanskiy soldiers. They taught them how to serve dinner and pour the wines. His food is tested the same as mine. They even look for radioactive elements. Impossible to get inside, even with a trained snake, an asp, which bit the breast of the Queen of Egypt. No. You've got to catch the wolf out of his lair. We know he is going to Rabat. To review his doughboys. They'll entertain him. They'll feed him their meat and potatoes. They'll play him music. A band. With a big bass drum.

What was the name of that trumpeter? The one we sent to Paulus's surrender. Victor Fillipovich! His instrument played just three notes: *Attention! Attention! Attention!* So the Germans let him through the Stalingrad lines. An idea circles inside my brain. The drum. The banging of the drum. Let us hope the Führer hears it. It is time for him to act.

What sort of man is this Herr Hitler? What does he see when he looks in the mirror? Yes, yes: a person who won't eat an animal. A person who won't, from a pipe, from a cigarette, take a single puff. And women? I don't think so. Look at the photos: he clasps his hands on top of his prick. He won't drink, either. A fanatic, then. And what if he is? It doesn't matter.

What I want to know is, when he looks in that mirror, does he say to himself, like the villains in the American movies, *Ho Ho! I make them suffer. But not enough! More! And more! Down to the last man on earth!* Is that how he receives his pleasure? People suffer because of Josef Vissarionovich, too. Plenty of people. But what if it's millions? It is for a better world. For the future. So in my mirror, at a certain angle, there is the face of a benefactor of mankind. And in his? He can't twirl his moustache, which is like a smear of dung on his lip. But does he see a man who recognizes the good—and then turns his back upon it? *Are* there such demons? To such a question the General Secretary of the Central Committee has no answer.

267

Hedda Hopper's Hollywood: January 1943, Los Angeles

Soon as Paulette Goddard finishes *So Proudly We Hail*, she's off to Mexico City. Wants me to go along as chaperone. Boy! That's one trip I'd like, cause I'd get a postgraduate course that Emily Post would never be able to give me. With her dark, Semitic looks, Paulette is going to fit right in, south of the border.

Ran into Art Silver at Ciro's, but when I hinted we make a night of it—easy to do now that Marcel Lamaze has taken over the club and hosts jam sessions to give us a little fun in this entertainment-starved town—Artie told me he had to get back to Burbank and work until dawn's early light changing all the trailers to *Casablanca*, which at long last is scheduled to open later this month. Seems he's been ordered to play down the love interest and play up how the destiny of the whole world depends on either that city or that film—I guess I had one too many of Marcel's French champagne mimosas to figure out which.

Speaking of the love interest, can you believe how Bogie the bogeyman has been cast as a sex symbol? "Heck," he told me, "I didn't do anything in this picture that I haven't done in twenty others. It's not me. It's Ingrid Bergman. When she looks at you, all of a sudden you're sexy." Let's hope that chemistry is still sizzling when they get done adding all this highfalutin political stuff. *Destiny*, indeed!

By the way, Paulette's trip down Mexico way is her first since getting that quickie divorce from Charlie Chaplin. He's been strutting around town with a big smile on that puss, as if the Little Tramp had just kicked some banker in the behind. That's what Charlie would like to do. He's no friend of the Capitalist system. He's on top of the world because of the Russian victory at Stalingrad. Sure, that's something we can all applaud. But has anyone thought about what will happen to our way of life if the Red tide rolls all across Europe?

A gal has to admit when she's made a mistake. Uncle Joe, as his fellow travelers call him, never left the Kremlin for North Africa. It seems that Mr. Pipe won't be puffing away with Mr. Cigarette and Mr. Cigar, if you get my smoke signals. Our American boys have done a wonderful job over there, and if their commander in chief is really out fishing in those waters, he ought to take a side trip and cheer them on. It's not so far from Casablanca to Rabat, where they are stationed—about as far as Los Angeles, so dull these days, to Santa Barbara. Go on, Mr. President. Take the salute! And strike up the band!

When Jean Arthur heard a bit player in *The More the Merrier* say that he was getting rid of his dachshund because of its German origin, she spoke up and said, "Wait a minute. A dog's a dog. If he was your friend before the war, he's the same today. I'll wager he never heard of Hitler and wouldn't know him from a fireplug." That's darn good thinking. The German people were our friends before the current hostilities and they are going to be our friends after. We might even need those "dachshunds." Remember what I said about the Red tide? *Somebody's* got to be around to put his finger in that dyke!

KK: *January 1943, Casablanca*

Two in the morning. No, three in the morning. The bed was empty. I heard rustling in the corner. There was Jack, hopping on one foot, trying to put on his trousers. His military trousers. Then, in his peculiar way, with his elbows out, fastening the buttons on his tunic. Even in the dark, his hair was shining. I could smell the paste in it. And, mingled with the nighttime flowers, his perfume. Perhaps I blinked. Or fell back asleep. All I knew was that one moment he was there and the next moment he was not. Dreaming? I checked the bed beside me. Not dreaming. He was gone. Where? Why? I knew why. The same thing happened on Briarcliff Road. Except that there, at the same hour, two or three in the morning, he would try to sneak in instead of sneaking out. All the cologne in Beverly Hills could not mask the smell of the woman. I went to the window. The words were in my throat:

Jack! Come back! I see you! I know where you're going!

I forced them down. I put a fist in my mouth. And bit. I feared the guards. The American boys. Then I heard the grinding of gravel and the rattling of pebbles in the tin cans. Next, out of the darkness, a ripping sound.

"Goddammit!"

And after that the howl of dogs. They have no accent. They bark the same in every language.

Impossible not to think of my father. The dogs snapping at his clothing, his hands, the slobber from their teeth flying in the yellow light of the streetlamps.

Next, silence: no shout, no rattle of pebbles in the clattering cans. Even the barking, from all those Amerikaner Schäferhunde, ceased. Suddenly the sound of an engine. The sound of tires on gravel. Jack L. Warner in heat. His bitch was waiting.

G. S. P., Jr.: January 1943, Casablanca

Had lunch at the palace and got to practice my French for three hours. The boy prince told me that when he becomes the sultan I am to be the grand vizier and that he will go everywhere in a tank. The current GV looked pretty glum, but the sultan himself happily grinned. His son as far as I can see probably goes to sleep with his fez.

Conference won't last much longer. Before it ends, Roosevelt insists on seeing the troops. That means a motorcade to Rabat tomorrow. With him in an open jeep, so he'll get plenty of photographs. I'll put the 3rd Battalion along the road. And arrange for air cover. So far the Luftwaffe has sat on its butt. The president refused my request that he move every forty-eight hours. He's too enamored of the luxuries in his villa. And we've had only two yellow alerts, one of them on the first night he arrived. He and the

PM wouldn't budge from their chairs. Just kept puffing and gabbing like nothing was happening. And nothing did. So far so good. Not a thing in our air space but the birds that Brooke, the British CIGS, is always looking for and writing down in a book. *By Jove, a Double-Breasted Booby-Hatcher!* But he is no booby himself, and it looks like his side has won the talking war. They wore us down with attrition. And better preparation. So no cross-channel invasion of France. No real second front. Just a slog up Italy.

I suppose that means I am a winner, too. If I acquit myself in the battle for Tunisia, I believe Ike will offer me the Sicilian command. I can stop twiddling my thumbs. I have only one wish in life: to go out and kill someone.

Goebbels: *January 1943, Berlin*

Our sources at the palace of the sultan tell us there is uneasiness at the prospect of American rule. They know that wherever the Anglo-Saxons go, their first act is to rescind the restrictions on the Jews—proof that in London as well as Washington this race acts the decisive role, even though it is one played backstage. You can't trust the Jews across the street and now they are to have the run of Africa.

Already our Arab friends regret our departure from Morocco. I think we shall have no lack of cooperation when the time comes to strike. But that time is running out. Tomorrow the American president plans to travel in an open vehicle. But how can we get a shot? He is far better protected than the Führer, who is at bottom a fatalist. We tremble at the risks he takes, both in the air and on land, but to our concerns he only responds with his deep, full-throated, manly laugh. It is impossible not to love one who laughs like that. But the president never removes his ever-grinning mask, as if the deepest matters of state, the fate of whole peoples, were nothing more than a pleasantry. You can be sure that along the route his Praetorian guard will have combed every tree of its coconuts, lest one fall by an act of Jehovah upon his head. We cannot wait for God. We must act ourselves.

Jack L. Warner: *January 1943, Morocco*

Déjà vu. That is what the Frenchies say when something happens over again. Except this time there is a twist. Sure, I'm driving in the dark to the palace and I'm also in a jeep. But before my pants were open in the front and now they're air-conditioned in the rear. Even at discount they cost forty big ones a pair. Made to order. With plenty of room for my equipment. "Left or right?" Loshak always asks. Sometimes I forget myself.

It wasn't the dogs, it was the wire. But one of those mutts got my ankle, which hurts like hell. Probably I'm going to catch rabies. Isn't there a shot for that? We made a picture about it. With Muni. What was that Frog's name? Pasteur! Like with the milk. Went around telling people wash your hands. Cured some kid with an injection. THE IMMORTAL STORY OF AN IMMORTAL MAN! Yeah, Muni got best actor, but I got screwed on best picture. GREATER THAN *DISRAELI*! If I spent two million like Metro did on *Ziegfeld*, I'd have gotten *two* Oscars. I'm bleeding! Bleeding! Don't those damned dogs have any gratitude? I made the whole breed famous. And I treated that bowser like a king! T-Bones from Musso's, for Christ's sake! Jesus, where the hell in these sticks can I get one of those shots?

It's black as the ace of spades out here. Not even stars. I might as well be wearing that blindfold. But I don't dare turn on the lights. I've had enough of those Ink Spots. Or those guys with hoods on their heads. Good thing I memorized the way. And I've got the plans of the palace inside my head.

Better step on it. If I don't get back before KK wakes up, I'll really be in for it. She'll never believe this is strictly business. Which it is, knockers or no knockers. What I put up with from that Blondie! Don't ask me why I do it. She scares me, to be honest. I'm pretty sure that one time she was going to throw herself out of a window. For fuck's sake, how was I supposed to know that Joe was going to blow his brains out? I've fired a thousand people—I would have canned Zanuck if he hadn't walked out—and none of them did a thing like that. And how do I know he did it? Those Nazis could have staged the whole thing. Didn't they beat the crap out of him once before? Because they didn't like Jolie singing in blackface? And that funeral cost an arm and a leg.

Wait a second. What's that up ahead? It's the sultan's joint, all right. Dark and still. I pull off to the side of the road and walk up to the same gate I went into and out of before. There's a little guard box on either side of it, like what you have at Bucktoothed Palace. But there's no one inside—hold on, there is, but both guys are fast asleep.

Here's the courtyard, the one that was filled with all those lawn jockeys, except they were real ones, on top of horses. With little red vests and sabers. All empty now. Lucky I remember my way around. I go in the door, they never heard of locks in this country, and up three flights of stairs. No mariachis this time. Everything is dead quiet. Not a sound. I ought to go on tippy-toe, but my ankle, where Fido sank his teeth right through my pant cuffs—there's *another* bill from the tailor—hurts too much.

Now I'm limping into that chamber where everybody had those funny socks on, and where I met the Ronald Colman stand-in—and there's his high chair, the throne, I guess, but there's no sultan on it. *Oh, ho!* sez I, in a stage whisper. *We know where YOU are.* For a minute I stand there thinking about how he must be rolling around with five or ten of those floozies—sheiks and shahs sure live the life of Reilly—and then I remember that's where *I'm* going, too. The harem! But I don't take another step because if they catch you in there it's *Off with his head!* Well, I've come this far. *Courage, mon ami!* That's why your name is on the water tower.

I know where to go. The corridors. The winding staircase. *Ouch, goddammit!* I can feel the rabies moving up my leg. It's a kind of tingling feeling. Ah, aha! The double doors! But no Strangler Lewis. No Nagurski. I yank them open. Yep, here's the pool and there's the steam coming off of it, just like before. But no babes are splashing around inside. My own head is doing some swimming. Was it because of going round and round on those stairs? Or maybe it's the water. I heard that with rabies just the sight of it can turn you into a fruitcake. Is this the end of J. L. Warner? Am I losing my mind? Let's see. Last year's grosses: *Yankee Doodle Dandy*, 11,855,221, in spite of all the dumb Epstein gags; *The Male Animal*, 2,444,131. The gags didn't help that one. *The Man Who Came to Dinner*, did those boys write *everything* last year? 4,998,724. Sharp as a tack! Plenty of marbles. Maybe I didn't get rabies from that mutt. Maybe it got double pneumonia from me.

Ohhhh-oooooooo!

What's that?

Oooooo! Ohhhhh!

Groaning. Moaning. Of a certain type. It's coming from over there, from those doors, the row of doors, at the end of the pool. That must be the super-private place, like an inner sanctum, where they keep the broads.

Still limping, trailing drops of blood—*my* blood!—I make my way to the first of the doors and put my ear against it. Not a peep. The next door. Ditto.

Ooooo-oh-wooooo!

It's coming from here, the door in the middle. It sounds like the sultan is having a frat party. But here's the problem: the two musclemen, Weissmuller and Atlas, are crouched in front of it. But they're asleep, too! It's like the sandman sprinkled his fairy dust. I step over both of these heavies and softly knock. *Tap, tap, tap.* No answer. I knock a little harder. "Yoohoo! Oumaima, honey? Are you in there?" Still nothing, except more moaning and more groaning and high-pitched shouts of *Marveilleux!* and *Formidable!* Some guys have all the luck.

I try the knob. The door swings open and even though it's dim and smoky I can make out the shapes of four or five ladies, none of them wearing a stitch, and all of them writhing around the shadowy form of the sultan, one at his head and one at his feet, another lying crossways, and still another seems to be hanging by her ankles. Uh-oh: I've been spotted.

"*You!* shouts the sultan. "The Jew!" At this all the girls let out a string of little screams.

"Ha, ha," I reply, because it's definitely an embarrassing situation. "You know what Confucius says?"

No one answers. They're all scrambling around doing one thing and another: somebody strikes a match and somebody else brings up a lantern.

"*Woman who fly upside down have crack-up!*"

All of a sudden the two bruisers are on their feet. Nagurski has my left arm and the Strangler the right.

"Hey, let go! I was only trying to lighten the mood."

Now the lamp comes on and right away I see two things. One: that it's not the sultan who is lying on a heap of cushions, it's the head of the Ku Klux Klan. Two: not one of these pinups is Oumaima. Not even close. Maybe okay for a bit part.

"Infidel!" says the grand vizier. "You have violated the Seraglio."

"The sore ankle-ow? And how!"

"No man can do that and live."

"Well, you don't have to make a federal case out of it."

"Do you know what fate awaits you?"

"Yeah. I saw *Marie Antoinette* at the Cathay Circle. Mayer spent three million on that one. He lost one-point-two. I'd rather lose my head."

"You think this is a joke? Guards! Take him away!"

"Hold your horses. This is strictly business. Everything's on the up and up. And I can prove it."

With that I wrench my arm free and reach inside my tunic, where I've got the studio documents all ready. Three hundred a week—though of course there are ways of earning a supplement. I hand it to the bully boys. Right away they put their fat heads together and begin to make clucking noises, which I guess is how you talk in Arab. One of them looks up and says, "Who is the subject of this cute photo? Lana Turner?"

Uh-oh. I'd grabbed the publicity shot of Sheridan that I promised to give to Michelier.

"Nah," I answer. "She's over at Metro."

The grand vizier snaps his fingers. "Bring it here," he commands. The wrestlers hand it over. The GV gives it a good, long look. Then he sticks it under one of his cushions.

"Hey," I say. "That's for the admiral. It's signed and everything."

"It is now part of the sultan's collection."

"Okay. But you've got to call Oumaima for me. That's why I'm here."

"Impossible. You showed her what no woman may be allowed to see."

"I couldn't help it. It was a reflex. Like a bull with a flag or a bee with honey, or—"

He waves my words away. "She has been banned from the hareem and put in a place with others who have been so defiled."

"What? She's not here? Where is she? In the Bouillabaisse?"

"The Bousbir? No, that is too good for her. What she has seen makes her no better than a Jewess. Thus she is now in the camp for Jews. You think your Roosevelt and your Churchill can free your people? We shall see. And you shall see, too. In return for this image of Mlle. Turner, you shall not be beheaded—"

"I told you. It's Sheridan. Didn't you see *Navy Blues*? MEET THE GIRLS! GREET THE GOBS!"

"Instead we shall put you in the same camp with those of your race. Not even the American army can get you out."

The two toughs grab hold again and start to lead me out. "Take it easy, boys," I say. "Didn't I tell you it's all strictly business? Look, I've got the contract right here."

Again I wrench my arm free and this time I pull out the right piece of paper. No sooner do I do so than a familiar face begins to materialize out of the gloom. The body is familiar, too. Oumaima!

"*Contract?*" she cries. "Oooh, la la!"

She comes up close and plucks the sheet from my hand. Then from off the top of her head—her hair is puffed up and parted, just like Lamarr out of the water—she takes a pair of glasses and sticks them on her nose. Her lips move a little while she reads.

"Three hundred?" she asks. "This is, in the capitalist system, an insult."

"Bonuses. Easy to earn."

"*Cindy?*"

"You don't like it? We can make it *Maureen.*"

And so, what a beautiful thing; she gives me this big smile—no bills from the dental department—and comes up real close. A dangerous moment. Lucky I told Loshak to leave plenty of room on the left.

"Bonjour," she says, right into my ear. "Bonjour, Monsieur Jacques L. Warner."

And then, within nothing on but those specs and a pair of pasties, she presses right up against me. Fade out with a kiss.

Josef Vissarionovich: January 1943, Moscow

Opportunities at the city of Rabat not seized. *Attention! Attention! Attention!* The sound of the trumpeter. The sound of the drum. But no one heard. What happened in that tropical heat? Wreckers have done their work. Naturally, we hear excuses. The wind changed. In other words: the gods, not saboteurs, intervened to save their darling. Little time remains. Sicily is confirmed. They expect the Peoples Commissar for Defense to be satisfied with such a decision. He is not. The conference is over. They trotted out the Frenchman, de Gaulle. Now the two plutocrats will depart for their hidden destination. They think my hands are tied. Well, we shall find this *Paris of the Sahara.* Then the hands will squeeze.

The Terrible Turk: January 1943, Rabat

A session with FDR before leaving for the capital of Rabat. No results, though of course the president said what he always says: "Better every day, Abdul. You're a magician! Take care you don't saw me in half!" I rode next to him in the Daimler. Before we got to the capital we stopped and I helped carry him to an open jeep. They set up a screen so no one could see. He sat sidesaddle, smiling and waving. I sat where I could catch him if anything went wrong. Thousands of soldiers lined both sides of the road, though far back from the edges. You should have heard the cheering!

We had lunch with the men. Boiled ham and sweet potatoes. I just ate the potatoes. My headache began to come on again when the band started to play "Chattanooga Choo Choo." It got worse with each new song. It felt almost like before. Like when my helmet was cutting into my scalp.

G. S. P., Jr.: January 1943, Rabat

Met the president's convoy outside of Rabat. He very cordial and complimentary. I did my best to reciprocate, but I was angry and anxious and not at my ease. It is not pleasant to take orders from those you know to be inferior, but I have the capacity to rise above my resentment only outwardly—and too often not even then. I know perfectly well that the Heinies are aware that the president is safe in his fancy Dar es Saada villa and is exposed and vulnerable only when he wishes to review the troops. And what does Clark concern himself with? Getting a bunch of Negro soldiers to parade in front of the president so they can take five million pictures—none for the glory of our men, all for the glory of FDR and Clark himself, when he can push himself into the frame. I consider this disgusting.

Even worse is that gumshoe, Reilly. He demanded that all twenty thousand soldiers be disarmed and stand at least three hundred yards from the road. Oh, they could keep their rifles, but they had to surrender the bullets. That made my blood boil. The Second Armored Division—so well turned out, eager, and fit—might just as well have been carved from wood. He thinks I did not notice that as the president passed by he ordered a dozen of his agents to keep their submachine guns aimed at American officers and men. I did not intervene. I bit my lip until it was bloody. This so-called Secret Service needs to be slapped down.

A pleasant lunch at the field kitchen. It could have been served at any good diner in America. The band played for our entertainment. The men relaxed and enjoyed it. Then who should show up and push the military bandmaster aside but the Kike! Amazing that Clark would allow a civilian up on stage; he made an exception for his co-religionist. Before anyone could do a thing, this fake lieutenant colonel was cracking jokes and introducing some Arab woman, a real floozy who was only half dressed, and of course the men became frenzied when she took the baton and pointed with it toward the trumpets and trombones, which was when the whole brass section broke into "Deep in the Heart of Texas."

Hedda Hopper's Hollywood: January 1943, Los Angeles

Looks like J. L. Warner might just be doing his best Bob Hope impression, telling his gags to entertain our boys overseas. My favorite little birdy told me that he even brought a stand-in for Dottie Lamour, a raven-haired beauty who could have come right out of some sultan's harem. She was wearing just enough to keep the Hays Office from shutting down the whole show. This gal has yet to have a screen test, but the boys in Burbank think she's destined to be their newest star.

Erich von Stroheim misses his native Austria so much he is going a little crazy. He blames Hitler and the Nazis for everything you can think of and says, "We'll never have peace until this generation of Germans is wiped out." He was so excited that the three double chins on the back of his neck started a rhumba. "The men who are fighting now are those who sipped the poison in each of their Führer's words." That seems pretty extreme to me. He is talking not just of his own homeland but that of Mozart and Goethe and Wagner, which means these men he insults share our values and in the future might help us defend them when they are threatened by the Asiatic hordes—and I am not talking now about the Japs.

At the Casa Manana Horace Heidt auctioned off a quarter pound of butter for sixty cents and a half pound of bacon for seventy-five cents. Hope the OPA won't come after him for raising prices!

Goebbels: January 1943, Berlin

I reported to the Führer that Operation Oasis has thus far failed to bring the desired results. Half our objective was nearly achieved at Rabat. It seems the plan with the American Volkslied was disrupted by nothing more than a shift in the wind. The strength of our leader, faced not only with that setback but with the latest cowardly request by Paulus to surrender, is remarkable. I could feel the force of his will flowing into me, as if we had been attached to one another by intravenous tubing. Of course Paulus's pitiable proposal was denied. The Führer even managed a joke. He said the only thing to do with such a coward was promote him. Thus this General der Panzertruppe will become a field marshal, since in all of German history no one of that rank had been known to surrender. He will have to kill himself instead.

As for the disappointment in Rabat, he also had a smile. "The wind blows one way, my dear Goebbels. Tomorrow it will blow another. The sailor who brings his ship to port is the one who knows how to set his sails."

And we do know how. I should never have trusted a Neger with a rifle. Our Mischling will succeed where he failed. Then we shall place the grand vizier on the Moroccan throne. And more: in exactly one week the Reich will celebrate the tenth anniversary of our assumption of power. Stalingrad will be lost by then. But I shall be able to announce a great victory: the annihilation of our greatest foes, the drunkard Churchill, the disabled Roosenfeld, and the Judeo-Capitalist culture they fought in vain to protect from German arms.

KK: January 1943, Casablanca

I have not been touched since the night we arrived. He doesn't bother to pretend. He splashes cologne on his back and strides out the door. He doesn't even take his camera. He is besotted. And last night he brought the girl herself to our villa. This has never happened before. Jack just laughed. "K-K-K-Katy!" he said. "Meet my friend Oumaima; she works in the library." Like a schoolchild I said, "She does?" And he said, "Sure! Every time I see her my circulation goes up!" While he was laughing at his own joke, I looked at the girl, and, with her dark, wet, wide-set eyes, she looked at me.

"Votre complice," she said in a whisper. "Demain."

"Accomplice? What do you mean?"

"Le chauffeur."

Tomorrow has arrived. The driver, a black man in an army uniform, drove up in the morning. Oumaima got in first. Jack hesitated. "Hey, I know this guy. Weren't you one of those Ink Spots?" Oumaima beckoned him next to her on the seat. The engine roared but I could hear him shout, "Hiya, Amos! Where's Andy?" They jerked forward, the gravel flew, and they drove away.

An hour went by. And another hour. I sit unfeeling now in the rays of the sun. A great event is occurring. Jack is about to be killed. I am unmoved. If only I were there to make sure. Of him. Of me. The sun beats down. I hear a sound. A cry. It is a gull. Then two gulls appear. There are more, calling to each other. I have not seen this before. What does it mean? It means the wind has shifted.

The Terrible Turk: January 1943, Rabat

The band was playing "The Missouri Waltz" and my head was splitting open, like a melon with the meat and the seeds. Then in a big surprise the Chief walked out onto the stage. He was grinning ear to ear. His teeth were flashing. The band stopped playing. Nobody knew what to do. Then he grabbed the microphone and said Hope couldn't make it, and anyway you should never listen to anyone from Paramount, and that this was the job and this was the moment he had dreamed of all his life. I could see the troops were looking at each other and asking *Who is this guy?* I wanted to jump up and tell them that this was Jack L. Warner, the vice president for production, but before I could say a word, the Chief began to speak for himself:

"It's a real pleasure to be here, boys, but the flight in that C-54 was really rough. Why it was so rough that the automatic pilot bailed out! Ha! Ha! Ha!"

He was the only one laughing. No, not true: the president, with his head tipped back, and that cigarette tipped up too, was grinning ear to ear.

"So I said to the real pilot, 'Gee, shouldn't we put on our parachutes?' And he says to me, 'Parachutes? The guys with parachutes jumped an hour ago!' Ha! Ha! Ha!"

Again, no one laughed. The bandleader started to get back on his podium. I thought that at any minute he'd raise his baton. I saw the Chief take out a handkerchief and wipe what in the business we call flop sweat off his brow.

"Ha, ha, ha! But was I scared? I just took out a novel and read it the whole way. And going back I'll read page two!"

Absolute silence. The bandleader gave a downbeat. I clutched my head, but before a single note could sound, the Chief began to wave his arm and a native girl in a revealing outfit came with a swish onto the stage. The thousands of soldiers went wild. Even the line of armed guards lifted their rifles into the air and started to holler along with the others. They didn't care that this was a Moroccan woman. Her hair came down to her waist and her breasts bulged up from her halter. That was all that mattered.

"Okay, boys," shouted the Chief into the microphone. "I wanted you to know what you are fighting for!"

When the tumult from that died down, the girl leaned up against him and in a thick accent said, "Oh, Jack, tell me because I am not certain. Have I come to the right place?"

The men whooped and yelled and some of them went *ooo-loo-ooo-loo-ooo* like Arab women. Finally, the Chief managed to say, "Don't worry about it, baby. If you haven't, they'll move the base."

The soldiers were in an even greater uproar. The girl gave the Chief a little kiss, which seemed to say *Aren't you sweet?*, and then she went over to the head of the band, who was standing as if in a trance, and took the baton out of his hand. She pointed it at the musicians and cried out so everyone could hear and in hardly an accent at all:

"'Deep in the Heart of Texas'!"

G. S. P., Jr.: January 1943, Rabat

The stars at night—
Are big and bright

Both armored divisions, twenty thousand men, were singing along. They all gave the traditional four claps. It was like artillery.

Deep in the heart of Texas!

The Moroccan girl led them in the next verse:

The prairie sky—
Is wide and high

Again came the clap-clap-clapping.

Deep in the heart of Texas!

I saw the Turk throw his hands over his ears. And then I saw something else. Something off to the seaward side. What was it? But with so much noise and tumult I could hardly think.

The sage in bloom—
Is like perfume

Off to the side, where the security unit—toothless without their ammunition—had lined up. Something wasn't right. What? I looked again, even though the shock waves from forty thousand hands was enough to knock a man down.

Deep in the heart of Texas!

I shaded my eyes. I peered ahead.

Reminds me of—
The man I love

There! *A black man, a soldier, in the line.* But all the colored troops had been taken for the separate review. We didn't have enough of them. Why, I'd even had to take Meeks—I hated to do this to him—and make him mingle with his own people. And all for show! Then who was this man? And why was he there in the middle of the guard?

Deep in the heart of Texas!

He was lowering his gun.

The cowboys cry—
Ki-yip-pee-yi!

He was aiming.
I swiveled round. There was FDR, sitting and grinning in his chair.

Completely exposed. And now he was clapping, *clap-clap-clap-clap*, along with everyone else. The sound was like bombs exploding.

Deep in the heart of Texas!

The assassin could shoot and the president could fall over, and no one would be able to hear a thing.

The rabbits rush—
Around the brush

Boom! Boom! Boom! Boom! The idiot drummer was actually joining in.

Deep in the heart of Texas!

I was halfway between the president and the shooter. Which way to go? "Stop him! Stop him! Arrest that man!"
No one could hear a word. I turned. I ran toward FDR. I made a silent prayer to my God to give me time to throw myself upon him and allow the bullet to strike me in the back of my head. That would be a good way to die.

The coyotes wail—
Along the trail

Again the thunderous roar. *Boom! Boom! Boom! Boom!* It was the sound, in my ears, of my own beating heart.

Deep in the heart of Texas!

It was no good. I knew I was not going to make it.

The doggies bawl—
And bawl and bawl

Knock! Knock!
That wasn't the booming. That wasn't the clapping. The Kike had grabbed the microphone.

"Knock! Knock!" he shouted again. No one replied, so he had to answer himself: "Who's there?"

He was forced to shout because the band was still playing and the men were still singing.

Deep in the heart of Texas!

"Augusta.

"Augusta, who?

"*Augusta wind will blow that man away!*"

And he pointed right to where the black man was standing with the pointed gun.

A big groan went up. It was the worst joke ever told. In the history of the world.

Warner went, "Ha! Ha! Ha!"

But no one could hear him. No one could hear anything. Sure, the band was still playing and the men were still singing. But the wind had suddenly shifted. It was almost as if it had been so shocked by what it had heard, the sacrilege of it, that it turned from blowing out to sea to exhaust itself instead over the desert sands. It carried with it in Aeolus's arms every human sound we made. I threw myself onto the president. But no bullet struck either of us. I looked back. The traitor had fled. He hadn't fired. He feared that in this sudden silence the report of his rifle would be heard.

"Mr. President," I said. "You were nearly assassinated."

"Now, George," he said. "Are you going to tell me one more time how you want to die with your boots on?"

Jack L. Warner: January 1943, Rabat

Assassinated? What's the big deal? I got assassinated when I was in the fourth grade. Got the measles anyway.

Speaking of lousy jokes, why did I tell that knock-knock just when things were going so well? I haven't heard that one since Youngstown. What I really wanted to do was sing "Sweet Adeline." Do you think the band knows that one? Jesus, what a voice I had. Ruined it with these cigars.

"Hey! Hey, listen everybody! Listen to this!

In the evening when I sit alone a-dreaming"

No one can hear me. Everything is breaking up. Everyone is running around. For a minute there I felt like a million bucks. I could tell those soldiers loved me. They were howling. Jessel never got an audience like that. So what if one joke bombed? Why are people shouting and carrying on? You'd think I'd let out a fart or something. Pay attention, soldiers:

"Of days gone by, love, to me so dear"

No good. Not a chance. Where is Oumaima? Gone off somewhere. Good thing I have her under contract. And Amos? My driver? Where did he get that rifle? And where did he go? Disappeared. Vanished. What the hell? No chauffeur. Am I going to have to walk all the way home?

21 } IN THE VAN

Josef Vissarionovich: January 1943, Moscow

The girl has been crying all day. She wants to see me. She wants to plead for the life of her lover. I won't take his life. He has value. We had to beat that value out of him. That is the royal road to the truth. I won't see her, but I did see him. We met last night. Not in the Kremlin. We do not allow such filth within these walls. And not Lubyanka. Let history record that the General Secretary never set foot in such places. There is no enjoyment in seeing one's fellow men suffer. Children exist who torture animals. They might burn a cat alive. Or put needles into the tongues of dogs. There is such a case in the works of Dostoyevsky. He knew, probably from the experience of his own life, that this is how the psychology of a person becomes warped.

No, I met our former agent—and if he spied for us when in Germany, does it not mean he could spy for Germany when he is here?—in a special van on a street blocked off by a bomb crater at one end and by our sentries at the other. There was enough light to see that our professionals had done a good job. No scars. No bruises. Even the wave in his hair was undisturbed. His clothing was also intact; it follows I could not inspect his torso or the backs of his legs.

We exchanged greetings like civilized people, and I put before him the proposition that he did not love my daughter but was using her to gain information for a foreign power. And what he said was that the only foreign power he worked for was the Soviet Union and that, more or less in his own words, "Svetlana Alliluyeva is a wonderful young girl, fresh and untouched, and I wished to open to her the world of poetry and beauty, which is necessary if one is to live a life that is not coarsened."

"Is it your suggestion, Comrade Engelsing, that I am such a coarse man?"

"Not at all, Comrade Stalin. It is well known that you go to the ballet."

"An objective person would definitely conclude that you have not answered my question. Perhaps I should ask it in a different way. When you were in your own country—did you enjoy life under the Hitlerites?"

"Germany was my country. The Nazis were not my government."

"And did that enjoyment include a romantic affair with a German-born citizen?"

"She was the daughter of a dear friend and—"

"And how old was this woman?"

"She was young."

"How young? You seem to have a fondess for innocent children, Alexander Wilhelmovich. But that is not in your confession. Why not? This shows lack of attention by our interrogators."

"Josef Vissarionovich, I do not—"

"Excuse me, Comrade. I only want to ask whether it is true that she is the one you love and not this poor Russian girl you dallied with."

"I loved the German. I did not dally with the Russian."

"And did you not follow this—this Karelena Josefovna to Hollywood? To make propaganda there?"

"You have been misinformed, Josef Vissarionovich. She followed me. Our relations soon ended."

"What difference does it make who followed and who led? Why do you bring up trifles?"

"No difference, Comrade."

"And did you not become aware that this innocent maiden, as you call her—"

"I believe it was you who called her that, if you will excuse me for making such an observation."

"Of course we excuse you. Why shouldn't we excuse you? Did you not become aware that she was acting on behalf of Gestapo Intelligence?"

The spy did not answer. He looked at the shoes on his feet. The act of a guilty man.

"It is necessary to remind you that you have already confessed to possessing this knowledge and that your signature is on the confession."

"I was compelled to confess. By physical force."

"You seem in excellent health to me, Comrade. Of course, if you wish to file a complaint about your treatment, that means is open to you. Then we must begin the interrogation again, as if what you have experienced never occurred. We have a constitution that guarantees this right to all our citizens. And noncitizens, too."

Now he raised his head. "I wanted to protect Karelena. She was acting in a strange manner. She was a different person. Something happened in Berlin. I did not learn what."

"And did this new person seek from you certain information?"

"I had no information. I was an actor. And soon I was not even that. My part was taken by another. I came to the Soviet Union, which had been betrayed by Germany. I wanted to join its struggle. The struggle for Stalingrad."

"Yes, you struggled—to seduce a blameless Soviet girl. I see on your back at this instant, at this moment when the battle is still raging, I see what uniform you fought in. And the Tretyakov Gallery. That was your battleground."

"I can only repeat to you, you who are her father, Josef Vissarionovich, that I was touched by Svetlana Alliluyeva. So eager to learn."

"She has Model School Number 25 to learn in. They teach her everything she has to know."

"Not everything, in my opinion."

"The opinion of a sybarite and a womanizer! I wish to get to the point before dawn arrives. Were you in touch with the German woman, the Jewess Kauffman, after your arrival in the Soviet Union and are you in touch with her now?"

Once again the subject failed to answer.

"Why do you look at your shoes? Are they pinching your feet? Please remove them if that makes you comfortable. And consider, Comrade—I should say, Herr Engelsing: I am asking you only to repeat to me what you have already told our men at Lubyanka. Are you in contact with the Hollywood actress? By mail? By radio? Is there a secret code? Has she made certain requests? Did she, for example, wish to know if the General Secretary and the People's Commissar for Defense intended to fly to the African continent?"

"You are asking the wrong person, Comrade Stalin. You should ask Warner. The head of her studio. Their relations are intimate."

"And these lovers are in North Africa now. Would you care to confirm this known fact? Why do you hesitate? Why is speech difficult? We have it all written down. In your own words. If you like, I can produce the document. Let me tell you another fact, my dear Herr Engelsing. We aren't going to kill you. You will have a different fate. But you'll never see Svetlana Alliluyeva again. It's done with my Little Housekeeper. So. Now. They are in Africa? Roosevelt. Churchill. Warner and his bitch."

"Yes. Africa."

"Where?"

"Casablanca. The conf—"

"Casablanca! We know about Casablanca! The whole world does. Old witches write about it in gossip columns. The Hitlerites know it, too. There are more Germans in that city than Arabs. *Where*, that's what we want to know. The conference is ending. We have to know where they go next."

"Where? I don't know where. Could it be America?"

"You disappoint me, Alexander Wilhelmovich. You know what I am asking. If I want to play games, I have a table for billiards."

"I have told you what I told the others, Comrade Stalin. It is all I know."

"*Others?* Those little shits at Lubyanka? Look. Here is what you told them. Everything is written down. Look—not at your shoelaces, you fucking Yidiy. Here: What name appears on this document?"

"I regret to inform you that I am not of the Jewish per—"

"You were asked a question. Is this not your signature?"

I took the confession from my pocket and held it in front of his face, his smooth face, his actor's face. The curl in the hair. The dimples like a girl.

"It is. You already have what you want. What is the purpose of such repetition?"

"Because—" My voice dropped low; and the more I wanted to rip the skin off his skull and see his teeth go flying, the softer and calmer and even sweeter it became. "*Because, if you don't tell it to me, it does not exist.*"

He was nothing, a peshka, a speck of dust. But the dust dared to speak: "Yes, you are correct, Comrade Stalin. What you hold in your hand does not exist. It is worthless. And I will repeat myself: I said what I said and signed what I signed because I was beaten."

"I'll cut off your balls, you fucking faggot! I'll stuff them down your mouth! Stand up! It's an order! On your feet! See that window? Go over there, and please forgive me for losing my temper. It is a definite flaw in my nature. Just push aside the curtain. No, no, push it along the rod. That's right. Is it dawn? No? Well, it doesn't matter. There is enough light. Would you be kind enough, my dear Sasha, to tell me what you see?"

This is what the academicians call a rhetorical question; no need to respond to it because the person who asks already knows the answer. I am fond of this form of speech. It is often employed when discussing dialectical materialism. This is what he saw: the suka, Svetlana—on her knees, with her arms twisted behind her back. And her own blood running down her own cheeks.

"Sveta! Svetlana, poor girl! Poor darling!"

He called these words out to her through the glass, but of course she could not hear. This van was especially equipped. The windows were double-thick and completely soundproof. He could not bear the sight. He swept the curtain closed.

"I was *not* correct, Herr Comrade Engelsing. I was mistaken. You did get to see her again."

"Comrade Stalin, do not torture this girl. She is innocent. If I knew what you want to learn I swear I would tell you."

"This is most unusual. It seems possible that the General Secretary has been mistaken a second time. Perhaps you do not care for this cunt of a girl, after all. But you are still Onkel Engel to your Hollywood whore. We won't torture her. She is already under a sentence of death. Your face goes pale, Comrade. Are you ill? Would you like water? The cure is to tell us the location of this *Paris of the Sahara*? Of course it is a code name. For what? An order of death can be canceled. Human beings have been known to change their minds. I am not an infallible pope. I wear on my head a plain cloth cap. What? Speak up. You must speak up. Only the General Secretary has the privilege of speaking softly."

The speck of dust was trembling. He could barely move the tongue in his mouth. If another person were present he would not believe that Comrade Stalin leaned forward to hear another person's words.

"*I am loyal. I wish the victory of the Soviet Union. Do not kill her.*"

"This is a rare day, Alexei Wilhelmovich. You have seen what no other living person has. The General Secretary made a third error. I told the former Little Housekeeper that you would be digging coal for five years. I meant to say ten. Five for what you have witnessed. And five more for what you do not know."

22 } EIGHT HOURS

The Terrible Turk: January 1943, Casablanca

They sent me back from Rabat to Casablanca in what they called an Austin Saloon. It looks like the conference is over. They made up their minds about everything and at their press conference announced they were demanding unconditional surrender. Now the president wants me to help him get ready to leave. He and the prime minister are going off in the Daimler. No one knows where—not even me, though Mr. FDR usually tells me everything. It's all top secret. One rumor is that Mr. Churchill and the president are going somewhere else in Africa or maybe to Turkey. What a pleasure it would be to go with them. I could look up my cousins in Harpoot. That isn't in the cards. I guess I'll have to pack up everything over there in the Chief's villa. Not only his stuff, but whatever belongs to both the women. We'll all go home together. It will be nice to be in pajamas. To pick up from my doorstep the *LA Times*. The toast popping up in the toaster. Just thinking about that makes my headache go away.

KK: January 1943, Casablanca

The gulls circled over the villa through the afternoon, then into dusk. The wind continued to blow in from the sea. The open jeep returned from Rabat just as the moon was rising. An American soldier was driving. A half dozen more servicemen were stuffed into the seats. Whooping. Cheering. Spilling their liquor over the side. Oumaima was sitting on somebody's lap. The vehicle came to a stop and she slid from it. Laughing, waving, moving her hips. She blew them kisses. She was dressed like a belly dancer.

"Les cochons dégoûtants!" she said as the jeep swerved off over the cobblestones. She moved past where I stood at the door of the villa.

"What's this? Eh?"

She pointed to the bags I had started to pack.

"The conference is ending. I'm going back to Hollywood. With Mr. Warner. With Jack. And you? I suppose you are, too?"

She threw her head back, so that her hair fell to the hollow of her back. She gave a high-pitched laugh. "Jamais!"

"I thought you had a contract—"

"Un contrat! Three hundred dollars a week. I am paid ten times that sum. And not for belly dancing."

"I think I can guess what for. The chauffeur. How did you know about the chauffeur?"

"Le grand vizier: he works for les Allemandes. The same as you."

"And you? Are you not paid in German marks?"

She laughed again. "Au contraire, my sweet girl. Rubles. But I would do my duty if I did not receive a single kopek. Does this seem strange to you? A believer in Islam, a believer in the Soviet Union?"

"Not as strange as that you and I are in this room together."

"Oui, deux ennemies dans le harem de M. Jacques!"

It was my turn to laugh. But Oumaima put a finger to her lips, then used it to beckon me through the living room and into the tiled kitchen. She picked up a knife, a big one, with a serrated edge. "You see this? Last night I picked it up. Do you know why? To go to your chambre, yes? And put it deep in your back and into your heart. Les ordres, you understand? Du Kremlin."

I did not say out loud the words that were moving in a smart parade through my head: *I wish you had.* Instead I said, "Why didn't you?"

"You can answer that as well as I. We are not enemies, we are allies. At least pour le moment. We have the same mission. We failed today; on the next occasion we must not."

"The chauffeur?"

"A loss of nerve."

"But there won't be another occasion. Everyone is leaving. We go back to America. Churchill? The president? They are leaving, too, but no one knows where."

"True. But we shall find out. You, Karelena. I, Oumaima. Together, we have that power."

"*Together?* Do you mean Jack—?"

She lifted her chin; she closed one long-lashed eye in a kind of wink.

Then she held out her arms. Was it because she was a beautiful woman? I stepped into them. We embraced. "So you see," she said. "We have made a new Ribbentrop pact."

Jack L. Warner: January 1943, Casablanca

Here it is. The fucking house. I need a drink. I need more than that. A fifty-mile hike! I should get a medal. Like Jesse Owens. Hell, he only ran a hundred feet. The Jews in the desert didn't go as far as me. And they had Jewesses. No pussy! All day. All night. It's a world record! Where are the girls? This is torture! Like that Chinese water business. Drop by drop. Minute after minute after minute. After a while you lose your mind. Dum-doodle, dum-doodle. "Ladies! Ladies! Open up! Jackie's home!"

KK: January 1943, Casablanca

Jack came back to the villa at four o'clock in the morning. Howling outside like a beast of the jungle. I felt Oumaima shudder. I am sure she felt the tremors that moved through me. The front door crashed open. He tromped this way and that, stumbling against the walls, against the furniture.

"Ouch! Goddammit! Who put that suitcase in here?"

Then a terrific pounding. Against the far bedroom door.

"Blondie! Open up! You won't believe what I've got to show you. For Christ's sake, open the door. Loshak wouldn't believe it himself. KK! You fucking Kraut! Have pity! Ooooo. I'm a suffering human bean! Ha, ha, ha! Listen. I'll do it backward. Ooooo. Whatever you want!"

I heard the door bang open. Who would not feel at least a pinprick of pity on hearing, as we did, the pitiful moan.

"Empty! The bed's empty! Help me, Jesus! Hey! Hey! Where is everybody? Hello? Hello, ladies? Hello?"

The stumbling. The crashing. The Soviet agent held the German one, tight, as the steps, like the footfall of a giant, a bear, an Ungetüm, arrived inevitably at our door. The pounding now seemed against our own skulls, our own flesh.

"Open up! Open up! I'm a hero of the Soviet Onion! You've got to have pity! You don't know what I'm going through. Forget eight hours.

Twenty-four! That's two times—er, ah. That's four times, um, um. Never mind! An eternity! That means forever! Girls! I'm on my knees! I mean as a manner of speaking. Open up! My name is on the water tower! You women don't know! You don't know! Ooooo! Ah! Okay? Okay? You want to play rough? I'm turning into an animal! Like Chaney in *The Wolf Man*! Here goes!"

There was a crash. A thunderclap. Another crash. And the door flew open. The first light of dawn was coming through our bedroom window. We saw him standing there: a silhouette, the outline of his human body. We clung together in the bed.

"Aha! What's this? A pas de trois? Fantastic! Just what the doctor ordered. I can manage à squaw. Two of them! What's the matter with these pants? Why all these buttons? That's why some great man invented the zipper. Say, didn't we make this picture? Sure! *Honeymoon for Three*. IT MAY BE A HONEYMOON FOR THREE. There! Are you ready girls? Take a look at this! Oh, boy! I can't believe my luck. BUT ONE OF THEM IS A REDHEAD!"

In three strides he was beside the bed. He reached for me. He reached for Oumaima. He was climbing onto the mattress. The next instant he let out a yell and leaped back, both hands in front of his crotch.

"What's this? Cindy! What's this?"

"Not a step closer, M. Jacques. Not one."

That was Oumaima. She had the serrated knife in her hand. "Comprenez-vous?"

Jack was pressed against the farthest wall. "What the hell? Is that a—a—a knife? With a blade? I should have known. That *Honeymoon* was an Epstein picture."

"Go. Sleep in the other room. Allez vous en!"

"What do you mean, the other room? Is this some kind of Lysa—Lista—? Listerine act? Haven't you any pity? Look at me! Look what I'm going through."

He then began to beat himself on the head. Bubbles came from the sides of his mouth. His legs twitched and trembled, so that his pants, in creases around his ankles, writhed like a nest of snakes. Finally the spasms ceased. He grew calm. Hunched over, he looked up at the two of us. "Maybe tomorrow?"

"Peut-être," said Oumaima.

"Huh? Boot-end her? I'm not into that, but if you really—"

"It means *maybe*, Jack. Maybe tomorrow."

"Oui. Ca dépend. On whether you take us to where M. Churchill and M. le president are going."

"I'll take you girls wherever you want. How about Vegas? Or maybe Ciro's. There's a little place on Briarcliff that—hey, wait a minute. Those guys aren't going anywhere. We're having our big premiere right here in Casablanca. It's a Command Performance."

"No, no, M. Jacques. They are leaving today, tomorrow, the following day. But no one knows the destination. It is un secret d'État. So, l'Anglais. L'Américain: you will find out where they are going, and we will go there with you."

"Now you're talking! It's a great idea. Like *The Three Musketeers*. Naw, Fox made that one with the Ritz Brothers. But we'll stick together. *All for one and one and, and*—Never mind. When do we start?"

"The question," I said, "is *where*. You know how to get the answer. You and Abdul. Come see us then."

"Demain. Tomorrow. No later. Now leave us. You need sleep. Do so in the other chambre. Go now."

Jack, with his pants still down at his feet, and still with his back to the wall, inched his way to the door. The rays of the sun lit up the only part of him that was standing straight. "Well," he said, as he looked down toward this phenomenon. "It's not a total loss. Ha, ha, ha. At least I can't roll out of bed."

Jack L. Warner: January 1943, Casablanca

I woke up at ten in the morning. Things were no better in South America, if you catch my reference. Little pains, they felt like electric ants, were sprinting up and down the runway, as if they'd found a banana split or whatever else they like to eat for dessert. And they were biting, too. A terrible thought came into the mind of the vice president for production: *Maybe better if that fucking harem girl had gone to work with her knife.* I grabbed my hat and put on my pants, which was no cinch. I tippy-toed into the hot sun of the day.

That's when I had a bit of the same kind of luck that has come my way ever since I was ten years old and pulled the rabbi's nose. Who should be walking by but Dickie Schotter, one of the photographers who all along had been taking pictures of the big shots, like de Gaulle shaking hands with some Frog general and with Churchill and so on and so forth. "Shutter!" I called out, because that's what I used to call him when he was one of the stills guys on the lot. "*Shutter!* Fancy meeting you here. What say I make a reservation for the clay courts? Want to play a couple of sets?" It was a sucker invitation, since I could always beat Dickie left-handed—as long as he wanted to keep his job.

295

"Can't, J.L. I've got to get a shot of FDR. The story is, he's driving away with the PM any minute now."

"What? Leaving already? Any minute? But how can they do that? Everything is set up. We're showing our new picture tonight. I need you to take all the publicity shots. Oh, by the way: You wouldn't happen to know where they are going?"

"Haven't a clue, boss. But I'm pretty sure they're taking off. If you run over now, you can see they've got a case of Scotch sitting next to the Daimler."

I ran all right, but not to where they were supposedly loading the car. I hightailed it over to the president's villa, and what to my wondering eyes should appear—that's Shakespeare—but that traitor, Abdul the Turk, who was pushing FDR in his wheelchair down the ramp.

"Abdul!" I shouted. "Where the hell do you think you're going? You can't run out on me!"

"Sorry, Chief. It's an order. I can't say a word."

"Oh, yeah? If you two think—"

The next thing I knew somebody tackled me around the knees and somebody else grabbed me around the throat and I couldn't breathe. It was like an asbestos curtain was coming down on the life of the executive producer of Warner Bros., only it was a black one, not a white one: yes, curtains indeed for the son of Benjamin and the former Pearl Leah Eichelbaum. *S'shma Yisroel!* I couldn't see. I couldn't breathe. I couldn't even talk.

"No, no! Let him go, boys. It's my old friend Jack-o."

The goons loosened their grip and one of them even picked up my Panama-style hat.

Reilly, the head of those boyos, said, "You know better than to run up on the president like that, Mr. Warner."

"Yeah? Well what do you think *he's* doing? I'll tell *you*. Sneaking out! And I've got a million bucks sunk into this production."

"You'll have to forgive me, Jack, old man. Winston raves about this spot he calls the Paris of the Sahara—and since we won't be seeing Paris itself, at least not until the liberation, I thought I'd take a peek. It's only one night. Then off we go to home!"

"You want Paris? You'll get plenty of Paris in our picture. Cafés and a train station and the Awful Tower and a street scene on the back lot. *We'll always have Paris.* You like that line? I wrote it. CASABLANCA: WHERE EVERY KISS MAY BE THE LAST! We're going to show it tonight, and you're going to sit there and watch it and Dickie will take photos and then we're going to release it worldwide."

"Not tonight, old boy. It's the sunset. I've got to see the sunset, Winnie says. The rose and the pinks on the Atlas mountains."

"Listen, this is a Command Performance. And I'm giving the commands. Or would you like to see another movie, one about the attack on Pearl—"

"Oh, Mike!" the president called to his gumshoe. "Take your men over to the parked car, will you? I'll be along in a moment. Abdul, why don't you go with them?"

The Turk, so-called, pushed the wheelchair to the bottom of the ramp and went off with everyone else. I turned to FDR.

"I don't think you'll be going to any mountains, Mr. President. I've got the keys to the car."

"Why, Jack. What on earth—?"

"What I am seeing, see, is Technicolor. Never mind the expense. It's all in my head: maybe Gable. Maybe Sheridan, now that I've reined her in. We'll have to use Chinks to play the Japs. Or Lorre. Mr. Moto without the blinkers. And who will play the great man in the White House? I know! Cagney! A little short, sure, but no one will mind. Want to know why not? Because he'll never get out of his chair."

"Really, sport, I don't know what you're getting at."

"You don't, huh? Well, here's how I see the trailer. Zeros diving. Tojos grinning with their buckteeth. White scarfs blowing around their necks. And down below: smoke coming up from the USS *Arizona*. From the

USS *Oklahoma*. Maybe the *West Virginia*, too. Close up on Cagney. Tag line: WHAT DID THIS MAN KNOW? WHAT WAS HIS TERRIBLE SECRET? Still don't get it, pal? HOW MANY LIVES DID HE LOSE?"

I ran out of breath. To tell you the truth, I surprised myself. This is how I talked to people when we were drawing up contracts. I'm not sure FDR was breathing, either. Then he said:

"You know, Winston likes motion pictures. He's always talking about *That Hamilton Woman*—"

"Forget it. Plenty of nominations, but what did it win? Best *sound*!"

"And the Marx Brothers. He says laughing at them saved his life."

"You want laughs? Try Bugs Bunny."

"The point I am trying to make is that Winston likes the movies as much as his mountains. Why can't we give him both? Eh, Jack-o? You and I? We won't see your new picture here. But we can see it tonight, just as we planned, but in Marrakesh. Will that do? Have we an arrangement? And have I now the keys to my car? You know how much I enjoy going for a drive. Well, isn't this a good compromise?"

I didn't reply. That's because I was already off and running. Here was the path to the villa. Here was the villa itself. Hooray! The door was open. "Cindy!" I called. "Blondie, you fucking Kraut! Jack has got the answer! The answer!"

They came half-dressed in their eagerness toward me.

"Marveilleux!" said the one with the bigger boobs.

"What is it?" cried the one with the smaller ones.

I put an arm around one girl. I put an arm around the other. Then I told them it was the same answer I always gave to my little darlings, Barbara and Joy, even though she was only a stepdaughter: *Marry cash! Marry cash!* Then I slammed the door behind the three of us.

22 } COMMAND PERFORMANCE

Hedda Hopper's Hollywood: January 1943, Los Angeles

Ran into Mrs. Moses Taylor, the reclusive socialite, on one of her rare trips
to our Golden State. Usually she winters in faraway Marrakesh, but this
season she has rented her famed Villa La Saadia to some very special guests
and is seeking the sun in little old San Clemente. I couldn't help noticing
that when she mentioned those visitors she wrinkled up that button nose
of hers. "You don't mean—" I started to say, but she quickly put her finger
to her lips. Ever the worm in the apple, I said, "Well, I happen to know on
good authority that *that man*"—which is how her set refers to FDR—"has
gone on quite a fishing trip and may have cast a line in your oasis." She only
gave a knowing smile, so the worm burrowed deeper: "Now, Edith, I can't
believe a granddaughter of Ulysses S. Grant and a staunch Republican,
too, would rent her beautiful home, with its minaret and gardens, to a person like that." That did the trick. The former and oh-so-glamorous Edith
Bishop burst out in indignation. "Do you think I had a choice, Hedda? And
do you think they are paying me rent? La Saadia, which I so treasure, was
practically requisitioned! It's like soldiers sleeping in a barn. Why, I'd just
as soon have my home taken over by storm troopers! At least they wouldn't
drop their filthy ashes all over my antique sofas and rare Persian rugs."

Seems to me this gal she has a point. Why are we fighting a war if
our leaders behave like conquering heroes and barbarians? Of course we
haven't any *proof* that Mr. Churchill and the president, not to mention
that other cigar smoker, the long-lost Jack Warner and the lovely Karelena
Kaiser, have actually taken up quarters in that paradise.

Can you guess how Hedy Lamarr fell in love with John Loder? It was
while watching him slice turkey last Thanksgiving at the Hollywood Can-
teen. There must be some symbolism there somewhere, but I'll be darned
if I can find it.

Goebbels: *January 1943, Berlin*

So it is Marrakesh. Our source in California as much as tells us so: *Its minarets and gardens.* More: this confirms what we have heard from our sympathizers at the sultan's court. So be it: the last great battle of the war will take place in *that paradise.* Even the Führer recognizes that the battle for Stalingrad is lost. The little airstrip at the Stalingradskaya flight school has been taken. No matter. If we are triumphant at Marrakesh the defeat at Stalingrad will be a footnote in history. A history that we, as the victors. will write.

So our pretty little birdy has landed in Marrakesh. I once held her in my hand. And let her fly away. But if she is at this Taylor Villa, we won't need ice cubes or darts or radioactive rays. We have in this last year become quite expert in the use of das Gas.

The Terrible Turk: *January 1943, Marrakesh*

The trip from the villa in Casablanca to the one in Marrakesh took four hours. It would have been shorter if we did not pull to the side of the road. We had an English picnic. Boiled eggs. Ham sandwiches, more lettuce than ham, which I don't touch anyway. Tea in canisters. Mince pie. Even wicker baskets and tablecloths checked red and white. I thought about the illusions in pictures. The way they make you think what you see is real. A picnic on the grass: but ours was on sand, with soldiers everywhere, the way makeup people and grips are always standing around; and airplanes buzzed over our heads like the arc lights in the days before sound. Back then was when my headaches really began, when Jimmy Jeffries banged me up against the ring pole. Lights out for Sniffy! I think my war wound only made it worse. I should have got the Purple Heart for *One Round Hogan.* At every picnic there are ants, whether you see them or not.

Jack L. Warner: *January 1943, Marrakesh*

Hell of a joint. Palm trees and bushes the same as in Beverly Hills, plus all kinds of marble and tiles and what they call arabesques like in a Jewish bathhouse. Also fountains and a pool with flower petals on top. They put the girls in one room and me in another, but there's a connecting door, and if I close my eyes I can tell myself this is a one-night stand in the Garden of Allah. Sunset and Havenhurst. Listen to these birds! They can drive you nuts.

G. S. P., Jr.: *January 1943, Marrakesh*

God knows what our little joy trip is going to cost the American taxpayer, not that this socialistic aristocrat gives it a thought. Nor does he care about the risks he is taking. We found forty-five scorpions on the grounds of this tarted-up villa and a half dozen inside—right under the cushions where A-1 and B-1 will be sitting. I don't know if this was a natural occurrence. We're the intruders in their habitat; they're not the intruders in ours. But they could have been planted before we kicked out all the French butlers and Arab servant boys. Frankly I prefer the scorpions to the local burghers.

Somewhere I read that these arthropods attained their present state of development hundreds of millions of years ago. My observation of the Arab race makes me wonder if the same sort of arrested development might apply to them. How else do you explain the stupidity of the male of the species, who sits in front of his hut staring vacantly into space hour after hour? As for the women, we should be thankful they hide their features with a veil. All of them may be immune to the bite of the scorpion through centuries of adaptation. But to the president and the prime minister, those creatures are living knives.

On arrival, B-2 insisted on climbing the six-story tower on the premises. He wanted, he said, to see the loveliest sight on earth. I arranged for Prettyman and Meeks to make a cradle of their hands and carry the president to the observation deck at the top. The Kike and his women, two of them now, came along. He must have some hold on the commander in chief. Some hypnotic power, the way snakes are said to mesmerize their prey. Why else such an affinity for a figure who strikes me, as do most of his breed, to be as subhuman as the Arab? I have to keep my eyes on him. Pathetic the way the legs of our leader dangled down, like those of a wooden puppet or an old rag doll.

No sooner had our party reached the sixth floor than the PM started in like an orator. "The mountains," he said. "Come and look. Do you see the snow on them? Do you see how they blush in the setting sun?"

The sun *was* setting. A breeze, surprisingly cool, sprang up. I gather that on some nights the water in the fountains will freeze. The two black men hoisted the president onto the parapet, so that he could look out over the city and to the Great Atlas range.

"Magnificent. You were right, Winston. It is the most glorious scene in the world."

"Worth the trip, eh? I hope you'll stay another day."

"I only wish I could. What do you say, Jack-o? Isn't this just grand?"

"Not so grand. It reminds me of the Paramount logo. I'm freezing my ass off—pardon my French, ladies. What time is dinner?"

The wind did have a bite to it. The president, I saw, gave a shiver. I did not like any of this. Prettyman had FDR by the arm, but his legs hung over the edge. "Mr. President, I don't want you to catch a chill. May we escort you to your quarters?"

"Oh, Abdul will give me a rubdown—won't you, Abdul? That and a good old-fashioned will keep the doctor away. I never get a cold, you know. It's because of my good Dutch constitution."

We all fell silent, undoubtedly with the same thought: this was the man who had already caught the worst cold in all of history. The same idea must have occurred to him as well, because—it wasn't a shudder, so much as a sigh. "A pity, but perhaps we'd better go down to—"

"Moment. Un moment, seulement." It was one of Warner's women, the dark-haired one, who had come onto the stage in Rabat. "I make you warm," she said—and before you knew it this substitute Lamour had peeled off her sweater, which of course revealed her chief assets, and the president swiveled his head around—yes, very much like that on a puppet—and this big grin began to spread across his face in a way that was all too human; the girl started striding toward him going, *Permit me, si'l vous plait*, and *You must to wear mon pull*, and then everyone gave a quite audible gasp because she stumbled forward and both her arms shot out and it was clear that she was about two seconds from hitting the president with a jolt that would send him sixty or seventy feet down to his death on the hard earth below.

Meeks, Prettyman, Warner, Churchill, the bald-headed infantryman who claimed to be a Turk, and I, G. S. Patton, Jr., a two-star general of the United States Army: we all stood as if turned to stone. Only the blond mistress of the Kike turned aside, so that she would not have to witness what was about to happen. The president, himself, seemed to be aware of nothing but the full-breasted woman careening toward him.

"Watch out!" I cried. "Mr. President!"

At that instant, as if in response to my voice, though I have to confess it was more likely in response to the sun at last going down: the electric lights atop every minaret in Marrakesh flashed on, twinkling everywhere. The sudden illumination had the effect of a gong, calling the faithful to prayer. All at once the Lamour lady was flat on the ground with her arms outstretched, but whether she was praying to Allah the Most Compassionate and Most Merciful and Master of the Universe or whether she had simply fallen flat on her face it was impossible to tell.

KK: *January 1943, Marrakesh*

I do not know what happened in the tower. I could not bear to watch. I turned away. Did Oumaima lose her nerve? Did she realize she must not carry out such a mission at the hour of the sunset prayer? All I can say for certain is that when I turned back she was on the ground, with the sweater in her hand. It is possible that she understood she was about to fulfill only half her assignment. So she went down. Oh, the look on Jack's face! The Jack L. Warner I know so well that I guessed what he was going to say before he said it: "Goddammit! I don't think even Busby could teach that girl to dance."

The Terrible Turk: *January 1943, Marrakesh*

I gave the president a rubdown, just like he said. But when I asked him if he wanted a full session he just gave a little wave of his hand and said it wouldn't be necessary. This was something new in my experience. Well, I did see what looked like some sort of sigh, or maybe a sob, high up in the tower. Is it the desert air? You see too clearly in it. But I don't like that he is maybe giving up. Better to see what also appears in the desert: the shimmering mirage. So I asked if he was sure and he said he was and that he wanted to rest a bit before dinner and that he had a long night ahead of him. What with the Chief's new picture and the communiques he had to write to Premier Stalin and Mr. Chiang Kai-shek, who are our main allies, and with his plane leaving first thing in the morning he wondered if he would get any sleep at all.

"I am sorry to have taken you from Mr. Warner," he said. "I am going to release you from the army so that you can go back to him. You do him a world of good, you know." And here he gave the old sunshiny smile. "Just as you have done a world of good for me."

Now I realized that while we were up in the tower, other guests had arrived: Mr. Harriman and Mr. Hopkins; and Mr. Wilson, Churchill's physician; and Sir Alan Brooke. Also that thin-faced grand vizier. We all sat down to dinner at around eight. The president had KK and the native girl on opposite sides of him. That brought back his spirits. We had a real feast: lobster, filet mignon, and a dessert built out of nougat that was three feet high with a candle in the middle and the Atlas Mountains all around the bottom made out of spun sugar. The president grinned and told Mr. Churchill that he could stay and paint the view but that he, himself, would be digesting it at ten thousand feet. Everybody laughed, though of course that happened whenever the president or the prime minister said anything.

The Chief, I saw, did not. He was frowning down at his plate. I leaned over to ask him was something wrong, but before I could get the words out he crushed his cigar into the middle of it. Then he stood up. "All right," he said and right away repeated himself. "All right! Let's quit stalling. What do you say, Mr. President?"

Without blinking an eye the president answered him: "Why, Jack-o: I say, *Let's go to the movies!*"

Jack L. Warner: January 1943, Marrakesh

I thought they were going to spend all night chewing the cud, like cows, and then chewing the fat, like at the writers' table. It was time to get the show on the road. A bunch of chairs had been set up in a room on the third floor, with sofas for the hotshots. The screen was a sheet hung up in front of the big plate-glass window. FDR came up in the little elevator, but everyone else climbed the flights of stairs. Most of them were half-tipsy.

Old-fashioneds before, brandy after, wine in between. I didn't have a drop. I noticed every bottle was already open. Tested for poison, like everything else. But no system is perfect: thirty bucks was all it cost to sneak Dickie inside. He was popping away at FDR, like I told him to. Me and the Prez together. Me and Churchill, too. I gave them the big smile, choppers brighter than the flashing bulbs.

I figured FDR would watch from his chair, but they shifted him to the sofa. Then I saw why. He patted the cushion and Cindy didn't waste a minute plopping down beside him. Then he patted the other cushion and gave KK the eye. But she wasn't going anywhere because I had hold of her arm. She knows how to give the special treatment. Hell, I'm at an age when I can't sit through a picture without it. This is what is such a delight about our industry: sitting in the dark, with people all around you, you can hear them breathing, and you can eat Milk Duds or some other kind of delicacy that melts in your mouth, and men and women twenty feet high are kissing with their lips in front of your eyes, and all the time some babe you don't have to look at or talk to and maybe you can't remember her name is going to work. I'm a Jew in good standing at the Wilshire Boulevard Temple and also at Temple Israel, just to hedge my bets, and generally speaking we as a people do not dwell too much on the afterlife. But if you ask me, this is heaven.

The room was packed. The doors were shut. I nodded my head. Off went the lights. Everything was pitch-black, darker inside than outside because outside you have the moon and the stars. I didn't wave to the Signal Corps guy who stood at the projector because people were jabbering at each other, just like at the dinner table. Jokes and wisecracks and off-color remarks, so you would not believe these were the leaders of the United Nations. After awhile I could not take it anymore. Even though a king or a queen wasn't in the audience, this was a Command Performance. I jumped up, checking to see whether my fly was already open. "Quiet! You and you and you! Nobody paid for a ticket. Nobody's got a right to talk!"

That shut them up. Everything was hushed. Time for the high sign. I gave it and sat back down with a smile on my face when the projector started up and the words *Jack L. Warner, Executive Producer* appeared on the screen.

The Terrible Turk: January 1943, Marrakesh

I was ready to enjoy the motion picture. When the Chief's name came up there was polite applause, which you couldn't hear anyway because music was playing. Next came a map of Africa and on top of it in big letters the names *Humphrey Bogart* and *Ingrid Bergman* and *Paul Henreid*. Then a tiny word "in" above the title, which turned out to be *Casablanca*, which made the music become more exotic, like you hear with a belly dancer; and then, in smaller letters, the names of other actors, and next, in even smaller ones, the rest of the cast, including the French blonde I saw plenty of times in the Chief's suite. After that came the words *Screenplay by Julius J. and Philip G. Epstein*.

"Neither one of them worked an honest day in his life," grumbled the Chief, who was sitting in the row behind me.

After the titles we heard a voice saying, *Many eyes in imprisoned Europe were turning hopefully, or desperately, toward the freedom of the Americas*, and right after that we learned that two German couriers had been murdered and two letters of transit stolen and that all suspicious characters had to be rounded up and searched. Then the police started blowing their whistles and hustling people off and one gentleman ran away, so they took out their guns and shot him dead, right under a big poster of Marshal Petain. The poor guy.

G. S. P., Jr.: January 1943, Marrakesh

It's a freezing-cold night, and the heat in this room is on full blast; but that's not why I am in such a sweat. I don't like this business of watching a Hollywood picture in the dark. I told the president I wasn't going to allow it. So did Reilly. Anything can happen when the lights are out. But neither of us could persuade him. So there he sits, his big head thrown back on the cushions and one arm thrown around the native woman, who is wearing a modest Muslim shawl over her hair, though the rest of her is only half dressed. He is lit up in the projector beam: it might as well be a spotlight on a target. There! A gunshot. I know it's up on the movie screen, but I jump out of my skin nonetheless. It is part of the nature of the human species that we don't learn from what has occurred in the past. But you'd think even an ape would make an adjustment after what happened—or nearly happened—at Rabat. Talk about dumb luck. A shift in the wind meant more than all the preparations of the Secret Service and the Third Army. The bad luck was that the spade with the gun got away. I doubt he acted alone. You find one of them in the woodpile, there's bound to be more.

Watch out! Shots! Two, three, four! It's that little worm, Lorre: he's shooting at the police. Now they're taking him away. If there's an assassin here now, he'll know to use the fake shots to cover up the real ones—the way they used the music at Rabat. Hell, they've got music here, too. The one they ought to shoot is the piano player. Everybody is knocking on wood, just like that *clap-clapping* during "The Heart of Texas." Why should I listen to the president? The Kike has him under his thumb, and I'm damned if I'll take orders from *him*. The next time there's shooting, I'm going to shut this carnival down.

KK: *January 1943, Marrakesh*

It is going to happen. Oumaima is there, on the couch. I can see her in the light of the projector beam. She is ready; in a few minutes she will rise. Jack has his hand on me. He thinks no one can see. I have him in my hand, too. He can last through a double feature. On the screen, the man who was supposed to be played by my poor Alex. Victor Lazlo—the perfect hero, with a scar where they beat him. The way they beat Joe-Joe in the street. Why wouldn't he take me to the Gloria Palast? So he could sit in the dark. With a gun. But we always sat together. We watched the girls in the Wasserfall. They were like floating diamonds. They were like pieces of glass. Ein Kaleidoskope. *By a waterfall, I'm calling you-oo-oo-oo.*

Ah, there is the woman who stole my role. Annina, the pure Bulgarian, so upset, the dear thing, at sleeping with Captain Renault. That was my part. It was promised to me. Look at her. They had to paint those tears in her eyes. What a joke! *Ha!* Don't laugh, little Mädschen. I put my hand, my free hand, over my mouth. But it *is* funny. It's what we Americans call a scream. If only I could tell Frau Hopper. *Guess what, Hedda: the orders of both the Führer and the General Secretary will be obeyed. The great men of the world are about to die. But your little birdy is all aflutter, she can only think one thing:* that the boss's daughter got her part! *Isn't that hilarious? Isn't that sensational? Ha-ha-ha! It's an exclusive! It's a scoop!*

Jack L. Warner: January 1943, Marrakesh

What is this skirt laughing at? What's so fucking funny? Not what's up on this screen. How come, if the Epstein boys are supposed to be such wits, with repartee and all of that, there isn't a single good gag in the picture? What am I paying them for? Thirty-five grand! And all I hear is one lead balloon after the other. I knew it! I knew it! We've got a world-class flop on our hands. What did Renault just say? Did I hear that right? *If he were a woman he'd be in love with Rick?* Jesus H. Christ! And at the end they'll go off together, practically holding hands. Didn't I say all along this was a picture for fruits?

Now what? Oh, yeah, that flashback to Paris. *A franc for your thoughts:* Now *that* is what I call comedy. I insisted on it. I made them put it in. I should have written the whole damn script myself. I mean, this is a disaster. A *disaster!* So what if we timed the invasion? So what if we timed the big conference? Nobody gives a damn about shit like that. They want laughs! They want romance, real romance, something hot, not all this yakking between Bogie, who's about three feet tall with a lisp, and some Swedish dame—look at that nose, for Christ's sake: they should have cast her in *Dumbo.* And with an accent to boot. I *told* Wallis: use Raft, use Reagan. Sheridan, she's your babe! At least she's got a pair.

How am I going to explain this to Harry? A cool million. What a bomb! What a dud! We're going to lose our shirts. *And* our pants! What's going on? Huh? What's going on? The girl is pointing a gun at the guy! *That's* amour? Go ahead, pull the trigger. Put the bullet in my head. We're washed up. We're ruined. It's all over.

G. S. P., Jr.: January 1943, Marrakesh

That girl, Ilsa, has a gun in her hand. Is this it? What they are waiting for? We can't take chances. If it goes off, we'll stop the show. I've got a man stationed right by the projector. We'll tell everybody the machine broke down. It's late. Almost one in the morning. These people should be home.

Safe in their beds. In a few hours I'll take the president to the airport. Then this job will be done. I'm nothing but a glorified security guard. Or a kind of entertainer. That's what everybody at home is reading in the papers. Oh, okay, good: she put down the gun. Now for a kiss. There it is, right on cue. Yes, the papers and the newsreels say that G. S. P., Jr., has been busy regaling the leading lights of the world. Dinners and parades and now the movies. Amusing people is not my game. Thank God it'll be over in the morning. Then I am going to go out and kill someone.

What is that woman doing? The Lamour stand-in. Cindy, the Kike calls her. She got up from the sofa. Now she's walking around, going up to every person. Like some kind of usherette. Selling candy or something. It's hard to see. She's leaving a trail behind her, a trail of little lights, as if she were wearing a gown with rubies. Oh, I get it: people are lighting up. She's the cigarette girl.

KK: *January 1943, Marrakesh*

Oumaima is up. Selling her cigarettes. Wait for the moment she leaves the room. Wait.

The Terrible Turk: *January 1943, Marrakesh*

What a great picture. It's got everything. Drama. Intrigue. Suspense. A real love story. And I can't help laughing all the time, like with Abbott and Costello. The Chief's ecstatic. He's got a real hit on his hands. "Listen, Chief," I whisper over my shoulder. "Isn't this a terrif—" But I am interrupted by the harem girl. She's got a big selection of smokes.

"Old Golds," she says. "Chesterfields, Pall Malls."

Her boobs are hanging into the tray.

"Sorry," I say. "I'm a nonsmoker. From my days in the ring."

She does not hear me. She seems to be in some kind of trance. "Winstons, Avalons, Du Barry De Luxe. Fatimas, Atikah Cigaretten. Have a Viceroy. Have a Kool. A Wizard, the Wonder Cigarette!"

"Hey," says the Chief, right behind me. "What am I? Chopped liver? Give me one of those Cohibas. Don't have one? Okay, a Montecristo. And lean over a little more, will ya?"

"Je suis désolé," she says in the French language. "I am out of the cigars. Give me a moment. One moment. I shall retrieve them. Montecristos, my dear Jacques. Always for you."

Off she goes, with her headdress trailing behind her, and out the door of the room.

Jack L. Warner: January 1943, Marrakesh

What kind of cigarette girl is that? No cigars. Take a gander at those buns. Like a mixmaster. I like that religous act, with the scarf or whatever it is on top of her head. Nothing left to the imagination with the rest of her. We can market that. Everybody in his heart of hearts wants to fuck a nun.

G. S. P., Jr.: January 1943, Marrakesh

Why is it so cold in here? A minute ago it was hot. Now it's freezing. You'd never know know we were in the middle of a desert. No wonder there's snow on those mountains. Windows shut. Doors shut. Not a breath of air. They must turn off the heat at midnight. That's the only explanation.

The Arab woman is back, still dressed like a slut. Except now the scarf isn't on top of her head, it's over her face like a veil, with only her eyes showing.

The Terrible Turk: January 1943, Marrakesh

I put my eyes back on the screen. This is an exciting part of the picture. Bogie's got a gun pointed right at Claude Rain's heart, and Rains tells him that is his least vulnerable part. What a good joke! I wonder why more people aren't laughing. I guess it is because most of them have fallen asleep. It has been a long day. Too bad. They are going to miss the ending. I don't want to miss it. But I can hardly keep my own eyes open.

G. S. P., Jr.: January 1943, Marrakesh

Another gun. It won't go off. All they do is point those things. They don't understand the feeling when you shoot your foe. It is pure. It is cleansing, when the fight is a fair one. It isn't in the genes of these motion-picture people. If they aren't Jews, they have been Judaized. A merchant class. That's why they are hated. It has nothing to do with religion. It's because in every deal they come out on top. But a soldier knows.

Just what I thought: nobody shot anybody. Now the whole bunch of them are off to the airport. That's where I am taking the president in the morning. If I never see that grinning mug again, it will be all right with me. Where is he? There. Slumped over the arm of the sofa. Fast asleep. And the PM? Also out like a light. It seems like half the room is catching forty winks. Can't blame them. This Hollywood garbage, it's worse than a sleeping pill. Stay awake, Patton! That's an order. Dereliction of duty. Sleeping on watch. You can get court-marshaled for that.

Jack L. Warner: January 1943, Marrakesh

What the fuck? Look at FDR. Look at Churchill. Some place in dreamland, the two of them. The big cheese of a general looks like he's nodding off, too. Okay, the movie's a stinker. But they can't get away with this. Not at a Command Performance. "Hey! Hey, you bums! Wake up! Nobody sleeps at a Jack L. Warner Production!"

The Terrible Turk: January 1943, Marrakesh

Somebody is shouting *Wake up*. From far away. From Anatolia. But it's hard to wake up. Look. Look, everybody. Now they are at the airport. And the girl, I forget her name, is going off with the man in the white suit. I forget his name, too. And here comes the German and he is upset and he has a gun and—is that Bogie? He has a gun and they are aiming at each other—

KK: January 1943, Marrakesh

Yes, it is happening. It is happening now.

G .S. P., Jr.: January 1943, Marrakesh

What's going on? That Nazi. He has a gun. He's shooting at Bogart—and Bogart, my God, he's shooting at him. No need to worry. It's only a movie. I can close my eyes for a moment. Haven't we thought of everything? Every bite they ate. Every drop they drank. Nothing radioactive. No explosives. Insects. Reptiles. Scorpions. Above all, we have put our faith in God. All will be well. He honors the brave and the just.

Wait. The girl. The cigarette girl. What's she doing? Kneeling at the door. That scarf. That veil. She's stuffing it into the crack. The crack at the threshold. Gas! The one thing we didn't think of! Where's my gun? Here's my gun. This Arab: she's the assassin. In my sights. There! And there! A crack shot. A rabbit at two hundred yards.

Jack L. Warner: January 1943, Marrakesh

"What have you done? Schmuck! She's under contract!"

The Terrible Turk: January 1943, Marrakesh

This isn't in the movie. This is real. The harem girl. She's bleeding. But no one is moving. They are all asleep in their seats. The man at the projector is sleeping, too. He's knocked the machine on its side; the picture isn't on the sheet anymore; it's half on the wall and half on the ceiling. It doesn't matter. Here comes that great line: *Round up the usual suspects.*

Jack L. Warner: January 1943, Marrakesh

Huh? I *still* don't get it. *Round them up for what?* I told Wallis. I told everybody. They wouldn't listen. We need a new ending...

G. S. P., Jr.: January 1943, Marrakesh

Warner is down. He's out cold. And so is that Turk. The whole room is unconscious. All of them gassed. From CO. A carbon atom. An oxygen atom. How could we protect ourselves from such a tiny, a teeny-tiny, foe? And then? All these lit cigarettes: they'll blow us up to hide the evidence. Very well, General: no excuses. I know what to do. A bullet into the brain. An honorable end for a soldier. I'll do it. I'll do it. If only I could lift my arm...

KK: *January 1943, Marrakesh*

All is quiet. All is still. What does Rick say in the film? *The whole world is sleeping?* And so it is. And so am I. Every thought leaves my head.

Except this: *Him.* With the girl. And the girl, the young girl, with her Wolfie. The glass. The other girls. The other women. All of them. Every one. Selbstmorde! And every man, too. Everyone. Everybody. Everything. That's what he wanted: the whole world with its fire and bombs and all the shit in it must fall on his shoulders and his face and his head. He succeeded.

I glance down. Here is a thing no one on earth has never seen. It is a marvel. A freak of nature. Jack Warner is dead. But this thing, his sex member, is still alive in my hand, as eager as it was in life. It is filled with blood, like a reanimated corpse or a creature from *Dracula.* And the bodies in this room? They lie in the moonlight of the projector's beams, like the victims in *Doctor X.* The nightmares of a young girl after the movies.

From this horror I am running, running toward the sheet, which is now blank, which is now white, like the bedsheet that Joe-Joe used to hold over my bed, *You see? Nothing can harm you,* and I go through it, so that it winds itself around me, and then I go through the glass, the pane of glass, the pain of glass, so that it shatters, and I fall through the air, the clean, fresh, sweet-smelling air that will fill the room and wake the dead and I am nothing but a small notice in HEDDA HOPPER'S HOLLYWOOD: *Karelena Kaiser, born Karelena Kauffman, the daughter of Joseph Kauffman, former director of the Warner Bros. offices in Berlin, fell to her death at the Villa La Saadia in a terrible accident.* But it wasn't an accident. Sooner or later the Moon Killer arrives at the door. Oh, see how the sheet spreads around me. How white and how wide. Like a pair of wings.

The Terrible Turk: *January 1943, Marrakesh*

The picture is just about over. The guy tells the girl that their lives don't amount to a hill of beans and then she goes off with the other guy in a plane and Bogie and Rains are walking through the puddles on the runway. A breeze is blowing in. An icy breeze. It's like a cold shower that's waking people up. I turn around. The Chief is blinking and shaking his head.

"Where's Karelena?" he mutters. "Where's KK? That's one beautiful broad."

Others are stirring, too. Churchill is lifting his head. And there is FDR. He's pushing himself onto to his feet. He is taking a step. He is taking another step. I get up. I've got to get to him. But he is waving his arms. He has a grin that goes all the way around, it seems, to the back of his head. "Look, Abdul! Look! At last we've done it! It's a miracle!"

And up on the ceiling, and on the wall, all I can see is this:

313

THE END

〜

[A Warner Bros.–First National Picture]

PART IV

~~~

OUTTAKES

24 } THAT'S ALL, FOLKS

Stalin: January 1943, Moscow

Four days ago Hitler promoted Paulus to the rank of Generalfeldmarschall. Here is an example of fascist thinking: no field marshal in German history has ever surrendered; Paulus is a field marshal; therefore Paulus will not surrender. It is a deduction that has held true for the junior officers: many shot themselves or committed the soldier's suicide by standing upright in the trenches and allowing our lads to do it for them. Paulus, however, decided that he was not going to shoot himself for a Bohemian corporal. He prefers a trip to Moscow, where we shall make him welcome. The battle for Stalingrad is over.

Roosevelt and Churchill have returned to their own countries. At Casablanca they declared they would accept only an unconditional surrender. To me they made more excuses about the second front. Perhaps I should have flown there after all. Nothing would have happened to an American airplane. And it seems our agent from the harem failed to accomplish her mission; a good thing she killed herself or we would have performed that task for her. Nor were the Hitlerites able to squeeze the living creatures they held in their hands. I am told their agent lost her nerve. Or the Americans threw her out of a window. It does not matter. Not after Stalingrad. We are free to move west, and we shall do so.

How amusing it would have been to watch the plutocrats do their dance when they were forced to tell me, *for the hundredth time*, there would be no second front. *Sicily!* That word would stick in their throats like the bone of a fish if they had to utter it to my face. I must be content with the dance that is performed at the Bolshoi instead.

The girl smiled at me this morning. A smile means nothing. Who dares not do so after Stalingrad? But I note that she wore the modest skirt of a Soviet woman. That means more. I allow myself to think she has already recovered from the loss of her lover. She does not need his poetry or his tours of the Tretyakov Gallery. My Little Housekeeper knows enough and more than enough to please her poor old Paposhka.

Hedda Hopper's Hollywood: March 1944, Los Angeles

The most amazing thing happened last night over at Sid Grauman's picture palace. When the Best Motion Picture Award was announced—and in the opinion of yours truly it is a crying shame that beautiful and spiritual *Song of Bernadette* did not receive the honor instead of the forgettable *Casablanca*—Hal Wallis walked onto the stage as the maker of the dark-horse winner. At that moment a disturbance, more like a stampede really, broke out in the front row. Jack Warner was stepping on everybody's toes and elbowing everyone out of the way and in two blinks of an eye he was up on the stage and snatching the Oscar out of Hal's hands and holding it up over his head. He had a real Cheshire cat's grin on his face, but the expression on the real producer's face could have curdled that kitty's milk.

It was quite a night for the Burbank boys who made that picture. When Mike Curtiz accepted his award, he said in his usual king's English, "So many times I have a speech ready but no dice. Always a bridesmaid, never a mother." Incidentally, when poor Jimmie Hilton presented the Best Screenplay award, the Epstein twins never walked up on the stage. Turns out they were back east, where they seem to be more comfortable among their own people than with their hardworking colleagues in Tinseltown. If you ask me, this kind of ingratitude sets a very poor example.

Marlene Dietrich is off on her overseas jaunt with a heap of new clothes made featherweight. She can only take fifty-five pounds along. But if those black-lace nighties that have become evening gowns don't make our soldiers gasp, I'll eat one of my hats.

Los Angeles Examiner: September 1944, Los Angeles

HOLLYWOOD, Sept. 9

(AP)—Abdul Maljan, 62, who as "Abdul the Terrible Turk" once contended for the light-heavyweight boxing championship, died of a cerebral hemorrhage Thursday night. Maljan, who lost to Philadelphia Jack

O'Brien in the title bout, had been a bit actor and physical conditioner at movie studios for many years.

He left his house at 10440 Camarillo Street, Los Angeles, and the rest of his estate to "My only true friend, Jack L. Warner." Warner Bros. Studios has announced that all these sums will be distributed to older boxers now down on their luck. Burial will be at Forest Lawn Memorial Park, Glendale.

Goebbels: May 1945, Berlin

The Garden. The Führer. Frau Hitler. She is the last of the women to end her own life. Fräulein Kauffman—Karelena: next to the last. Because of that single night in his bedroom. I feel nothing for her. She failed us. It would have been best if I had never seen her. In that lighthearted film. In that bathing suit.

Magda bites into the capsule. Not a word of farewell. She falls. She is still. Perhaps it could be said that she is the last, though I do not believe she had any experience with the Führer. In truth, it may be said that I am the final victim. I have the capsule. I have the pistol. And I have Schwägermann, should I fail. In truth I am no different than any of these women. I loved him, too.

Our ideals, the idea of National Socialism: all will return in fifty years.

William Schaeffer: March 1946, Burbank

To: Mr. Groucho Marx
From: William Schaeffer, on behalf of Jack L. Warner
Date: March 22, 1946
Subject: Infringement of rights

Dear Groucho,

Our legal department has learned that you are about to make a new film entitled *A Night in Casablanca*. They have advised us that such a venture would almost certainly involve an infringement of our intellectual property rights and large financial investment in the property *Casablanca*, which went into wide release three years ago. Jack has asked me to write to you with the request that you change the name of the picture, and that you do not make a parody of what was an important patriotic motion picture from which we still derive considerable revenues.

With Jack's best wishes and mine to you and your brothers,

Bill Schaeffer
P.S. A formal letter from legal is attached to this note.

Groucho Marx: April 1946, Los Angeles

Dear Warner Bros.,

Just a few days before we had planned to announce our new picture, we received a long, ominous letter from your legal department warning us not to use the name *Casablanca*.

I don't understand your attitude. Even if you plan on re-releasing your picture, I am sure that the average movie fan could learn in time to distinguish between Ingrid Bergman and Harpo. I don't know whether I could, but I'd certainly like to try.

You claim that you own Casablanca, which was apparently discovered by your great-great-grandfather, Ferdinand Balboa Warner, while looking for a shortcut to the city of Burbank.

Do you also claim to own the words *Warner Brothers?* You probably have the right to use the name Warner, but what about Brothers? Professionally, we were brothers long before you were—and even before that there had been other brothers: the Smith Brothers; the Brothers Karamazov; Dan Brothers, an outfielder with Detroit; and Brother, Can You Spare a Dime?

Now, Jack, how about you? Do you maintain that yours is an original name? Well, it's not. It was used long before you were born. Offhand, I can think of two Jacks—Jack of Jack and the Beanstalk and Jack the Ripper, who cut quite a figure in his day.

We are all brothers under the skin, and we'll remain friends till the last reel of *A Night in Casablanca* goes tumbling over the spool.

Sincerely,
Groucho Marx

Alexander Engelsing: *March 1953, Leningrad*

So Josif Vissarionovich is dead at last. The crowds in Moscow are prostrate with grief. They kill each other trying to get close to the coffin. He was wrong about some things; he was right about many others. He said I would never see Svetlana Alliluyeva again. But I did, not long ago. He said I would be laboring for ten years in the mines; and that I did. *Your poor fingers,* Sveta exclaimed. *They were so long, so delicate. The hands of an artist.* I thought she was going to cry. *Now they look like potatoes.* Of course they do. One lump of coal, forced from the ground. Then another. Not to mention my hair. It had turned completely white. She did cry over that.

Another mistake of the General Secretary: I never spied for Germany. I was loyal always to the Soviet Union, which means I was, even under torture, loyal to him. But he was right about the main thing: I did love his daughter. Yes, for her sweetness, her purity, her eagerness to learn. Breathless to learn, I should say. But one time, in the war, in Moscow, we did spend one night with our bodies bare and together. Kind Comrade Klimov sat with a newspaper over his head, on the other side of the hotel door. When I removed my clothing she looked at that part of me. *So this is what they make such a fuss about,* the young girl said. Then she sighed. *To think there is such inequality in the Soviet Union.*

I said we met again. That was only months ago, after my release, and at the Black Sea. She had by then a son and a daughter. Also two husbands. Like a doomed couple in Chekov we talked and talked. The day and the night went by in words. But my mind, my thoughts, were on Joe Kauffman's daughter. She was, in the Hollywood phrase, *the love of my life.* Sveta and I said good-bye at the first rays of light. Her hair was still an attractive sort of reddish brown. She told me what she had learned: "The attempt to be happy is a mistake."

My bags are packed. I am at the Moskovsky Station. They are letting me go to Berlin. Of course to their sector. I shall find a way to the American zone, and then to America itself. What do I want to do with my life? I want to make movies.

New York Times: January 1947, Washington, DC

Washington, Jan. 26th—The War Department today revealed the awarding of the Medal for Merit to Jack L. Warner, the head of Warner Bros. Pictures, Inc.

Mr. Warner was honored not only for the great number of training films and recruiting subjects produced at his Burbank studio but for the many feature motion pictures distributed to our forces in the field.

He is further cited for his notable heroism in North Africa, where with no regard to his personal safety he filmed our troops in action and where, at the Casablanca conference of 1943, he performed valuable service to the president.

Fewer than two hundred citizens have won the medal since it was created by George Washington in 1782, and Mr. Warner is the first from the motion-picture industry. The medal was presented by General Arnold at March Field and was concluded with a flight of P-80s. Mr. Warner served with the rank of Army Air Force Colonel during the war.

Variety: October 1945, Los Angeles

Variety—October 7, 1945

WB VICTIM OF VANDALISM

Famed Sign Defaced after Riots

BY BERNARD KATZ

At some time over the weekend and in the wake of the "Black Friday" riots that sent 47 set decorators and other members of the CSU to the hospital with serious injuries, some person or persons defaced the well-known billboard outside the Burbank studios of Warner Bros. In what seems a clear reference to the tactics of the studio in dispersing the picketers, tactics that included tear gas, water hoses, armed deputy sheriffs and their baton-wielding squads of strikebreakers, the sign, which had read:

Warner Bros: Combining Good Picture Making
With Good Citizenship

was overnight replaced with the following motto:

Warner Bros: Combining Good Picture Making
with Good Marksmanship

Studio Exec Jack Warner would only say, "I know who these two jokers are and I know how to make them pay for this."

By Monday morning the sign had been returned to its original condition, and the picketers from the union had returned as well.

October 1947, Washington, DC

MR. STRIPLING, CHIEF INVESTIGATOR, HOUSE UN-AMERICAN ACTIVITIES

Committee: Now, Mr. Warner, you have indicated that you wished to include the writers Julius J. Epstein and Philip G. Epstein in the list of names you have supplied us. Do you feel that they, too, have introduced Un-American Communistic ideas into their motion picture scripts?

Mr. Warner: Yes, I do. Those fellows did very good work at one time but they fell off. They are always together. They are never separated. And I would like to add that their work habits are Un-American, too.

Mr. McDowell: I would like to ask the witness a question.

The Chairman: Go ahead, Mr. McDowell.

Mr. McDowell: Mr. Warner, during Hitler's regime they passed a law in Germany outlawing Communism and the Communists went to jail. Would you advocate the same thing here?

Mr. Warner: Maybe it's a good idea. I don't like that taking from the rich part, even if it's giving it to the poor.

Mr. Stripling: May I return to the subject of the Epstein brothers?

The Chairman: You may, Mr. Stripling.

Mr. Stripling: Mr. Warner, you said that the writers Julius J. and Philip G. Epstein introduced Un-American language and ideas into their scripts for your studio. Can you give the Committee an example of this kind of work?

Mr. Warner: Well, the way they write the rich man is always the villain. It seems to me they are Un-American because they are always on the side of the underdog. Besides we already made that picture: *The Adventures of Robin Hood*. THE GREATEST BANDIT THE WORLD HAS EVER KNOWN! Well, they never met Harry.

Robert E. Stripling: November 1947, Washington, DC

Committee on Un-American Activities
House of Representatives
Eightieth Congress
Regarding the Communist Infiltration
of the Motion Picture Industry

J. Parnell Thomas, New Jersey, Chairman
Karl E. Mundt, South Dakota
John S. Wood, Georgia
John McDowell, Pennsylvania
John E. Rankin, Mississippi
Richard M. Nixon, California
Hardin Peterson, Florida
Richard B. Vail, Illinois
Herbert C. Bonner, North Carolina
Robert E. Stripling, Chief Investigator
Benjamin Mandel, Director of Research

To Julius J. Epstein and Philip G. Epstein:
Pursuant to a possible subpoena by this committee, you are required to complete the following questionnaire. It consists of two parts:

Part A:
Are you now or have you ever been a member of a subversive organization?

Part B:
If so, name that organization.

Sincerely,
Robert E. Stripling, Chief Investigator for the Committee

Philip G. and Julius J. Epstein: November 1947, Los Angeles

Dear Mr. Stripling:

We are happy to complete your questionnaire.

In response to Part A, <u>Are we now or have we ever been a member</u> <u>of a subversive organization?</u>, the answer is: YES.

In response to Part B, <u>If so, name that organization</u>, the answer is: WARNER BROS.

Sincerely,
Julius Epstein
Philip Epstein

Jack L. Warner: December 1943, Burbank

To: The President of the United States
From: Jack L. Warner
Date: December 22, 1943
Subject: *Passage to Marseilles*

Dear Mr. President:

I am writing to tell you that in about three months Warner Bros. will be releasing a new picture entitled *Passage to Marseilles*. For this feature we have assembled many of the cast you so much enjoyed while in Casablanca: Humphrey Bogart, Peter Lorre, Sidney Greenstreet, Claude Rains, and Michelle Morgan, who we considered for *Casablanca*, and who in my opinion should have used as the leading lady instead of Miss Bergman. So you can see we have invested a good deal of our financial and artistic resources into this new motion picture.

I am writing because I have heard through numerous sources, including a well-placed columnist at the *Los Angeles Times*, that after the current campaign in Italy is completed you intend to direct the United Nations forces to open a second front across the English Channel, probably in Normandy. In my opinion this would be a big mistake. It is much better to continue the soft underbelly strategy you have been pursuing and launch the invasion in the area of Marseilles. In fact, I must insist upon it. Launching the attack in Northern France might lead to the kind of debacle we experienced at Pearl Harbor, if you get what I mean. A debacle that could have been avoided.

I hope you will take seriously this suggestion, which I make as an American citizen who wants only the best for his country.

Sincerely, your friend,
Jack L. Warner

P.S. I have not yet heard about the Medal of Merit I mentioned some time back. It would be the greatest honor of my life if I were to receive it. And soon.

New York Times: January 1947, New York

> January 17th, 1947
> CORRECTION:
> Jack L. Warner, vice president of Warner Brothers, Inc., served during the recent conflict at the rank of *lieutenant* colonel. This is a lower rank than that of colonel.

VOICE-OVER:
That's all, folks

~~

END

Speaking Parts

PRINCIPAL PLAYERS (in order of appearance)

— Hedda Hopper: Columnist
— Abdul Maljan: Former boxer
— Karelena Kaiser: Former German actress
— Jack L. Warner: Vice president for production and executive producer, Warner Bros.
— Josef Goebbels: Reichsminister für Volksaufklärung und Propaganda
— Josef Vissarionovich Stalin: General Secretary of the Soviet Union
— George S. Patton, Jr: Commander, Western Task Force, Operation Torch

THE SUPPORTING CAST (in order of appearance)

— Martin Bormann: Private Secretary to Adolf Hitler
— Adolf Hitler: German Reichskanzler
— Joe Kauffman: Head of Warner Bros. Berlin office, father of Karelena
— Magda Goebbels: Wife of Josef Goebbels
— Franklin Delano Roosevelt: President of the United States
— Hannelore Kaiser: Wife of Joe Kauffman, mother of Karelena
— Max Kimmich: German film director
— Alexander Engelsing: German actor, producer, director
— Julius J. Epstein: Screenwriter, Warner Bros.
— Philip G. Epstein: Screenwriter, Warner Bros.
— David O. Selznick: Hollywood film producer
— Rydo Loshak: Costume designer, Warner Bros.
— Herr Doktor Kunz: German dentist
— Joachim von Ribbentrop: Reichsminister for Foreign Affairs

— Baron Hiroshi Oshima: Japanese Ambassador to Germany
— Hermann Göring: Supreme Commander, the Luftwaffe
— Admiral Wilhelm Canaris: Chief of the Abwher, German military intelligence service
— Walter Schellenberg: High Sicherheitsdienst official, head of German foreign intelligence
— Winston Churchill: British Prime Minister
— Admiral Harold Rainsford Stark: Chief of Naval Operations, United States Navy
— Max Aitken, 1st Baron Beaverbrook: British Minister of Aircraft Production and War Supplies
— Sir John Dill: Field Marshall, British Imperial General Staff
— Lord Hallifax: British Ambassador to the United States
— Maxim Litvinov: Soviet Ambassador to the United States
— George C. Marshall: Chief of Staff, United States Army
— Charles Wilson, 1st Baron Moran: Personal physician to Winston Churchill
— Eleanor Roosevelt: Wife of President Roosevelt
— Harpo Marx (in his own language): American entertainer
— Ann Page: Wife of Jack L. Warner
— Joy Page: Daughter of Ann Page
— Ernie Glickman: Portly production assistant
— Mike Curtiz: Film director, Warner Bros.
— Hal Wallis: Film producer, Warner Bros.
— V. M. Molotov: Minister of Foreign Affairs, the Soviet Union
— Svetlana Stalin: Daughter of Josef Stalin
— Georgy Zhukov: Marshal of the Soviet Union
— Alexander Poskrebyshev: Head of the Special Section of the Central Committee, the Soviet Union
— Averell Harriman: Special Envoy to Britain and the Soviet Union
— Alan Brooke, 1st Viscount Alanbrooke: Chief of the British Imperial General Staff
— Admiral H. Kent Hewitt: Commander, Amphibious Force, Atlantic Fleet, United States Navy
— William Meeks: Master Sergeant, US Army; orderly to George S. Patton

— William H. Wilbur: Colonel, US Army
— Hobart R. Gay: Colonel, US Army; Chief of Staff
  to George S. Patton
— Sultan's Guard (aka "The Ink Spots")
— Man in Bugs Bunny suit
— Peter Lorre (*Clang! Clang!*)
— Slapsie Maxie Rosenbloom: Jewish boxer
— Sultan's horsemen
— The Sultan of Morocco: The Sultan of Morocco
— The Grand Vizier: The Grand Vizier of Morocco
— Oumaima: Busty harem girl, under contract, Warner Bros.
— Admiral Félix Michelier: A French naval officer
— Box-office girl, Hollywood Theater, Avenue A
— Kurt Zeitzler: Chief of German Army General Staff
— Alfred Jodl: Chief of Operations Staff, German Armed Forces
  High Command
— Albert Speer: Reichsminister, Armaments and War Production
— Michael Reilly: Head of President Roosevelt's security detail
— Dick Schotter: A photographer, employee of Warner Bros.
— Robert E. Stripling: Chief investigator, House Un-American
  Activities Committee
— John McDowell: Of Pennsylvania, a member of that committee

All Mentioned Films (in order of appearance)

— *Tortilla Flat*, Metro-Goldwyn-Mayer
— *Strawberry Blonde**, Warner Bros.
— *Tales of Manhattan*, 20th Century Fox
— *One Round Hogan*, Warner Bros.
— *Twenty Million Sweethearts*, Warner Bros.
— *Fashions of 1934*, Warner Bros.
— *42nd Street*, Warner Bros.
— *Where the North Begins*, Warner Bros.
— *The Man with Two Faces*, Warner Bros.
— *Gold Diggers of 1933*, Warner Bros.
— *Footlight Parade*, Warner Bros.
— *Dracula*, Universal Pictures
— *M*, Nero Film
— *Doctor X*, Warner Bros.
— *Algiers*, United Artists
— *Dive Bomber*, Warner Bros.
— *Maltese Falcon*, Warner Bros.
—*You're in the Army Now*, Warner Bros.
— *The Man Who Came to Dinner**, Warner Bros.
— *Confessions of a Nazi Spy*, Warner Bros.
— *Yankee Doodle Dandy**, Warner Bros.
— *Zu neuen Ufern* (*To New Shores*), UFA
— *Andere Welt* (*Another World*), Tobis
— *Die Umwege des Schönen Karl* (*The Roundabouts of
   Handsome Karl*), Tobis
— *Der Tiger von Eschnapur* (*The Tiger of Eschnapur*),
   Tobis
— *Heimkehr* (*Homecoming*), UFA

— *Snow White and the Seven Dwarfs*, Disney
— *Annelie*, UFA
— *Virtuous Wives*, First National
— *The Great Dictator*, United Artists
— *In the Navy*, Universal
— *White Zombie*, United Artists
— *Battle of Hearts*, Fox Film Corporation
— *Merry Melodies* (as a group), Warner Bros.
— *Now Voyager*, Warner Bros.
— *Singapore Woman*, Warner Bros.
— *The Male Animal**, Warner Bros.
— *The Jazz Singer*, Warner Bros.
— *Happy Go Lucky*, Paramount
— *Girl Trouble*, 20th Century Fox
— *Star-Spangled Rhythm*, Paramount
— *La Cucaracha*, Pioneer/RKO
— *The Gorilla*, 20th Century Fox
— *The Gorilla Man*, Warner Bros.
— *Desperate Journey*, Warner Bros.
— *Blood and Sand*, 20th Century Fox
— *Casablanca**, Warner Bros.
— *The German Route before Moscow* (aka *Moscow Strikes Back*),
  Artkino Pictures
— *The Bride Came C.O.D.**, Warner Bros.
— *Law of the Tropics*, Warner Bros.
— *Captain Applejack*, Warner Bros.
— *Misbehaving Ladies*, Warner Bros.
— *Nanook of the North*, Pathé Exchange
— *Three Faces East*, Warner Bros.
— *A Night at the Opera*, Metro-Goldwyn-Mayer
— *Gold Dust Gertie*, Warner Bros.
— *Captain Blood*, Warner Bros.
— *Raiders on the Mexican Border*, Warner Features Co.
— *The Sea Hawk*, Warner Bros.
— *Murder in the Big House*, Warner Bros.
— *Peril of the Plains*, Bison Motion Pictures (Warner Bros.)

— *The Keyhole*, Warner Bros.

— *Open Your Eyes*, Warner Bros.

— *Edge of Darkness*, Warner Bros.

— *City Lights*, RKO

— *Gone with the Wind*, Selznick International

— *Three Cheers for the Irish*, Warner Bros.

— *It All Came True*, Warner Bros.

— *The Mysterious Doctor*, Warner Bros.

— *Girl Crazy*, RKO

— *Queen Christina*, Metro-Goldwyn-Mayer

— *Road to Morocco*, Paramount

— *So Proudly We Hail*, Paramount

— *The More the Merrier*, Columbia

— *The Story of Pasteur*, Warner Bros.

— *Disraeli*, Warner Bros.

— *Ziegfeld*, Metro-Goldwyn-Mayer

— *Marie Antoinette*, Metro-Goldwyn-Mayer

— *Navy Blues*, Warner Bros.

— *The Wolf Man*, Universal

— *Honeymoon for Three**, Warner Bros.

— *The Three Musketeers*, 20th Century Fox

— *That Hamilton Woman*, Alexander Korda Films (United Artists)

— *Dumbo*, Disney

— *Song of Bernadette*, 20th Century Fox

— *A Night in Casablanca*, United Artists

— *The Adventures of Robin Hood*, Warner Bros.

— *Passage to Marseilles*, Warner Bros.

*These motion pictures were written after 12:00 p.m.